Shadows

of the

Emerald

City

Edited by JW Schnarr

*To Carrie,
From your #1 Fan.*

Jan 3/2010

Northern Frights Publishing

In the Great White North, Blood Runs Colder...

www.northernfrightspublishing.webs.com

Northern Frights Publishing is proudly Canadian.

This book is a collection of fairytales, and as such they are
fiction. Unless of course, you believe in the magic that
brings fairytales to life; in which case all bets are off.

This is a collection of short fiction based on the Public
Domain work of L Frank Baum and his Wonderful Wizard
of Oz series. The characters, names, and places in many of
these stories are derivatives of the original work.

FIRST PRINTING

ISBN: 978-0-9734837-1-0

For Aurora,
who still dreams in technicolour.

ACKNOWLEDGEMENTS

In no particular order, thanks to my daughter Aurora for letting me use her laptop when my computer crashed, and thanks to my sister Janice for supporting both the company and myself in our first endeavour. Also thanks to Jacob Kier at Permuted Press and A.P. Fuchs at Coscom Entertainment for helping a noob out with advice (namely me) and showing the new kids how it's done.

Of course, this collection would be nothing without the artists and authors that contributed to make it so special, and to you, the reader, go the biggest thanks of all.

—JWS.

TABLE OF CONTENTS

"Whenever I feel blue, I start breathing again."
—L Frank Baum

DR WILL PRICE
AND THE CURIOUS CASE OF
DOROTHY GALE

by Mark Onspaugh

Kansas was far hotter than Will remembered.

His new dress shirt was sticking to his back by the time he reached the institute. He figured his jacket would hide the circles of wetness under his arms, but he didn't like that sticky, clingy feeling of the fabric against his skin.

The dealer in Chicago had assured him that the Pontiac's air conditioner was state-of-the-art, but the damn thing had burned out halfway across Missouri. He had driven all the way to Topeka with the windows down, wearing only his shoes, pants and undershirt. He had stopped at a Mobil station ten miles from the institute and used the restroom to change. At twenty-five his brown hair was already beginning to thin a bit, but his face was unlined, and he possessed the same easy good looks as singer Tommy Roe, who had a hit that year with "Sheila". He smiled as he remembered the three high school girls in a red convertible who had kept pace with him until he crossed the Illinois state line, convinced he was Roe on the way to a gig. Then, remembering the importance of his appointment, he ceased to smile and put on his dress shirt and tie.

Will pulled up to a pair of massive wrought iron gates, flanked on either side by rough hewn columns of stone that were part of a massive wall overgrown with ivy.

An enamel sign affixed to the right column declared itself in brilliant white with crisp black lettering.

Clear Springs Asylum of Wichita

There was a small guard kiosk on the other side and Will showed the guard his identification and letter from Dr. Carlton Fisk, the director. The guard gave him a tip of the hat as he returned Will's documents. The gates swung open soundlessly and he drove in. He told himself not to be nervous, but he could feel the perspiration dripping from his pores as if he were a large sponge being squeezed by the heat.

He passed the visitor's parking area and entered a small lot designated "Institute Staff Only". He felt a flush of pride when he found the space labeled "Reserved – Dr. Price".

The grounds were green and well-tended, and small paths meandered around flowerbeds and out to a duck pond surrounded by willow trees. Only two patients seemed to be out, which wasn't unusual, given the heat. They were seated on a bench by the pond and were feeding the ducks small bits of bread. A large orderly watched them from a discrete distance. He saw Will, surmised he was a new doctor, and gave him a small wave. Will waved back.

The main entrance of the institute was a colonial *façade* marked by large columns and a pair of sturdy oak doors. Will entered and was relieved to find it much cooler inside.

The interior was light and airy, with terrazzo tiles, white walls and high ceilings. Barred windows in the lobby let in sunlight filtered through gardenia bushes.

The admitting nurse, a rather plain woman in her forties, gave him directions to Fisk's office. The director was a big man, easily four hundred pounds, with a close-cropped crew cut and ruddy face. He looked like a former quarterback who had gotten fat from rich food and alcohol. Will was careful not to make any assumptions. His professors had assured him that Dr. Fisk was a brilliant man.

Fisk beamed when he saw him, and stood up, extending his hand. This was very different from the more reserved protocol of Chicago, but it was familiar to Will, who had once made a home among these garrulous, hard-working people.

"Dr. William Price, I presume!" Fisk boomed, then laughed at his own joke.

Will laughed, too. The man was so jolly it was impossible not to, and they shook hands. It was like shaking hands with a bear, and his not-so-small hand was engulfed in the other's massive paw.

"How was the drive from Chicago?" Fisk asked.

"Hot," Will answered honestly.

"I can have some lemonade brought in, or iced tea?"

"Iced tea would be wonderful, thank you."

Fisk called to his assistant in the hall, not bothering with an intercom or phone. He saw that Will was startled and laughed.

"Many of the patients are comforted by this trumpet of mine," he laughed. "If I tone it down they begin to worry!"

A young man with a name tag identifying him as *Patient Greg Stevens* brought in two ice teas on a tray with a small dish of sugar cubes and another of lemon wedges, as well as spoons and cocktail napkins. Though the tray rattled slightly, he managed to dispense the beverages and incidentals without spilling anything.

"Thank you, Greg," Fisk said.

The young man smiled, and then looked at Will.

"Thank you, Greg. This is just what the doctor ordered," said Will.

Greg looked confused for a second, and then Fisk laughed heartily. Greg joined in, his laugh more of a bray, then exited with the tray.

Fisk and Will fixed their drinks and enjoyed them in silence for two minutes. Will had a feeling Fisk was measuring his sense of security, whether he needed to fill silence with trivial conversation.

After a moment, Fisk nodded and smiled.

"Doctor Price, you come highly recommended. Dr. Stanton is a long-time friend and colleague, and he couldn't be more impressed with you. I am, as well."

"Thank you, Doctor."

"I'm sure you're tired and would like to see your quarters."

Will hesitated, then took the plunge.

"If you wouldn't mind, Dr. Fisk, may I see her?"

Fisk smiled, but his eyes were keen, watchful.

"Ah, yes. She was the subject of your dissertation four years ago."

"Yes, sir."

"I read it. Most of the staff did."

Will looked at Fisk, waiting to see if the man was going to comment on his work.

Fisk smiled, took one last sip of his tea, then stood up.

"Let's go meet her," Fisk said.

Will, unsure what the man's silence regarding his paper meant, was nevertheless caught up in the excitement of this moment come at last.

Fisk led him down the hall and to an elevator with burnished bronze doors.

"She's downstairs," Fisk explained. "Most of the older patients are. We tried to move some of them to the newer, more modern wing, but many insisted on staying where they felt safe, secure."

The elevator creaked into service and rocked slightly when they reached the lower level.

Fisk exited briskly and Will followed. The linoleum here was clean but worn, its bright spots of blue and green now scuffed and rubbed into the gray of a stormy sea. The walls were freshly painted, though, and there was no hint of malfeasance or neglect.

Each of the patient's rooms had a small window of wired glass. They passed rooms brightly lit, others that seemed pitch black.

"We've had some attrition over the years," Fisk explained. "Eventually this entire ward will be given over to support services and file storage."

Her room was at the end of the corridor, the last one on the left. There was no patient opposite her, just a maintenance closet and a fire exit.

Fisk gestured to the window. Will had hoped to actually meet her, but knew there was a protocol in place to which he must adhere. He stood before the door and peeked in.

She was dressed in a faded blue shift and sat in a straight-back chair next to her bed. She was in her seventies, with long, wavy hair of silver with some white. Her hands were big and gnarled, the hands of a pioneer woman, and they were clasped in her lap. Her eyes were large, their color unknowable at this distance. Her nose was a bit lumpish, as if it had been broken and crudely set a long time ago. Her lips were moving wordlessly.

The picture she was staring at was a child's rendition of a rainbow. A smiling sun shone overhead, and the colors of the rainbow were slightly off, the red missing and the green twice as large as the other bands. Under it, very small, was a green blob sat that sat atop a thin vertical line of yellow, crosshatched with black.

"Hello, Dorothy," Will whispered, then glanced at Fisk to see if he had heard.

Fisk smiled. "Did you notice her feet?"

Will looked again, almost expecting shoes that were covered in red glitter. She was wearing unremarkable flats, hospital issue.

Then he saw them move.

She was clicking her heels, three times in succession.

The first two months were busy ones for Will, and he only saw Dorothy Gale on two occasions, both with Dr. Fisk.

His predecessor, Dr. Vincent Colby, had left without notice two months before. Will found that odd, especially in light of Dorothy's case, but Fisk was unperturbed.

"Colby was a good man, but his heart wasn't in it," Fisk confided as they observed Dorothy. She was sitting near the duck pond, but stared at her hands, unmoving.

"I read a couple of his papers," Will said. "He seemed rather... *clinical.*"

Fisk nodded.

"Skinnerian," he said, his rosy face wincing as if he had smelled something bad. "I'd take the whole lot of them with their rats and black boxes and dump them in the Arkansas River."

"But in light of Dorothy's family, the farmhands..."

"I know what the papers say," Fisk said. "But they never found bodies, did they? I think they were lost in the tornado, and the trauma of seeing that is what reduced Dorothy to catatonia."

"I think that theory has merit, Doctor," Will said. "But it's that lack of bodies that makes me question the disappearance of Doctor Colby."

"I would imagine if you called around to various psychiatric institutions, you'd find he was practicing in another state," Fisk insisted. "Perhaps even in Europe."

"But, to leave his belongings behind..."

"Doctor Price, the truth is I feel we are well rid of the man. Unlike you, he was a heartless bastard that felt all of Man's maladies could be removed by a scalpel or some operant conditioning. If it gives you any comfort, there was no tornado the day he left, not even a slight breeze."

"Still..."

Fisk chuckled.

"You think she killed him, buried him on the grounds somewhere. The police thought so, too. Had bloodhounds out here for three days. They scared the patients and the ducks. And before you ask, they checked Dorothy's room, too. No one walled up behind the lath and plaster, *Montresor!*"

Will was unsure.

Fisk clapped him on the back.

"You haven't left the grounds in weeks. I'm taking you out for steaks and a round of martinis at *The Brazier.* Doctor's orders."

Will looked over at Dorothy, but she continued to regard her hands, as if waiting for them to reveal some great mystery.

The case was already something of an urban legend when Will first heard about it as a youngster in Bramble, a small town west of Topeka. It was the summer of '46 and he had just turned nine, the same age as Dorothy when she was found wandering miles from her home in Dryden after the big tornado of 1900. The little girl was unharmed, but everyone at the farm where she lived had disappeared. In Will's time, the popular versions were that Dorothy had butchered her family and fed them to the hogs or that a ravenous monster had devoured them, driving poor Dorothy mad in the process.

There was no reference to Oz.

The story stayed with him, and he was plagued by nightmares for weeks. As a result, he remembered details of the legend long after his friends had forgotten it.

When he was fifteen, Will went to the public library in Lawrence and researched newspapers from that fateful summer in 1900.

FARM FAMILY STILL MISSING – GIRL DECLARED INSANE

"WICHITA – *Authorities have been unable to find any trace of local farmers Henry and Emily Gale, who disappeared some time during the devastating tornado that struck the region on June 5, 1900. Also missing are three farm hands who had been with the Gales for three year, Ed "Hunk" Chaffee, Clyde "Hickory" Ferris and Leo "Zeke" Mayer and a neighbor, Elmira Gulch.*

The farmhouse itself was mostly undamaged by the twister, though local Sheriff Charles Morgan said that it had been shifted on its foundation "slightly out of true". Locals know the capricious nature of tornadoes, and it is not unusual for one house to remain intact while all around it are destroyed.

What has authorities puzzled is that the Gales, their hands and neighbor have vanished without a trace. The only exception is young Dorothy Gale, the nine year old niece of Henry and Emily.

Dorothy was found wandering three miles from the house, confused and bearing evidence of a blow to the head. The child first told how she had been taken in by a gypsy fortune teller known as "Professor Marvel", but authorities have been unable to corroborate the existence of such an individual in the area. It was suspected that Dorothy had been abducted by some third party who had also abducted her friends and family, then subsequently escaped.

The story became more puzzling when the girl began to insist she had traveled via the tornado to a magical land "over the rainbow", and that her friends and relatives remained there.

The land, which she calls "Oz" is supposedly a place of witches and dwarves, talking scarecrows and animals, monkeys that fly, roads of gold and palaces of emerald.

Experts in the field of psychiatry now believe that Dorothy witnessed the murder of the six adults and has experienced a "psychotic break", allowing her to believe they live happily in a colorful fairy land. Rumors that the child herself may have been involved in the disappearances have been called "ridiculous" by Sheriff Morgan, although he has admitted that the child had an ongoing conflict with her neighbor, Elmira Gulch, and her aunt and uncle over the disposition of her pet terrier, Toto, also missing.

As the child has no other relatives willing to care for her, she has been made a ward of the state and has been placed in the Wichita Insane Asylum for treatment. Doctors are not hopeful."

Will had been fascinated by the story, mostly by the land the traumatized child had conjured up. To think someone so young could create such a vibrant, compelling delusion! This fascination stayed with him through high school, and led to his pursuing psychiatry as a career.

Now he looked again at his favorite patient, once again seated before her drawing and mumbling as she clicked her now-calloused heels.

It was the only time she appeared animated, other than when the skies became gray and stormy. Otherwise, she exhibited all the classic signs of catatonia, and had to be fed, dressed and washed.

In his first week, Will had leaned close to her to try and discern what she said as she regarded the painting, which he learned she had done in her first year at the institute, back when it was crudely labeled an "insane asylum".

It was just five words, and she repeated them like a mantra.

There's no place like home
There's no place like home
There's no place like home

In the spring of 1964, when the country was still reeling from the death of President John F. Kennedy, Will went to Dr. Fisk with a proposal.

He found the big man sniffling at his desk. Fisk held up a copy of *LIFE Magazine* which contained a picture of Kennedy's young son saluting his father's casket.

"It's a hell of a thing, Will," Fisk said, putting the magazine down and blowing his nose on an enormous handkerchief.

Will agreed, but his sorrow was tempered by excitement.

"Doctor Fisk, I…"

"Son, you've worked here now for nigh on to two years. I wish you would call me 'Carl'."

"You're right, *Carl*, I should."

Fisk beamed, and wiped an errant tear from the corner of his eye. He then looked at Will expectantly.

"I would like to sign Dorothy Gale out for a day."

"For what purpose?"

"I have been doing some reading in *Die Deutsche Fachzeitschrift fur Psychisches Wissenschaft.*"

Fisk smiled.

"I haven't gotten my translated copy, yet." When he saw the younger man flush with embarrassment, he waved him off. "A joke, doctor. I remember from your résumé you speak German and French."

Will almost mentioned that he also spoke Italian and a smattering of Russian, but thought better of it.

"There's an interesting article by Friedrich Leuchte concerning what he calls '*erschüttern der bekannten*', or '*the shock of the familiar*'. He cites numerous case studies where some catatonic individuals have been shocked or jolted from their stupor by familiar surroundings. In Dorothy's case, I'm thinking the Gale farmhouse."

"But Dorothy was returned there after being found," Fisk said. "Doctor Walshe, the psychiatrist who initially treated her, also took her to other familiar surroundings. None of the attempts proved successful."

"But those trips were taken while she was still in the process of fabricating her fantasy world. She hasn't been outside these grounds for over fifty years. In effect, she has spent all that time 'in Oz'. Now it's the farmhouse that would seem new and exotic, something both known but forgotten."

"A shock of the familiar."

"Exactly."

Dr. Fisk sighed.

"There are many who would say the old woman is at peace, leave her be."

"If that's true, Carl, then why not just load up every patient with tranquilizers and sit them in front of the television or the duck pond?"

Fisk considered this and nodded. He pulled a form from his desk, and began filling it in.

It was a brilliant May day when Will and Dorothy set out for the farm in Dryden.

The drive was just over an hour, and Will had gone there on his last day off to make certain there was enough of the farmhouse standing to give Dorothy the necessary jolt.

She sat in the front seat, her large hands clasped in her lap. For all her lack of affect, she might be sitting out on the duck pond bench. She was far more animated in her room than she was now.

Her demeanor changed only once. Will heard her gasp slightly and saw her lean forward.

There was a young girl on a bicycle, a white wicker basket of flowers mounted on the handlebars. When it became clear it was only a young girl, Dorothy returned to her vegetative state.

Elmira Gulch had ridden a bicycle, Will remembered. It was funny, he knew the Gulch woman had had an altercation with Dorothy shortly before the tornado hit. He had thought of hiring an actress to play the woman, perhaps to come charging out of the house when they arrived. But he could find no pictures of Elmira Gulch, and realized the shock of seeing her double might be more than Dorothy could bear. One of the lessons he had learned in his residency was that results did not always come quickly. "*Patience for patients*" was something his instructors mentioned time and time again.

They were about three miles from the town of Dryden when Will took a dirt road off to the left. He thought he saw Dorothy's eyes flicker, but he had to keep his eye on the rough and rutted road.

They passed one large working farm and two smaller spreads that had gone to seed, their houses and outbuildings slowly caving in to rotted piles of lumber and nails.

Then came the Gale farm.

The barn was burned down, and the pigsty and chicken coops were gone, but the house stood, seemingly little changed from that infamous day in 1900.

Will glanced at Dorothy, and was rewarded to see that her eyes were alert, her hands unclasped.

They passed the rusted ruin of a mailbox and parked in the dooryard.

The house was indeed crooked on the foundation, as if a giant had lifted it and then replaced it carelessly on the foundation.

It was a sad and plain gray house in a colorless landscape. Even the brilliantly blue sky seemed bland and charmless in this barren and desolate place.

My God, Will thought, it's no wonder her fantasy world is so filled with bright colors and rainbows.

The two of them sat there for a moment, the only sounds the ticking of the cooling engine and a big dog barking somewhere in the distance.

"Dorothy?"

She turned to him, and he noticed for the first time that her eyes were an amazing shade of green, like the ocean as the sky clouds up. Though he had seen many pictures of her over the years, he realized that in her youth she must have been extraordinarily beautiful.

"Do you want to go in?" he asked.

She nodded slowly, looking again at the house as she did so.

As if it might disappear.

Will got out first, and went to help her out. Her hand was strong as it clasped his, and despite her age there was no hint of weakness or palsy.

The front door was open, and he and Dorothy walked in.

The house had been cleared of furniture and *bric-a-brac* decades ago. Only a pair of faded gingham curtains remained in living room. Still, for a house standing vacant for sixty years, there was no sign of vandalism or decay.

How could that be?

Will realized he must have spoken this thought aloud, because Dorothy was looking at him.

"I was thinking," he said. "The house looks remarkably untouched for one so old and abandoned."

"It was touched by Oz," Dorothy said, as if this was obvious.

She walked over to the curtains and touched them tentatively, then leaned in to smell them. She smiled for the first time since Will had known her, and it was a beautiful smile.

"I... I can smell her perfume," Dorothy said, her voice the whisper of an acolyte.

"Whose, Dorothy?" He wished now he had brought a portable tape recorder with him, but he had a feeling Dorothy's days of silence and immobility were over.

"Auntie Em," she said, and suddenly wiped at a tear in her eye.

"Where is Auntie Em, Dorothy?"

"She's waiting for me, back in Oz with Uncle Henry and the others."

"And Elmira Gulch?"

Dorothy's smile disappeared and her eyes flashed.

"Her? My house crushed her sister and I melted her. Good riddance!"

Will couldn't believe how well it was going. True, she was persisting in her fantasy, but it was carefully crafted over years of inactivity and lack of stimulation. That was all going to change.

The dog barked again, but now it sounded different. It was closer, for one thing, and it...

"*Toto!*" she cried, her face lighting up like a child's a Christmas. "Oh, Toto! Toto, I'm here!"

She ran toward the back of the house. The barking had sounded more like the yip of a terrier, but surely that was a coincidence.

He hurried after her, not trusting the ancient floor to support her.

She was in a back bedroom, spare and empty, with one window. She held something in her hand, and looked at him, her eyes shining with tears.

"This was my room, Dr. Price, when I was younger."

She remembered his name! Surely this was a breakthrough!

In her hand was a single poppy, its bright orange petals satiny and vibrant. The flower looked as if it had just been picked from a field, yet the land for miles around was too hot and dry for poppies.

Will wanted to ask her where it came from, but then she smiled and blew on it, like a dandelion. Shining pollen like diamond dust swirled and eddied, each mote a tiny star suspended between them, and both of them were inhaling it before he could protest.

Suddenly, there was a roaring all around, as if some great beast had discovered the long-empty house was now occupied. Will felt a sickening lurch in his stomach, that kind of giddy, nauseous joy experienced on elevators and roller coasters, and the room began to spin. Will's knees buckled, and his vision blurred.

As he lost consciousness, he heard the yapping of a small dog growing louder, more urgent. Everything went Kansas gray, and then he slipped into a darkness that seemed to have been waiting the whole time.

Something wet touched Will's face, and for a moment he thought he was out in the rain.

Eyes dark and merry were regarding him as he opened his own. He sat up, and the small, dark terrier barked and capered around him.

"Toto, let him stand up!" Dorothy called out, laughing.

The dog ran to her and whined until she picked him up. Will's head was throbbing and he wondered if she had bludgeoned him. Perhaps he had been drugged?

"Oh, Doctor Price, it's so wonderful, so incredibly wonderful!" Her cheeks were flushed, and again he noticed that she had once been an incredible beauty.

"Hit my head," he said, framing it midway between a question and a statement.

"I'm sorry," she said, kneeling near him. "The first trip is always the most difficult."

"Trip?" He remembered the poppy and wondered if he had ingested

LSD somehow. Perhaps Dorothy had spiked the lemonade he had bought them at the fruit stand down the road from the insitute. The idea of her having access to hallucinogens explained a lot, but would also mean someone at the institute was her accomplice and supplier.

Dorothy looked at him, her face filled with concern.

"You don't believe me, do you? Oh, Doctor Price, you must! Please, come to the window and see!"

"See what, Dorothy?"

"Oz, of course! We set down near the outskirts of Munchkin Land! They've been keeping Toto for me, and..."

"Dorothy, you must know that's not your dog," he said gently. "This is a puppy, and your Toto would be over sixty years old. No dog lives that long."

"But this is Oz, Doctor Price, Oz. It's a wonderful place, please come to the window and see!"

Will knew this was a crucial juncture in her therapy. If he went to the window, he would be giving her fantasy some credence. It might undo all they had achieved here today, and put her back in that delusional state of isolation and confinement.

"Dorothy," he said slowly, "I will come to the window if you tell me if anyone at the institute has been supplying you with hallucinogens."

Dorothy looked at him, puzzled.

"I'm not sure I know what that word means, Doctor Price."

"It's a chemical that causes you to hallucinate, to see and/or hear things that are not there."

"Like a dream," she said, the animation leaving her face.

"Yes, but a waking dream."

Dorothy hugged the dog, and the little animal wagged its tail furiously and licked her neck.

"The Scarecrow told me you wouldn't believe," she said sadly "He said you're too concerned with your brain to listen to your heart."

"Dorothy, I only want what's best for you."

She looked at him, and put Toto down. She stood and offered him her hand.

"Please, Doctor Price, come with me. My friends will protect you."

"From what, Dorothy?" He tried to project as much compassion and empathy as he could. Patience for patients, the golden rule.

"*From the Witches*," she hissed, her eyes darting nervously as if some hag might even now be crawling along the ceiling.

"But you told me both the witches were dead," he said calmly. Gently, he reminded himself, she has had years to craft this fantasy, but there are flaws. Oz for all its grandeur is merely a trauma-inspired house of cards.

"New witches always arise in the West and East," she said. "Please, come with me to the North, where Ozma and Glinda can look after you."

"And what about the Wizard?" he asked.

"Wizard," she spat. "He's the reason I came back. He convinced me that this is where I belonged. He was a horrible man and Oz is well rid of him."

He heard a flock of crows cawing outside, their raucous din a reminder of their location, a dreary and deserted farmhouse in Dryden, Kansas.

Dorothy tugged on his arm.

"Please, we must leave now!"

Will shook his head, ready to deliver another gentle gust of reason to bring down her playing card construction.

But Dorothy would hear none of it. She scooped up the terrier and ran from the room. Will stood up, and reeled from a bout of vertigo. Whatever had been given to him was still having an effect. Still, he was responsible for the old woman and could not allow her to hurt herself.

He lurched out of the bedroom and down the cramped hallway. The house creaked and swayed under him as if it had become unsettled, and he chalked this up to some residual effect of the drug.

He came out onto the front porch, but there was no sign of Dorothy. A quick check of the car and the house revealed nothing but the flat dry earth surrounding the gray structure.

Will reentered the house, thinking Dorothy might be hiding or had relapsed back into catatonia. He began to search each room, checking the closets and the pantry as he went.

As he was coming out of the kitchen he heard laughter and barking coming from her old bedroom.

Will entered the room, but it was empty. He crossed to the window and looked out.

Impossibly, the rear of the house now looked out onto verdant fields filled with fantastic flowers of gold, orange, red and yellow. Beyond this were meadows with grass so green it hurt his eyes, leading to mountains that disappeared into thick, fleecy clouds.

And there, on a path of shining gold bricks, were Dorothy and the terrier. They were running to three creatures that Will remembered from Dorothy's descriptions of her traveling companions in Oz: a living scarecrow, a metal woodsman and a large lion with a bow in its mane. They waved and called to her, even the lion.

If he had had any doubts he was under the influence of some psychedelic drug, he was sure now. What he was seeing was impossible, preposterous. He had memorized every aspect of Dorothy's make-believe world, and now her delusion was informing his drug-induced fantasy.

As if a final proof was needed, Dorothy seemed to shrink as she neared her friends. By the time she reached them she was a good eighteen inches shorter, and her hair had darkened to a chestnut brown, tied in pigtails with bright blue ribbons that matched what was now a crisp, gingham dress. Transformed into a little girl of eight or nine, she skipped to the three denizens of Oz and hugged them happily while the little dog capered and barked.

Will shook his head, wondering how long it would be before the chemicals in his system were absorbed. He certainly couldn't drive like this, and he had told Fisk he and Dorothy would be back by dinner time.

Looking out the window, Will decided that the only things that were actually there were Dorothy and the dog. Though his perception of her was altered under the influence of some unknown substance, he hoped he could still communicate with her.

"Dorothy!" he called, and she turned to look at him. She waved to him sadly, and he noticed that her friends were frowning at him, even the lion.

The scarecrow whispered in her ear, and she nodded. She waved to Will one more time, and then she and her companions began to skip away along the golden path. They began to sing a song as they moved away, something about Ozma, the goodly queen of Oz.

Will ran from the bedroom, intent on preventing her from wandering off. He cared for Dorothy and was worried about her, of course, but at that moment he was more concerned how these events might reflect on his position at Clear Springs and his reputation in the psychiatric community.

He ran for the front door, barely aware that the house was beginning to pitch and roll under him like a ship caught in foul weather. He tripped as he hit the front porch, and flew out into the dooryard, landing painfully on something hard and smooth, something that broke under him with a loud crack.

He lay there for a moment, gasping for breath and feeling pain in his knees and elbows. The ground under him felt cool to the touch, and he was shocked to find he was lying on a sheet of glass as black as ink. The areas that had taken the brunt of the impact, elbows, knees, now was marked by spider web patterns of cracks. He looked up, and discovered the "sheet" was in fact a vast plain of black glass, stretching out in all directions. The car was gone, and he heard a slight snapping sound behind him. He looked back, and the house flew up into the sky without a sound, diminishing to a tiny dot within seconds, then it was gone.

His mind was reeling at the strangeness of what he was experiencing, but there was also a part of him that was calm; quietly observing what happened, coolly collecting data to form a rational hypothesis.

This was not like any hallucinogenic state he had ever read about.

It must be a lucid dream, he thought, one composed of all his fears and anxieties about treating Dorothy and advancing his career. Yet the pain he felt was intense and real, unlike anything he had experienced in dreams. It was also accompanied by that certainty of consciousness one has when awake.

He couldn't decide whether it was real or a compelling mirage.

But... what if, just for the sake of argument, it were real?

Dorothy.

If they were in such a place, then he must help her.

Will stood, wincing at the pain in his joints. He saw the verdant fields and the golden path, but they were much farther away, now, as if he had traveled in the house to some more hostile region of Dorothy's fantasy world.

Our world now, he amended.

He could just make out the four figures and the little dog, about to crest a small rise and then be out of sight.

Will cupped his hands and shouted as loud as he could. "Dorothy!"

He saw her turn, and wave. Was she hoping he'd follow?

He ran, trying to catch up to them. It was difficult to run on the black glass, and he was grateful he had worn tennis shoes today rather than his customary Oxfords. After a couple of minutes of hard running he realized that the fields did not seem to be getting any closer. Thinking this must be some kind of optical illusion Will ran even harder. He ran until he got a stitch in his side and collapsed, crying out in pain and frustration.

Will remained on all fours until he caught his breath, drops of sweat falling from his brow and pooling on the obsidian glass.

When he stood at last, he was confronted by yet another anomaly.

He was now standing before a great wall of black stone set with crimson mortar. The mortar was shiny and appeared wet. He touched it gingerly with an index finger.

It was blood.

Now he could discern skulls half buried in many of the bricks, their empty sockets peering out from some battle or catastrophe, their vacant orbits even darker than the stones that housed them.

Not all of the skulls were human, and he felt an atavistic chill run down his spine.

The wall ran toward the horizon in either direction, and was at least a hundred feet high. There was a large sign just over his head, and he had to back up several yards to read it properly.

TAKE HEED!
ALL FROM THE BLASTED LANDS AND
DEADLY DESERT ARE HEREBY BANNED
FROM THE EMERALD CITY OF OZ AND ALL
ITS PRINCIPALITIES AND TERRITORIES!
TRESPASSERS WILL BE MAGICKED!
BY ORDER OF OZMA, QUEEN OF OZ,
LOCASTA, GOOD WITCH OF THE NORTH &
GLINDA, GOOD WITCH OF THE SOUTH.

There was no way to follow Dorothy now. Will nearly collapsed as tears filled his eyes, but the horrific nature of the barrier was too much for him to bear. His heart heavy, Dr. William Price, formerly of Bramble, Kansas and Chicago, Illinois, walked back the way he came over the plain of black glass.

Though Will and Dorothy had arrived at the Gale farm at noon local time, he figured it was nearing that here in…

Go ahead, say it.

Oz, here in Oz.

He still felt ridiculous saying it, and in that self-criticism he felt a tiny spark of hope, that perhaps this was unreal, and he would, at some point, find himself back at the institute.

But as doctor, or patient?

He walked for at least two hours, and the plain of glass began to thin. The time element was guesswork on his part because his watch had ceased to function, the hands spinning crazily in opposite directions.

There were patches of what looked to be grass, though it was scarlet in color with tips of indigo. Bright cobalt blue flowers with stamens of silver and crimson grew in bright clumps within the grass. He bent down to smell one, but some corrosive chemical in the grass produced angry blisters on his fingers and palm. He instinctively sucked on the injured fingers, only to blister his lips.

Terribly thirsty, Will found shallow pools of tepid, stagnant water. It was ghastly and had a sharp, metallic taste, but he drank it anyway. It made his stomach cramp momentarily, but he was able to keep it down.

The glass gave way to rocky ground, and the scarlet grass and cobalt blossoms gave way to gnarled bushes of black wood with silvery leaves.

Berries grew on these bushes, plump and pink with small orange and white dots. By now he was ravenous, but ate cautiously, afraid of something corrosive.

The berries had an unpleasant taste like meat just shy of spoiling, but they did fill his stomach. Some were infested with bright green worms. Remembering a documentary he had seen of Air Force survival training, he ate these as well.

He found himself walking through a small canyon threading through immense gray and black hills. Will didn't know if he had dozed while walking or if the terrain had suddenly altered as dream landscapes are prone to do.

A large boulder lay in the path, and scrawled on it in a childish hand was the message

BEWAER THUH WEELURRS

Will was trying to figure out who or what were "*weelurrs*" when he heard a piercing, high-pitched shriek from up in the hills. The scream echoed throughout the canyon and was answered by others.

Will heard a strange whistling, and looked behind him.

Coming out of the hills was something that seemed to be a man on all fours with wheels at the ends of his arms and legs. He was dressed in some sort of patchwork leather tunic and breeches, and his hair was long and woven into a dozen braids which whipped behind him like frenzied snakes. His eyes were large and dark, no more human than a shark's.

The worst part, though, was his mouth.

It was large, abnormally so, with upper and lower serrated plates instead of teeth. From that horrid mouth a banshee shriek bellowed forth as the creature approached him, faster than any accomplished human skater Will had ever seen.

Will ran through the canyon, looking in vain for a place to hide. The peculiar whistling the creatures' wheels made as they crunched over the sand and gravel echoed in the hills around him, as was the terrible wailing of the Wheelers.

Will knew now he was being herded by a pack of the creatures, but didn't know enough of the terrain to evade them. Any possible deviation from his desired path was quickly cut off by one of the creatures who would wail and snap at him until he returned to the main trail.

He saw with dismay that the canyon ended in a dead end, a sheer cliff face with no protrusions or gaps where he might gain purchase.

Will stopped at the wall and turned to face his pursuers, his heart thudding in his chest.

It's an illusion, he told himself, *a psychic test. These are your fears made manifest.*

Face them and you will conquer them.

Eight Wheelers rolled to within ten feet of him and stopped. The Wheeler he had first seen stood slightly in front of the others, and was obviously the leader. Two of the creatures were smaller and more delicate, but Will could not determine whether they were adult females or children.

The lead Wheeler moved forward and snapped at him, its eyes wide and fever-bright. Saliva flew from its mouth in viscous droplets.

Will touched his chest.

"Will. Friend."

The Wheeler watched him, as if trying to decide whether this was a trick.

Will repeated the gesture.

"Will. Friend." He then pointed at the Wheeler and said, "Who are – "

What happened next was so fast he could barely register the motion. The Wheeler struck like a snake and bit off most of his index finger. Will screamed in agony as blood spurted from his ruined finger and was quickly absorbed into the barren ground. He was sickened to see one of the cobalt flowers spring up, its seed obviously lying dormant until blood was spilled.

The other Wheelers shrieked and jostled one another as the leader gulped down his finger with same bobbing motions a crane makes swallowing a frog.

Will pulled a handkerchief from his pocket and wrapped his hand. The wound was throbbing and burned with a searing pain. He wondered what infection was even now coursing through his system.

The lead Wheeler looked at the others and shrieked something in five harsh bursts. The others wailed back at him, then all eyes were on Will.

It was clear they meant to tear him apart.

There was a hollow booming sound then, and a roar of a lion.

It's Dorothy, he thought, *she's come to get me.*

A cunningly camouflaged door opened in the canyon wall, and a metal man and large animal emerged, but they were not Dorothy's companions.

The metal man he had seen earlier had worn a gentle look and was burnished to a mirror-like shine. This thing was covered in rust, parts of it actually eaten away by corrosion. Its movements produced squeals and protesting shrieks that were nearly as abominable as the Wheelers. It carried a sort of halberd, the blade side serrated and the other a long spike with a barbed end. Its eyes were blue flickers like gas flames, and steam issued from a grille fashioned to look like a sadistic smile.

The Rust Man's animal companion was a huge patchwork dog. It's variegated hide was crazy quilt of furs and hides from some twenty different animals, including tiger, elephant, zebra, ocelot, crocodile, cheetah and snake. It's mouth and teeth were enormous. For it to swallow Will's head would be no more inconvenient than a man taking a whole apricot into his mouth. Its eyes were dark like the Wheelers, and it wore a collar of small skulls strung together.

Children's skulls, Will realized, and felt sick.

The Rust Man beat on his chest with one great fist, producing the low booming sound.

"I am the Rust Man," he bellowed, "and this formidable creature next to me is Mr. Manyteeth, the Patchwork Jackal!"

The Wheelers muttered but did not advance.

The Rust Man gestured at Will.

"This man is property of the Wizard," he roared. "Go or face the wrath of Nyx the Terrible and Merciless!"

"Eece him," the lead Wheeler exclaimed, pointing to his own mouth while he drooled copiously.

"Go," the Rust Man repeated.

"Eece man, tayse gud! Maybay eece yoo toos!"

The Wheelers shrieked in agreement until Mr. Manyteeth the Patchwork Jackal decapitated one of the smaller Wheelers with one quick bite.

The Wheelers shrieked in fury but the Rust Man readied his weapon. The Wheelers, knowing they were outmatched, turned and rolled off into the hills, shrieking insults and promises of reprisals.

While the Patchwork Jackal finished the Wheeler in a series of sickening, crunching bites, the Rust Man approached Will.

"Thank you," Will said, "I was sure –"

"We have to go, Will, the Wizard is expecting you."

"How do you know me?" Will asked. "Did Dorothy send you?"

"Dorothy," the Rust Man said, and looked at the Patchwork Jackal, who merely growled low. "Dorothy is the reason I am no longer in Kansas."

Will gaped at him, then saw within the scabrous visage a face he knew.

Dr. Vincent Colby.

Dorothy's former therapist.

"How…" Will began.

"If I knew that I would have gone back!" said the Rust Man, his voice filled with the angry squeal of shearing metal. "I took away that damn drawing she was always staring at and found myself here. Now… Now it's too late to go back."

Will looked at the creature, afflicted with a leprosy of oxidation, and realized there was no hospital in the world that could make him human again. What had been done was the most awful magic, and only magic might restore him. Then he realized what he was thinking and chided himself.

Magic. Superstitious wish-fulfillment.

The Rust Man's smile grew wider, which was a terrible thing to see.

"You think you are dreaming, or drugged."

Will smiled. He had just realized his hurt finger was uninjured in the sober, waking world.

"Of course, Dr. Colby, I…"

"*Don't call me that!*" The Rust Man screamed, bits of red flakes and foul-smelling oil flying from his grille as he approached Will with his battleaxe held high.

"Sorry, I didn't mean to offend you!"

The Rust Man nodded and lowered the halberd.

"We don't go by our Kansas names." He saw the puzzled expression on Will's face. "To the indigenous people of Oz, our world is known as '*Kansas*'."

Will was still convinced he was dreaming or hallucinating, but had no idea how long he might be in this state. Since he could feel intense pain here, he decided he would do everything possible to make his experience free of discomfort.

It seemed his best option in that regard was to gain the trust of the Rust Man and the Patchwork Jackal.

"Dorothy likes me," he began. He saw the Rust Man tense, so he continued quickly. "If we can find her, I'm sure the Wizard or Ozma could undo this um… enchantment you are under. Then the two of us can figure out how to return to Kansas."

The Rust Man looked at him as if he were an idiot, and Mr. Manyteeth the Patchwork Jackal snickered.

"We are banished to the Deadly Desert, Doctor Price, don't you know that? Don't tell me you missed her sign, the one as big as the side of a barn?"

"But, I haven't done anything," Will protested.

The Rust Man and Mr. Manyteeth laughed.

"You haven't done wrong, my friend, you *are* wrong. Your type is an anathema to all the sweet creatures of Oz… You have to come to Oz with an open mind, doctor. An open mind and the heart of a child. You, you're an intellectual. You believe that only what is reasoned and rational is worth consideration. But don't worry, our Wizard wants to put you to good use."

The Rust Man whistled, a shrill, unpleasant sound. Several bent and misshapen gnomes emerged from the cliff. Four grabbed Will and wrestled him to the ground where they held him fast. Will shouted and struggled, but the gnomes were far too strong.

A fifth gnome appeared, bent under the weight of a large basket filled with the caustic scarlet grass.

Will's clothes were torn from him, and he saw with horror that the Rust Man was now sharpening the blade of his halberd on a portable grinding wheel. Sparks and smoke filled the air and the Patchwork Jackal sneezed, his skull collar rattling.

"What are you doing?" Will cried, but the Rust Man ignored him until his task was done.

He stood over Will, an oxidized parody of a man, the only part of him shining and new the terrible weapon.

"You're going to be the new Scarecrow of Nyx," he announced. "To accomplish this, I am going to split you open," he told Will matter-of-factly. "Mr. Manyteeth the Patchwork Jackal will dine on your entrails while my gnomes stuff you full of firegrass. Don't worry, we're going to leave that wonderful brain of yours intact."

The gnomes tightened their grip. Mr. Manyteeth licked his chops as the Rust Man raised his halberd.

Will saw with sudden clarity that it was all real. Tears sprang to his eyes and he began to convulse with fear as he cried out to his former colleague.

"*Please, please! How can you do this?*"

The Rust Man chuckled bitterly.

"It's easy... when you don't have a heart."

THE END.

PUMPKINHEAD

by Rajan Khanna

M r. P walked out of his pumpkin-shaped house and paused on the edge of the garden path. Even in the waning light, I could tell that the colour in his face, which should have been a bright, glossy orange-gold, had faded to a dull fuscous hue. The skin sagged with a grayish cast. I had only picked that one a week earlier.

He bent his round head to the side and tapped it with one gloved hand. When he righted it again, he stared at me a moment before speaking. "I think there's something wrong with this one," he said.

"It's deteriorating," I said, smoothing down my dress. "But it looks like it still has some life in it. A few days at least."

"No, it's...it feels a bit odd on the left side. And my vision...I think I'll need a new one right away. I keep...seeing things."

"Okay," I said, not knowing what else to say. "I'll get you a new one right away. Do you want me to take it to her to carve?"

"No," he said. "There's no time. I'll have to do it myself."

I nodded and went to pick a new pumpkin. The blight was getting worse. I would have to step up my efforts.

Luckily for me, I wasn't dependent on the usual growing times that such pumpkins would require. While it would normally take months, Mr. P had supplied me with packets of Dr. Nikidik's Magical Powder of Growing, obtained from one of his high-placed connections, which meant I could cultivate a new crop in less than a week.

I walked among the golden rinds, finally selecting one that was suitable for my employer's purposes - large, evenly shaped and firm. I picked it, then brought it inside.

Mr. P sat at the table, his sagging head leaning against one gloved hand. It was tilted slightly to the side and he was waving the free fingers of his other hand in the air.

"Mr. P?" I said.

He tilted his head toward me. "Call me Jack," he said, for the hundredth time. But I couldn't. He was my employer, but more than that, he was a celebrity, and a close personal friend of the queen. In fact, if it wasn't for his imminent need, she would be the one about to carve this pumpkin for him. He was basically part of the royal family.

He held out his hands and I placed the pumpkin into them. His arms, which he kept covered at all times, were little more than wooden sticks, like broom handles, but they were strong and sturdy and he pulled the pumpkin closer, cradling it for a second before placing it on the table in front of him.

Fascinated, I longed to watch as he carved it, to see how it was done, but it was such an intimate act, so very personal, and I couldn't bear to intrude upon it. As the knife penetrated the rind and into the tender inner flesh, I turned and left the house and returned to the field where I belonged.

I left the farm not long afterward, able to do very little after night fell and, truth be told, somewhat stumped as to a next step. I thought that some sleep might help, so I returned to the boarding house in which I stayed nearby in Winkie Country. That part of Oz was still strange to me, raised as I was in Quadling Country. But the queen had asked for the best, and word reached her that it was me. I won't say that I wasn't pleased to hear this, for I took pride in my accomplishments, but it also made me nervous and I feared being shown to be a fraud.

These thoughts continued to rattle around my head – my fears, my pride, my frustration at being unable to solve the problem before me – until I found sleep at last. When I awoke, early the next morning, I returned to Mr. P's farm and bent down to the task once more.

My process was simple. Because I had the powder to aid growth, I had planted the seeds in batches, two at a time. One would be a test group, the other a normal group to compare it to. As each pair of batches matured, another would be a few days behind it and so forth. This allowed me to try out different techniques and theories as to what might be causing this.

The first thing I ruled out was infestation. For one, there were no signs of critters on or in the pumpkins. However, this being Oz, I didn't trust my eyes alone, and so borrowed a pair of magnifying spectacles. But the only insects afflicting the crop were the flies hovering over the rotten pumpkins on the other side of the field. Every so often I would find a specimen that had been punctured or torn – the growth powder sometimes accelerated things too much - and my hands would punch through the rotten rind, into the maggot-strewn interior. I was used to critters of all kinds – snakes and worms and crickets and toads – but this challenged even my resolve.

Not all the rotten pumpkins lay at the other end of the field, though. Those that Mr. P took for his heads, no matter how short a time he wore them, he buried, in a plot of land adjacent to the pumpkin fields. In the last few months the number of graves had increased severely so that it looked like the graveyard of a small town, much like the town I grew up in. Looking at that field of buried heads made me think of my parents and how much I missed them. Their graves lay far away in Quadling Country.

If critters weren't to blame, I thought, it might be the soil. So I planted some other crops beside the pumpkins – some squash, some beets, some cucumbers. All turned out fine. It was only the pumpkins that seemed to be affected.

It stymied me. As I tended the current crop, they looked good to my critical eye, plump and glossy, heavy to the hand. It seemed only when they were picked that they started to deteriorate, turning to mush within weeks. Once, Mr. P had told me, a head would last months for him. Possibly up to a year if well cared for. Some property in his body, or perhaps the force that animated it, kept them hardy. But recently, it was weeks, if that. The last had only endured for nine days. I thought about what it might be like if I had to change my head every week and I wondered how I could function.

"How's it coming?" came Mr. P's voice from behind me.

I bent over the pumpkins, running my fingers across the creases. "I'm making progress," I said. "But not as much as I would like."

The voice came closer. "I feel better today," he said. "The new head seems to help."

I nodded, unable to face him. I couldn't overcome the thought that I was letting him down. That I was failing him.

"Thank you for helping me," he said. "I know you're doing your best."

I bowed my head.

"No. Really," he said. "Please." I stood up and turned to face him.

And almost screamed.

One of Mr P's eyes sunk low on his pumpkin face, as if flowing down, as if made of wax. The other jaunted at an unusual angle, casting that side of the face in a demonic light. That eyebrow was high and menacing. The other was a deep, crude gash in the face. The nose was a mere slit, the mouth a vicious sneer tearing across the lower curve of the pumpkin.

"What is it?" he said, stumbling back.

I shook my head, unable, unwilling to speak the words.

I swallowed, trying to suppress my horror, to spare his feelings, but I was apparently ineffective, for he ran off, his wooden limbs pumping to put as much distance between us as possible.

When he was gone, I turned and collapsed among the pumpkins, running my fingers through the dirt to console myself, inhaling the earthy, mineral scent. My tears watered the soil, partially from fear, and partially from the knowledge that I had hurt my employer.

The day's activities, like every day, left half moons of dirt beneath my fingernails. Some days the combination of soil and pumpkin pulp left a reddish cast like blood, and I was once again reminded of my parents.

They died when I was barely a woman, though I had already spent long years toiling in the garden. A disease swept through the Quadling countryside, a red disease like everything in that place. I was spared, but my parents bore the full brunt of it, stiffening and reddening until they looked like radishes laid out in bed. They, like the others stricken with the disease, were taken to the graveyard and buried. There were memorial services and solemn vigils, but none of these did anything to soothe the ache that sprouted and bloomed through me in those long weeks.

Only one thing could. I did what came naturally, drawing out seeds I had long saved and nurtured for a garden of my own. These I planted and watered and watched for the first shoots from the earth. When they appeared, I watered and cared for them until the others in the town recognized what it was I had done.

By then, it was far too late to stop it, and green vines and leaves spread throughout the town graveyard, strong and verdant, striving to escape the dark gravity of the earth. Soon, the graveyard bloomed with flowers and with thick fruit - cucumbers and tomatoes, peas, beans, and strawberries. All of these shone red on the vines, as most crops in our land did. The townsfolk gathered, and talked of rooting it, of pulling all the plants up or setting fire to them. But in the end, they left them. They feared disturbing the dead, their loved ones entangled, embraced by the reaching, yearning roots. So they left it there, a dark, red garden the likes of which no one had ever seen and none would again.

Instead, they made me leave. And though I missed it, the garden I helped create, I knew that in some small way, a part of my parents lived again through it. I had done my part, the rest was up to the elements.

When I saw Mr. P again, a towel wrapped around his head leaving only narrow gaps for his eyes and one for his mouth.

"Mr. P," I said. "I'm...I'm sorry."

"No," he said. "I saw myself. I don't know what I was doing when I carved this one. It looked fine to me. But I don't want to abandon it just yet. So far it's fine, and I don't want to switch so quickly."

"I understand," I said, looking at my nails. "I'll get back to work right away."

"Linnaea," he said, tugging on the lower end of towel.

"Yes, boss?" I said.

His mismatched eyes bored into me.

"Never mind," he said, and turned away. "Carry on." He waved one gloved hand in the air.

I returned to my work. Having ruled out the soil and infestation, I considered the pumpkins themselves. Most of Mr. P's crop had come from seeds harvested from his earlier batches, which accounted for the yellowish, almost golden quality of the pumpkins. But I had brought some Quadling seeds with me as well, which now dotted the field with a darker, reddish orange than the original. All fell victim to the rot, with similar timelines. So the seeds were not to blame either.

That meant the situation was more complex. Either a combination of factors, or something beyond the normal difficulties of farming.

I considered magical causes. Mr. P was highly respected, a close companion of the queen. Afflicting him in this way would be dangerous, but at the same time, it could be a way to strike at Ozma.

I walked over to Mr. P's pumpkin-shaped house and knocked on the door.

"Come in," he called.

I entered. The boss was slumped over the table, the towel loosened around his head. In one of his hands he held a bottle of dark glass and he was pouring liquid, a little at a time, into his crooked mouth. He swiveled his head slightly so he could look at me out of one eye.

"Yes?"

"I just...I wanted to ask you a question," I said.

"Okay."

"Do you know of anyone who might be trying to harm you? Who might be doing this on purpose?"

He poured some more of the liquid into his mouth and I caught a whiff of alcohol. I wondered where it went. The only thing I could think was that the small amount was absorbed into the flesh of his head.

"I can't...I can't think of anyone," he said. "I have no enemies."

"But Ozma..."

"There are other ways someone could reach her," Mr. P said, now slurring his words.

"Why are you drinking?" I said.

He looked at the bottle in his hand.

"I should be grateful for the life that I have," he said. "And I am. But this..." he waved at his wrapped-up head, "makes that life less bearable. I think differently now. And things look strange to me. I have odd thoughts. I can't bear to go outside and be among other people. You're the only person I've seen in weeks."

I moved a step closer to him.

"I get very lonely," he said.

I sat down opposite him across the table. My hand, dirt-stained and calloused, rested scant inches from his.

"I tried to make a companion for myself once," he said, softly. "When the loneliness became too great. I commissioned a Winkie carpenter to make her body – a much finer one than I have, certainly – and I planned to give her a head like mine, though perhaps crafted with greater care. Only the Powder of Life, which gave me my vital spark, and also the Sawhorse and the Gump, was all gone long ago and the magician who made it had committed suicide by jumping off the side of a mountain."

"I searched for another magician to help me, hard because magic has been outlawed for all except Ozma and Glinda. But eventually I found one, hiding in a swamp, practicing his craft there. He gave me Powder of Life in exchange for some valuables I had – a jeweled belt, and a bracelet of gold, both gifts of my mother."

"But couldn't she have helped you?" I interrupted. "Since she can practice magic."

"She knew nothing of this," he said. "She still doesn't. I wanted it to be private. Personal."

I nodded. "I understand."

"Do you?" he said. "Well, I had the body, and I selected my finest pumpkin and carved her face myself. You may well wonder why I didn't get a famous artist to do it, but the truth is that I wanted to have that connection. It may not have been the most beautiful face ever carved, but it pleased me and that's all that mattered."

I nodded again. "So what happened?"

He bowed his toweled head, then poured more of the drink into his mouth.

"I laid her out in my bed, dressed in a nice yellow sundress decorated with daisies. And she was so beautiful, lying there. And I sprinkled..." His voice dropped to a whisper. "I sprinkled the powder on her."

I was almost holding my breath at the story.

"Did it work?"

He raised his head. "In a way. It brought her to life, her limbs started moving almost immediately, but," he took another gulp of the alcohol, "she had no sense in her. She was alive, but without any thought, without any brains. Mindless."

I said nothing, not knowing what to say.

"You can't imagine what it was like to see her, to see this beautiful creature, thrashing around without purpose, without any understanding of what was happening or where she was. She...she attacked me. Savagely. I ran to escape her. Outside into the pumpkin field, and she ran after me. I was only able to stop her by...by *hitting* her. With a shovel. She fell down, but still thrashed. So I grabbed an axe and I cut at her arms and legs, splintering the fine, sanded wood, ripping her yellow dress and cutting the pumpkin from her head. Then, when it was all done and she had stopped moving, I dragged the pieces to the graveyard and buried them beneath the ground."

His head lowered, propped against one wrist. I reached my hand across to his other, slipped my fingers over his worn white glove.

"I never told anyone that before," he said. "Not even my mother."

"I understand," I said. And before I could think about it, and perhaps in an effort to also share something I'd never told anyone, I told him about my parents' death and the graveyard and the garden I planted on top of it.

He nodded. During his talk and the drinking and listening to me afterward, his towel had come undone and his mismatched features were now revealed. A dribble of the liquor down his open mouth lent him a monstrous appearance, but I kept my face blank.

"There's more, though," I said. "The night I left town, I packed up my belongings, preparing to leave. But I snuck back into town, and over to the graveyard. I picked the fruit that grew there – long, glossy red squash and strawberries, whatever I could pick, and I took these with me. As I traveled, I ate them, thinking in some strange way that I was keeping a part of my parents with me. That I had taken something of them out of the town and into myself."

I sat back, suddenly drained and light.

"Is that wrong?"

"No," he said, shaking his pumpkin head. "No. I suppose if I could have eaten my companion – I never named her, I couldn't bear to – I might have."

I squeezed his hand, happy for the sharing. Then I slipped out of the house and back into the field.

That day brought no new results and this was beginning to worry me. I had gone to Mr. P to help him with his problem, and so far I was no closer than when I started.

Maybe that was why I walked the fields looking for the best pumpkin I could find. This I carefully removed and took with me back to my room at the boarding house. Carefully, with all the skill I could muster, I wielded the knife, carving a face into the pumpkin. I gave it bright, kindly eyes, a strong, patrician nose, and a wide, happy smile.

I lightened it slightly, removing some of the pulp from behind the carved features, but kept a nice, dense seedy section inside. By all accounts, Mr. P relied on the seeds for his brains. When I was done, I looked it, pleased. I could never be accounted an artist, but I was good with carpentry and I'd made many a scarecrow.

The next morning, I arrived early for work, my gift in a reed basket, wrapped in a tablecloth. When Mr. P appeared, stumbling ever so slightly, his head still covered with the towel, I brought the basket to him. Trembling, on shaky feet, I held it out to him, wordlessly.

He took it, tilting his head to one side, and unwrapped it with his gloved hands. When it was uncovered, he had to pull the towel to one side to see what it was. Then he looked up at me.

"I thought...since you had some troubles with the head you have now...," I swallowed. "I can't guarantee it will last. Not yet, but..."

"It's perfect," Mr. P said. "Absolutely perfect." He looked at me. "Thank you," he said.

I smiled and returned to the fields as he carried it into the house to do whatever it was he did to change heads. I found myself wondering what he looked like without a pumpkin on top of his neck. Did he lose his sight when it was taken off? Did he feel that separation?

I continued to work in the fields, trying to gather more information about the blight.

Sometime after midday, I smelled a delicious odor wafting from the house. It was my habit to take a small lunch when I was working, usually a salad or a loaf of fresh bread and farmer's cheese, but I had become so engrossed in my notes that I'd forgotten. My stomach growled at the smell.

Then Mr. P appeared in the doorway to his house, my pumpkin on his head, looking happy and almost regal. "Come in, Linnaea," he called.

I did so to find the table laid, and a pie steaming on the tablecloth. "I made it," he said. "For you. From my old head. Please, sit."

I took the chair that was offered, noting that the other chair had no place setting. "The rot wasn't so far advanced that it was no good," he said. "And I hated to see it go to waste, even with its problems. Plus, I wanted to thank you."

I sat down and cut a slice and moved it to my plate. Next to it was a bowl of fresh cream that he must have just whipped up. I plopped a dollop on top of the creamy crust. I wanted to ask him to join me - it seemed wrong to enjoy it on my own - but I thought that might seem to strange to him, eating of his own self. He'd always buried his heads before.

I placed the pie into my mouth, chewed and swallowed. It was sweet and earthy, and I dreamt of the taste later that night.

That evening, I brought my notes to Mr. P and we sat across the table again. "Thank you again for the head," he said. "This one feels better than any I've had in recent months. I think better with it, and I haven't been plagued by any strange thoughts since putting it on."

"I'm glad," I said. "I've been reviewing the notes I've made, and I've ruled out a problem with the soil, with the seeds, and with any kind of pests."

"So what does that leave?" he said.

"I want to do another test," I said. "I want to try a new pumpkin. One that wasn't grown on this farm. One grown on another farm."

"But I have such a wonderful head now," he said, the disappointment plain in his voice.

"I'm glad you like it, boss, but it won't last. And I want the next one to be from another farm."

"I wish you would call me Jack," he said. "Very well. If you think it's for the best. But I think that this is the one. I think this one will break the curse. You'll see."

I smiled, but I didn't believe him. It would start fading in about a week or two, then he would need another head.

"I'll ask around tomorrow, see if there's a farm nearby where I can find them. Then when the time's right I'll take it and, if you like, carve it for you and we'll try it for next time.

"Okay," he said. "Thank you, Linnaea. If it wasn't for you, I think I might lose my mind."

I blushed, then said goodnight. I went home with the leftover pie in my basket.

Over the next few days I continued my experiments, but I also roamed the countryside, asking around at farmer's stalls and at the market. It turned out that Mr. P's pumpkins were so readily available (for he couldn't use all of them for heads) that many of the nearby farmers had stopped growing them.

I was forced to roam further afield, taking the better part of the week to find a farmer who was still growing them, and at sizes that suited my work. When I did, I was disappointed to discover that they weren't part of his current crop rotation and if I wanted them, I would have to use some of the Growing Powder, which I'd left at Mr. P's house.

By the time I returned to his farm, I could already see the signs of the rot in his face. The color, originally a nice amber-gold, had faded already, and it sagged slightly on his neck. The features I'd carved, while still pleasant, had lost some of their sharpness.

"Any problems, boss?" I asked.

He shook his head, merrily. "None at all," he said. "I'm telling you, this is the one."

I decided not to pierce his swollen hopes and instead set about retrieving the Growth Powder. Tucking the little brown paper packet into the pocket of my coat, I returned to Mr. P. "I'll be gone for a few more days," I said. "You'll be okay?"

"I'll be right as rain," he said, bowing. "I'll be fantastic. But hurry back. I thought we might have dinner on your return."

I blushed, but nodded and said okay.

It took several more days for me to return to the farmer and for the pumpkins to grow, even with the help of the growth powder. The farmer must have thought me a queer sight when I sprinkled the powder onto the sprouts, saying the magic words (which always felt strange in my mouth). But soon the vines were stretching out across the field and the tiny yellow orbs of the pumpkins themselves had started to grow.

By the time the crop was ready, the farmer bade me thanks for the help, let me select the best of the batch, and then I was off back to Mr. P and his farm.

I kept the pumpkin whole for the trip, though intending to carve it before he wore it. He'd seemed to like that. I carried it in my basket.

Mr. P came out to greet me when I called, his head in worse shape than I'd hoped. The color had almost completely faded, now brownish-grey, and it sunk low on his neck, the bottom squashed against his wooden shoulders. Tears had appeared in the skin, and his once proud features were distorted yet again.

"Linnaea," he said. "It's so good to see you."

"Mr. P," I said. "I brought you a new head." I held out the basket to him.

He looked at it without taking it. "But this one is working just fine," he said. "This is the one you made for me."

"I know," I said. "But I can make this one, too."

He shrugged and took the basket, placing it down on his porch. "I'll look at it later," he said.

I scratched my head. "Okay," I said. "But we should probably see to it soon. To see if anything changes."

"Never mind that," he said. "How was..." He trailed off, looking at a point above my head.

"Mr. P?"

His eyes returned to me, as if he'd just woken up. "How was your trip?" he said, as if nothing had happened.

"Long," I said. "It took days just to get the crop in shape. But now we have the sample. And I'll be able to see how it reacts to you."

"Yes..." he said.

"I'm going to go check on the crops here," I said. "Then I'll come back and we can do something about that head."

Mr. P bowed again, and I saw the deteriorating crown of his head. "I will get to work on dinner, then," he said.

I walked down to the fields with my notebook and made a record of how things were progressing. The crops seemed in fine shape, as well as I would expect them to be. What would be important now would be how Mr. P reacted to the new head. If that succeeded, then there was something systemic to the whole field, despite the fact that the fruits and vegetables flourished before being used as heads for Mr. P. If it failed, then it was something else. Some property of the process, perhaps?

For many years Mr. P's heads had been fine. So something had changed. Something that affected the field, or...

The field.

I looked at the rows of grave markers, walked over to them. Most of them bore a simple marker. *Here Lies the Mortal Part of JACK PUMPKINHEAD* and the date which it spoiled. That is until the end. Because the heads were spoiling so fast, they had been tossed into something like a mass grave, piled on top of one another with no marker. The last marker bore a date near to when the troubles started happening.

Between this marker and the mass grave, was an unmarked plot of earth. I looked back to the house - Mr. P was nowhere to be seen, probably busy with dinner - so I grabbed my spade and started digging.

It wasn't long before my spade hit something, and as I bent to see what it was, my hand closed on something long and wooden. I pulled it from the damp earth, to find that it was an arm, with a hand, lovingly crafted and jointed, on its end. I turned it over, wiping the dirt from it to admire it.

The arm had been sanded smooth, letting the natural color of the wood beneath come through, but something in the earth had grown over it, ropy strands of mucous-green vines or roots lacing up over the wood.

Then it moved.

I dropped it and scurried out of the hole I'd dug. Then, as my panic subsided, I chided myself for my silliness. It had probably just flopped over as I turned it. I crouched down to retrieve it again, this time, picking it up by the wrist.

The hand swiveled and gripped my arm. I swatted at it with my free hand, but it held firm. Then it began to squeeze.

Pain shot through my arm, and I felt the pressure on my bone. I slammed the severed arm against the ground, but that only caused a white blossom of agony that almost made me pass out.

I reached for the spade, closed my hand around the part where the shaft met the metal blade and brought it down on the arm. Each strike sent blinding pain streaking through me, but I closed my eyes and hammered at it until I heard a splintering sound that I hoped was the wood cracking.

The hand loosened and I yanked my arm back, scrabbling out of the hole. With my feet, my good hand, and then my body, I pushed the exhumed earth back into the hole on top of the still-moving limb. Before it disappeared, I thought I saw more wooden fragments pushing themselves up through the soil.

I ran for the house, my left arm useless, dangling at my side, each step sending new pain ringing through it. I thought it must be broken.

I ran into the house, to Mr P. He was busying himself with some food, fussing near the oven.

"I know what it is that caused this," I said, breathless, and wincing with the pain.

"What?" he said.

"Your companion. The one you made. Whatever was in that powder, it went horribly wrong. That thing is still alive. And when it attacked you, I think, something must have happened. To you. To make your heads rot and decay. I think that's what it is."

Mr. P tilted his head to one side. He clasped his hands in front of him, and I saw that they were bare, with no gloves. The wood of the arms and fingers, little more than branches with crude extensions, was riddled with strands of sickly yellow. They wove up the arms like turgid veins.

"Mr. P," I said. "Jack. You need help. Maybe Ozma, or someone, can help you. It might be possible to fix this."

"It doesn't need fixing," Mr. P said. "You're here now. That other one, she was a mistake. I didn't need to make her, I just needed to find you."

"You're not listening to me."

"I have something for you," he said. "Come." He grabbed my hand and pulled me into his kitchen. There, on the counter, was the pumpkin I had brought him, carved. Like his old mismatched face, its features spread across the skin of the pumpkin, the eyes jagged gashes that skewed apart from one another, the nose little more than a slit, the mouth a grotesque slash.

"What is that for?" I said.

He looked at me, the smile stretched across his face, the way I had made it. "Why for you, of course."

I stared, uncomprehending. I shook my head. "I don't understand."

"So you can be like me," he said. "So we can be together." He reached down below the counter and brought up an axe. "We just need to get rid of the head you have now."

I screamed.

I ran.

He stumbled after me. I ran for the fields, for the open sky.

"Come back," he called. "We can be together."

I pushed my legs as hard as I could, but he was taller and his legs longer and I felt him crash into me, and push me down to the fresh soil. He rolled me over, straddling me with his wooden legs. Up close, I could see that the wood beneath the cuffs of his trousers was also covered with the same veiny growths.

"Hold still," he said, his voice still merry. "It will only take a moment."

His sagging face hovered over mine, the smile wide. A brown slug slithered from his open mouth, like a tongue, dripping slime. It plopped onto my neck, writhing.

I screamed again.

My left arm was useless, broken, but I pulled my right hand free and clawed for his face. I hooked my fingers into his right eye cavity, and pulled. Great chunks of rotten pumpkin pulled away. The sickeningly sweet scent of rot filled my nose. I saw into the dark cavity of his head. Maggots squirmed and wriggled through the decaying pulp.

He gripped my broken arm with his hand and pain roared through me. My eyes rolled up in my head and everything went black for a moment.

When they flickered open, he was standing over me, the axe in his hand. "It will only hurt for a moment," he said. "Then we'll be together."

I scrabbled with my free hand for something, anything that could help me. I stuffed it down into my coat pocket.

"You've eaten of me," Mr. P said. "I'm already inside of you."

My hand closed on the Powder of Growth. I threw it at him and screamed the magic words. But the wood of his body was long dead and the pumpkin, too.

He brought the axe back. The veiny growths pulsed along his arms. They spread, coursing across the wood.

He toppled back.

I scrambled up and, using my good hand and all my weight, pulled on the axe gripped between his twig fingers. It came free. Then, turning, I brought it down on him. Again and again. Wood splinters flew into the air. Then maggot strewn pumpkin pulp. I hacked and hacked away at him until he was all splinters.

Then I thought about passing out. About giving into the pain and the weariness that gripped me. But I couldn't.

Instead I gathered the splinters and other pieces together, using the shovel to push them into a pile on top of the tablecloth. Then I took them inside to the oven and pushed them all in to burn.

I would have to leave. To flee. Mr. P was a close confidant of the queen and I wasn't sure that anyone would believe me as to what had happened. So I snuck out in the night again, thinking that perhaps I should visit Munchkin or Gillikin country for a change. I would need to find a doctor at least to set my broken arm which I bound in place with some cloth.

It was only later, days after I'd left the pumpkin fields, that I remembered the wooden limbs in the unmarked grave still moving, ceaselessly moving, beneath the soil.

THE END.

TIN

by Barry Napier

He watched her as she slept, being careful not to make a sound. His joints had been making the occasional odd noise ever since he had started walking again and at times, he felt as if his legs weren't his own. So he knelt there, his old knees against the ground, watching the sleeping girl.

Her dog lay curled beside her. Its ear had twitched for a moment as he had approached and there was a panicked moment where he feared the dog had heard him. But the mongrel had settled down and remained asleep by the girl's side.

He watched the girl breathing—in and out, simple yet somehow so complicated. He admired her for her anatomy and the way her mind worked. She was rather daft at times but there was a brilliance about her that he did not understand.

After all, he was not made of flesh. He was pretty sure he *used* to be, but that had been a very long time ago.

The closest thing to human anatomy he possessed were his hands. The joints were flawless and moved like the human girl's. When he had been created, much detail had gone into his hands. At one time, they had been his most imperative feature.

But not now. Now he was old, decrepit and of little use.

Or so everyone thought.

He grinned. His face made a slight sound as his mouth moved but it was so miniscule that not even the dog heard it.

He watched them a bit longer—the girl from a place called Kansas and her annoying little pet—as he tested the reflexes of his hands.

He tested them by squeezing the handle of the axe he held. His axe, just like his tin body, reflected the moonlight in a peculiar shade of white.

He could do it now, if he wanted. He could just plunge the axe into the girl's chest. He could squash the dog into a bloody mess with his heavy foot. It would be over in a matter of seconds.

He peered back over his shoulder, his neck making another of those slight rusted sounds. The Scarecrow was several yards behind them, snoring and oblivious. By the time that imbecile got to his shaky feet and rushed to the girl's rescue, it would be done.

His shoulders seemed to flinch in anticipation of raising the axe into the air and driving it into the girl's body.

But something inside of him told him to wait.

He looked away from the Scarecrow and focused on the copse of trees that they had selected to camp behind. He could see the magnificent yellow glow of the road through the trees. He wondered if the bricks of gold that comprised the road were speaking to him, telling him to wait and to properly fulfill his destiny.

Looking at the road made him feel sick. He may not have a heart, but he knew pain. And to him, the Yellow Brick Road was nothing but pain and suffering.

He looked back to the girl and her dog. He clenched the axe one final time and then relaxed his grip.

In time, it would be done. But not just yet.

Hundreds of years ago, when Munchkinland had been nothing more than a bald spot within the forest, there had been plans to unify Oz. According to the Wizard of that time—a beloved man by the name of Rondolpho—and his council, it was illogical for such a diverse scope of citizens living in such seclusion from one another. For Oz to truly be great, it was believed that everyone in the land should live as one rather than as individual societies.

It was also believed that witches, Munchkins, common folk and all races in between should be able to live in a harmony that was befitting of the Land of Oz. There had been talk of clearing out much of the forests and connecting the villages and small towns with the rest of Oz. For Munchkins that needed to travel to the Emerald City, there was no sense in having to hike for eight days through the grueling and terrifying forests. There should be an easier way, a way for everyone to share the same conveniences of travel.

The Tin Woodsmen had been hired to work with transportation personnel from the Emerald City. Together, over a very tiresome period of four years, a great portion of Oz's woodland was knocked down. As the Tin Woodsmen chopped down the trees, Emerald City employees followed behind them, leveling the earth and laying down brick. When work was not going as fast as planned, mill workers and magicians from the Emerald City worked overtime to create *new* Tin Woodsmen.

It was a gruesome process, one that required actual human woodsmen to be transformed. The legs and arms were magically altered into large chunks of tin, molded to resemble something akin to human appendages. Most of the real work had gone into the eyes and hands—the finest detail ever created by the wizards within Oz.

And that was how he had been made.

Formerly a man named (rather aptly) Nick Chopper, he remembered very little of his human life. With his transformation into a Tin Woodsmen, he had easily forsaken his mortal memories for a life of immortality. But his was a life that hadn't been worth remembering.

His shrew of a wife had broken his heart and left him with nothing. So when the Wizard's men came calling, he gladly accepted the task. It gave him purpose and made him feel important for the first time in his life. And from what he could tell, the majority of the other Tin Woodsmen were there for the same reason—to escape a life that had been less than hospitable to them.

Of course, when the offer had been extended to Nick and the hundreds of other participants, they'd had no idea that they were agreeing to participate in a life of servitude.

The first glimpse of this life of slavery came two and a half years into the construction of the Yellow Brick Road. The crew at that time consisted of just over eight hundred Tin Woodsmen and three hundred employees from Emerald City. They had come to a clearing in the woods that, according to the topographers and mapmakers of Emerald City, had never been discovered.

The clearing was specked with small huts and shanties and was populated by a race of Munchkins that Nick had never seen. They were actually a bit smaller than typical Munchkins and looked rather like trolls. As the Tin Woodsmen awaited instruction, Nick heard murmurs from those around him.

"I've seen these creatures before," said a Tin Woodsmen named Alzo. "Several years ago in the village of Yull. There were perhaps a dozen of these creatures living among the people. They are called Woodkins."

"Are they creatures of magic?" another Woodsman asked.

Their answer came from behind them. One of the Emerald City employees was peering into an odd ocular device and studying the Woodkins. "No, they have no magic. We simply believed them to have gone extinct."

There were whispers behind the Tin Woodsmen as the Emerald City men discussed their plans of action. Nick and the other Woodsmen stared out to the little creatures and it was in that moment that Nick Chopper felt the last surge of dread that his heart would ever endure.

He knew even before the command came what they would be asked to do. And even as his heart sank at the thought, he found his strong hands wrapped around the axe handle, ready to obey.

Then the command came from behind them.

"Level it. *Leave no one alive.*"

There was only a moment's hesitation before the forest was alive with the clinking of eight hundred Tin Woodsmen tearing into the clearing, the makeshift armor of their bodies shining dully in the sunlight that crept through the treetops. They entered the clearing with their axes raised. The first blows had fallen before the Woodkin people could fully grasp what was happening.

Nick remembered very little of the event. He had swung his axe in a blind frenzy at anything that moved. His head and dwindling heart had been very aware of the hollow sounds of skulls crunching under his feet and blood splattering against his chest and arms. The Woodkins had only rocks, crude clubs and spears to defend themselves with and they fought with little enthusiasm; they knew the battle had been lost before it had even begun.

The battled ended rather quickly. The forest had been filled with the childlike squealing of the Woodkin people as they were massacred. But even those horrendous sounds had been so brief that it had scarcely disturbed the birds and other woodland creatures nearby.

There were exactly eight hundred and six Tin Woodsmen that surged into the Woodkin camp that day. The Woodkin population, they found after the melee was over, had been only one hundred and thirty.

Once the camp had been cleared, construction on the Yellow Brick Road continued. As they made progress, they buried the tiny bodies of the Woodkin people in shallow holes that were then covered by shining bricks of gold.

Several months later, the Tin Woodsman that had once been a man by the name of Nick Chopper woke up screaming. The Tin Men were allowed three hours of rest per day and ever since pillaging the Woodkin camp, those daily three hours had been haunting ones for Nick. He screamed into the night, the sound of his voice from his tin throat like that of a wounded mechanical monster.

Others stirred beside him but said nothing. From elsewhere within the campsite, one of the Emerald City men barked, "Back to sleep, you!"

But even when he was awake and at work, Nick's mind would wander. When he swung his axe into a tree trunk it felt like he was hacking into flesh, spilling blood and pulverizing the bones of the Woodkin people. His work began to suffer and he became far less efficient. It didn't take long before those from Emerald City took notice.

One day, as the army of Tin Woodsmen neared the thicker regions of forest to the west of Munchkinland, several of the Woodsmen had been rounded up and asked to step aboard a peculiar looking carriage. A robed man in a mask sat at the helm of the carriage, hidden by the large flanks of four white horses. He eyed the group of Tin Woodsmen as they stepped aboard but said nothing. Nick had met the man's gaze as he and his co-workers boarded the carriage and he knew from that single glance that there was trouble ahead.

Along with eight Tin Woodsmen, a single human also boarded the carriage. As the horses pulled them back towards Emerald City on the very road they had helped build, the man held out a crystal ball that glowed a pink light into the carriage cabin.

"Think of yourselves as privileged," the man explained. Nick stared at that pink hue along the surface of the crystal ball and knew right away that this man was a sorcerer. He had never seen this man in the ranks of the work crew, but his demeanor alone spoke volumes. He appeared to be a high ranking official in Emerald City—perhaps even the Wizard's own personal magician.

"You see, not only have all of you taken part in the building of this amazing road," the magician went on, "but now, as we return you to Emerald City, you are also the very first to travel it."

"And why are there only eight of us going to Emerald City?" one of the eight asked.

"To state it simply, you are defects," the magician said without emotion. "You see, when you were morphed into Tin Woodsmen, there were certain things about you that were supposed to cease to exist. Among those things were moral reasoning, the bulk of human emotion and your hearts. Of course, as with all creations, there were a few in the batch that didn't perform as they should."

Nick thought about how he had felt during the Woodkin massacre. He had felt something similar to regret, a heavy presence in his chest where his heart, even now in the back of the carriage, beat slowly. To Nick, it felt as if his heart wasn't sure that it was supposed to be beating at all. It felt out of place, alien within the tin housing of its owner.

He also thought about the dreams and how he would wake up screaming. If he had been robbed of a moral compass, surely those dreams would have never surfaced.

"What will become of us?" Nick asked.

But as he stared into the crystal ball, he saw nothing. There was only the pink glow of light from its surface. He could feel something in his head growing heavy. He felt exhausted all of a sudden...so very tired.

A loud *clunk* to his right broke his gaze from the ball. As he turned to see what the sound was, he let out a loud yawn. The clunking noise had been one of the other eight Woodsmen toppling over. He appeared to be dead but it was very hard to tell the difference between sleep and death when observing his tin body.

"He is merely sleeping," the magician explained. He opened his mouth to add to this but was interrupted by another loud crashing sound. Another of the Tin Woodsmen slid against the carriage seat and bumped into the Woodsman beside him. He had also fallen dead asleep.

Nick opened his mouth to protest. He even felt his fingers gripping tightly to his axe handle so that he could plunge the blade into the magician's head. But he was too tired. He couldn't even move his tongue to speak.

"You will all sleep," the magician went on. "The Wizard is a kind man and cannot bare to see anything destroyed. You have worked well to this point. It's just...well, your hearts are getting in the way of your purpose."

Purpose, Nick thought as sleep wrapped its velvet fingers around him. *What purpose is there to come after this? I had no purpose as a man and now my purpose as a Tin Man has come and gone. How dare he speak of purpose to me?*

That question went unanswered. He felt his heavy torso lean to the right. His head clinked against the side of the carriage and the last thing Nick Chopper saw before sleep took him was that pink glow from the crystal ball.

Sometime later he heard the sounds of metal on metal. Beneath the clamor, there was heavy breathing and a woman's voice uttering curses under her breath. He tried to move but felt incredibly sluggish. Not only that, but when he moved his arms, he felt stiff. His arms, his legs, even his head felt as if they weighed tons.

It took a while for him to come around, for his muddied mind to figure out what had happened. He had opened his eyes to that woman's voice and had resorted back to the life he had lived as a man. His waking mind had temporarily forgotten his other life—the life he had lived as a Tin Man. His arms and legs felt heavy because they *were* heavy.

But it wasn't just that. He felt weighed down, as if something were on top of him. With a great effort, he opened his eyes and saw only darkness. He opened his mouth to call out but the task was too much.

From somewhere very close by, he heard the woman again.

"Wretched tin," she was saying. "Who thought of such nonsense?"

He felt a clamor as her voice neared him. There was a thunderous crash from somewhere as the reverberations of her movements reached his frame. They coursed through him, tickling him in a peculiar way. He tried to open his mouth again and realized what the weight on top of him was.

He was in a pile of discarded Tin Men. They lay all over him, pinning him down to what was either the ground or other bodies. A pain shot through him and he opened his mouth to let out a weak cry. He had meant to say *help me* but what came out of his tin throat was only a desperate mewling sound.

"Who's there?" the female voice said again.

"Here," he said. His voice sounded like sand on metal. "Help...please."

The woman's movements quickened and she grunted as she worked. It occurred to him then that this woman was digging her way through the pile.

"Bang on something, would you?" the woman asked. "It's hard to find you in this...this *mess*."

He flexed his right hand and was aware that he had held on to his axe through whatever had happened to him. He raised it as much as he could and pounded on the nearest surface.

"Ah, there you are," the woman said.

He felt a slight movement in front of him and then his eyes were assaulted by an intense white light. He closed his eyes against it so he only caught the briefest glimpse of the woman.

"Finally," he heard her say. "A live one."

He only groaned in response.

"Give me your hand," she told him. "Let me help you out of there."

Blindly, he did as she asked. He offered her his hand, waving it about until she grabbed it. Her hand met his in a surprisingly firm grip. Her hands were delicate, almost bony, and cold to the touch. Even through his tin structure he could feel her chill.

"You may want to wait for your eyes to adjust," she said. "You'll need to watch your step."

He did as she suggested and allowed his eyes to grow accustomed to the light. When he opened them, he saw his savior standing awkwardly before him. She was standing in a haphazard fashion, one foot poised on the back of a Tin Man and the other between two bodies on some unseen appendage of a third.

Nick looked around and saw that they were standing in a heap of tin bodies. He was essentially standing in a Tin Man grave yard—a scrap heap of sorts. He and the woman stood roughly four feet from the floor, standing on a pile that filled the far wall of a large chamber. He did a quick estimate and thought that there were easily three hundred Tin Men at their feet. There were more further up, past his former position in the pile. He didn't bother looking back to see their numbers, though.

He was more interested in the woman. She wore a peculiar hat on her head from which a sleek mane of black hair flowed. Her face was petite, her nose and chin rather sharp and her eyes seemed to bulge slightly. The black robe she wore seemed to flow over the bulks and shapes of the fallen Tin Men like oil.

"Where are we?" Nick asked the woman.

"Emerald City. This is one of the Wizard's warehouses. Although—and please don't take this the wrong way—I can't imagine why they kept all of you. It's been *years* since that damned road was built. And if they couldn't find a use for you after that, you'd think they would have just scrapped you."

"What are you talking about?" he asked as they slowly and carefully made their way down the heap of bodies.

"The way I understand it, all of you," she said, waving her arm wildly around the room, "were defects. The transformation from man to Tin Man didn't completely take."

He thought about this for a moment and nodded. "I remember bad dreams. We...we slaughtered a Woodkin village. And then there was a magician with a crystal ball and I—,"

"*Yes, yes,*" she said. "I have spoken with the Wizard about this. I told him I was in need of someone or something to assist me with clearing out a new property within the woods. For a fee, he let me come back here to see if any of you were still in working order."

"And I'm the only one?"

"Who knows? But you were the first one I found. The Wizard said that if the defects were brought here due to physical deformities, they may still be, um, *alive*. But the majority of you were brought here because you were simply overworked and broke down."

They were on the warehouse floor now, having descended the pile of tin bodies. Nick took a moment to look back to them and he felt that old tremor in his chest, the faint stirring of what was left of his heart.

"There are so many," he said. 'My God, how long have we been here?"

The woman looked away from him and headed towards the door. She cocked her hat slightly on her head, reached beneath her robe and withdrew a broom.

"I'm not sure you want to know the answer to that."

He took a few clunking steps towards her. Tin or not, he still felt as if he had muscles and those muscles had not been flexed in a while.

"I do. Tell me."

The woman sighed and began plucking the bristles on the end of her broom. "Well, records vary, but it's been somewhere in the neighborhood of one hundred and sixty years."

What little of his heart was left sunk within his chest. That crystal ball had put him to sleep for *that* long? How much longer would he have slept if this woman had not come looking for help? He peered back to the heap of useless tin bodies and wanted to collapse to the floor. Seeing them heaped together like that, discarded and of no use, made him think of the Woodkin village.

"Why has this happened?" he asked the woman. He knew that he could not cry, but he tried his best.

"I don't know. But looking at you right now, I think I know why you were brought here—why you were of no use."

"It's because I still think like a man," he said. "After the Woodkin village, I...I don't know. It affected me and I don't think it was supposed to."

"Come here," she said, beckoning him forward.

He was walking towards her before he realized it. There was a pull to her, a magnetism that he didn't understand. But he assumed, from her wardrobe and the broom, that she might be a witch. They were pretty scarce when he had been human, little more than legends. But that was almost two hundred years ago. There was no telling how much had changed in Oz since then.

As he came to her, she placed a hand on his shoulder and ran her other palm along his frame. She started at his brow and made her way down his cheeks, his neck, his chest. Her touch was cold but there was still something nearly sensual about the examination.

"Ah ha," she said as she neared his chest. "Your heart still beats. As I understand it, the transformation into a Tin Man should have removed it."

He thought of the Woodkin village and of the wife that had left him in his other life.

"I wish it had," he said softly.

"You know, dear," the witch said lightly, bringing her sharp face closer to his. "I can fix that if you want. Come with me—*work* for me—and I can fix it. And then, without a heart, you can live a very long time. There are Tin Men that worked on the Road with you that are still alive today and making very good lives for themselves. They show no signs of aging, no signs of guilt, remorse or regret. Many people actually envy them."

"They remained in Oz when the Yellow Brick Road was finished?" he asked.

"Oh yes. The Road is legendary now. Those that helped build it are held in high regard. You could be among them. All you have to do is let me take your heart."

He didn't have to think long. He felt it within him even as she mentioned it. It felt foreign. Part of him knew that it no longer belonged to him. The moment he stepped into that Woodkin village with his axe raised he had forfeited his heart and anything else human that remained within him.

"I'll come with you if you'll just take it away."

When she smiled at him he once again found himself wanting to be rid of his heart. Her smile chilled him; a chill that seemed to pierce the wretched muscle that stubbornly remained in his chest.

"We can work with that," she said, turning her back to him and heading for the door.

He followed her out of the warehouse, thinking of what the magician had told him about purpose so long ago. And as he trailed behind the witch through the streets of Emerald City, he was very aware of the faint beating inside of his chest. He counted each one, knowing that they would be his last.

She had rescued him from the pile of bodies and told him that she needed a place in the woods cleared. She had plans on building a new cabin out there where she could marry a man and raise their children.

This had turned out to be a lie. As she lay him down on a mat in her cottage and placed several emeralds on his chest, she explained it all to him. There was a slight hesitation within him as she told her story but he fought it off. If what she said was true about the Tin Men that had helped with the construction of the Yellow Brick Road, then there was nothing to think about. He might even be able to put those missing one hundred and sixty years behind him.

"Our time is incredibly short," she told him. "This spell should only take about an hour to work. Once your heart as been removed, I believe you will need about another hour or so to rest. Once that is done, I need you to go out onto the Yellow Brick Road and stand by the entrance to the woods. Pretend that you have rusted—like you have been there for a long time."

"Why?"

All of the emeralds were aligned as she needed them and, ignoring him, she took a moment to close her eyes and meditate. In the corner of the room, three monkeys sat in a corner watching her. They had wings on their backs and something about the way they looked at him made Nick think of bats.

"Earlier today, something happened in Munchkinland," the witch finally said. "I believe it was the Great Funnel Wind that did it. A house just dropped out of the sky, you see. Any other day, I'd say it was just some sort of tomfoolery put on by the Wizard to strike fear into the Munchkins.

"But the house landed on my sister. It killed her dead as anything and I got no explanation. Some little bitch came out of the house, totally unscathed, and said it was an accident. She played dumb...like she had no idea."

"Who is she?"

"No clue. She says she's from a place called Kansas. I've never heard of it and I've been a great many places, mind you. Those ungrateful Munchkins...you'd think some great God had dropped from the sky. They were praising her and dancing and singing. Meanwhile, my sister lay squashed under that damned house."

"What do you need me to do?"

The witch sighed. "I'd better wait to tell you after your heart is gone. I don't know how it will react."

Nick nodded.

"What I will tell you is that the stupid little girl is awfully desperate to get back to this Kansas place. The Munchkins have her following the Yellow Brick Road, thinking that the Wizard can help."

Nick had a good idea of what she was going to have him do. And while it did make his heart tremble, it simply reminded him of how badly he wanted it out of his body.

"Are you ready?" the witch asked him.

"Yes."

She spread her hands out and began muttering something under her breath. Nick watched as a fine mist of reds and oranges rose from his chest and gathered around the emeralds that she had placed there.

Moments later, Nick's heart thumped a single time and then settled in his chest. When it left his body, he smiled lightly. As he lay there and waited for further instructions, he was sure that he could hear its pounding echoing in his head.

If the stupid little dog hadn't have perked its ears up in its sleep, Nick would have never sensed the other presence in the night. He turned slowly, wondering if the Scarecrow had awakened. But the figure that stood behind him was slender and draped in a robe as dark as the night itself. Even if he hadn't have figured out the identity of the stranger from these details, the broom gave it away.

"Don't torture yourself over it," the witch whispered to him. She then waved her hand upwards and flexed her fingers. A brief flicker of light filled the night and then the Tin Man actually heard the breathing patterns of the girl, her dog and the Scarecrow change as they fell into a much deeper state of sleep.

The Tin Man studied the witch's face for a moment as she looked to the girl named Dorothy. There was malice in her stare but faint traces of awe as well. "I fear you may have to accompany her for the duration of her pointless little trip," the witch said.

"She's going to Oz, you know," he told her. "She wants to see the Wizard."

She grinned at him. He never noticed until then, looking at her in the shaded moonlight, that her teeth were yellowed and sharper than most people's. "And do you know why?" she asked him.

"It's like you said. She wants to return home. She seems sincere about it."

"I'm sure she is. And what about the Scarecrow? I understand that they'll be asking the Wizard for his brains, too?"

"Yes."

She walked closer to him and placed her hand on his chest, her palm touching the left side of his tin plate. "And what about you? Are you having any second thoughts about our trade? Is there anything you may be asking the Wizard for?"

"No," he said quickly. As he said this, he found himself gripping his axe. He didn't want to attack the witch, but he wanted to hurt *something*. Perhaps he'd slice the dog in half. Or maybe he could tear into the Scarecrow.

No. If he was to carry out any violence in the future, it would be on the girl.

"You know," the witch said. "You'll likely come to the place in the woods where you helped slaughter the Woodkins tomorrow. Are you ready for that?"

"I believe so."

"And there are all manner of odd creatures in that area of the woods these days. Cranes, wild horses and those insipid lions. I'm sure *Little Miss Kansas* will end up attracting someone else to your traveling party."

"If you don't mind my asking," Nick said, "if she bothers you so much, why can't I simply kill her right now while she sleeps?"

"I'd love nothing more," the witch said. "But she needs to make it to Oz. She needs to see that moron of a Wizard."

"Why? Do you want her to succeed now?"

"Hardly. It's just that she gives people hope. You should have seen those Munchkins bowing and dancing around her. So foolish. But they adore her and the hope she provides."

"Well then, what would you have me do?"

"Wait until you get to Oz. Wait until the Wizard is fawning all over her like the Munchkins. Wait until she *knows* she is going home. And *then* attack."

"Won't I be arrested and punished?"

"Likely. But you're made of tin and your heart is no longer an issue. What's the worst they could do to you? Besides, politics in Emerald City are shadier than people think. I am certain I could pull a few strings. Not *everyone* is in love with the little bitch."

The Tin Man nodded. He looked to his axe and regretted that he would not be using it.

"Okay then," he said. "I'll wait."

The witch nodded to him and straddled her broom. She looked to him almost lovingly as she floated from the ground. As she gained momentum and faded into the distance, he watched her lift her hand, removing the sleep spell she had cast upon his companions.

The Tin Man looked to Dorothy. The spell broke. She sighed in her sleep and the faintest traces of a smile came to her face. Her dog chuffed and settled its head onto its paws. It awoke slightly, cast him a curious glance with one beady eye and then returned to sleep.

Nick sat up the rest of the night. He sat perched on a fallen log, looking to the outskirts of the forest. The Yellow Brick Road barely showed through, casting a sickly glow into the night.

To Nick, it would never be a road, but a graveyard.

He thought of the Woodkin bodies beneath it and a hollow place in his chest filled with something akin to heat. He gripped his axe tightly, looked to the girl from Kansas and scowled at her.

He wondered what it would be like to murder the girl and not feel those

old stirrings of guilt and remorse from within. He knew beyond a shadow
of a doubt that his heart was gone now; the thought of killing the girl
neither bothered nor elated him. He simply saw it as a task to be
accomplished.

Still, he peered out to the Yellow Brick Road and wondered if the ghosts
of the Woodkin people knew he was here. With the thought of feeling
those phantom eyes on him, he wondered if fear was linked to the heart.

And he wondered if ghosts would even bother haunting him if they
knew he was without it.

As it turned out, the witch had been right. The following day, their group
grew by one. The lion had pounced out of the woods at them, terrifying
the girl, her dog and the wobbling scarecrow. But Nick had planted his feet,
gripped his axe and was ready to strike. When he realized how harmless the
lion was—he was, in fact, as terrified of the girl as she was of it—Nick
eased up.

And even though Nick did not attack the gentle beast, he knew right
away that the end was near. He was pretty sure that Emerald City was still at
least three days away and there was no way he could continue to act merry
in the presence of these idiots. He remembered the magician in the back of
the carriage so many years ago, speaking to him about purpose. Well now
that he finally had a purpose—a *real* purpose—he was bursting to fulfill it.

As he walked quietly behind the small group of odd travelers, he
thought of the witch and what she was asking of him. Basically, she was
asking for his services…for him to carry out her dirty work. Hadn't he
been subject to similar treatment many years ago? Hadn't that same
treatment caused him to be junked, to be stored away forgotten while
Oz took pleasure in the horrors and hells he had endured for the sake
of that damned road? What was the point in submitting to servitude
again when he knew where it would eventually lead? Was this newfound
evil purpose worth it?

Sure, the witch had made her promises to him, but he knew full well
the breaking capacity of promises. When he had been a man, his wife
had broken them. When he had been a productive Tin Woodsman, the
Emerald City workers had broken them. Why would the witch be any
different?

As they walked through the low hanging branches of the forest, Nick
glanced into the trees. He knew that something was moving around out
there; the longer he stared, the more certain he became that the forms
in the shadows of foliage were the witch's winged monkeys.

Fine, he thought. *You watch all you want, witch.*

Yet, as he observed the shapes in the tops of the trees, he became
more and more aware that the posture to their forms was somehow off.

The shapes up there were not the bodies of the witch's minions...they were more rounded, more agile somehow.

A sound from the ground broke his attention. He looked down and saw one of the yellow bricks of the road protruding up, pushed from its underside. To his left, another brick did the same thing. He studied this one as it popped into the air and clattered to the ground. When the brick was free, revealing the ground below, four small fingers tipped with brown cracked nails tore through the soil.

"What is *that?*" he asked. He readied his axe, prepared to lop off the fingers.

"What is it, Tin Man?" Dorothy asked him. She was looking to him and then to the ground, back and forth, perplexed.

"There! Do you not see it?"

The girl shrugged. Even her dog seemed to be confused. Similarly, the Scarecrow and the Lion stared at him as if he had lost his mind. Nick looked to the ground and the fingers were still there, reaching and pulling. To both sides, more of the bricks were coming undone as something pushed its way out of the ground. The dirt shook and trembled and Nick could feel the movement in the hollow shapes of his legs.

Whatever it was that he was witnessing, the girl and their companions were not seeing it. Even the little dog, which seemed to have a higher sensitivity to unseen things, was unaware of anything happening.

Nick looked behind him and saw that thousands of the bricks were being jarred from the ground in similar fashion. And with each brick that was unearthed, a reaching hand took its place. The hands were small and the wrists and arms to which they were attached looked as thin as twigs. Still, there was something menacing about them.

Finally, he understood.

He looked back up to the trees and saw that the shapes had begun to descend. They were swinging from branches and scaling down the bodies of the trees. Their faces were hidden in shadows that came as if from nowhere, broken only by the menacing white of their smiles. And despite the shadows, Nick recognized the appearance of the Woodkins right away.

As they gathered around him, surrounding him and chanting in some woodland language that he did not understand, his traveling companions still saw nothing. It was in that moment, as Nick began swinging into the air with his axe, that his question was answered.

Yes.

Ghosts *would* haunt a man despite the absence of his heart.

Nick swung at the small figures as they approached. To the girl and her new friends, he was merely swinging at air. Realizing this only pushed Nick further to an edge of angst and hate that he didn't understand—even if he had his heart, he didn't think he'd be able to fathom the sensation.

He turned to them and swung with blinding purpose. The Lion reacted first, his cowardice forgotten in the face of a threat to the girl. But before he could raise so much as a paw, the blade caught him just above the left eye. There was a cracking sound followed by the creature's yelp of pain. The lion reeled back, his paw going to his face as he tottered to the ground in a spray of crimson.

The dog came next, barking nonsensically at Nick's ankles. Nick barely noticed the mutt at all. He was swinging at the shape of an approaching Woodkin. Its body had deteriorated; its face was a smear of color and wrinkled, its limbs caked with rot and stale dirt. As Nick brought his axe around only to watch it pass through the Woodkin's form like mist, the end of the axe came down upon the dog like a club. There was a cracking sound like branches snapping and then the dog went limp. It happened so fast, the dog was unable to let out even the slightest squeal of pain.

"*Toto!*"

The stupid girl came rushing forward, her left arm raised to ward off his blows, her right one extended towards her crushed pet. Behind her, the Scarecrow looked as if he wanted to attack, to prevent Nick from further damage, but his legs seemed to fail him. He shivered with fear, the straw of his torso slowly unraveling and fluttering to the ground in frail strings.

Nick raised his axe over his head. The world was nothing more than a melee of moving Woodkin phantoms and this girl—this haphazard savior to the miracle land that had betrayed him—and it was all too much for him.

He screamed. Before the axe fell in a mad swoop, he saw the Scarecrow cringing at the scream. To Nick, his own rage-filled wail sounded like the shrieking of metal on metal in a violent collision.

But the sound he heard when the axe fell heavily on the girl's shoulder drowned it out. There was a pop as her collarbone snapped in half and then a wet tearing sound as her entire left side was torn and fell away. For a moment, the face and neck of the girl from Kansas seemed to hover in midair and then collapsed with the rest of her split form.

Nick watched as her blood pooled on the ground, trickling between the bricks of the road.

The bricks…

The road was whole again. The yellow bricks he had seen popping from the ground were back in their rightful places. The Woodkins were also gone.

Only, as he stared down the Scarecrow and raised his axe again, he knew that they were still with him. He could feel them watching from the shadows of the forest. They were waiting for him.

Faced with death the Scarecrow was unable to move. He opened his oddly shaped patch of a mouth and let out a cry of anguish. Nick swung his axe around in an arc that could actually be heard on the air. The blade tore through the soft body of the Scarecrow. It tore him in half. His legs stood stubbornly for a moment before collapsing in a heap of straw and fabric. The upper half of the body twitched a bit in response. Nick watched contently as one of the idiot's button-like eyes drooped from the surface of its face.

He looked to the girl's body once more, her blood cascading over the yellow bricks. It seemed fitting, somehow. Had he the capacity to do so, he liked to think that he would have grinned.

Looking away from her, he walked to the edge of the Yellow Brick Road. He carried his axe by his side sternly as he felt the lure of the Woodkin dead from the shadows. He sensed them ahead of him, leading him somewhere. He wasn't sure where at first, but as the forest grew deeper and darker, he began to understand. It was easier to think clearly with that damned road behind him.

The witch had taken his heart and for that, he was grateful. But in the end, she had expected something of him. And while he had done that duty— although not to her standards—she was expecting something from him in return. And Nick Chopper was done with being used.

Nick Chopper, he thought. *I remember him. He certainly was a foolish man.*

As he walked further into the woods with the ghosts of the Woodkin people ahead of him, he thought of the witch. He thought of what it was going to feel like when he plunged his axe into her guts.

And with that thought, he actually managed something similar to a smile. The shadows of the forest squeezed in and overtook him completely. As a parade of Woodkin ghosts led him towards his next kill, he left Nick Chopper behind to die in the shadows.

His heart was what had defined him as a man. Now it was time to be defined by the axe, the darkness and the tin.

THE END.

FLY, FLY PRETTY MONKEY

by Camille Alexa

Madrigaard is closest to my heart. I hold her to my breast, croon to her. I stroke the sparse hairs on her misshapen head, soft like crow feathers but fine and ill-rooted.

"Fly, pretty monkey," I tell her. I lean far out the open window of my turret. Wind whips against my cheeks and neck, tugs cruelly at my hair, rakes my clothing from my body until it billows out in webby tatters like a banner of my imperfections, announcing that the Wicked Witch is home.

I kiss Madrigaard's warty head once more and toss her into the whipping wind.

Her tiny stick arms flail helpless at the air. She tumbles like a small black stone.

Fly, I silently urge, not shutting my one good eye against the sight of her plummeting body, out of respect. *Fly, pretty monkey*.

I expect to hear the wet smack of her small body against the stones far below, but her tiny wings like scraps of rotten leather unfurl from against her shivering body. They flap feebly. For a moment, I'm certain she'll not make it. The rocks beneath my tower are littered with the tiny skulls of her siblings, her cousins, her foremothers—generations of their bones lying stark and naked and lovely, picked clean by keening birds swirling the cliffs near the waterside not far from these bony spires of my keep thrusting upward between sky and landlocked inland sea.

But her flapping strengthens. At the last instant before death on the rib- and femur-covered rocks, her bat-scrap wings slow her descent. She clutches at the nothing of wind and space, her tiny newborn body shriveled and fragile. She flaps and flaps and flaps, slowly rising on one of the bitter currents gusting from the inland sea. When she finally draws up level with me, I smile. In my hopes for her, I've bitten clean through the thin skin of my lip, and ichor trickles down my chin, wending toward the tattered open neck of my rotted black lace gown.

Flapping, hovering, she dips her tiny monkey paw into what my blood has become. She holds it to my mouth, as though I must kiss my own hurt better, and when I croon, "What a pretty girl, a clever girl," she wraps her stick arms around my neck and sighs her tiny monkey sigh into my ear.

My sister's murderer has been sighted in the poppy fields on the other side of that Green Monstrosity that Oz calls home.

I know those poppy fields well. In his younger days, Oz would meet me there on lazy, sunlit afternoons. He had a fascination for the flowers, a weakness, a longing for their sharp juice and numbing powers. Poppy juice turned out to be more addictive for him, in the end, even than his love for me. We always love most that which has the greatest power to destroy us.

I was beautiful then, and young. We both were: me, and that strange bright-eyed boy from somewhere over the boundless oceans of desert. We would lie under the large drooping heads of flowers at the edge of the field. A game, he called it: to see how long we could resist sleep, lying on our backs side by side with our long hair mingling, and our breaths. We'd laugh as we drifted in and out of consciousness, our minds floating, daring each other to see how long we could last before the poppies claimed us both too completely for one to drag the other to safety. It was always he who succumbed first. I'd watch the tinted shadows of poppy-reflected light play across his sleeping features, and I'd trace his lips with my finger. I've always been stronger than I looked, and when he became well and truly senseless from poppy fumes, I'd lift him gently and carry him well past the flowers' influence. I'd lie down beside him and wait for him to wake, and when he did, he would always kiss me.

Don't ever leave me, my beautiful young Oz would say in a poppy-drowse murmur; *or I'll send people to find you, and tell them to kill you.*

Even now a smile brushes across my lips at the memory of him. My smiles are rare these days, most of them spent on my dear pretty monkeys. Especially the babies, with their delicate skulls and unformed features and mewling cries. I always did love the babies.

A slight scratching comes at my door and Madrigaard's sharp little fingers stab into my neck at the sound. I stroke her with one hand.

"Come," I say.

Baarg opens the door and enters, tray balanced in one hand, the other dragging the floor like a cane or a third leg as he hobbles into the room. His ancient ruined wings lie in tatters more ragged than my gown. If he didn't hold my special favor, the other winged monkeys, warriors all, would have killed him long ago. Resources are scarce around here: food and space and love. Monkeys are not quite as jealous as other people, but they come close.

Baarg slides his dented silver tray onto a nearby table and sidles under my free hand where it dangles off the arm of my chair. I absently pat his wisp-covered skull, feeling without intending to the fragility of the bone beneath my fingers. I'm keenly aware that I could crush his brain between my fingers if I chose to. As he sighs and leans into my touch, I wonder if the same awareness runs through his monkey mind as well. We always love most that which has the greatest power to destroy us.

I give Baarg a last stroke and turn my attention to the silver tray. He has, as always, collected everything just so, arranged it with inhuman precision on the tray in the same order: the candle, the strap, the spoon, the needle. A small dribble of wax rolls down the side of the taper, and when I touch it with my finger it burns, though not enough. I move my hand into the flame, and though my skin reddens and the air fills with the scent of burnt lace, it's still not enough.

I lean forward even more, causing Madrigaard to whimper and grasp more tightly at my neck. When I pick up the spoon and needle, she buries her face in my high lace collar and tucks her wings tight against her bone-ridged back.

The bowl of the spoon has just a few drops of water reflecting from its bottom, a deadly mirror. With the powerful sight in my one good eye, every detail of the room is reflected in that small curved pool: the dark stones arching heavily across the ceiling, dry-rotted, crumbling; the beady glow of Baarg's eyes as he watches my slow movements with worry, with eagerness, with love; the tattered black muslin billowing at the ogee windows, breezes of this high turret bringing salt from far below, stripped of moisture. All the moisture I can physically withstand is in this one little spoon.

I pass it across the candle's flame a few times, warming it to room temperature, but not above. I want the burn to come from water, not the heat of a mere candle. When I draw the water into the syringe, letting Baarg tie the strap around my arm, I can think of nothing but the sinuous way the poison slips up the needle: secretive, seductive, almost alive.

When it enters under my skin, I slump in my chair. Madrigaard looses her grip on my throat and tumbles to the floor but I barely notice. Baarg is untying the strap, blowing out the candle, picking up the empty syringe where it has rolled from my slack fingers to clatter onto cold flagstones beneath my chair.

But all I can think about is the fire roiling in my veins; the few drops of that poison, water, cooking me with a slow acidic burn from the inside out.

We always love most that which has the greatest power to destroy us.

The assassin and her metal paramour have murdered my wolves. All forty of them, with their handsome long legs and eyes like diamonds and teeth like polished ivory. I called them to service with my silver whistle, and because of this they've died. The land is a far poorer place for their loss.

I know the murderess still comes for me; there's nothing in her shallow heart that isn't selfish or cruel. She killed my sister Sally, and when Oz heard of the death he couldn't help sending her against me as well. My Winkie spies in the Green Monstrosity have confirmed as much.

I weep for them now, the gorgeous wolves, the ichor of my tears stinging rivulets down my cheeks, tainted with the poisonous clean water of yesterday's indulgence. It's all I can do not to call for Baarg and his tray here and now.

The silver whistle around my neck is suddenly a heavy thing, burdensome and cold. Grasping it with both fists, I tug, silver links snapping across the back of my neck, showering to flagstones in a glittering rain. I heave the whistle out past the curtains into thin air, where it arcs away from my turret spire. I imagine it falling to the rocks below, picture it mingling with the broken bones of a thousand newborn monkeys not strong enough to survive life among their own.

But a small black streak shoots out the glassless window after it.

"Madrigaard!" I cry, running to the sill to lean out far above the water of the brine sea lapping at the base of my aerie, my prison, my home.

The small ball of wadded leather unfurls, becomes my darling baby monkeychild. She plucks the silver whistle from the air and flaps, flaps, flaps her small sad scraps of wings, and when she reaches my outstretched arms she lets me clasp her to my chest. Her heartbeat and mine clamor against each other, separated by our ribs, our sheaths of skin, my tattered lace and her sparse wisps of monkeyfur. When she squeals for breath I let her go, and she shoves the silver whistle between my lips.

For a brief instant, I imagine the whistle is covered with sea spray. I imagine natural water burning my lips, my teeth, my tongue—burning all the way down into my heart.

But no. It's merely cold from the high altitude, from the air, from the hard winter sun that offers no warmth. I glance at the hourglass, but the sands are against me; I can't endure another shot until the top is emptied of its burden of time. Here is the image hovering always near the surface of my consciousness thoughts: a large amount of water, not a mere spoonful, but an entire bucketful, with the most glorious burning imaginable . . . just one brief flare of agony, and then no more pain forever.

Madrigaard chirps in query and taps the whistle between my lips. I've cried out all the lingering traces of water from yesterday. Through my ichor tears I nod at the small monkey and blow the whistle twice, and immediately the sky begins to darken with wild black feathered birdwings, as though with clouds bringing poison rain.

They are all murderers. The grass man callously stood without expression or regret, killing one by one every wild crow he saw. With my good eye I see them lying broken in a heap at his feet where he tossed them after twisting their necks.

Poor, lovely wild crows.

The hours haven't filed from my glass yet, but I ring the bell for Baarg, regardless. While I wait for him to bring his tray, I blow the silver whistle three times.

The buzzing starts small at first, but quickly swells to a crescendo. The gorgeous black swarm roils just outside my window, thousands upon thousands of bodies rubbing together in a dark chitinous whirr. I lean out across the stones, the air, too far perhaps for good balance, and thrust my arms toward the sky. The bees land on my hands, my face, the places on my throat and arms where the black fabric of a gown I've not removed for longer than I care to remember has rotted and fallen away.

This gown was meant to be my wedding dress once, though it turned from white to black with the unhinged magic of my grief when Oz left me waiting for him at the place and time of our arranging. His poppy-scented dreams had replaced my love in his heart, and when he came to his senses from his trance and found my door closed against him and guarded by winged monkeys, he holed up in his Green Monstrosity with its gaudy glitter and its artifice, and I in my tower. He lives a life of brittle lies, while I embrace the brittle truth. Both are sharp as razors.

Bees buzzing in my ears, my open mouth, the corners of my eyes, I shout into the roiling cloud about the murderess and her paramours, who crushed my defenseless sister, who show such careless disregard for the magnificent wild creatures of this land as they cut their swath across it, killing and looting on their journey to assassinate me in my own home. When I'm through, the swarmcloud wheels upward and away, surging over the landlocked sea toward Lake Quad and the forest of the Fighting Trees. As always, I'm grateful that my bad eye blocks from my long distance sight the toxic blighting glow of the Green Monstrosity where it mars the land.

Before Baarg is able to mount the stairs to my high turret, all the poor bees lie broken and dead, heaps of cinders at the murderess's silver-shot feet. I close my farseeing eye against the sight and slump to the stones.

The two winged monkeys watch me with large eyes, silent. Baarg lopes over with his carefully balanced tray, and though I want the sting of water flushing through me more than anything else in the land, when I open my eyes, I knock the tray from his hand so it goes flying against the wall in a frightful clatter of metal and stone. Candle wax has splashed across my hand and the skin turns red as I watch, but it's not enough. Not nearly enough.

I scoop Baarg and Madrigaard into my arms and hug them with a fierceness that both excites and frightens them. Their leathery wings and the hollow twiggy bones inside shudder with their response to my affection. I let them go, gently shove them from me though they both reach for me again with gnarled sticklike paws.

"Go," I tell them. "Send the Winkies to parlay with the murderess. Perhaps the similarity of their humanesque form to hers will inspire her mercy."

The Winkies have failed. They say the murderess refused even to listen to their pleas, and sent the largest of her paramours after them with teeth like daggers and breath like swampgas as he roared. They're not the bravest people, Winkies. The winged monkeys showed their disgust in the way they do: with feces flung, delivered with taunts and sneers and laughter. The Winkies have no doubt already embellished the tale in retellings amongst themselves, so that their list of grievances against the monkeys and myself probably now involve me beating them with sticks when they returned, or the monkeys pelting them with hot oil or stones rather than the simpler, more scatological reality.

With heavy heart, I fetch the Cap. It symbolizes the covenant between myself and my friends. The winged monkeys are a fierce and loyal people, but it's time to release them from our bargain. Do they serve me because they love me? Or do they love me because they serve me? We always love most that which has the greatest power to destroy us.

I perform the ritual, donning the Cap and speaking words in the ancient language of the treaty. All my pretty monkeys have gathered to witness the event. The arching walls of my turret room are covered with them clinging to the crevices between the stones, their hard eyes glittering, their needle teeth bared. With their black wings hanging down they look like bats. They jockey for position on the wide stone windowsills, shoving each other out into the air, laughing and screeching, fighting for perches on the backs of chairs and the tops of tables. Madrigaard and Baarg cling close to my skirts, intimidated by the raw unchecked ferocity of their own kind, the violence and the cruel humor. They are all magnificent.

They rarely speak to me, but the largest of them steps forward. I don't even know his name. Their leader in any given year is always the strongest, the most agile, the most virile of their number. They've had many leaders since they came to live in the keep beside the landlocked sea.

"You invoke the ritual," says the largest, unfurling his wings to add to his impressive stature, to increase even further his physical dominance in the room. This display is for the other monkeys, I know, and has nothing to do with me. "Why do you do this, knowing it brings an end to the covenant you struck with our people all those generations ago?"

His voice is like gravel on the shores beneath my tower: sharp, hard, and littered with bones.

I feel the sadness of my own smile.

"An unstoppable assassin is on her way to kill me," I say, lifting my voice so all can hear. The screeching and laughing has quieted, but scuffles continue along the windowsills and the passage beyond the door to the twisting stairs. "I don't know what's going to happen," I tell them, "but I want you to be long gone from this place. It's the only way I know to keep you safe. After this last task, your people are free to go."

The screeches are deafening. Monkey fists beat monkey chests; wings rub against each other like rustling dead leaves; teeth are bared in pleasure or sorrow.

The leader waits for the clamor to die down. He stares into my face, his expression inscrutable. When the room is completely quiet, he says, "What is this last task?"

And into that same quiet, I answer:

"Bring her to me."

The winged monkeys are gone.

They destroyed two of the murderess's paramours in the battle, though I'm certain they lost a greater number of their own. They're warriors, fierce and violent and proud. I will miss them, bitterly.

The monkeys tied the prisoners in the courtyard at the base of my keep and left without another word to me. Some few lingered to pelt the leonine paramour with their filth, to taunt him with their screechings from the top of the wall. There's another, much smaller four-legged paramour the murderess keeps in attendance at all times, who has proven himself most vicious. And then there is *her*.

She's so ugly that she's stunning. I can see why men follow her to their deaths.

Each night she goes to lie with the prisoner in the yard. She bares herself to him and whispers in his ear, and they look up at my tower. I feel their gazes even through the dark, even through the stones. And with my good eye, I can see them as they twist together in the moonlight, making plans to kill me for good and take my land for themselves.

It is merely a matter of time. The certainty of this weighs on me. The fickle, cowardly Winkies have all fled to the countryside. The few winged monkeys left behind when their people departed continue to serve me: the infirm, the elderly, those too young to fly. I'm very grateful to Madrigaard for going with them, and pleased with myself for teaching her to be strong, to survive. Baarg is loath to leave my side, and spends most of his time perched in the window overlooking the courtyard, glaring at its leonine resident. He leaves the turret only twice each day, bringing back his candle, his spoon, his silver tray.

I no longer pay any attention to the sands in the glass. I take the water as often as I want, playing with its fire, feeling myself burning on the inside, burning hot enough to melt me into the stones of the floor, to make me nothing that couldn't be swept out with the dust and dirt. What a relief that would be.

And *her*. Each day she taunts me, plays her cruel mindgames, knowing I'm a prisoner in my own home. No doubt the history books will tell it differently, but history is always written by the victors.

But she certainly is exquisite. I watch her from my high window now, stripping herself in broad daylight to lie with the shaggy man, as Baarg tightens his strap around my arm and gently pushes aside the rotting black lace covering my skin. I grit my teeth as water blossoms its heat in my veins, and see again her bitter beauty as she writhes naked in the courtyard beneath, doubtless counting the days to my destruction.

We always love most that which has the greatest power to destroy us.

THE END.

A HEART IS JUDGED

by Kevin G. Summers

In the Land of Oz, in the country of the Munchkins, there is an abandoned town along the old Yellow Brick Road. It was once called Munchkinville in the time before outworld historians began chronicling the histories of that strange fairyland. Farmers and merchants once thrived in the tiny hamlet, selling their wares and minding their business. Children were born. Grandparents died. Families huddled together in the night, fearful of dark magic in the world outside. But if you visited Munchkinville today, you would find only ruined buildings, the streets littered with debris, and not a soul in sight. Munchkinville is a ghost town.

It was ten years before Dorothy Gale dropped a house on the Wicked Witch of the East. Munchkinville was still a thriving community at that time, and on that spring day the people the entire town had gathered together for an annual event called the Festival of the Covenant. It was much the same in villages all over Munchkinland. The people were commemorating the decades-old bargain they'd struck with Orpah, the Wicked Witch of the East.

Only one man in all of Munchkinville wasn't participating. Robin Plumly sat on a wooden bench in the only prison cell in town. He sat in near perfect darkness; the only light, slipping through the cell's single iron-barred window, formed a slow-moving square on the floor. Before long the sun would reach its zenith, and life as Robin knew it would be over.

Robin was tall for a Munchkin—as tall as a human adolescent. He had black hair and striking blue eyes. Robin broke the hearts of most of the girls in town when he married, but those other girls were fools. He'd only ever had eyes for Cordelia Snow, the love of his youth.

They'd been married happily now for almost two years, and over the winter they'd been blessed with a baby girl. It broke Robin's heart when he thought of her—the child he would never again cradle in his arms. He shifted uncomfortably on the wooden bench. The lighted square on the floor moved another fraction of an inch.

Sheriff Rozzco had been using the cell as a corncrib and he wasn't happy when the Mayor of Munchkinville ordered him to clean it out. Rozzco made his feelings perfectly evident when he arrived at Robin's house the previous afternoon.

"Gonna spoil the whole crop," Rozzco complained as he bound Robin's hands behind his back with a pair of iron shackles. "Been drying all winter. Now tell me, how'm I gonna feed my animals when…"

"How can you do this?" Robin demanded. "They're taking my little girl, giving her over to that witch. You're the sheriff, how can you stand by and just let that happen?"

Cordelia stood in the doorway of their little house the whole time, weeping. She was a beautiful creature—porcelain skin and hair like creamed corn. Robin wasn't exaggerating when he called her the loveliest woman in Munchkinland. Cordelia held a baby in her arms, wrapped in a blue blanket. Dot, the child, whimpered as her mother's tears fell upon her face.

"You know why we have to do it," Rozzco said. "Ain't nothing personal. Your name was drawed in the lottery, that's all. It could have been me or Nimmie Amee or anyone." The sheriff gave the end of his curled mustache a twist. "Besides, you threatened to burn down Mayor Torin's house."

Sitting in his lonely cell, Robin couldn't comprehend how his people could willingly surrender their children to the Wicked Witch of the East.

The tradition, it was said, began in the distant past, when the witch Orpah first enslaved the Munchkins. It was, in fact, the *reason* for the season. The covenant between the Munchkinlanders and the Wicked Witch of the East guaranteed that every year on the first day of Spring, each Munchkin settlement would deliver to Orpah a girl-child under the age of two. It had been going on as long as anyone could remember, and none that had been given over to the witch had ever been seen again. Each winter, the names of all the new parents in Munchkinland were written on scraps of paper and placed in a hat. Whoever's name was drawn was forced to give up their child for the good of the country. Before he was a father, Robin found the practice revolting. Now, when he thought of little Dot and her dark curls, the idea made him absolutely murderous.

"I won't let this happen," Robin whispered. Across the cell, a rat squeaked at him furiously and then scurried through a tiny crack in the wall.

Before long, the sun blazed directly overhead. There was a commotion outside. Not wanting to watch but unable to help himself, Robin rushed to the cell's single window and pressed his face to the bars. His heart breaking, his vision blurred by tears, he watched the horror unfold. He could not look away.

The witch came from the east, traveling along the Yellow Brick Road in a palanquin carried by four hulking giants. The brutes moved with surprising grace considering their size. Their arms bulged with muscles as big around as Mayor Torin's ample belly, and the shortest of the giants stood as tall as five Munchkins standing on one another's shoulders. Their eyes were close set. Their foreheads formed into sharp brow ridges that made them appear both perpetually angry and perpetually stupid. They never spoke, but sounded out with an occasional throaty grunt. If the sounds meant anything, no one could say, but they seemed to comprehend when a frigid voice issued a command from inside the palanquin.

"*Halt. Set me down.*"

The giants complied, easing the litter to the bricks with amazing gentility. A door opened in the palanquin a moment later, and a pair of legs arrayed in red and white striped hose appeared. At the bottom of her shapely calves, the witch's feet were shod with silver slippers. These were said to possess great magical power, and so long as she wore these shoes, the chances of overthrowing the Wicked Witch of the East were non-existent.

She stood before them as a being of seemingly limitless power. The Munchkins, trembling with terror, fell down upon their faces and worshipped her as a god.

Orpah was beautiful for a witch. For any woman for that matter. Her hair was bright red, and her skin as pale as the sands of the Deadly Desert that surrounded the Land of Oz.

No Munchkinlander knew the history of Orpah, and they rarely saw her except when she appeared to claim her annual sacrifice. But they feared her. Occasionally, a brave soul would defy the witch, and their death would be swift. The head of the last such agitator was still rotting upon a spike near the town's western gate.

"Another year has passed," said the witch. Her voice sent chills down the spines of everyone present. "Will you Munchkins fulfill your bargain, or shall I turn your entire people into jitterbugs?"

"We will honour our agreement," came a familiar voice from deep within the throng. The crowd parted, and Mayor Torin stepped forward. He was a fat little man dressed in a suit of fine blue velvet. He motioned to Sheriff Rozzco, who led Cordelia and Dot through the crowd. When they reached the witch, Cordelia looked up through watery eyes at the woman who would take her child away.

"*Please,*" Cordelia said. "Please don't take my little girl."

Orpah's nostrils flared. Her green eyes, dyed in the finest spa in the Emerald City, narrowed.

"Silence your pleading," she hissed, "it annoys me."

Cordelia dropped to her knees. "I'll do anything, mistress. Please, don't take my..."

The witch bent down and grabbed hold of the child. Dot wailed in protest as Orpah wrenched her away from her mother. Cordelia lunged at the witch in a sudden fit of madness, but before she could land a blow, one of the giants grabbed her by the arm and lifted her high in the air.

"Kill her," ordered the witch.

The giant reared back, and then hurled Cordelia as hard as he could to the ground. Her skull shattered as it smashed against the Yellow Brick Road. Blood poured from the open wound, staining the bricks.

Not far away, a wretched wail ripped across the village. It was Robin Plumly, watching in horror as his wife died in the street. The people of Munchkinville watched silently, too terrified to even utter a sound.

"Let us be gone," said Orpah. She stepped casually over Cordelia's body, and then slipped back into her palanquin with Dot tucked under her arms. The baby's pitiful cries echoed back to the village as the giants carried them out of sight.

The next day Robin heard keys jangling in the cell door. A moment later, the door swung open and blinding light poured in. The light stung his eyes. Robin had cried all night, until his heart pounded and the tears simply wouldn't come anymore. He slept on the hard floor, and remained there long past the breakfast hour. He simply didn't care what happened next.

"Robin," said an unexpected voice. "I hate to see you like this."

The prisoner had been expecting Rozzco, and indeed the sheriff was standing right there in the doorway. But beside him, as round as a balloon, stood Mayor Torin.

Robin pushed up off the floor and rose quickly to his feet. His clenched his fists. He narrowed his eyes. He grated his teeth.

"What do you want?"

Torin smiled nervously.

"I wanted to tell you that I'm sorry about your wife and..."

Robin took a menacing step toward the Mayor, and was quickly intercepted by Rozzco.

"You don't wanna do that," said the sheriff. He placed a steadying hand on each of Robin's shoulders. Robin didn't resist, but his hate-filled eyes never waivered from the Mayor.

"You're a coward," said Robin. "Both of you. You've allowed that witch to terrorize our people for years."

"What would you have me do?" The Mayor's voice throbbed with sudden anger. "How could our people hope to fight those giants of hers? And what about her magic? She could kill us all with a word."

"Better to die than to live like this," Robin said.

The Mayor shook his head in frustration. How many times had they had this exact conversation? Ten? Twenty?

"There's nothing I can do," Torin said at last.

"Why are you here?" Robin demanded. He stepped back, and Rozzco relaxed his guard.

"I've decided to drop all charges against you," Torin explained. "You're free to go."

"Why would you do this?" Robin knew very well that the punishment for threatening a government official was exile from Munchkinville.

"Because you've been punished enough already," said the Mayor. "Please, I want you to know how sorry..."

Robin darted across the room, and before Rozzco could intervene, he punched Mayor Torin in the nose. The fat little man staggered back a few steps and slid down the wall. He sat upon the wooden floor, blinking his eyes furiously as he tried to regain his senses.

Rozzco rushed toward Robin, but stopped when the prisoner assumed a fighting stance. In truth, there was very little need of a sheriff in Munchkinville. The people were reasonably well behaved, and other than the times when the Wicked Witch of the East came to town, this was one of the easiest jobs in the country. Unaccustomed to violence, Rozzco covered his head with his hands and scurried toward the back of the room like a rat.

Robin knelt beside the stunned Mayor.

"I don't want your apology," he whispered. "I want my daughter back. And I want you to know that I'm going to get her, and if it costs the life of every soul in the Land of Oz then so be it."

Robin stood, and without looking back stepped outside the jail. A few minutes later he was standing over the body of his beloved wife. No one bothered to bury Cordelia. They didn't even cover her with a shroud. Crows had come in the night and eaten her eyes. She stared at him with two empty red holes in her face. A line of blood was dried upon her lips.

"How could you let this happen?" she seemed to be saying.

"I'm sorry." Robin collapsed beside her broken form. "I promise to avenge your death," he cried. "And I will hold our daughter again." He wept uncontrollably.

Robin Plumly stood once his sorrow abated. He lifted Cordelia's body in his arms, took a final look around at the village that had been home his entire life, and then started west along the Yellow Brick Road.

Robin buried Cordelia near a small cottage that stood vacant beside the Yellow Brick Road. The place was overgrown with trees, and many Munchkinlanders claimed it was haunted. A statue of a tin man stood not far from the house, his hands clenching an axe and his body corroded with rust. When Robin was a lad, he remembered his friends daring him to touch that hideous statue. He'd come within five paces of the thing, but his courage failed and he made a hasty retreat.

Drawing near the tin man now, Robin heard what sounded like a deep groan. He peered at the statue, considering the implications, and then shook his head. Black trees whispered all around them.

"My mind is playing tricks on me," Robin said.

Cordelia lay in an open grave at his feet. Using a shovel he'd retrieved from the cottage, Robin piled dirt over the woman he loved. He worked furiously, never stopping until Cordelia was cold underground. His heart pounding, Robin fell to his knees.

"It's time for me to go," he said once he'd caught his breath. He placed a wild rose he'd found growing nearby upon the grave. "Farewell my love."

Before long Robin was marching along the Yellow Brick Road again, toward the only person in all the Land of Oz who could help him rescue his daughter.

Under any other circumstances, the Emerald City would have awed Robin Plumly with its sheer size and beauty. The city was gigantic by Munchkin standards, and every stone glowed a beautiful green. A high wall surrounded the city beyond which Robin could make out the emerald tower where the Wizard of Oz held court.

Robin slowed as he approached the city's gate. A crooked man in black robes stood beside the door. A long, white wizard's beard poured from the mouth of the cloak. He leaned heavily on a wooden cart, and though the man's face was cast in shadow, Robin had the distinct feeling that this stranger was a dangerous man. They passed each other on the road a dozen paces from the city gate. Robin kept his eyes averted, not wanting to become distracted from his task.

"I'd turn back if I were you," the crooked man hissed.

Robin paused in spite of himself. "Excuse me?"

"Do you seek counsel with the Wizard of Oz?" The kept speaking before Robin could even answer. "He won't see you, I can promise you that."

"How do you know?"

"He's a humbug. A liar. Nothing but an *illusionist*." The crooked man spoke the last word with utter contempt.

"What do you mean?" Robin demanded. His every hope rested on the Wizard's magic. The Munchkin took a step nearer the crooked man.

"The Wizard of Oz rarely sees anyone," he explained, "but he knew me as a powerful wizard, so he was willing to meet with me."

"So?"

"*So*... he appeared as a giant, floating head. That's the oldest trick in the book. My dog could do that trick. And while he was ranting and raving, begging me to slay the Wicked Witches, I realized that he had less magic than an ordinary laying hen."

"The Wizard..." Robin shook his head. "No, that can't be."

"It is, lad." The Crooked Wizard gestured over his shoulder toward the city. "If you're looking for a wizard, don't bother going to the Emerald City."

Without another word he began walking once more, headed in the direction from which Robin had come.

The Munchkin took several steps toward the city, and as he drew near he noticed that the Emerald City wasn't made of emeralds at all. It shone brilliantly from a distance, but up close, he could clearly see that the walls were only cinder blocks painted with green sparkle paint.

"It can't be," Robin said aloud. He reached toward the button that would summon the Guardian of the Gate, but hesitated. What if the Crooked Wizard was right? Dot was running out of time, and Robin might waste days inside the Emerald City.

"*Wait!*" Robin shouted. He turned around and ran back the way he had come. The Crooked Wizard was a hundred yards away now, moving along at a surprising pace, with his beard waving from side to side. He paused at the sound of Robin's call and began to fiddle with a long pipe that he produced from a pocket of his robes.

"Can you help me, sir?" Robin said as he drew near the wizard.

"That depends," said the Crooked Wizard, his back still turned to Robin. A puff of smoke drifted over shoulder. "What sort of help do you require?"

Robin took a deep breath, trying to maintain his composure. This man was Dot's only hope, and if he refused to help, he had no one else to turn to.

"My daughter has been taken hostage by the Wicked Witch of the East," Robin explained. "The witch murdered my wife."

He felt the tears burning in his eyes, but he refused to give in to weakness. He didn't have time for weakness. He should have taken Cordelia and Dot and fled Munchkin country as soon as their name was drawn out of the hat. Instead he turned to diplomacy. He tried to argue that his people should rise up against their oppressor, but the Munchkins refused. They were all cowards, and Robin considered himself the worst of the lot.

"That is most unfortunate," said the Crooked Wizard.

"Why does she do it?" Robin demanded. "Every year she comes to Munchkinland and steals one female child from each village."

The Crooked Wizard nodded. "It is an ancient spell," he explained. "She uses the life force of the children to keep her young and beautiful. Have you seen Orpah? She is beautiful, is she not?"

"In a way," Robin admitted. In truth, the Wicked Witch of the East was quite beautiful, but hers was a haunting, vacant beauty. Not like his Cordelia, whose smile could light up a room. When he thought of Orpah, Robin's blood burned. She was a sensual, gothic creature, the kind of woman Robin's mother had warned him about.

"Orpah is the oldest of all the witches in Oz," the Crooked Wizard said. "They're all sisters, did you know that? Glinda, who rules the Quadling Country of the south, Denslow, who is called the Wicked Witch of the West, Locasta, the Good Witch of the North, Mombi, who *has* no country, and Orpah, the Wicked Witch of the East."

"Five sisters," Robin said.

"Five sisters," said the Crooked Wizard, "and every one of them is a bitch. I used to have a thing with Orpah once upon a time, but she left me for another man. When we broke up, her sisters cursed me. Well, Denslow and Mombi did anyway, but the others didn't do anything to stop it. They made me the broken old man you see before you."

"I'm sorry..." Robin began, but the wizard cut him off again.

"Keep your words, they mean nothing to me. You want me to help you get your daughter back?" The Crooked Wizard took a shaky step toward Robin.

"Yes."

"It'll cost you. Are you willing to pay?"

"I don't have much gold," Robin said. "But I'll give you everything..."

"I don't want your money." A cruel smile formed inside the Crooked Wizards hood. "But there is something else."

"I'll pay anything," Robin said.

The Crooked Wizard removed his pipe and blew a smoke ring into the air. It drifted lazily back toward the Emerald City, finally catching on the point of the wizard's tower and dissipating.

"When the witches left me, they stole my heart. I'm not talking figuratively either. The Crooked Wizard pulled open his robes, revealing the pale skin of his chest. There was a purple scar over his left breast. They cut it right out, used it in one of Mombi's nasty spells. I haven't felt anything since that day. If you ever want to see your daughter again, laddie, then the price you must pay is your heart."

Robin's hand went instinctively to his own chest. He could feel his heart thumping below the skin. He had known nothing but sorrow since the day his daughter's name was drawn in the Munchkin lottery. Every dream he and Cordelia had ever dreamt had turned into a nightmare. There was no future he could envision besides one of pain. It would, in truth, be a blessing to relinquish his heart to this old wizard.

And what of the future? What of his life with Dot once she was returned to him? *If I don't do it*, Robin thought, *then Dot will never have a future. There is no choice. I must do this.*

"Fine," Robin said. "I will give you my heart."

"*Fine*," the Crooked Wizard said. "I will help you rescue your daughter."

The Crooked Wizard lived in a cave in the Gillikin Country, and it was to this cave that he and Robin traveled once their arrangement was struck. By the time they reached the cave, the Crooked Wizard had arrived at a plan for rescuing Dot.

"Let's hear it," Robin said.

"There's no possible way we can defeat the witch in her castle," the Crooked Wizard said. "She is far too powerful. Even for me."

"What can we do then?"

The wizard grinned wickedly.

"This is the brilliant part. *We lure* her *out of the castle.*"

Robin thought about it.

"If she's so powerful," he asked after a few minutes, "won't she be able to win no matter where we battle her?"

The Crooked Wizard glared at Robin.

"Of course, don't be an imbecile. We have no hope of defeating the witch, what we're really trying to do is buy time so that you can free your daughter. That is what you bargained for, correct?"

Robin nodded slowly.

"Well then, listen carefully and try not to say anything stupid." The Crooked Wizard mumbled something under his breath that sounded like a curse. "We'll lure the witch out of her castle by writing her a nasty letter from the Mayor of Munchkinville. We'll call her a *cunt*, women hate that. She'll come with all her giants, ready to squash those little bastards. Meanwhile, you can sneak into her castle, rescue your daughter, and then do whatever it is fathers and daughters do."

Robin stopped in the middle of the road.

"It'll never work," he said.

"What's that?"

"The witch and her cronies will overrun the town in minutes. I won't have enough time to rescue Dot."

The Crooked Wizard turned back, staring at him incredulously.

"You're not worried about the Munchkins, are you?"

Robin shook his head. "They sacrificed my wife and daughter to protect themselves. As far as I'm concerned, they can all burn in hell."

The Crooked Wizard smiled.

"Very well," he said. He reached into his pockets and removed a glass jar full of white powder. "This is the Powder of Life. With it, I can bring to life anything I desire." He gave the jar a gentle shake.

"I don't understand..."

"I told you," snapped the wizard, "if you have nothing intelligent to say, then keep your mouth shut. We will go through with my plan, but in order to buy you some more time, we will build an army to distract the witch."

"Build an army?" Robin asked. "From what."

The Crooked Wizard thought about it for a minute, and then his eyes sparkled.

"From straw." He began to laugh, a wild, psychotic laugh that made Robin's hair stand on end. This man was dangerous, perhaps as dangerous as the Wicked Witch of the East herself, but Robin had to trust him.

Finally, they came to the black mouth of the cave.

"This is it," said the old man. He pointed to an opening that was draped in hairy vines that might have been poison ivy.

Robin closed his eyes, his thoughts tracing back to the little cottage he had shared with Dot and Cordelia. How long ago those days seemed, and in truth, only a matter of days had passed.

They stepped inside the cave. It was a terrible place–dank and wet and reeking of bat guano. The chamber was piled high with books and crates full of spell components. Animal cages covered nearly every surface–*was that a pig?*–and the stench inside the cavern was unbearable. Several dusty shelves lined the walls, and upon these Robin observed what appeared to be human body parts floating in cloudy yellow liquid. A small, rusted cage rested upon a desk in the center of the chamber. Within the cage was a large black crow that cawed demonically when the Crooked Wizard entered the room.

"Abra," the old man said with something like tenderness in his voice. He produced a large insect from a pocket of his robes. The creature's legs raced as the Crooked Wizard dangled it over the bars of the cage. The crow flapped its wings and squawked until its master dropped the writhing insect into its mouth.

"Come on," said the Crooked Wizard. "We have a lot of work to do."

The scarecrow stared at Robin with vacant, unblinking eyes. It had a puzzled expression on its burlap face–an expression better suited for a jester than a soldier. The first of the twenty scarecrows Robin had assembled wore a veteran's scowl, but as the days wore on, Robin's attention to detail waivered. And, quite frankly, he wasn't much of an artist to begin with.

Now his task was almost complete. Nineteen scarecrows lay scattered all about the tiny cave, and this one, dressed in a suit of blue clothes, lay atop a wooden table. Robin dipped his paintbrush into a can of black and finished painting the eyes.

"It's done," he said. "That's the last of them."

The Crooked Wizard, who was sitting behind his desk, looked up from a spell book. His pointed nose and prominent forehead gave him the look of a bird of prey. He wore small, round spectacles perched on the end of his nose. "Took you long enough," he said.

"It would have been easier if you would have helped," Robin mumbled.

"I *heard* that," said the Crooked Wizard. "And you must remember, we each have our own role to play. I've been preparing the spells that will bring our army to life."

"I thought that powder was going to do that." Robin lifted the scarecrow from the table and leaned it against one wall of the cave. His back was to the wizard.

"It will," said the old man. "But there are some magic words involved, and they must be said with great precision. And there is the matter of our little arrangement..."

Robin shivered as he thought of the bargain they'd agreed to. Unconsciously, he placed his right hand over his heart.

"When?" he asked in a quiet voice.

"What was that?"

"When do you mean do to do it?" Robin said, this time loud enough to be heard. "When will you take my heart?"

"Once you've been reunited with your daughter," the Crooked Wizard said. "I'll allow you a chance to hold her one last time."

"Last time? But she'll be free..."

The Crooked Wizard grinned wickedly.

"You're planning on stealing from the Wicked Witch of the East. Even if you succeed, and believe me, that will be a miracle, the chances of you being able to hide with your girl in peace are practically non-existent." He leaned forward, seeming to enjoy this a little too much for Robin's comfort.

"She will search for you," he continued. "Orpah will never rest until she finds and destroys you."

Instinctively, Robin knew he was right. "What can I do?"

The Crooked Wizard tugged on his white beard.

"There is something." He motioned to a distant corner of the room, where a heavy blanket covered a huge picture frame. Robin walked to the frame and tugged on the blanket. It slipped away, revealing a dusty mirror.

"What is it?"

The Crooked Wizard came up behind Robin. He smelled worse than the cave, if that was possible. "A portal to the outside world—a place where all the magic has died."

"Another world?" Robin had never heard of such a thing.

"Actually, it's part of this world," the Crooked Wizard explained. "The Land of Oz has been hidden from the eyes of the rest of the world. If you take your daughter there, to live as an ordinary, albeit short, human, she will most likely be safe from Orpah. Of course, you can never truly be safe in this world, and people usually have a way of returning to the place where they started. In any case, the choice is yours. Once you return from Orpah's castle, I will claim your heart and your ability to lovingly raise a child will certainly be compromised."

The Crooked Wizard smiled again. "Now, let's bring this army to life."

The Crooked Wizard stood over the last of the straw men. He pinched something from a vial that hung around his neck and sprinkled the white powder over the scarecrow. Next, the old man shoved his left pinky finger into the air and said "*Weaugh!*" Then, waving his right hand over his heard, he pointed his right thumb upward and said "*Teaugh!*" The air in the cave began to tingle as the wizard pushed both hands over his head, spread out all his fingers and said "*Peaug!*"

Tiny flecks of powder began to glow all over the scarecrow. The straw man sat up, looked around, and then smiled stupidly at the old man.

"Are you my father?" the scarecrow asked.

"Of course not," snapped the wizard. "Don't ask such foolish questions you brainless sack of hay." The Crooked Wizard grabbed the scarecrow by the arm and flung him toward the door of the cave, where the rest of his brothers stood waiting. The youngest of their lot stumbled into the company, and several of the straw men toppled to the floor. They were up again in a second, brushing each other off and all the while jabbering.

"So fine to meet you."

"And you also."

"Say, does anyone have an idea what we're doing here?"

"*Shut up,*" the Crooked Wizard ordered. The army fell silent. "This is why I hate using this stupid spell," he mumbled. "Everything the Powder of Life animates turns out to be a complete moron. Now, I want the lot of you to stand there and keep your traps shut. I don't want to hear a peep out of you. Am I understood?"

The scarecrows, as one, nodded silently.

"Now that's done, it's time to work on the letter." The Crooked Wizard sat down at his desk, drew a sheet of paper from a drawer, and began to write. After scratching for a few minutes, he handed the letter to Robin.

The munchkin took the letter and scanned it. It read:

> *Dear Orpah,*
> *As Mayor of Munchkinland, it is my duty to inform you that we will no longer stand for your tyranny. We have sacrificed our own children to your wickedness, but no more. From now on, the Munchkins will stand against you and your cruelty. Though it means our deaths, we declare that we would rather die than to live as your slaves. Our agreement has come to an end. You are a fucked up cunt bitch, and I hope you die. The next time you appear in Munchkinville, we will consider it an act of war.*
>
> *Sincerely,*
> *Mayor Torin*

"What do you think?" the Crooked Wizard asked.

Robin considered for a moment.

"I think it will provoke war," he said.

"Grand." The Crooked Wizard snatched the paper and refolded it.

"What happens next?" Robin asked.

The Crooked Wizard moved to Abra's cage. The crow began flapping its wings and pacing frantically as the old man opened the cage door.

"What a pretty bird you are," he hissed. "Will you do me a little favor my pet?"

The bird leapt through the open door of the cage and fluttered to the wizard's shoulder with two flaps of its wings. The Crooked Wizard removed something that looked like a worm from the fathomless depths of his pockets and dangled the treat before the crow. The bird immediately swallowed the worm, and the old man's fingers up to his knuckles.

With his thumb and index finger still buried in the crow's mouth, the Crooked Wizard stared intently into the bird's eyes.

"Take this letter to Orpah," he ordered.

As her master removed his fingers, the crow croaked something that might have been "I will." She seized the letter with her beak and exploded into flight. Robin watched as she soared from the cave and into the Gillikin country beyond.

"Now it's your turn," the Crooked Wizard said. Robin glanced back at the old man and saw him gliding toward the hog pen at the far side of the cave. The creature's presence within the small space was likely the source – at least one of the sources– of the horrendous stench. Still, this was the Crooked Wizard's plan, and without him Robin would likely be still sitting in a waiting room in the Emerald City. He took a few hesitant steps in that direction.

"Behold the *Pigasus*, the most marvelous, wonderful and otherwise incredible creature in all the Land of Oz." The Crooked Wizard gestured sardonically into the hog pen, and he noticed something he hadn't seen before. The creature, gray with dried mud and shit, had wings.

"What the hell am I going to do with that?" Robin asked. He hadn't meant to speak out loud, but somehow the words spilled out of him anyway. The Crooked Wizard spun on him in instant.

"Steinbeck here is going to fly you to Orpah's castle," he snapped. "That is, if you treat him with the respect he deserves. Otherwise, you can walk there, but I think the witch will probably be back by the time you arrive. The choice is yours."

Robin sighed. The idea of riding upon that vile creature was appalling, but what other choice did he have?

"Fine. That's fine. Let's do this."

"I'm pleased you see it that way," said the Crooked Wizard. He unlatched the door of the hog pen and started making kissing noises at Steinbeck.

The Pigasus followed the old man out of the pen and through the cluttered mess of the cave. Once they passed through the gate of poison ivy they paused in a small clearing just outside.

"What now?" Robin asked.

The Crooked Wizard rolled his eyes.

"Get on the Pigasus and fly away."

"I mean, how do I control him. Her? And where do I go?" It took all of Robin's restraint not to lash out at the old man. Why did he have to be so difficult?"

"Just get on his back, tell him where you want to go, and hang on."

"That's it?"

"That's it."

Robin threw one leg over the animal's back and settled on top of the pigasus. He leaned forward, wrapped his arms around its neck, and spoke into its ear.

"Listen now you rancid beast, take me to the castle of the Wicked Witch of the East."

Robin was amazed at the rhyme that came out of his mouth. He looked at the Crooked Wizard as the pigasus began flapping its wings.

"I almost forgot," the old man said. "So long as you're on Steinbeck's back, everything you say will come out in Poesy."

"Does Poesy mean I'll speak in rhyme? Watch out, *Steinbeck*, for that pine."

They were now several yards above the ground and moving east. The Pigasus swerved violently, dodging a large tree. Soon they were high above the ground, flying headlong toward the most dangerous person in all the Land of Oz.

Munchkinville was quiet on its final morning as a habitable community. The villagers rose early as usual and went about their business. Farmers and merchants tended their fields and shops. Children played. Parents watched proudly as their wee ones took their first step or mastered a new word. Around ten o'clock something strange happened. An army of straw men marched into town along the Yellow Brick Road.

They walked in bumbling, stupid silence, their painted-on eyes focused on the road ahead of them. Each scarecrow held a spear or a short sword or a garden implement at the ready.

"What in the world," Sheriff Rozzco wondered. "Looks like they're fixin' to have a war." He was standing outside the jail, which had lately returned to its more traditional use as his corncrib. Rozzco was sure that war was out of his jurisdiction, and frankly, he didn't like the look of these scarecrows. He quickly returned to his work, ignoring the situation as overtly as possible.

The straw army stopped abruptly when they reached the town square. One of the scarecrows, the Crooked Wizard had called this one *General Vapid*, began barking orders.

"You and you, hide over there. You three get behind that wagon. *Not you Puck*"

Before long, he had distributed his entire force in small pockets throughout the town. Only Vapid and Puck remained, and they were soon hiding in the alley between The Shady Pig Tavern and The Lamb & Blue Hand dye shop. They were just in time. Not five minutes passed before a palanquin borne by four giants appeared from the east.

Orpah was fuming mad. The look on her face alone was enough to send Mayor Torin scurrying across town to greet her. The rest of the Munchkins, to their credit, were hiding under tables or peering anxiously through their curtains. It was clear that something had happened, though no one in Munchkinville would have suspected what it was.

"Queen... Madame...." Torin's face was bright red, and the armpits of his blue suit were soaked with sweat.

"*Shut up*," snapped the Wicked Witch of the East. She grabbed Mayor Torin's tie and pulled him close to her. Their foreheads were only an inch apart, and it seemed to everyone watching that she might burn holes in him with her eyes.

"I got your letter," Orpah whispered. "Would you care to repeat your sentiments to my face?"

"I... um, excuse me?"

Orpah gritted her teeth.

"You called me a cunt," she hissed. "And now I'm going to teach you a lesson that you'll never forget." Standing up straight, the witch motioned to her giants. The brutes started lumbering toward a nearby house.

"I don't understand," Torin pleaded. "I never called you..."

His words ended in a scream of agony as Orpah raked her nails across the Mayor's face. Blood oozed from four deep scratches on his left cheek.

"*You watch!*" she screamed. "*You watch what you're foolish letter has done!*"

Orpah grabbed him by the head and forced him to watch as her giants slammed their huge fists again the tiny cottage. It splintered in a thousand pieces, collapsing upon itself and the helpless Munchkins inside. But their work was far from done. The brutes tossed the devastated lumber aside, revealing an attractive young couple that had been in the throes of passion before their lovemaking was forever interrupted.

"Please don't hurt us," said the girl as she tried to cover her half-nakedness. One of the giants grabbed her by the hair and lifted her off the ground. Her lover made a desperate leap for her, but another giant kicked him hard, crushing his sternum and sending him flying into a nearby apple cart. Fruit was scattered everywhere as the boy breathed his last.

The girl screamed as she watched her lover die. But her grief quickly turned to horror. The Wicked Witch of the East pointed at the girl and said *"Kreon!"* A bolt of lighting shot from Orpah's finger. It arced across the town square and hit the girl directly between her small breasts. A moment later, a blackened, unrecognizable form hit the ground with a thud.

"Now," said Orpah to the Mayor, "do I have your attention?"

Torin was nodding stupidly when General Vapid and Puck suddenly charged out of their alley.

"Attack!" Vapid ordered. He was pointing his spear at Orpah and shrieking a blood-curdling battle cry. Puck was a few steps behind him, holding a short sword by the blade and swinging the handle recklessly at no one in particular.

The element of surprise was almost enough to win the day and forever change the political landscape in the Land of Oz. But Orpah reacted quickly and used her magical silver slippers to fly across the square and evade the attack. Vapid was now standing amidst the four giants. He lifted his spear and plunged it into the thigh of one the brutes. The giant yelped in pain, and was quickly set upon by three more scarecrows. They hacked him with their swords and axes, spraying his blood all over place. The giant collapsed face first to the bricks. He was dead.

Another giant, the largest of the bunch, took a step toward his comrade. The scarecrow army set upon him as well, and he soon joined his friend in death.

Nearby, Mayor Torin suddenly realized that he was free. Not only that, this mysterious army of straw men actually appeared to be winning. Torin smiled, hoping that the enslavement of his people had finally come to an end.

Unfortunately, this hopeful future was cut tragically short when Orpah shouted *"Flamack!"* and a fireball exploded on the town square. Three scarecrows, the bodies of the half-naked lovers and Mayor Torin were all instantly consumed.

Puck, the stupidest of all the brainless scarecrow army, somehow managed not to be incinerated by Orpah's fireball. He was several feet outside the blast radius, attacking a giant with the hilt of his short sword, when the brute snatched him up like a sack of hay (which he essentially was) and tore him in half. The remains of Puck's body were tossed in a water trough and forgotten.

Battle raged across Munchkinville. Several structures were destroyed when the scarecrows took down the dark-haired giant that was responsible for the death of Cordelia Plumly. His legs were cut out from under him, and when he fell, he took down a bell tower–the tallest structure in town. This tower collapsed onto the Mayor's house, leveling it.

Seeing her escorts defeated so soundly, Orpah began to wonder if her own safety was in jeopardy. She considered escaping–the silver slippers would return her to her castle in three jumps if she wished–but decided against it.

"I'll make an example of this town," she muttered under her breath. Grinning cruelly, the Wicked Witch of the East began hurling fireballs in every direction. One by one, the scarecrows burst into flames. They stumbled frantically about the village, spreading destruction from house to house and shop to shop. Within minutes, the entire town was burning.

Munchkinville was doomed.

The land surrounding the castle of the Wicked Witch of the East was unlike anything Robin had ever seen. It was twisted and scarred with blackened trees and stagnant bodies of water. Orpah's castle was a terrifying golgotha amidst all this ruin. The structure actually looked like a skull, with the nose and eye sockets serving as windows, and the open mouth as the front door.

"What kind of crazy, evil bitch," Robin said to himself, "would want to live in a place like this?" Fear nearly paralyzed the Munchkin as Steinbeck began his slow descent. *What if the witch is still inside? If so, then I will surely die. And if she's left her guards behind? On my flesh they'll surely dine.*

It was only the horrible realization that he was actually thinking in Poesy that caused Robin to slide off the Pigasus the moment that the creature landed. He heard something crunch beneath his foot, and when Robin looked down, he realized he had stepped on a skeleton. The bones were gray with soot, but they were unmistakable–this was the body of a Munchkin child.

Rage flushed whatever fear remained from Robin's nervous system. His little girl was inside that awful place, and he was determined to rescue her or die trying. Either way, his fate lay beyond the grinning teeth of the witch's castle.

"Stay here," Robin said. He knelt beside Steinbeck and patted the animal on top of its bristly head. The Pigasus stared up at him with troubled black eyes and whimpered.

"I'll just be a few minutes," Robin said. "Just long enough to find my daughter." The Munchkin stood, faced the castle, and walked right up to the front door.

As he approached the door, Robin noticed a lion-headed doorknocker.

He had to stretch to reach the huge, metal ring in the lion's mouth, and Robin was tall for a Munchkin. He slammed the ring against the door only once, and immediately a small opening appeared in the door. A green-skinned, pointed-nosed goblin peered through the opening.

"Who are you and what do you want?" the creature demanded.

"My name is Robin Plumly," Robin said, "and I've come to rescue my daughter."

A smile spread on the goblin's ugly face.

"You can't..."

Robin's hand shot out like a crossbow bolt. He grabbed the goblin by the nose and twisted. The creature squealed in pain as Robin began to pull him face-first through the tiny hole in the door. "Let me in," he ordered, "or I swear I'll tear your nose right off."

"I can't," the goblin shrieked. "She'll kill me."

"*I'll kill you.*"

Several moments passed like this before the goblin finally conceded and allowed Robin into the castle. The door swung open slowly, the hinges screaming in protest, and finally revealed a large open foyer lit by a hanging chandelier. A treacherous staircase wound along the back of the foyer, and the walls were covered with expensive, if dusty, tapestries depicting famous historical and political figures in compromising positions. The tapestry closest to Robin featured Princess Langwidere of Ev performing fellatio on the Nome King. The Munchkin had little time to ponder the many levels on which this offended him, however, because the goblin stepped in front of him, and blocked his entrance. He was wielding a small cudgel in his right and smacking it threateningly into his left.

"You wanna try that again?" the goblin asked.

It was at this moment that it occurred to Robin that perhaps he should have brought a sword or gun or some other weapon along on this mission. Up until that point, he considered his fists and his anger enough to ensure victory, but now he was wondering how he could have been so stupid. His only hope was the element of surprise.

Robin lunged forward, taking a single stinging blow from the goblin's cudgel before the fight turned into what every fight eventually turns into— a wrestling match. Robin finally gained the upper hand by slipping a finger into each of the goblin's nostrils and pulling with all his might. There was a sickening pop as the creature's cartilage tore away, leaving its nose hanging between its eyes by only a small flap of skin. The goblin screamed in pain and fury as blood pumped into its mouth.

Robin grabbed the goblin's cudgel, slipped behind the creature, and ended its miserable life with a single blow to the back of its head. It yelped one last time and then fell forward on its face.

When no other guards came running, Robin moved to the stairs at the back of the room. His heart was racing, and somehow he knew that Dot was still alive and that he was going to see her again. Taking the stairs two at a time Robin noted the chain that allowed the chandelier to be raised and lowered. It was held in place by a single bent nail.

At the top of the stairs was a door, and beyond that, a large room lit by two circular windows. The eyes of the skull, Robin realized. He glanced around the room and found it strikingly similar to the lair of the Crooked Wizard. Dusty bookshelves dominated the room from floor to ceiling, and in fact actually seemed to be holding up the roof in places. Several tables covered with yellowing papers were pushed together near the left wall. In the center of the room hanging from the rafters were five Munchkin-sized cages.

"Dot!" Robin dropped the cudgel and rushed across the room. Immediately he examined the cages. The children inside were naked and filthy—they'd been sitting in their own excrement for days. They stared at him with wide, vacant eyes. Unfeeling eyes.

Robin's stomach turned. He leaned forward and vomited on the wooden floor. His knees buckled.

Dot.

Robin scrambled to his feet and pushed his way through the cages. He tried to ignore the horrible site before him as he search for his little girl. The nausea hit him again when he found her.

Dot was dead.

A sound like a scream ripped through the castle; it was the hinges on the door downstairs. *The witch*, Robin thought frantically. *Orpah has returned.*

Acting on pure instinct Robin ripped open the cage door that held Dot's body. He scooped her stiff form under his left arm and raced toward the stairs. Perhaps he could escape the castle.

If I can make it back to the Crooked Wizard, Robin thought, *then maybe he can use the Powder of Life on Dot.*

He was halfway down the stairs when he saw the Wicked Witch of the East. She knelt in the middle of the room, cradling the goblin's body in her arms. Her shoulders hunched forward and back as sobs wracked her lithe frame. Orpah looked up when she heard Robin on the stairs. Black lines of mascara streaked her face, and she looked like a demon bent on destruction.

"*You!*" she shouted. "You murdered him. You did this." Orpah stood holding the goblin's body before her like a groom carrying his bride over the threshold. Her eyes began to glow as she chanted something under her breath in the language of magic.

Robin, cradling his own lost child to his breast, realized two things at that moment. Orpah was standing directly underneath the chandelier, and he was standing right beside the lowering chain. The Munchkin shifted Dot's body, and with his free hand, he plucked the chain off the bent nail.

Orpah was glowing all over when the chandelier crashed down on top of her. She collapsed under its weight. Her black robes instantly burst into flame when they came in contact with the still-burning candles. Her screams filled the castle, and Robin smiled for the first time in weeks when he walked calmly past her flailing body.

Steinbeck was waiting outside. Whether he hid when Orpah returned or if the witch simply ignored him, Robin could not say. He climbed on the animal's back, positioned Dot's body between his legs, and nudged the Pigasus into flight.

As much as Robin Plumly hoped that his story would end with everyone living happily ever after, that is sadly not the case. He returned to the cave of the Crooked Wizard and begged the old man to bring Dot back to life.

"I won't do it," the wizard insisted. "Wasn't part of our original bargain."

At this point, Robin held a dagger to his own chest, the tip pressed right over his heart.

"If you don't," he said, "I'll deny you the thing you hold most dear." There was an eerie calm in Robin's voice, and the Crooked Wizard was convinced he wasn't bluffing. Fifteen minutes later, Dot came screaming back to life.

Robin held her close, crushing his child against his chest.

"I love you," he whispered. "I missed you so much." Dot closed her eyes and nuzzled against her father's neck.

Unfortunately, the happy ending lasted for only about thirty minutes. That's when the Crooked Wizard stood up, checked his pocket watch, and stomped over to the corner of the cave where father and daughter were hugging and snuggling and weeping heartbreaking tears of regret.

"It's time," the old man insisted. "Take her through the portal and come on back."

Robin considered breaking his agreement with the Crooked Wizard, but deep down he knew that this was Dot's only hope of ever escaping the Wicked Witch of the East. Orpah would come for her; it was only a matter of time. So he stood, stared at the dusty mirror for a moment, and then stepped through into another world.

It was a flat, gray country on the other side of the mirror. Not a tree broke the broad sweep of flat country that reached to the edge of the sky in all directions. Only a single house could be seen, and it was upon the doorstep of this house that Robin left his sweet little innocent Dot, swaddled in an old gray blanket and asleep in an apple crate. He left a short note that read: *This is my daughter, Dorothy. Please take care of her.*

It occurred to Robin that he might also remain in that gray land and escape his bargain. But the thought of a lifetime fleeing not only Orpah, but the Crooked Wizard as well caused Robin to reconsider this course. Dot was better off without him. Resigned to his fate, Robin returned through the portal to find the Crooked Wizard waiting for him.

The old man's hand darted from the folds of his cloak, and before Robin could move there was a wet cloth over his nose and mouth. He struggled against the wizard, he struggled to breathe, but his vision blurred with each breath, and his sinuses were burning.

Robin dropped to his knees. He tried to rise but it was no use. The old man guided him to the floor, placing his head gently upon the cold stone. Robin closed his eyes.

Many miles away, a single soul stirred amongst the smoldering ruins of Munchkinville. It was Sheriff Rozzco, who had buried himself deep inside his corncrib when Orpah decimated the village. Every man, woman and child in Munchkinville (save Rozzco of course) was dead. The sheriff, *ex-sheriff*, stumbled through the charred bones of his form jurisdiction. He wept openly, wishing that he could have been brave enough to die with his people.

Finally, Rozzco came to an overturned water trough where he discovered the remains of one of the scarecrows that defended the town. He picked up the straw man's head and was amazed when the thing began to speak.

"Excuse me," said the face on the burlap sack, "but I believe that if you stuff my clothes full of straw, I'll be able to function again."

Rozzco looked down and saw the still-damp suit of blue clothes to which the scarecrow was referring. After a moment's consideration, the sheriff gathered the clothes together. Most of the straw was gone, burned up in the witch's fire, but he was certain he could find some along the way. This was the Land of Oz, after all, a place that was full of magic and crows. Before long, Rozzco and the scarecrow were headed for the next town, following the path of the Yellow Brick Road.

You know the rest of the story right? Rozzco settled in a town called Munchkinburg, where he set up a small farm. His fields were kept safe from crows by a certain talking scarecrow. The Crooked Wizard and his Powder of Life went on to be involved in several adventures. And Dot? She became the most famous adventurer of all. She grew up in that strange gray country, but eventually returned to the Land of Oz and killed the Wicked Witch of the East by dropping a house on her. She never saw her father again, however, because Robin Plumly died on the operating table just minutes after the Crooked Wizard extracted his heart.

Robin's name was vilified in the Munchkin newspapers. They claimed he was responsible for what Orpah did in Munchkinville. And perhaps he was, who can say? But in a way, he was also responsible for the death of the Wicked Witch of the East and the redemption of Munchkinland. Either way, hero or villain, the story of Robin Plumly is done.

THE END.

Mr Yoop's Soup

by Michael D. Turner

King Gob Ghab was worried. Normally being King of the Munchkins was quite a pleasant job. He got to wear fine clothes with fancy buttons and excellent boots that were made just for him, instead of being picked from a tree like everyone else's. He got to wear a crown.

His was a particularly nice one, a gift from the emperor of the Winkies, made of light and shiny tin with delicate gold-foil flowers tastefully decorated with thimble-sized sapphires. True, he had to sit in his court and settle any disputes his Munchkins brought to him, but his people were by-and-large a peaceful, settled folk, so he only had to do that an hour or so every other week. The rest was just making speeches at holiday festivals and having dinners with important Munchkin citizens. Not today though. Today was one unusual thing after another.

The first thing was a mysterious hole in Mob Cobi's roof, accompanied by the disappearance of his prize cleaver. Mob Cobi was Munchkin City's most popular (and only) butcher, and the cleaver—an enormous two-handed affair that dated back before the time of the witches, had not been used in many years. Instead it had hung on a stout wooden peg above Mob Cobi's counter. Today the peg was still there but the cleaver had disappeared...apparently through a hole torn in the shop's roof!

Theft! Burglary! Vandalism!

Such a thing had not happened in Munchkin land in many, many years.

Then there was the missing goose-girl. Nemi Omsbi was the daughter of an important farmer and by all accounts a most responsible girl. Every day for as long as anybody could remember she'd risen early, ate breakfast, and then taken her geese out to the meadows near her father's farm. She tended the geese all day, usually knitting clever sweaters and scarves with patterns of blue geese in them to pass the time, always returning just before dinner time. Only today she hadn't. *Returned* that is. Her geese were found milling in the meadows, calling for her. Her knitting was under a tree nearby but no sign of her. Most Munchkins assumed she'd finally run off with some lad but her geese said not, and her mother believed them and insisted there was foul play.

Foul play! In Oz!

Finally, for certain that in fairy counties such things always happen in threes, a most alarming report came in.

"Your majesty," Vorodi, the High Chancellor, wheezed, "Mr. Yoop has escaped!"

"*Whoop?*"

"Yoop, your Majesty. Mr. Yoop, the giant cannibal who was caged along an unused road to the Winkie country long ago, before the time of the witches! He's out; his cage is broken and empty! He escaped."

"How?" asked the King. "When?"

"I . . . I don't know, your Majesty," the chancellor said, a worried look passing over his normally round and cheerful face. "A passing Jay had taken to taunting the giant every few weeks. Today he went to taunt and there was no giant. I don't know how he escaped."

"No matter," the King clapped his hands in front of his ample stomach, the result of dining with too many important Munchkins. "This is too much for us, Vorodi. Holes in roofs, missing cutlery and goose-girls. Now a giant! We must send word to Ozma's court and ask for help. Perhaps Princess Dorothy or Nick Chopper, will be about, to come lend us a hand."

"Emerald City is a long way off," observed the chancellor. "What are we Munchkins to do until help arrives?"

"The King paced a bit and then declared, "Send the constables around to every village and farm. Tell my people to stay indoors or in large groups."

"You want the people to huddle in fear, while we wait for help?"

"That's right," the King agreed, "most sensible thing to do, really."

"If we send out the constables, who will we send to Ozma?"

"I'll go myself," the King declared. "Get someone to hitch up the goat-cart." King Ghab knew he was much too fat these days to walk all the way to Emerald City.

"As your majesty commands," said Vorodi.

Soon the constables were scampering about, and Munchkins were huddled into their homes and cellars, waiting further news, while King Ghab was settled in his cart behind a goat named Nick, after the Emperor of the Winkies, that placidly munched vegetables hung before him on a pole, heading steadily down the yellow brick road to Emerald, capital city of Oz.

The king had not traveled very far beyond the edge of Munchkin City, his capitol, before he got to the edges of the great Munchkin forest. It wasn't the largest forest in the Land of Oz but it was large enough, and home to many wild beasts. The forest was very quiet, which neither the king nor the goat took note of. The goat had been chosen for its phlegmatic personality and as long as its mouth was full it was content to plod along pulling the cart until the vegetables ran out. The king was just preoccupied.

The forest was unnaturally quiet because Mr. Yoop, the giant, was running loose in it. He was one of the most dangerous things to ever run loose anywhere in the land of Oz, and the beasts, living in a less refined but more natural state than city folk, were very sensitive to such things and not inclined to put themselves at risk by running about with a giant on the loose. King Ghab lived in the city however, and was more careless about such things.

So it was that he didn't notice the cart was passing two suspiciously hairy tree trunks. The giant, whose legs those tree trunks were, was used to snatching unwary travelers who passed his cage and he snatched King Ghab up the same way. He wrapped his hand 'round the King's head, shoulders, and arms and lifted him right out of the cart as quick as you could blink. The goat Nick never even noticed and continued on for several miles while he worked through a large, juicy turnip currently hanging on his stick.

In three great strides the giant had them out of sight of the road. Thirteen more of his gigantic steps and they were deep inside the blue-tinged forest. Gob Ghab struggled in the giant's grip, kicking his legs and even trying to bite the giant's leathery palm, but he might as well have been wrapped in stone. The giant walked a long way into the woods before he stopped.

After he stopped he shifted his grip so King Ghab's head poked out of the top of his hand and the King could see.

Nothing he saw did much to encourage the King. They were somewhere deep in the forest under an enormous Hickory tree. A low fire burned on a stone hearth laid near the tree's trunk and over it simmered a huge iron pot, it's outside quite rusted. Beside the pot was a rough hewn trestle table on which sat a coil of heavy rope, a pile of onions and what had to be Mob Cobi's cleaver.

"Unhand me!" Gob Ghab demanded of the giant. "I am the King of this land! Put me down!' This might have made more of an impression if he'd not squeaked so in the middle of "down!'.

Mr. Yoop simply grinned and plucked the great gold-foil and tin crown off Gob Ghab's head. He held it up to his eye.

"The king you are of those I hate, a fine meal I'm sure you'll make!"

"Don't be ridiculous. The king is supposed to eat fine meals," Gob protested, "not be eaten as one! Put me down! Let me go!"

Though the Munchkin King continued to protest it didn't matter to the giant at all. In a twice he had King Ghab trussed up and tied down across the table. He then proceeded to pluck and pull off the King's fine clothes, starting with his splendid tooled boots.

"Hey!" Shouted Gob. "Careful with those, they're custom made! Ouch! That pinched!" Mr. Yoop finally shut him up by stuffing a fine knit stocking into his mouth. He finished undressing the Munchkin before Gob managed to spit the stocking out.

"Why are you doing this to me?" Gob cried.

Mr. Yoop paused to consider the question before replying,

"One hundred years in a cage, you can not comprehend my rage. No one to eat, nothing to gnaw. Now I'll try you in my jaws." He reached for the cleaver.

Gob Ghab, King of the Munchkins, howled as Mr. Yoop did his work. The giant's cleaver was sharp enough to split hairs, and the blade caused a deep burning sensation as the giant slowly drew it through the King's flesh, as if it were white hot. Tears welled in the King's eyes as Mr. Yoop leaned in to complete his first cut, severing Gob's feet just above the ankles. When the giant saw the tears he grinned and paused in his cutting long enough to wipe one on to his finger, thick as a fence-post, and touch it to his lips.

He then went back to his labor, cleaving every joint and splitting King Gob's torso up the middle like a chicken. This did not kill the King, of course, because very few things can actually kill the residents of the fairy realm of Oz, but it was very, *very* painful and the giant worked his knife slowly and deliberately, saving Gob's head for the very last cut so the King could fully appreciate the giant's work.

King Gob didn't appreciate any part of Mr. Yoop's work, however.

"Enough, enough I say! Oh, this is awful. Stop doing this to me, please!" Mr. Yoop just grinned and lifted the lid off the great iron cauldron. He tossed the king's left foot into the pot, and then his right forearm. He made a game of it, standing behind the table and flinging a thigh and buttocks, still attached together, back up from behind his head. It rattled around the rim before falling in with a splash, which was followed by a high-pitched "*oomph!*" from inside the cauldron.

The giant's grin widened and he snatched the king's head up and held it over the cauldron so he could see in. In the steaming stock inside Gob could see a girl, or parts of a girl, floating and bobbing along with the parts of him just placed. Her head came out from under his thigh, looked him square in the eye and spat out a mouthful of broth.

'Oh my," King Ghab said. "Are you Nemi Omsbi?"

Mr. Yoop frowned at him and crammed an onion in his mouth, but the girl's head answered.

"Yes, I'm Nemi Omsbi. Oh, this is terrible! Watch out!" This, just as the giant stuffed his head into the simmering broth. The liquid was scalding of course, and also heavily spiced with pepper. It burned in Gob's eyes and reddened his skin and made his ears itch inside, which was all the worse for having no hands and arms attached to scratch with. His face impacted something soft, which floated to the surface with him. He managed to spit out the onion and work his face around with jaw, tongue and eyebrows until he could see. His head was floating on top of Nemi Omsbi's chest. If Gob had not already been scalded red he would have blushed.

"Look out!" Nemi Omsbi said, just as the rest of his parts started raining down. The stock splashed and Gob was knocked off Nemi's chest and ended up somewhere near the bottom of the pot. It was much hotter there. Gob Ghab felt his eyes and ears swelling in the heat, so much so he was glad when the giant stirred the pot with a big wooden ladle and brought his head to the surface again.

The grinning giant was waiting for him. Once both heads were floating on the top of the broth he proceeded to pelt them with onions. Nemi was struck hard in her left eye, which immediately teared up. This delighted the giant.

"Don't cry, Miss Omsbi," Gob said. "We'll get out of this, somehow."

"Idiot!" the girl replied. "I've got onion in my eye! And the only place we're going from here is down his gullet."

"The girl is right, you're in a spot." Mr. Yoop said. "Nothing can pull you from my pot." Then he pasted Gob between the eyes with the last onion and put the lid on, plunging the cauldron into a sweaty darkness. This sent the stock to boiling and for quite some time afterward all the two heads could do was scream.

Bosky Boq was a famous wrestler. He'd been champion wrestler of the Munchkins for as long as anyone could remember, since the days of the witches. He still had, in his backroom where he kept such things, a silver rod set with sapphires awarded to him by the Witch of the East for his first championship. He seldom displayed any of his trophies for in truth he had very few friends, but in his heart he valued that one the most, not the least because it had come from one of the feared wicked witches.

Like those witches, Boq was not well liked but was well respected and feared. He was a true Munchkin from Munchkin City and so only about half as tall as most Ozites, but what he lacked in height he made up for in lean hard muscle. Broad shouldered, barrel chested with legs like stumps and a neck fully as thick as his thigh, he'd spent his lifetime taking on bigger, or at least taller, opponents without suffering more than a handful of defeats over a very long career.

He reasoned that his skill and experience at wrestling ought to stand him in good stead against a giant. While he was too small, or at any rate the giant was too large, for Boq to exert much leverage against his arms or legs, he might be able to work something against the fingers of his hands. Footwork was going to be a problem though. He'd even consulted with a copy of his friend Col. Wyndel Wynkaisser's "How to fight like a Winkie" for ideas on that.

Winkies were indeed the most ferocious fighters of all the Ozites, but no Winkie had ever matched him at wrestling, which was why Wyndel had asked him for his input on the chapters on wrestling and ground work. He'd been proud to be asked and gladly contributed, for while no Winkie could out wrestle him he'd decided long ago to stay out of any contest conducted under Winkie rules. A low center of gravity and superior leverage were scarcely enough to counter all the punching, kicking, stomping, chopping and gouging dished out in Winkie fighting. After all, he was a wrestler.

He was working on a few ideas he had in the big, open yard behind his house. Let his neighbors cower in their cellars and wait for help from Emerald City. Boq believed in solving his own problems and thought Munchkins as a whole should do the same.

Practice had always been a key element in his success. What he was practicing now was a sort of twisty, low spread jump designed to move him out of the giant's grasp while positioning him to get behind a descending hand and maybe let him get a grip. It was harder than he'd thought it would be, with all the squatting and turning, and Boq had to concentrate very hard to avoid tripping his own self up. He was much surprised when, in the middle of a twisting leap, he ran smack into something very large and very hard right in the middle of his yard, and fell backwards on to his bum.

He stared stupidly for a second at what he thought was a big, hairy tree someone had planted in his yard while he wasn't looking. His eyes and his mind both regained focus then and he tilted his head back farther to stare into the swarthy, grinning face of Mr. Yoop.

"In the pot are pork and veal," the giant said. "I want your beef to fill my meal!" The giant made a snatch for Bosky Boq, but the wrestler was ready for him. As the giant's hand shot down the wrestler leaped up and twisted. Mr. Yoop's hand closed on air, except for his little finger which

Boq had bent backward. The wrestler twisted the finger further and pushed it down into the ground and the giant over balanced and planted his weight on his empty fist.

"Ha!" Boq cried in triumph.

"Grrr!" Mr. Yoop growled deeply as he swung around with his other hand. Boq saw it coming but he hadn't quite worked out what to do about the giant's other hand, and before anything occurred to him Mr. Yoop had snatched him up. The giant sprang to his feet and held Boq high in the air and shook him fiercely. Just when the wrestler thought his eyes would pop out Mr. Yoop flung him on the ground very hard.

Boq's backyard was covered with a thick, springy turf over hard earth, and Boq landed face first so hard he left an impression on the dirt beneath the grass. He didn't move. The giant grinned as he peeled him up and carried him off.

The dove flew straight through the open window at the back of the throne room and began to circle wearily around the small girl seated on the throne, cooing distress. The girl, who was not really a girl but was, in fact, Ozma, a powerful fairy and queen of the Lands of Oz, held up a finger for the bird to land on. It did and immediately began cooing out its message.

The girl Queen allowed no distress to show on her angelic face, but rose at once, placed the dove on the arm of her throne and motioned to her Royal Chamberlain.

"Have Princess Dorothy meet me at my magic picture," She commanded.

The Chamberlain bustled off to find Dorothy, and Ozma left right behind him.

"There was no point to your going off to Emerald City," Nemi Omsbi said. "Queen Ozma is perfectly capable of keeping track of what's going on without your help. Glinda will have read about Mr. Yoop's escape in her magic book and sent word to the Queen by magic or messenger bird. For that matter *you* could have sent a bird. It's much faster than a goat cart."

King Gob Ghab spat a mouthful of broth at the goose-girls head.

"Maybe so, but I didn't think of it."

"No," the girl agreed. "All you thought of was how much safer it'd be in Emerald City with a giant wandering around Munchkin Land! Get your face off my bosoms."

"How?" the King asked. The giant had left the lid only slightly ajar, to allow the broth to cook down a little, and the King could barely see, especially with the pepper still burning in his eyes. The spicing didn't seem to bother the girl's eyes. She saw every transgression.

"Just open your mouth—let it fill up—and spit it out in a stream. Like this . . ." The girl opened her mouth to demonstrate, bringing her face to face with a favorite part of Gob's" anatomy, which caught the brunt of her spray as she propelled her head across the cauldron.

"Hey, watch that!" Gob objected. He didn't like the silly way it looked flapping around at the end of hiss torso, with no legs to keep it in place.

"Ha!" Nemi laughed. "I'll bet you wish I'd gotten closer."

"Not at all," said Gob. "It's the Queen's favorite part of me. Sometimes I think it's the only part she really likes."

"If we get out of this I'll have to have a talk with her Majesty." Nemi spat a little broth to turn her face toward Gob's. "About her standards."

"It's not exactly displayed to best effect in here." Snapped Gob.

"Quiet," the girl replied. "Mr. Yoop is coming back."

"I think he knows we're in here." Gob quieted down anyway. They could hear the giant bustling about the table. This went on for some time. Suddenly there was a shriek, followed by a long string of the foulest swearing either of them had ever heard, and then the giant removed the lid, releasing a cloud of steam. He leered down at them over the rim.

"This one put up quite a fight, but I know how to cook him right." He held up his latest victim's head. Gob's crown was crammed, points down, over his bulging forehead. Unfortunately it didn't cover his mouth.

". . . *motherless, dog-dicked arse-lipping nome-knocker! You tree fucking, pig-pimping, turd-faced*—," the giant dropped the head into the pot where, thanks to the crown, it sank right to the bottom and stayed.

"Now that I have dealt with that, its time for a little snack." Mr. Yoop poked his massive finger into Nemi's face, not put off a bit by her attempt to bite him. He didn't seem to like what he felt. "Heads take longer for to cook, I'll just settle for a foot."

Fish out a foot he did, and a leg and a thigh and bum to go with it. All of them belonging to Nemi Omsbi.

"Ohh! That curd-spoiling, silage slurping vat of monkey-shit!" She exclaimed. "I wish he hadn't sunk that other head. That fellow sounded like he could really swear. Right now I'd take lessons."

"You were doing just fine," Gob assured her.

"Do you really think so?" Nemi asked. "I've never sworn before."

"Perhaps you should save the next batch for when old Yoop shows his face over the side again."

Just then the giant reappeared, fork in one hand and cleaver in the other. Nemi Omsbi didn't hesitate at all.

"*You goose-shit snorting, pond-scum gargling erb buggerer! Whimsey-brained*

Growlywog slut-slave! Self-fornicating, Kalidah baiting—yeagh!—" Mr. Yoop poked Nemi in her left eye with the fork. It popped like a half-poached egg and her head sank under the broth. The giant grinned and said,

"The maiden's bum was juicy sweet! Let's see how you are to eat." His fork jutted down at Gob's torso, clear across the cauldron from his head. "A tiny bite of you I'll try, and then I'll eat her other thigh." He speared Gob's penis and nicked it off with the tip of the cleaver. Quick as that he was grinding it with he molars like a tough piece of gristle.

"Oh, the Queen won't be pleased with that."

As Mr. Yoop speared Nemi's other thigh her head resurfaced, missing an eye and most of the surrounding cheek.

". . . *son-of-a-wogglebug*. Put that back, you circus geek!"

The giant withdrew.

"Watch out!" Gob warned her, without stopping to wonder just how a half-cooked floating head would go about doing that. It began raining pieces of the other Munchkin. He was a bulky cusser; the huge pot was growing full.

"Too much time you take to stew," the giant said as he lifted the lid back into position. "I'll add some wood to boil you." He placed the lid firmly over the cauldron with a clang. Gob could barely hear him moving about, but he definitely felt it when the giant built up the fire.

"Shit," he said aloud, "we really are doomed."

"I wish I could hear what they are saying," Princess Dorothy said.

"The situation is clearly worse than I'd hoped," Ozma replied. "Mr. Yoop has already seized several of my subjects and is cooking them."

Dorothy twirled a blonde ringlet for a moment, thinking.

"Send for the *Nome King's Belt*, Ozma! You can use it to turn old Yoop into a stone and we can send someone round to fish those Munchkins out of the soup."

The Fairy Queen sighed.

"No, Dorothy. We can not just solve the problem from here with magic. If we did that, the people would soon come to rely on us to protect them always. They might grow so confident in us as to fail to take responsibility for their own safety. Why, if they did that the Munchkins would still be going about their business instead of sensibly huddling in their cellars in fear, waiting rescue. It's not enough to protect the people of my realm," the Girl Queen explained. "We must be seen to protect them. I'll send a party to deal with Mr. Yoop."

"Ugh!" Dorothy had just watched Mr. Yoop eat Nemi Omsbi's butt.

"Too late for that girl's ass. Let me go, Ozma. Please. If I wear my magic belt, Mr. Yoop won't be able to harm me. Let me deal with him."

The fairy smiled at her oldest, dearest friend.

"No, sweet one. Mr. Yoop is a crafty old cannibal, and if you go there is a chance, however small, that the wicked giant could get you out of your belt. If that happened, you might end up in his pot, and he might end up on my throne."

"He wouldn't fit," the farm girl replied.

"Perhaps not," Ozma agreed. "We won't chance it, though. I'll send a party of people he can't eat to deal with him. Who among my not-meat subjects is at court?"

"Hmmm, lets see." Dorothy pulled a scroll from the pocket of her smock. She'd been Ozma's intelligence secretary for decades now. "Scraps and Scarecrow are still at the corn palace, and haven't been back for months. *Haven't left his crib for months*, that anybody's noticed. Jack Pumpkinhead should be back soon, he always comes in between planting and harvest, but he's not here yet. I don't think he'd be right for the job anyway." Ozma nodded her head in agreement. "Nick Chopper's just come from the Winkie Country, and he brought the Tin Soldier with him. They've both had quite a polishing. The Glass Cat is around somewhere, of course . . . and the Sawhorse is in his stable, naturally."

"Yes, that's enough." Ozma tapped her perfect lips thoughtfully. "Nick Chopper knows that forest, he cut wood in it for years before he was tin. He can go, and the Soldier as well. The Glass Cat too, of course. She can scout, there's no where in Oz she hasn't been. They'd best take the sawhorse and the red wagon." She looked at Dorothy, who was trying not to pout. "See to that, sweetling, while I get the wizard to prepare something for Mr. Yoop."

"Of course, Ozma dear." Dorothy gave the magic picture another glance. "Ung! The Munchkin Queen won't care for that!"

Just when Gob Ghab didn't think things could get any worse his crown came loose from Bosky Boq's head, which floated to the surface.

". . . *stinking result of a gang of Winkies and a Gillikin crone. Dung pated, oversized—*'"

"Who are you? The King asked.

"Huh?" the other head started. "I'm Bosky Boq, champion wrestler of Oz. Who the hell are you two?"

"I'm Nemi Omsbi; my father has a farm south of Munchkin City. The other is our King, Gob Ghab the First." Gob was amazed at the amount of sarcasm the girl could get out of half a face.

"That explains the crown," Boq said. "Hey, are those yours? Nice tits."

"Yes, they're mine. They've been stewing in here so long they've swollen up."

"It's as hot as a nome's smelter in here." Boq declared.

"Tell me about it," Nemi managed to say, just as the rest of her cheek sloughed off. "I was going to ask, since we don't have much else to do, could you teach me to swear like that?"

"Sure."

"Now, Miss Omsbi," Gob said. "What would your father say to your learning to swear?"

"Nothing compared to what he'll say when he finds out what *you* let happen to me!" the farm girl replied. "You're the King! You're supposed to protect the Munchkin people. What were you doing while that giant ate my ass?"

"Floating in the pot." Gob replied.

"The giant ate your ass?" asked Boq.

"Yes."

"Can't fault his taste." The wrestler's head was bobbing alongside Nemi's chest. He suckered up to it like a leech and bit off a bit. "Or yours."

'Stop that!" Nemi cried.

"Why should the giant get it all?" Boq asked.

Nemi let out a long, detailed string of invective detailed the wrestler's ancestry, eating habits and sexual proclivities, going both forward and backward through several generations.

"*. . . to wallow in the puked-up remains of your own feces while fornicated with your mother's children!*"

"See," Boq said, "there's nothing too it."

The lid rose off the pot and Mr. Yoop grinned down at them.

"Now my soup's smelling sweet. I think that it is time to eat." The giant stood over the pot, fork in one hand and a huge ladle in the other. Nemi and the wrestler began to swear but the giant just grinned and ladled Nemi's head into his mouth. She screamed as he slowly slurped the remaining flesh from her face.

Bosky Boq fell silent as the giant crunched her skull in his jaws. If Gob had still been attached to his stomach he would have vomited. "Mmmm." Said the giant as he thrust his fork at the wrestler's head. Boq let out a spray of broth to dodge and the giant ended up spearing a larger chunk.

"Hey, that's my chest!" exclaimed the King. Mr. Yoop just grinned as he bit off a large chunk. He slurped as he ate, and pieces dropped out of his mouth and off his beard to fall back into the cauldron and onto their faces. He missed Bosky with the fork again but caught him up in the ladle.

Crunch, crunch, crunch, crunch

Gob Ghab was alone in the pot. Oh, bits and pieces of the others remained. Nemi's chest, Bosky Boq's ridiculously muscular thighs and buttocks, the King's own rather spindly knees and calves. The pot was two-thirds empty before Mr. Yoop had eaten his fill.

"I think I'll cook you down to stock. The others have all filled me up."

"Hey," Gob called. "That didn't rhyme!"

The giant shrugged and spat one of Nemi Omsbi's teeth into his eye. The lid clattered down, and the Munchkin King boiled alone in the dark.

"Slow down!" The Glass Cat shouted. "Its just ahead here, beyond the bend."

The cat hated traveling in Ozma's wagon, especially when the Sawhorse was in a hurry. There were no limits to the wooden beast's speed, but the wagon could only go so fast and remain upright. Every time she was forced to travel in it she was sure she'd be dashed against the road as if shot from a cannon and shatter into a thousand pieces of glass. In fact she was certain the Sawhorse disliked her, and would like nothing better than to smear her pretty pink brains all over the road's yellow bricks.

Gold-shod hooves slowed from a blur to a rickety trot just as they came to the curve, and the Glass cat had managed to survive another insane journey. Both tin-men had secured a wrist to the wagon's rail with a silk rope but the only thing that frightened the Glass cat more than being thrown from the wagon was being thrown down on the road with it tied to her, and so she was secured to the seat-cushion only by her sharp glass claws. She was happy to get off.

"This way," she started off into the woods almost before the Tin Soldier had cut the rope holding him and the Woodsman to the wagon.

"Wait for us," the Woodsman said.

"Ozma said to hurry," the cat replied.

"Yes, we know." This from the soldier. "We're coming."

The two tin men clacked off into the woods right at her heels.

They made good time under the trees, what with the two tin men's tireless sword and axe making quick work of the brush. With all the waking and clattering of metal limbs, the Glass cat didn't see how Mr. Yoop could miss their coming, but when they found the enormous hickory tree with the huge iron pot cooking under it, the giant was no where around.

"He must have gone off," said the soldier, "to hunt more victims."

"Those poor people," the woodsman cried.

"Now, don't start." The Glass cat admonished as she climbed on top of the giant's table. "Go see who's left in the pot."

It took both tin-men to lift off the lid. King Gob Ghab's head sat miserably on top of his dented crown amid a sea of boiling gravy and body parts.

"Who is it?" the head inquired.

"Don't worry," the Tin woodsman said. "Ozma sent us."

"Yes," the Glass cat added from the table. "We're from the government, and we're here to help you."

The Tin Soldier looked over the rim of the pot.

"Where's Mr. Yoop?"

"Not in here," King Ghab replied.

"We'll have to wait until he returns," the Tin Woodsman said. "Let's hide."

"What about me?" Gob asked. "Get me out first, don't leave me!"

"You're already pretty well cooked," observed the soldier. "We don't want to alert the giant by disturbing anything."

"At least fish out my head," pleaded the King. "So it isn't devoured like poor Nemi Omsbi's and that wrestler fellow's"

'No time," the Glass cat declared. "I think I hear the giant now."

The Tin Woodsman stepped behind the hickory tree while the Tin Soldier eased back into a holly bush across the camp from it. The Glass Cat used her strong, sharp claws to scamper up the tree and out onto a branch high overhead. For all the noise the tin men made walking when they stood still they were very quiet indeed, which was to the good as not a minute later Mr. Yoop came out of the forest with a familiar wizened figure wrapped in his grip.

Unc Nunkie, beloved of Ojo the Lucky and a favorite at Ozma's court, had been quietly tending his farm on the other side of Munchkin City when the giant had snatched him up. He still had his old hoe in his hands, its handle tangled in his long grey beard inside the giant's hand. Seeing this the Tin Woodsman sprang forward, his axe a blur in his right hand, and shouted,

"Unhand that farmer, you wicked, gluttonous giant!"

Mr. Yoop shifted Unc Nunkie to his left hand and said,

"*You*, I remember from my cage! You'll be the next to feel my rage!"

He reached for the Woodsman, who promptly brought his axe around and severed the giant's little finger. Mr. Yoop snatched his hand back, launched a kick that caught the Woodsman's arm, sending both it and his axe off into the trees. Poor Nick Chopper sat down in surprise, staring at where his arm should be.

Mr. Yoop wasn't given time to gloat. The Tin Soldier stepped out of the bushes behind him and ran his saber as high as he could reach into the giant's backside. He was just short of reaching the giant's buttocks and instead sliced through his trousers to impale a more delicate area.

"*Ahroo!*" Bellowed the giant, who dropped Unc Nunkie and bent to clasp both hands on his jewels. This brought his head directly beneath the Glass cat, which landed on his face just as the tears began to fill his eyes.

"*Aarrgh!*" The giant lashed out with heels and hands, knocking the Tin Soldier back into the holly bush while tearing The Glass Cat, along with most of his eye lid, off his face. Lucky for he cat, glass can be quite slippery when covered in blood and she managed to wiggle out of his wounded hand before the giant dashed her into the tree. She landed lightly and quickly dashed from the clearing.

The Tin Woodsman made good use of their distraction, removing his tin hat and picking up the object he'd carried there. A golden egg, entrusted to him by Ozma and the little wizard. Somewhat awkwardly he tossed it at the giant, and it shattered on his belt buckle.

"*No!*" shouted the giant, all thought of rhyme dashed from his head as he rapidly began to shrink. He managed to straighten up some and began to run when Unc Nunkie thrust the hoe between his feet. He tripped and sprawled out on the ground. Writhing in pain and terror, he began to change shape as well as size. His limbs retracted and he sprouted scales. In less time than it takes to tell he was a snake, not much longer than a tall man's leg.

He tried to slither into the forest, but the Glass cat had known what Ozma had prepared for him and expected this. She'd come 'round the camp as she ran, and bounded into the clearing to pounced the snake, pinning it to the ground with her hard, sharp claws. The snake coiled around her and tried to bite, but her glass body was much less vulnerable to snakes than giants, and she kept him pinned until the Tin Soldier came over to take him in hand.

The Yoop-snake bit the soldier as well, with little more effect than to mar the fine polishing of his arm he bit him over and over until, in despair of his fine finish, the soldier shoved the snake's own tail into its mouth. This didn't deter the former giant one bit. He chomped down on his own tail, worried at it a moment, and bit down again a little farther along. Within a minute he'd downed half his own body, which was no longer a mass of coils but now a single loop. The loop got smaller and smaller until it was balanced in the soldier's hand, and then it disappeared entirely.

The Tin Soldier stared at his empty palm. So did the Tin Woodsman. The Glass cat stared up at the back of his outstretched hand and, after a moment asked,

"What happened?"

"He swallowed himself whole," said the soldier.

"I don't think that was part of Ozma's plan," said the woodsman.

"Someone, please, let me out!" Gob Ghab cried faintly from the cauldron.

"You two empty that," the Glass Cat indicated the huge metal pot with an ear. "While I go find your missing arm."

The two tin men shouldered the cauldron over, knocking the lid off and spilling its contents all over the grass. Gob Ghab gasped with the sudden relief, the cool verge seemed like heaven after his time in the pot. At Nick Chopper's suggestion Unc Nunkie began sorting out the various pieces.

"Looks like we won't be needing the tinsmith," the old farmer said, "There's a whole person here, or parts enough for one anyways."

The Glass Cat emerged from the trees with the woodsman's arm, still clutching his axe, in her mouth. She dropped it at the woodsman's feet.

"That's good," she said. "Dorothy packed some flesh glue under the wagon's seat. She thought it might be useful."

"We still have to visit the tinsmith," The woodsman said. "I'll need him to fix my arm. I haven't seen him in years, you know."

"Let's fix King Ghab up first," the cat said.

King Gob Ghab was worried. Being king of the Munchkins wasn't a very hard job, *usually*, but it did require being able to command a certain respect from one's subjects. Gob Ghab suspected he no longer had that respect. In fact he suspected he was a laughingstock. Nick Chopper and the others from Emerald City had done what they could for him. He supposed it was better than ending up in a giant's belly. It was just that there'd been so little left to choose from when he was rescued.

His head now sat on Nemi Omsbi's full and finely formed chest. None of his own arms had survived, only one from each of the others. The wrestlers left arm and the goose-girl's right. He had them both, but unfortunately the wrestler had been right-handed, the girl left-handed. Now both his arms were so uncoordinated he could barely dress. He couldn't manage tableware beyond a spoon, and so the Queen alone dined with important Munchkin citizens. She didn't seem displeased with that.

The queen was less happy with the rest of him. The only other original Gob-parts had been his lower legs and feet. His upper legs, belly and thighs all came from Bosky Boq. Along with his package. That was the one part the queen did like, which vexed Gob all the more because he'd thought she liked his original equipment so, and she didn't seem to miss it at all.

He should resign, but he knew he wouldn't. He was the fourth Munchkin King since the death of the Witch of the East. All the others had resigned when they grew tired of the job. Gob Ghab would not resign though. He thought it better to be a laughingstock and king than just a laughingstock. It was either this or join the collection of freaks at Ozma's palace. If he was to be useless, hanging around all the time being laughed at, he'd rather do it in his own palace.

THE END.

EMERALD CITY CONFIDENTIAL

by Jack Bates

Keep me out of the Emerald City.

A light green rain splashed on the windshield of my mono-dragon chariot. The gyros and the wheels squeaked from the splash. It was a warm rain, the kind where a little bubble of sunshine bobbed in each drop. Most folks found the rain refreshing but I felt crushed under all of that heavy green optimism. Ahead of me I could see the great green castle shimmering in the rain and I felt the weight of all that optimism pushing down on me even more.

Queen Ozma had summoned me out of my semi-forced retirement back to the castle to meet with her and the Security Council. She knew what it would do to me to be back there, but *I* knew she couldn't be seen slumming around my digs where I now lived in Winkie Country. I also knew why she wouldn't travel to see me.

For about a week the *Emerald City Gem* had been running stories about the mysterious and violent deaths of Half-of-Talls from Munchkinland. Someone or *something* was eating them up. Literally. Reports had been coming from outlying farm areas where first it had been small livestock. Later there was the badly mauled body of a reclusive Half-as-Taller. Then villagers reported horrifying screeches in the night, and wild, lonely screams. Then the severity of the attacks intensified. Half-as-Tallers were fleeing from Munchkinland City in droves and many were finding the road dangerous.

What started with the supposed attack of a feral animal wanting a quick meal became a life and death struggle for the fleeing Half-as-Tallers. One victim was said to have been found stretched out to three times his size, frozen in a death crawl, his entrails unraveled like a ball of twine covered in slime between his two halves.

Whatever was happening was enough to make the city elders want me back.

"You're looking good, Captain Jo Guard." Queen Ozma's words echoed around me, bouncing off the cool green walls of solid emerald. Ozma was looking good as well. Her reddish hair was longer and done up, a few pin curls dangling on either side of her smooth ivory face. Her hips and breasts were rounder and fuller, but not overly so. A dusting a sparkling green glitter covered the rolls of her cleavage and her green silk gown hugged tight along her hips. She had grown up from a princess to a queen before all of Oz.

She held out her hand for me and I took it, kneeling before her. I kissed the back of it. Ozma turned her hand over and cupped my cheek, lifting my eyes to see her smiling down at me. I stared into those dark brown eyes knowing nothing had changed in the year we had been apart.

"I'm so glad you're back," she said. Even in a whisper her words echoed around us. I brought her hand back to my lips, ran my tongue along the insides of her fingers, rolled it around down between the soft of two of them. I heard her tiny gasp followed by a slight moan.

I didn't want her to know I was glad to be back in the Emerald City, if just to see her. At one time I was her Senior Captain Jo Guard of Security. At least until our bodies got the better of us. We fucked nearly every night until the Security Council caught on and I was demoted and reassigned. Eventually they forced me out and I became constable in Winkie Country.

That's why calling me back meant that not only was Ozma scared, so was the Emerald City Security Council.

Behind me a great door closed. It was followed by the shuffling of slipper covered feet along the polished checkerboard floor. Ozma pulled her hand away. I stood up and turned to find the Security Council gathering around us.

"Captain Jo Guard," Security Prime said to me. He voice was whispers caught on cobwebs.

"Not anymore, Security Prime." I said.

He smiled a wrinkled smile at me and raised eyebrows that hung like sandbags

"Nevertheless, the Security Council is pleased you have returned." The six Security Trustees whispered a murmur of approval. It echoed like the hiss of snakes.

"Your welcoming makes me think the Security Council is doubly worried as Queen Ozma." I said. We hadn't parted on the best of terms.

Security Prime pushed his agenda along.

"You have no doubt seen the papers. Farm livestock decimated. Half-as-Tallers attacked and murdered. Munchkinland is in total disarray."

"I've heard."

"At first we thought there was a logical explanation. Perhaps a group of rogue Scoodlers looking to increase its food supply."

"Scoodlers? I thought all their heads were at the bottom of a pit."

"Which is why, as the attacks increased, we began to ponder other theories."

"Such as?"

Security Prime turned from me and looked at the six trustees. Their heads nodded. They encouraged Prime to tell me.

"Two nights ago Mayor Gerrld of Munchkinland City disappeared."

"Disappeared? How do you mean?"

"One minute he was there, the next he wasn't."

"No, Prime. I mean—was he using a *Teleporting Cloak of Invisibility?*" Prime narrowed his eyes.

"It would be difficult to determine," he said. "As it would be invisible."

I let it go. It wasn't the time to get into a pissing match with the old man.

"Any ransom?" I asked.

"Just this." He handed me a note. *We have the Mayor* was all it said.

"Any reason to think the Half-as-Tallers are the target of something the mayor knew about and he split on his own?"

"That's what we were hoping you could find out, Jo Guard." Ozma said. The concern in her voice softened me. I gave her a reassuring smile and she returned the gratitude. The energy between us seemed to echo as loudly as her words.

Prime cleared his throat. I turned around to the suspicious glares of the Security Council. I tried flashing the same charming smile I shared with Ozma but they weren't having anything to do with it. After an awkward moment, Prime reached into one of the deep pockets of his robe and withdrew a small mahogany box.

"Do you recognize this, Captain Jo Guard?" Prime asked.

I took the box and held it.

"Sure do. *The Great Mahogany Box.* It holds the *Lead Button.*" I shook it. My face fell at the silence. I looked at Ozma. Fear filled those dark brown eyes of hers. "The Imp?" I asked.

"Gone." Security Prime said.

"He apologized? After all this time?"

Ozma shook her head, the pin curls bobbing around her narrow face. Her beautiful, narrow face.

"No." she said. "I didn't release him."

Escape was supposed to be impossible for the Imp. The Impertinent Imp had been Oz's public enemy number one. When it was finally caught, it was changed into a lead button and was to remain that way until it apologized for its crimes. When it did, the button would change to aluminum and Ozma or Glinda the Good Witch would be able to rejuvenate the creature.

"Then how did the Imp—?"

"I don't know." Ozma said. Her voice was heavy with panic. "I picked up the box one day and noticed it felt different. I thought perhaps the lead had changed to aluminum but when I opened it, the button was gone." Ozma threw herself against me. "Oh, Jo Guard. You have to help me. I'm so afraid of the Imp. You know it wants to eat my heart." Her face fell against my chest. I felt her sobs and beneath those I felt her breasts pressing against my chest through the heavy wool of my old uniform. Her soft auburn hair lay beneath my nose and I drew the musk of roses mixed gently with spring water and orange melons. I pulled her closer, a familiar strength and firmness growing between my legs. Ozma put her arms around my neck, pressed her hips against me. Our eyes met. "Please." she begged.

"Of course," I said softly. "Of course."

How could I refuse? She had saved my life when the Security Council wanted to feed me to the Scoodlers' heads in the deep, deep pit. Those hideous, two-faced heads: One side black face with white hair, the other yellow face with purple hair but always those razor sharp teeth chomping.

"Then perhaps you should be on your way, Captain Jo Guard."

Ozma and I turned our faces. Prime and the council stared objectionably at us. It didn't matter. When I finished this assignment; when I saved her from the Imp; when I returned with the answers Ozma would take me back and this time it would be for good. Regardless of what Prime and the council decided.

Before I left, I asked the trustees for access to the Storage Room where I procured a few necessary artifacts, one of which was the *Magic Carpet*. Prime accompanied me. He stayed quiet for most of my rummaging. When it looked like I had everything I wanted, he spoke to me.

"Jo Guard." he said. His lips were closed and tight making his smile all the more disturbing. "While I don't approve of the behavior you and our queen exhibited, I am glad you are going on this mission for us."

"For her." I said. His smiled became a straight line.

"Something dark is happening in Oz." he said. "Darker than has ever settled here before. I don't quite know for certain what it is. Be careful, Jo Guard. Trust no one."

"Not even you, Prime?"

I knew there was only one place the Imp would want to go upon being released. Someplace dark and vile. Someplace that would make the Green Skins squeamish. Someplace deep in the heart of the Oogaboo.

The Oogaboo.

The outhouse hole of Oz. All sorts of sewage flows through its streets. Nobody wants to live there. There's an old maxim about the place: All roads lead out of the Oogaboo. Even if I wanted to take my mono-dragon chariot, it would be days on the road and I was pretty sure the sands of the desert would gum up the gyros and sprockets of the mechanical dragon. A Teleportation Cloak of Invisibility would have gotten me there in a blink but no one could find it in the Storage Room.

Most people like to sit upright, legs criss-crossed, while riding on the Magic Carpet. Me? I have to lie on my belly clutching the two front corners of the rug. Even then I still feel vulnerable. The sag in the thick weave gives me the impression I'll slide right off the back end. I know that won't happen because the carpet *won't let it happen* but that doesn't stop me from thinking it could. I roll the corner tips around my wrists and hold tight.

Besides, falling off the carpet was the least of my worries. Flying monkeys, walls of solid air as thick and hard as emerald walls, or even rounds of grapeshot fired from the musket-trees provided more danger than riding on a flying carpet. Even if the carpet flew at ten thousand feet and faster than a zephyr. More disconcerting than any of it, though, were ivory bone underbellies hanging over the Oogaboo.

I let the carpet know it was time to descend and where I wanted to go. I was looking for a little Outlander-run dive called *Dorothy's*; a B-girl joint that opened shortly after Miss Gale's untimely departure from the wonderful world of Oz. Seems a lot of the Green-Skins had a thing for the Kansas virgin, and not because she murdered two of their own. They found her tenacity and spunkiness alluring. Now a Green-Skin could rent his or her very own by the hour or for the night. Word on the street was that a group was thinking up ways to lure Kansas girls into Oz.

I hovered over a narrow street thinking it was an alley. Then I remembered all of Oogaboo was nothing more than a series of alleys. Dark, narrow alleys that stank of spoiled eggs and mechanical oils. A flying monkey perched on the roof of a seedy looking office building. It puffed on a smoker, keeping its eyes on me. A flying monkey this deep in the Oogaboo meant only one thing: It was a rogue off on its own.

A couple of Green-Skin tramps looked up at me. One of them held open her top, flashing me her double nipple titties. The other had her red and white gingham dress over the head of a Half-as-Taller enjoying the pleasures between her green thighs. I could see his stubby little fingers poking out from under the hem, clutching at her ass.

"Hey, look up there, Detrita." The titty flasher said. "We got us a law-like official keeping an eye on us."

Detrita took a drag off a smoldering brown roll of tree bark and poppies. She exhaled towards the Half-as-Taller giggling between her legs. Detrita's hips rocked.

"What you think he wants with us, Archetta?"

"Maybe he wants to have a little fun. He a long way way from home." Archetta said. They cackled. "Or maybe he wants a little cut of our action."

"He ain't getting no cut of my pie." Detrita took another drag on her smoker. Her eyes slid closed and then she exhaled at me. "And I don't mean the pie my little man down there is gobbling up." They cackled again.

The hidden Half-as-Tall slapped Detrita's ass and she yelped.

"Feisty one." The cackling was wicked. Detrita's eyes narrow and she grimaced. She straightened her arms and placed her palms against the brick of *Dorothy's*.

I stood on the carpet as it lowered me to street level. Once down I bent over and picked it up by the corner. It was thinner and easier to fold down now, into a small square I tucked inside my jacket.

Detrita's head shook and she moaned. Archetta came over and took my arm. She winked at me and whispered in my ear.

"Must need a little relaxing after that long ride." Archetta said. She moved in closer and whispered in my ear. "'Sides, honey. I think Detrita needs a little alone time with her man, you dig?"

"I dig." I said.

"Take me in, Captain Flyboy. Buy me a drink?"

"Make you a deal," I said. I held open the door. "I give you something, you give me something."

"That's the plan."

"I'm giving you the wrong impression. What I need is information."

"You Flyboys are all business, aren't you?"

"Not at all." I said and slipped my hand under the black leather straps and belts covering her round green ass. I cupped the fleshy area between her legs, a little taken back by the coolness of it. I wiggled a finger up into her and pulled her closer to me. Her hands were up behind my neck and our lips fell against each other.

"We going in for a room or ain't we?"

"What's wrong with right here? Detrita is enjoying it."

"I ain't an exhibitionist like Detrita is. Come on."

"All right." We went inside *Dorothy's*.

It was pretty much how I imagined it would be. Dark. Smoky. Blue and white and ruby and green lights cut through the haze, pulsed to the disharmony of the pipe music. A Green-Skin in a Dorothy costume clutched a crystal pole and raised her self up on it, her legs extended and spread apart, revealing a tangle of black hair between them. She swung out over the heads of some Half-as-Tallers and a couple of sailors. As she passed by, a puff of green-gray juice sprayed out at the men. At first they grimaced, then laughed, then seemed to settle into some weird sexual funk.

"Can you do that?" I asked Archetta.

She laughed, nowhere near a cackle.

"Takes some practice. But we can certainly give it a try." Archetta slid her hand along the outside of my coat. Her fingers tried to undo the buttons. I took her wrist and pressed her hand against my erection.

"You want in somewhere," I said. "Get in here."

Archetta licked my lips and smiled at me, her dark eyes sliding almost closed.

"We ain't talked price yet."

"I think I've got something you can use," I said. I reached into my pocket and pulled out a small pink ball. I held my palm open. Archetta put her finger on it and rolled it along my skin. Little shocks poked at my palm as she did it.

"What is it?" She asked.

"It's called a *Pearl of Protection*. Protects you from danger. Loaded with ten charges. When the tenth one is used, the pearl crumbles into dust."

"What I gotta do for that?"

"Just tell me something."

"I'd rather blow you, Flyboy."

I laughed. "You might get to yet."

"Whatcha wanta know?"

"Did the Impertinent Imp come in here tonight?"

"Imp?" Archetta lifted the pearl between her long green finger and her narrow thumb. She rolled it between the two. "It tingles."

I took the pearl back.

"The *Imp*," I said again. Archetta looked at me, but clutched the pearl. "Short guy. Ugly, narrow eyes a kind of piss yellow. Razor sharp teeth. Big nose like a tulip bulb. Dirty fingers he can pop claws out of." Archetta gave me a blank look. "Oh. And he has wings on his back like a dragon fly's."

"Oh. *Him?* He's the guy outside with Detrita."

I stuck my fist into my jacket pocket and dropped the pearl inside it. I went back outside the club, stepping into a puddle that hadn't been there when we went in. Detrita's body was face-first against the black bricks of *Dorothy's*, the apparent source of the oily green-black blood covering my boots.

The Imp hadn't been feisty; it had been hungry, and it ate Detrita from the outside in.

The wails and cries of the Imp made my skin ripple with gooseflesh. A heavy wet thud struck the black bricks behind my head. Sliding down along them was the green mush that had once been Detrita's heart. I looked up and saw it, silhouetted against the near full moon. The Imp hovered, its wings buzzing, while it chewed on some other internals taken from Detrita.

I shook out the carpet and jumped on it, taking off after the Imp. The little demon thought it was a joke. Its laugh a death rattle and it trailed over the night sky above the Oogaboo. The Imp flew higher, its double set of insect wings humming and buzzing and helping it to dart in sharp angles.

"*Imp!*" I yelled. "*Hold up!*" I knelt on the carpet, clutched my two favorite corners and held the front half of the rug up in front of me. This maneuver severely shrank the area beneath me. I clutched it tighter and rose higher. The carpet knew my every thought; it knew I wanted to overtake the Imp so it pushed itself further and faster, to the point where I could hear the unsettling rip of the fabric. "*Imp! I command you to halt!*"

"Not on that dead tramp's life." The Imp darted past me on his way back down, winked a narrow yellow eye at me. I could see the gristle between its fangs. "You want to turn me into that lead button again!"

The carpet dipped to follow.

"*No!*" I yelled. "I just want to ask you some questions." The carpet tipped sideways, wrapped around my ankles to keep me on. It followed the Imp through a series of the narrow alleys. I ducked my head before it got bashed and scraped along a wall.

"Rotten apples!" The Imp cursed. "I don't want to go back!" The Imp's voice trailed as it once again shot forward.

The carpet kept with it.

"*You won't!*"

"Not even for killing the Green Skin tramp?"

"*That's up to the Oogaboo,*" I yelled into the wind. "*It's their jurisdiction.*"

"Yippie!" The Imp yelled, spiraling into a barrel roll. The Imp knew as well as I did that the only thing that brought out one of the two Oogaboo police guards was money or booze. "It feels so good to be free!"

"I'll bet." I pulled up next to the Imp. It sat cross-legged in the night sky, its wings humming to keep it in place. I looked below. The moon felt too large from this spot, the people too small below me. I kept my eyes on the Imp.

"You have no idea," the Imp said. It smiled at the moon, then wiped the rest of Detrita's blood off its chin with the back of its stubby hand.

"So you apologized to Queen Ozma?"

The Imp looked at me with mirthful eyes.

"Not."

"Then how did you get released?"

"How do you think, Captain Jo Guard?" He leaned in towards me. "Only two people have the power to release me. One of them sucked your shaft. Oh, don't act so surprised. All of Oz knows you were poking her with your mighty emerald dick."

"All right, all right," The Imp could be so crass. "So who is the other one besides the Queen?"

"*Good* is a relative term," the Imp said.

I hated when the Imp spoke in riddles *almost* as much as when it was crass.

"Imp," I pleaded. "I don't have time for this. Someone or something is killing the Half-as-Talls and it's driving them out of Munchkinland."

"Oh that. I know about that. I'm one of them."

"You're eating Half-as-Talls?"

"They're not so bad with a little green salt." The Imp let loose with its death-rattling giggle.

"You said you're one of them? There's more?"

"Plenty more." The Imp opened its narrow eyes and smiled revealing its cracked and crooked teeth, its fangs, and its bifurcated tongue.

"Why eat the Half-as-Talls? There's food all over Oz."

"You want answers, Jo Guard?"

"I wouldn't be hovering over the fucking Oogaboo if I didn't."

"Then follow the Yellow Brick Road." The Imp straightened itself out, getting ready to fly away home. It opened its mouth to say something when we both noticed the wisps of smoke floating out. An orange circle began to glow in the center of its grey chest. The Imp clawed at the spot with his stubby fingers. It began to tremble.

"*No! No!* You just let me out! I didn't tell him anything! I didn't speak about you!"

The carpet pulled me backwards, wrapping itself around me in an attempt to keep me away from the impending explosion. I could still feel the shock and heat as the Imp disintegrated behind me. The concussion sent the carpet twirling. Unable to unfurl, it plummeted with me wrapped inside it. I kicked and pushed at the fabric, squirming to open it up before smashing to a pulp below. I had no idea of how close I was to that very event.

Smoldering fabric filled my nose. In addition to smashing on the streets of the Oogaboo I now had to worry about burning away like the black tree bark inside Detrita's smoker. I started rocking side to side until I felt the carpet unroll. That got it open and I crawled around slapping at the flames. The rug spun in flat circles, dropping faster and faster.

I tried to keep the panic out of my thoughts so the carpet could read my peace and straighten itself. The flames were engulfing it. I was dropping down along side of buildings and watching the pavement rising at me when I felt a heavy tug on my back. I was lifted into the air as the carpet flamed out, becoming little tendrils of red-hot glowing threads flittering to the ground.

It took me a few seconds to realize I was dangling beneath the hairy toes of the flying monkey I'd seen earlier. My nose actually cued me in before I looked up; flying monkeys weren't known for their hygiene. When I did, I found the monkey reaching down with a paw to hoist me up into a more secure position. I crawled around and got on its back, folding my arms around his neck. I had no idea where the monkey was taking me and it wouldn't have done any good to ask it.

Monkeys don't talk. They fly.

He carried me far away from the Oogaboo. I was thankful for that but would be even more thankful when my feet touched solid ground. He banked in a long, effortless glide. Ahead of us was a dark valley. Atop a precipice I could pick out two flickering pinpoints of firelight. The monkey took us in that direction and soon was landing along the cliff. At the end of the ride I clapped him on the back, showing him my approval and my respect for his gallantry. The monkey turned and hooted his appreciation. He turned and ran at the edge of the cliff and floated off into the night.

For a while I thought I was alone. It didn't take me long to realize I wasn't. Even though I couldn't see anyone, I had the impression there was somebody else there.

The high-pitched nasal drone of the invisible voice told me it was Mayor Gerrld of Munchkinland City.

"She sent you, I see."

I turned in the direction of the voice and looked at a shadow under the left hand torch. Slowly the Half-as-Tall mayor's head appeared. It was followed by his hand.

"So *that's* where the Teleporting Cloak of Invisibility went," I said. "Hiding out, Mr. Mayor?"

"For the moment. It won't be long before she finds me."

"Who?" I asked.

"Your whore of a queen." He said. There was a tone of anger I didn't know Half-as-Talls possessed.

"She sent me to find you."

"Of course she did. She wants you to bring me back so she can kill me."

"Why would she do that? She thought the Imp was going to get you."

The Mayor looked around at the shadows. He pulled his hands back into the cloak.

"The Imp? What would the Imp want with me?"

"He said he was part of an army sent to kill Half-as-excuse me. Munchkins,"

The Mayor shook his head. "Glinda let the Imp loose to go after Ozma, not me."

"Yeah, well, that isn't going to happen now."

"Why is that, Jo Guard?"

"The Imp is dead. Vaporized. Besides, Glinda knew the Imp could only kill Ozma once the charm she placed around her is broken. Why would she release the Imp if she's protecting her? Doesn't make sense."

"It does if you understand the royal lineage."

"Maybe you should map it out for me."

The Mayor pulled the hood up over his head and disappeared. The wind made the torches dance. I looked around at shadows. When the Mayor spoke again, he was behind me.

"Sorry. I had to jump away and jump back. Glinda has spies. She knows where I am."

"How?"

"Crystal ball. She's been watching you. Certain. She probably vaporized the Imp."

I looked around. Glinda could have seen the Imp with me. And now the Mayor? And if so, why hadn't she zapped him like she had the Imp? I asked the Mayor.

"Pearl of Protection. Down to six charges. It's pissing her off."

"Why does she want you dead?"

"Emerald City is choking itself to death. Ozma needs to expand so she's set her eyes on Munchkinland. Come on, everyone knows we Munchkinlanders don't put up much of a fight. Our biggest militia is the Lollypop Guild. They might be scrappy but that's about it."

"The Imp told me there were others—attacking the Munchkinlanders."

"There are. A whole guerilla unit made up Frogmen, Scoodlers, and that goat-fucking cowardly lion."

It wasn't making sense. Glinda released the Imp to go after Ozma. The Mayor's story made it sound like Ozma was up to the same dirty plans as Glinda, but for what purpose?

"How does Glinda fit into this?"

"Glinda was next in line to be Queen of Oz but the powers that be put Ozma in charge. Civil war is brewing in Oz, Jo Guard. Glinda is preparing to battle her sister for ultimate control."

"Ozma and Glinda are sisters?"

From somewhere in the valley came a loud screech. The Mayor looked to the skies.

"I can't make it any clearer than that, Jo Guard. I have to go."

"Wait. How do I get out of here?"

"There's a circus balloon inside the cave. You'll have to wait until morning to inflate it. It's a small balloon but it'll get you back to Oz. I have to go!" And like that, the Mayor disappeared.

The screeching in the valley sounded closer. I rolled the torches into the dirt, snuffing them. The night wrapped its cold arms around me. I slipped into the cave, moved back as far as I could. It was still cool inside but I didn't risk making a fire for warmth. I pulled the canvas of the circus balloon over top of me.

I lay there thinking about Ozma and all the nights we had stolen away to places like this to enjoy each other's flesh. I remembered her tear drop breasts and how soft they felt in my hands, how her back would arch as she straddled me and I let my tongue roll over her rock hard nipples. She would grind her hips with my girth deep inside her before falling down on top of me, her breasts against my chest. I always loved the feeling of being inside her and her breasts squashed between us.

It had been so good for us until Security Prime found out what was going on. If he hadn't wielded so much power I'd still be with Ozma and she might have been there with me. Glinda could have all of Oz for all I cared. Ozma would have been much happier without it. I was.

Then it hit me with such clarity it made me smile.

The Mayor had said '*the powers that be*' and even the Imp would have known who he meant. He meant Security Prime and the six trustees. For a group that was supposed to protect the Queen, it was doing a better job of *controlling* her. It made her appear weak and insecure. What better way to show her subjects she was a leader than to invade a neighboring country?

But the Mayor had said there was a civil war coming between two sisters, one of which was one of the greatest guardians in all of Oz: Glinda the Good. She was beyond wanting to be queen. And she loved the Half-as-

Talls. They were like the children she never bore. It didn't ring true with me but I didn't have the Mayor there to ask him how he knew Glinda wanted the crown.

If I wanted to know, I was going to have to ask her.

"Glinda." I said into the night. I closed my eyes and called out to her with my thoughts. I did this for over an hour before I heard the tinkling of bells. In between my silent calls, my mind wandered to thoughts of flying monkeys in cahoots with teleporting mayors. I was on the verge of making a connection between the two when the golden glow announcing Glinda's arrival brightened behind my eyelids.

"Jo Guard." Her voice was flower petals falling around my ears.

I opened my eyes. I saw her shimmering in her white body glove, the yellow diamonds scattered over the fishnet weave twinkling like the night stars. Her long blonde hair hung down over her shoulders. Her smile invited me.

"Glinda." I said. I held out my hand and she floated over to it, took it in her own creamy hand. I helped her down under the balloon canvas. "I'm sorry. I wish had something more comfortable."

In a blink we were in a bed of pillows, warm beneath furs. She hummed sweetly.

"Is this better?" She asked. Her fingers stroked my naked chest. Her breasts hung loosely along my side.

"Always."

"It's been so long, Jo Guard."

"I know. I apologize."

"You don't need to apologize. I know all about what has happened."

"It's why I summoned you."

She kissed me. It caught me by surprise. Tiny vibrations awakened my lips and my lust for her.

"I had hoped you brought me here for reasons you use to bring me to you."

"Tonight I have another reason."

"What is it you want to know?" Her voice sang. It was a series of pleasing bells, not heavy, not light.

"Mayor Gerrld of Munchkinland says you released the Imp to kill Queen Ozma."

"It wasn't me who released the Imp." She kissed me again.

"Only you and Ozma have the power to do that." I said.

"Then it was her."

"She knows the Imp wants her dead."

Glinda laid her head on my shoulder. Her hand tickled my chest, her fingernail traced a line down below my belly.

"Doesn't mean she didn't do it. And, as long as my charm lasts—."

"So you haven't removed it?"

She looked up at me with her probing brown eyes. They danced in the natural glow of her skin.

"Of course not. Why would I?"

"The Mayor said you were getting ready to go to war with Ozma over the rights to the crown and that you both want to invade Munchkinland. He said you've sent carnivorous mercenaries in to slaughter the Half-as-Talls."

Lightning flashed all around the entrance to the cave. The rocks of the cave rumbled and reigned down around us. Glinda sat up next to me in bed, her hair billowing out behind her. Fire raged in her eyes. I had heard it wasn't good to piss her off, that someone so gentle had a tempest raging beneath her calm demeanor.

"I control the balance of this world. Without me all of Oz crumbles and falls away. If I wanted to control it, I already would have."

The tempest evaporated. I lay there, raised up on my elbows. Glinda smiled warmly at me.

"I get it." I said. "So who is causing all of this to happen?"

"You already know that, don't you?"

I nodded and lay back down.

"Security Prime. Maybe some or all of the Security Trustees. Could Prime or one of them make Ozma do something like release the Imp?"

"Who better than they to get Ozma out of the way?" Her voice carried off in a singsong way.

"It would make more sense than you." I kissed her cheek. She turned and kissed me. Her hands went up over my chest and she pressed me down into the pillow bed. My hands traced along her ass, held her hips as she pressed into me and kissed me. I wanted her but I knew I just couldn't have her any more.

"Glinda," I said between rapid breaths. Her touch moved me in the right directions. My body tingled to the point I was ready to pass on, leave it entirely. "Glinda, I can't."

She sat up. There was hurt in her eyes.

"Because of last time?"

"You almost killed me." True. Her orgasm had been so intense the bed ignited. I had burns on my groin for months.

"You're back with Ozma, aren't you?" She was looking for my weak spot.

"I'm not back with anyone. If you want to know, in the last year there hasn't been anyone serious."

"I waited for you to call out to me, to just think of me. When I heard you in my thoughts tonight I hoped that——."

"I'm sorry. I just can't."

The warm golden glow of the room faded. The furs dried up beneath me. For a moment, my bare ass sat on the cold slab floor of the cave. Then my clothes reappeared on me. I sat on top of the canvas circus balloon and watched the light recede outside of the cave and then she was gone and I was alone.

In the morning I was stiff. Sleeping in a damp, cold cave with nothing but a canvas circus balloon over top of you doesn't offer much in the ways of comfort or protection.

I woke to the whistling of the northeast winds. At least they would be pushing me in the direction I needed to go. It was a bit of a struggle, building the fire to heat the tanks to inflate the balloon. Two hours after waking up and fighting against hunger and nature, I got the balloon filled and cut off the restraining ropes with a hand axe in the bottom of the basket.

The winds were strong and I was prepared for the sudden jerk of the balloon and the swing of the basket beneath it. I smashed the blade of the axe into the lip of the basket and held the handle with both hands. I knocked around inside the basket as it swung like the balls of an elephant on a hot day. Eventually I got carried into a calmer stream and the basket stopped swinging. It didn't lessen the fact that I just simply hated my feet not being on solid ground. In the last rotation of the clock hands I'd gone over Oz on a burnt up carpet, a flying monkey's paws, and an uncontrollable circus balloon.

The winds slowed once I was out of the dark valley. I settled down on the floor of the cramped basket, my knees up around my chin. It gave me time to think about the errand Ozma had sent me on. This wasn't the first time there were rumors of war or usurpation in the Emerald City. Last time it came from the Oogaboo. A weak attempt by the weak queen of an even weaker army. She had tried amassing troops of some of the more eccentric citizens of the land. They marched on the Emerald City only to cower in the green shadows of the tall, glistening and glittering gem walls.

What made this war different was it sounded like it was coming from the inside out. According to Mayor Gerrld it was Ozma hoping to expand the borders, a move that seemed highly unlike her and more along the lines of the Security Council. Gerrld also believed Glinda the Good was trying to fight back by forming a band of mercenaries whose inherent carnivorous tendencies had apparently gotten the better of them and were feeding wantonly on the weak.

But Glinda said that was bunk, which meant Prime and the Security Council were spinning it to make the Munchkinlanders think they had lost their greatest weapon of protection: Glinda the Good. Which meant that somehow Security Prime or a member of the Security Council had tricked Ozma into releasing the Imp in the first place, and then told Ozma that Glinda was moving against her.

Nothing like being in the middle of a couple of sisters a guy used to screw.

My legs were cramping. I hoisted myself up on the lip of the basket and peered out. Ahead I saw the first twinkling of yellowish-green sparkles off of the topmost towers of Emerald Castle. I could also see the faint wisps of smoke rising up from around the base of the walls. The closer I got, the clearer it became that during the night something grand and horrible had happened in the Emerald City. Fires burned around the parameters of the castle. Bodies, both Tall and Half-as-Tall, lay strewn in poses only created by the last ditch efforts of warring. The aroma of warm and burnt flesh filled the skies and I hovered in the thick of it, retching at the stench.

There were shouts beneath me. A long emerald tip bolt held taught in a crossbow was leveled at me. I stood up to wave them off, holding up the breast of my captain's jacket. The guard, still frenzied from the all night battle, fired the bolt. If I hadn't ducked it would have split my skull in two. As it was, it passed through the balloon canvas like a twig through a paper wrapper.

The basket became an anchor to the flapping dead ball above me. The tower came closer and closer and for the third time in a day I found myself plummeting. This time I had no carpet to carry me away; no flying monkey to catch me. The guards readied their bows. Tiny flecks of green glinted off their arrowheads in the morning sunlight. I braced myself against the far side of the basket just as the first arrowheads popped through the weaving in front of me. Two broke all the way through. One embedded itself in my shoulder.

The basket hit one of the parapets. I spun around and tipped forward before slamming backwards. It rocked me. Dazed me. The bouncing and jarring intensified the pain from the arrow. I saw flashes both bright and dark and my head dropped. I remember spinning left and right until at last the world rocked me into blackness.

I woke up once. I was in a cool, dark green room. A bald man bent over me. He wore glasses. A series of telescoping magnifying lenses stretched out from his face to mine. He struggled with something I couldn't see but I could feel in my chest. Sweat beaded on his crowning scalp. He grunted and tugged and as he did so, I felt a rush of warm liquid spill over me. Green bolts of electricity shot around my eyes. Then blackness returned.

The next time I awoke I was in a room with an open window. White lace curtains billowed in a breeze. Ozma sat on the windowsill looking out at the streaming sunlight. I attempted to sit up in bed. A heavy white bandage was wrapped around my shoulder from where the arrow had pierced it. My scooching to sit up aggravated the wound and I winced. Ozma turned to look at me. Her smile trembled.

"Jo Guard," she said. Her voice was as soft as the morning breeze.

"Queen Ozma."

She came to me, threw her arms around my neck and hugged me. Her sobs fell heavy on my neck and her gentle heaving was enough to make me see the green bolts of pain behind my closed eyes.

"Ozma," I said. "Ozma. The pain."

She sat back quickly, her eyes full of concern. Her face softened and she placed the palm of her hand on my cheek.

"I'm so sorry." She said.

"Never mind me. What happened here last night?"

"A riot. The Munchkinlanders took to the streets. It was supposed to be a peaceful march of unity, of showing whatever or whoever has been preying on them they weren't going to take it."

"But they got jumped."

Ozma nodded.

"It was horrible. Flying monkeys by the score descended upon them. Lions attacked from the shadows. There was blood everywhere."

"Where was Glinda?"

Ozma's eyes narrowed for an instant. Just long enough to let me know what she suspected.

"Where ever is Glinda when the Half-as-Talls need her?" Ozma stood and strutted across the room to the window. When she turned to face me again, she was full of concern. "I sent the guards to do what they could but we were greatly outnumbered. Fear works an evil magic on a mob. They turned on us. Three armies fighting for individual survival."

"Guess that changes your plans."

Ozma cocked her head at me. She gave me a bewildered smile.

"My plans?"

"Mayor Gerrld believes you've been launching covert attacks against the Munchkinland City. He says you want to expand the Emerald City's borders."

"Into Munchkinland? Everyone knows that's Glinda's territory."

"Maybe that's why you want it. Is it true Glinda was actually next in line to be queen but Prime and his cronies put you on the throne instead?"

"The throne is legally mine." Ozma stood in front of the window. The breeze blew her gown against her body, pressing it against her like a cool white layer of skin.

"Unless it isn't and that would mean either you or someone close to you wants you to protect the secret."

"Why would I summon you to Emerald City? Why would I ask you to find Mayor Gerrld? And as for the Imp, I don't think it will be much of a problem now, do you?"

I had answers for all of those questions but the one I hit on was the last.

"How do you know the Imp is dead?"

Ozma's face froze. Her eyes searched for an answer. She let out a held breath, smiled, and said,

"I assumed you killed him. That's why you came back."

"I came back because there was nothing out there in the Oogaboo except a frightened Half-as-Tall who wanted to know why his people were caught in the middle of two spoiled sisters. You knew I'd find him and so you kept an eye me through your crystal ball. That's how you zapped the Imp. That's how you would have zapped the mayor but his paranoia kept him jumping. That and his pearl of protection."

A shadow in the corner shimmered on the heels of a soft voice. A familiar voice, but it wasn't Security Prime's.

"I told you he was smart, Ozma." Glinda slid out and stepped behind Ozma. "Maybe you know why we sent you away?" Glinda slipped her arm around Ozma. It hung lazily around the queen's waist.

I had no reason to be concerned about the politicking of Emerald City. I wasn't a part of it any longer. I remembered the riddle the Imp had posed to me the night before. *Good is a relative term* It had said. I knew the answer. There was nothing good in the Emerald City. If these two evil sisters were teaming up for something bad, where was the good in the land?

Mayor Gerrld.

As Captain Jo Guard, part of my responsibility was to maintain order in Munchkinland when Glinda couldn't be summoned. Or *wouldn't* be summoned. Mayor Gerrld and I had our share of ordeals to handle while I was in charge. We were tight. That was why he was surprised when I showed up. '*She sent you*' he had said. So there it was.

It was Ozma and Glinda's idea to come up with the kidnapping ploy to have me find Mayor Gerrld, giving them the opportunity to direct a heat ray or some other death spell through a crystal ball and zap him like the Imp. Why they couldn't just locate him through their magic eluded me, unless the cloak also acted as a shield. They released the Imp, telling me it was after the Mayor, making me believe Ozma would be next on its list when it finished its job. The Imp was just a pawn. Those two sisters knew I would do whatever it took to find the Imp because those two sisters knew I still loved Ozma. With Gerrld out of the way, Munchkinland was ripe for the picking.

I told them my theory.

"And with the backing of Security Prime and the trustees, you were all set."

The women laughed. It reminded me of Archetta and Detrita.

"Prime is dead," Ozma said.

"Dead? When did that happen?"

"Right after you left," Glinda said. "I would have been to the cave sooner but I had some things to take care of." They laughed again. They laughed into each other's faces and then their gazed lingered in one another's eyes.

"The Security Council was getting wise to our plans," Ozma said. "We couldn't have that." She looked lovingly into Glinda's eyes. They kissed.

For Ozma, it was the kiss of death. I saw her hair smolder then the tips glowed like little lights at the ends of long fibers. I threw my heavy covers off the bed and swung my legs over the side. I stood up but the pain was still fresh. It rocketed through me. My legs buckled and I fell ass first onto the edge of the bed.

Ozma's body shook momentarily and then she was a pillar of ash, burned from the inside out. The breeze rolled into the room and the ash crumbled and blew in swirls. When it cleared, Glinda stood alone.

"Now you can be Queen of Oz," I said.

"And you can be my king."

I shook my head.

"There's nothing for me here now."

Glinda produced a ruby red horseshoe from a pocket of her robe. She pointed it at me.

"There's plenty here for you," she said.

I felt the dark attraction return to her. I saw her long blonde hair blowing off and around her shoulders, revealing a long ivory neck. Her dark brown eyes drew me in. I stood on shaky legs and stumbled around the edge of the bed to her. My arms went around her and my lips went against hers. Her narrow hands came up on my shoulders and pressed down on them, pushing me lower along her body. I took her breasts through her shimmering white gown, cupped her firm ass with my hands. I was on my knees before her as her dress slid upwards. A thin trace of hair the color of honey and the shape of a lightning bolt rose up above her warm spot. My tongue traced around her lower lips. Her fingernails scratched my head and tugged on my hair.

"Yes, my king. Yes," Glinda moaned. Her body tensed, trembled, and she let out the most horrific gasp I've ever heard.

Her hands fell away from my head and her body tumbled backwards. The ruby read *Love Magnet* horseshoe clanged on the marble floor. Something warm and sticky seeped around my feet.

Mayor Gerrld stood over Glinda's body. At least parts of him. His head and hands floated in the air, disjointed from the rest of his body. In one hand he held a long, moon-curved dagger. He shrugged and as the cloak fell from him and became visible, so did the rest of him. It took me a moment to realize he was giddy. Before I knew it, he was kneeling on her chest and working the dagger's outer edge across Glinda's throat, pushing it deeper and deeper until it touched the stone floor beneath it.

"What—what are you doing?" I could barely choke out the words.

The Mayor could only look at me through his narrowed eyes. Frenzy gripped him as he grabbed the blood soiled locks of Glinda's hair.

I fell back against the end of the bed. My hands were covered in Glinda's blood. My fingers trembled before my eyes. I looked again at the Mayor. He carried Glinda's head to the window and held it out. Below there was a loud, if somewhat nasally cheer. Gerrld opened his fingers and let Glinda's head drop. He wiggled his fingers and smiled at the crowd below then turned around to face me.

"All right, so maybe the cunts weren't sisters. More like step-sisters. That's where all that legal bullshit about who was going to be queen and who wasn't came in," he said. He stepped out of the Teleportation Cloak of Invisibility. "But it doesn't matter now, does it?"

"No," I said. I felt oddly remorseful over both of their deaths even though I was more than likely going to die the same way Ozma had gone.

"Oh, what are you so broken up about? Ozma played you like harp. She knew all she had to do was tell you she was in trouble and you'd go running back to her."

He had me. I stared at him, wanting to say something in my defense, but my mouth dried up and seemed stuffed with something gritty. I hoped it wasn't Ozma's ashes. Finally I shook my head.

"Why call me?" I asked.

"Ozma knew sooner or later the Security Council would bring you into it. You're the only Jo Guard anyone of them would have trusted even if you were diddling their virginal queen. Eventually the murders were going to go into Winkie Country. It was better to bring you in on a bogus kidnapping to look for me and cover it up with all that hogshit about the mystery murders of Half-as-Tallers."

"So they were both in on it."

"They weren't going to stop at Munchkinland, you know. Munchkinland was a training ground for their troops.

"Training for what?"

"They were looking for the portal."

"Portal? You mean to Kansas?"

"To the Outer World. Kansas was the first stop. Oz was small pockets. They wanted total control of Dorothy's world."

I looked around at the emerald walls, the sparkling gold furniture, and the fine silk paintings.

"They had everything they needed here."

"And it wasn't enough. War gets in the veins like a drug. You just keep it going because you get such a rush from it."

A rush from war. I was Captain Jo Guard of Emerald City and I had had my share of war. It was no drug I wanted to become addicted to.

"Emerald City is going to need someone to lead it out of this dark chapter," Gerrld said. "Someone everyone in it and around it can look to for strength and leadership."

My head felt heavy. My stomach turned like It had in the balloon basket. Glinda's blood and Ozma's ash made a horrible stink.

Gerrld kept talking.

"I know the citizens on Munchkinland and probably all the citizens of Oz would feel safe and secure under your guidance, Captain Jo Guard. Or should I say, King Jo Guard?"

"No," I said. The pain in my shoulder, the roll of my stomach, and the fog in my head all began to mix and swirl together. I got to my feet and scooped at a blank spot on the floor; an area made blank, I hoped, by the cloak. My fingers brushed the cool silvery threads and I pulled it over my head.

My mind flashed on a golden field beneath a blue sky. In the distance I saw a red barn and a young woman in sapphire dungarees and a white cotton blouse looking up to the sky, shielding her eyes against the sun as she watched the air above her ripple. Even the trials and tribulations of her outside world were more inviting than where I was.

Keep me out of the Emerald City, I thought. And soon enough, I was.

THE END.

THE LAST BATTLE OF TREWIS
by David F. Mason

The caramel apple orchard dripped with sweetness. The ground was gummy with it, and the west wind blew its October smell through the hills and valleys that crowded close. An old disused lane ran beside the trees. Beside that, a small cottage smoked blue and purple from its twisting chimney.

"Not long, dear wife," Trewis said after peeking out the window. "Harvest time draws near."

Celizabeth smiled and stoked the fire, sending flakes of bright orange ash wafting through the air.

"I'm sure they'll keep growing without you standing there gawking," she said. "Now sit down with me, my love, your old legs look like they could take a rest." She patted the cushioned chair next to her.

He sighed and felt the creeping ache needle at his shins.

Striving had warped his bones like a plank of wood left too long to the sky; years bound themselves around him thick. And he wondered how much the War had really taken from him—long days marched through the heat of the High Desert had left his skin leather tight, and nights under the dripping Jungle palms clouded his lungs. In those days all there'd been was fighting, fighting—ever fighting—killing in the trenches of the West.

He'd been a hero once, tiny though he was. A fudgewood flintlock rifle hung above his mantle, the only evidence of soldiering he let himself keep.

The rest moldered with the bones of the dead—those he'd killed and those he'd tried to save. Then, like a sudden eclipse, his thoughts turned dark. Cannon thunder from years passed filled his ears. Winged Monkeys screamed, hanging gory on Quadling spears. Friends he'd known and loved since youth gasped with gushing wounds. And he was defenseless against the memories when they came.

Celizabeth saw his face seize, and inwardly winced. *How many yesterdays lay like tombstones on his soul?* she wondered. She caressed his calloused hand trying to thaw the ice that froze him so.

The white-headed Munchkin drew breath till his lungs ached, and exhaled in release, letting himself heal in her touch.

The visions of battle faded.

It had never been for the glory that he risked his life. It wasn't even for freedom. *This* was why he faced the bullets and the swords, this was why he killed and soaked his hands in other creatures' lives. It was for his darling bride and their quiet life.

He sighed again. This time with contentment.

"I think I'll fetch water for the cooking," Celizabeth said, bolting up from the chair. Fifty-years of habit fueled her quick steps. Trewis leaned back and closed his eyes, letting the breeze through the window caress him. Satisfied, he slept.

He didn't notice that the wind turned cold.

Or that the fire sputtered.

Or that outside the sun bleached itself grey.

If he had been a soldier still, young and fresh, he would have woken, he would have known the signs, but he didn't.

The stillest murmur of a whimper reached his ears.

"Dear Heart?" he called out, fumbling awake, "Are you well?" The fire had burned low. How long had he slept?

When no answer came he bounded out of his chair.

"Love? Love? Is something wrong?" His heart rushed, but he held himself steady. Nothing could happen. Not now. Not on a day as wonderful as this. He walked through the hall and turned a corner into the kitchen. The sizzle of a skillet filled his ears.

Someone stood at the stove cooking a flank of something on the fire. He was tall, twice the Munchkin's height, and lank as a skeleton coated in wax.

"Ah, Trewis. It's been an age. How fare ye?" The man turned to face him. His skin was green- emerald as a corpse when it's pulled from the ground. And like a corpse its eyes had melted to gobs of pus, oozing in thick, wicked tears down his cheeks. Decay had taken his nose, and instead two hollow chambers looked out where nostrils should have been.

"Ozymandias? It can't be..." The Munchkin's words were strangled, ground out through gritted teeth. "I killed you. I *buried* you." Trewis stepped forward, seizing a knife from the counter. The weight of the blade sparked slumbering instincts awake, and his knobby hands remembered war. "I'll kill you again if I have to," he spat.

"Will you?" The man laughed. "It takes more than a kitchen knife to kill the Witchling King. And if death was unkind to me, life was no more loving to you. Forty years, eh? You look about as dead as I do." He paused, a smile blacker than shadow creeping out his mouth. "You'll excuse me. Rotting in a mound of sand and soil leaves a man hungrier than you'd expect. I couldn't wait on lunch. No worries, there's plenty to go around." He stepped aside, pulling back the edge of his dirt caked coat.

Celizabeth sat slumped over against the wall, her hands bound together so tight blood wept out from beneath her fingernails. Her mouth bulged, gagged full with the corner of her apron. Her glassy eyes seemed to peer down in disbelief at the side of her dress- it was cut away... *she* was cut away... so deep ribs showed their marrow. Her half gone heart hung limp.

Munchkin blood runs in rainbow shades; Celizabeth's was indigo, and it filled the floor around her like the sea.

Ozymandias looked down at Celizabeth's body then back at Trewis.

"What colour do you bleed, Little Father?"

Trewis' senses betrayed him. Mint tears drowned his eyes blind. Grief buzzed his ears deaf. As his lungs twisted themselves empty. His fingertips burned, the heat growing and growing till he knew the only thing that could quench the fire was the green man's brains laying in chunks on the counter. He slashed out, and a sick, wet sound filled the room as the knife-tip bit through the skin and muscle across Ozymandias' chest, leaving an angled gash from shoulder to sternum.

Trewis staggered back. Out of the wound a giant eye peered out, its iris thick and yellow and contracting. The skin on either side formed lids. Coarse black hair grew out like weeds, making spindly lashes for itself. It blinked and the pupil narrowed, focusing and reflecting the horror in the Munchkin's face.

Ozymandias shrugged.

"Death doesn't leave a man with many options. I had to make some rather... unsavory agreements. You wouldn't believe how crowded the grave is, how many things want out and how few bodies there are to go around." Ozymandias, drew a finger over the wound, closing it like a zipper. "No more of that now," he murmured. "Now, Trewis, back to the task at hand. If you want revenge, you'll know where to find me."

And Trewis *did* know. Onyx City—where the streets were a maze and black obelisks rose like talons to the sky. The blocks of its buildings were made of midnight stone, heavier than even a giant could lift; stones like marble but whose veins took the shapes of the screaming faces of dying men. It was a jigsaw city of madness and shadow, whose history lie in impenetrable gloom. A place where Sorrows stalked.

He'd only been there once, pursuing this wicked man. He'd sworn never to return, but it seemed that history was in the habit of repeating.

"Yes," Ozymandias whispered. "Onyx City. My capital. My crown," he shook his head, "...at least it should have been. *Would* have been, but for a turn of luck. Do you know how long it took me to even *find* the Lost City? More importantly, can your diminutive wit grasp an entire metropolis built like a lock to seal a Door? Can you imagine what that Door might hide?" He pointed a putrefied finger at the Munchkin. "The man who rules that city rules all things."

"I stand against you," Trewis choked through tears.

Ozymandias scoffed.

"*You* stand against *me*? *Faugh*. You and those traitorous daughters of mine, Lacasta and Glinda, built a ramshackle imitation with that Emerald ghetto. Do you truly think that there is power in it to fight your fate? Fool. No light can pierce the blindness that I bring, and this time you've no army gathered behind you to delay the inevitable. Remember, revenge waits where the horizon swirls darkest. But I won't wait long."

With his last words the witchling dissolved into nothing and Trewis let the knife clatter to ground.

He rushed to his bride and squeezed her clay cool hands.

Hours later, when the sun melted into night, he stood over her open grave, soaked in indigo and sick with the smell of the caramel apple trees.

Trewis shoved open the shack's door. Dust danced thick in the musty air. The only light came from chinks in the rough wood boards that comprised the ceiling and walls. Stacks of boxes towered high over his head, packed he was sure, with junk and scraps not worth saving.

He hadn't traveled days to sort through someone else's trash. *Where could it be?*

He scanned old crate labels, then shoved them aside with half snarled words. It had to be here somewhere. Then he saw it, tucked in a corner half covered by an old oiled tarp. He yanked it off and stepped back.

"He's returned," was all the Munchkin needed to say for the mechanical man to rattle alive. Inside it, flywheels groaned for oil and old iron gears spun wobbly on rusty axles, spinning faster and faster until they finally righted themselves and found their grooving. Its dented skin hummed as the propane burner in its guts burst with streams of blue fire, engulfing the water tank that filled its stomach.

A shrill whistle sounded and the Ticktock's ruby eyes lit up.

"*Your information is false. Ozymandias' body was recovered after the rebel's victory and verified deceased.*"

Trewis scowled.

"I know what happened. I was there."

"*For further investigation the evidence must be reviewed. The Organic Leaders must be summoned,*" its voice emanated from a music box in its throat, clicking out the words in odd, singsong tones.

"There *are* no others. Polychrome, Lacasta, Glinda, the China Princess, all of them—all the old resistance leaders—they're gone. Kidnapped. Probably taken to Onyx."

Inside the Ticktock's stainless steel guts something hissed. A jet of steam sizzled out its mouth.

"*If your statement proves true, the chances of their survival are outside the realm of possibility. Their organic functions will terminate.*"

Trewis rubbed the hilt of his dagger with a calloused palm.

"He mentioned a Door…"

The machine's eyes blinked a deeper shade of red.

"*You interfaced with the enemy and survived?*"

Its voice turned suspicious. As a Tin Soldier, detecting subterfuge was well within its programming. During the rebellion it had to be. Ozymandias had agents planted so deep, the resistance leaders could never allow themselves the luxury of trust, even with each other.

"The witchling killed my wife," the Munchkin said, then paused, searching for a phrase the Ticktock would understand. "My marital counterpart… "

"*If the information is verified,*" it sang. "*The enemy has the advantage of time and location of battle. He has destabilized your emotional capacity for logical war. The enemy's chances of success are well within the realm of possibility.*" It lifted an outstretched arm. "*But the possibility of life function returning to a terminated Organic is not within the realm of possibility. Ozymandias is dead, his vital signs nil. What is the purpose of this deception?*" The last words were a clamour, like all the keys of a piano struck at once. Green sparks razzed from its extended fingertips, charring the wooden floor where they landed. It took a tottering step forward on pole legs. "*Termination eminent.*"

Trewis scampered back, suddenly desperate. A knife, his rifle, none of them would do anything more than leave a smudge on the Tin Soldier's grey metal hide.

It never occurred to him that the Ticktock might think *he* was the enemy.

"What is your program directive?" the Munchkin asked as emerald fire freckled his face with welts. "*ACKNOWLEDGE!*"

The music box's delicate tones mixed with the *zzzzaaaa* of thirty thousand volts sprouting from its palm.

"To kill the Tyrant Ozymandias at any cost."

"I want the same thing," the Munchkin cried.

The machine stopped. The electrical fire sputtered out.

"Trewis?" It asked, recognition flooding its voice. For the first time it seemed that the mechanical man did more than imitate life. "Trewis? But... you're old," it said with dismay. "How long have I been stored?"

"A long time. Too long," Trewis said, trying to steady his breath. "For all you did you should have been allowed to live, but you were the last of the Soldiers, and they thought it'd be better to keep you locked away in this shed, for another day. Another emergency. Maybe they were right."

There was an awkward silence kept imperfect by the rhythmic ticking of the Ticktock's clockwork heart. Its program was filtering; checking, rechecking all apparent facts and eliminating all unlikely outcomes. Finally the Tin Soldier asked,

"There is no possibility of aberrant data? No falsification of facts?"

Trewis shook his head. If only it *was* a lie—or some fever dream, and soon he'd wake to find Celizabeth bathing his brow with a cool cloth and a gentle kiss.

"He stood in my house. He killed her," he said simply, and kept the rest to himself. No one else needed to know about the blood clotted dishes he'd found in the sink, or the pieces of her skewered on the ends of forks. That was between him and Ozymandias.   Him and his gun and the pieces of lead he'd prayed would pierce the witchling's tenderest parts.

"The Tyrant's previous objective was to locate Onyx City. This he achieved the day of his termination. His new goal will be to unlock the Door."

"What do you know of the Door?"

"Only what my programmers theorized and obscure legends state. The city was constructed in order to harvest the vast energies emanating from the site. The original inhabitants were ignorant of the fact it would alter them, eventually resulting in their death. Some believe it is a nexus, where layers of reality collide. But again this is only a theory. Some view it as preposterous."

Something icy slid down the center of Trewis' stomach.

"Would it be possible for someone like Ozymandias to use it to his advantage?"

The mechanical man's rust tinged neck squeaked raw as it nodded its head.

"That is obviously Ozymandias' hypothesis. There is no quantifiable data to support his conclusions, nor any to discount them. Yet it *is* within the realm of possibility."

"How would he open the Door?"

"A structural flaw is inevitable within any design and I am programmed to detect such weaknesses. When you pursued him into the City and I followed with the reserve forces, my sensors mapped the defects. Several charges, if located correctly would bring down the monoliths, designed as tumblers in the lock. The City would shatter."

A sound echoed from outside- a grunt mixed with the flutter of feathers and the sweep of wind.

"Gumdrops," Trewis cursed. It was too familiar a noise to ever forget. He rushed to the door, swinging the rifle off his back and pouring gunpowder and shot into the barrel as he ran. The Ticktock's feet clanked close behind. By the time he stepped into the sunshine the weapon was packed and ready to fire.

Trewis skidded to a halt. Every tree limb sagged with the weight of apes, their shoulders twitching with raven wings.

These were no flying chimps. These were Silverbacks. Gorillas. Once Trewis had seen one catch a cannon ball midair and throw it back. Flying monkeys were dangerous. *These* were death from above. He glanced at his gun. What would he do now? Their skulls were too thick for bullets.

"*Imminent danger*," the Ticktock warned.

Trewis spat.

"Thanks."

Suddenly the Munchkin tumbled forward, pain searing through his side. An ape pounded the ground where Trewis had stood, throwing dust and torn grass in the air. In the trees gorillas drummed their chests and howled.

"*DESIST*," The Ticktock commanded and threw up its arm to fire. The Silverback was too quick. It gripped the mechanical man's hand in its own and the Tin Soldier's metal fingers crumpled back like paper.

Trewis righted himself, spun, and fired sending a cloud of blueberry haze funneling from the muzzle. So many years had passed since the sweet and sour tang of gunpowder had invaded his nostrils it made his nose twitch. The lead shot struck just above the ape's frenzied brow, but did little more than madden it.

"*Let him go you filthy monkey!*" the Munchkin screamed as he reloaded.

The Silverback roared and swept its wing across the Ticktock, sending it crashing through the shed wall. A second later the ape charged, its mouth so wide Trewis could count every tooth.

Trewis held steady. There was only one chance. He wrapped his finger around the bronze trigger... felt the earth beneath his feet throb with the gorilla's gallop, but he held steady and studied his enemy. Probed the savage face. *Where was the weakness? Where was the flaw?*

Then he knew.

In his mind the ape's eye grew so wide he knew he couldn't miss, and as he aimed he willed it wider than the sky.

With one squeeze of the trigger the gorilla's entire body quivered. Blood sprouted where its eye had been—a curling stream, growing like a funeral flower out of a grave. The beast was dead before it hit the ground, but inertia carried the body forward until it collapsed. With a final convulsion it laid its limp hand at Trewis' feet.

Howls erupted from the trees. The gorillas spread their wings and flocked to the air, black like storm clouds and grey like ghosts. Trewis saw them coming, his hands working in a flurry to reload- but it was too late.

They surrounded him. A fist jagged his head back. Knees and elbows pummeled his sides. He heard snaps as his ribs cracked and an arm caught around his neck cinching tight, tinting the edges of his vision dark. It felt like he was swinging from a gallows made of muscle. Suffocation crackled through his bones, lighting up his brain like wildfire. He snatched the dagger from his belt and stabbed out until blood coated his hands, but they never let go.

Apes plunged into the shed and pulled the Ticktock out, hoisting it over their heads like a war trophy. The mechanical man swung a hand down and crushed one of their skulls, but the others took hold of its arms and legs and pulled them apart.

With swift wing beats they lifted into the air, still carrying the mechanical man between them and hooting victory with extended lips.

The last thing Trewis saw was a bright blue sky as his eyes rolled up and blackness vomit from the sun.

"He was *supposed* to be dead."

There was a grunt, and the sound of an open palm slapping the ground.

"No, no. This is better. You'll be paid appropriately. The Jungle, all of it—I bequeath you, and when I come again into my kingdom I'll give you power to make war over the Lions. Now tie him up and set him with the rest. Then you may go."

A moment later savage hands wrapped the Munchkin's wrists and ankles in leather cord and dragged his body backward, propping him up against a monolith.

"Good. Now off with you." When the apes were gone he knelt and leaned in close to study the curving wrinkles in the Munchkin's face. All that was left of the witchling's eyes had melted away. Just two, cavernous red sockets remained. "Wake up Little Father, you've been dreaming."

Trewis stirred half awake. The taste of iron flooded his mouth and a pain jabbed so sharp in his chest it felt like his organs were torn. It was all he could do to bite back the groans welling from his lips. *You're a soldier*, he told himself in the half-conscious haze, *even if you're an old one. What'd the War teach you, but that pain is a guest? Pain means you're alive.* Suddenly a smell caught his nose that twisted his stomach inside out. His eyes fluttered open and the witchling king was there, still hovering close.

"Morning, Sunshine. You overslept, you lazy thing. But you did a wonderful job of finding the mechanical man. Celizabeth would be proud." His wild hair blended into the darkening sky and maggots wriggled at the corners of his mouth. "Strange how things go, eh? Turns out you *weren't* the hero after all. Just a lovely little pawn."

Trewis sat silent.

Sometimes wrath makes a reckless tongue. Sometimes it lies patiently in wait. *Don't give him what he wants*, he thought, *Don't banter with fiends and devils. Let him grow as sick of his own voice as I am of it.*

And while he waited he took stock of his surroundings. To his right the China Princess, five inches tall, stuck out crooked from a block of concrete. On the other side of her a blur of colors bounced back and forth in a prison of prisms. *Polychrome*, he realized. *The Living Rainbow. He is a power if he can capture lig*ht. Then he saw Glinda and Lacasta, their faces ravaged with burns, and just beyond them the Ticktock, its truncated frame still smoking.

"What use would he have of you?" Trewis wondered.

They were in the middle of a city square bordered on every side with broken columns and spired buildings whose windows stood empty and staring. The air was still and heavy like it was crowded with ghosts, and the ground was paved with black cobblestones.

It was Onyx—the place the wise, of old called the Graveyard of Worlds.

Ozymandias sighed.

"Wasn't it wonderful, the day I died? It was like a song with a sorrowed end. My small band of loyalists against an ocean of rebels. Your army flooded the streets. And do you remember? This is where the waves broke." He pointed down the way. "That was where your lucky bullet scuttled everything. Poetic really. *You* killing *me*. But enough of that. Today someone *else* is going to share my luck." A few wide strides took him out of sight, leaving a confused Trewis alone with the others.

Nearly half a minute passed before he decided it was safe to try and free himself. He tested his bonds, turning this way and that, trying to wriggle free, but the knots were noose tight and his hands were already going numb.

Suddenly the windless air broke with screams. Someone sobbed. Another begged. The voices were high and young. Girls.

Ozymandias returned, dragging one by the arm and the other by long black hair.

"Little Father, meet Easter and Westerly. Recent orphans whose parents died quite tragically."

"*LET THEM GO!*" the Munchkin bellowed, writhing against the ground, trying to break the bonds on his wrist. "*DON'T YOU TOUCH THEM!*"

"Ah, so the cat didn't quite catch all your tongue? Good." Ozymandias turned and knelt near the girls. "My daughters were very naughty," he said, stroking one of their faces tenderly and leaving a shiny trail of rot where his fingers touched. "They had me killed. And I can't have that, can I? No. I need new ones. Wouldn't you like that? Wouldn't *you* like to be my new daughters?"

A fresh torrent of tears erupted from them both.

He frowned. Speaking in a tone that would have been soothing except for the horror of his words, he said:

"Did I scare you when I stole you out of your beds and you saw your parents all in pieces on the ground? When you're my daughters you don't have to be scared ever again. You'll be the ones to scare. You'll be the monsters beneath the bed. Doesn't that sound nice?"

They wailed and collapsed into each other's arms.

Ozymandias stiffened.

"You're just children," he snapped, "it doesn't matter what you want. You would have learned that if you'd have had a chance to grow up." Then a dagger flashed. Crimson flowed from one girl's throat, splattering the ground. The knife flashed again, this time rose-red, and sank into the other's heart. The girls' eyes were a canvas painted with ever colder colors until they faded into dark. Death rattled from their throats before they even knew that they were dead.

"There's a serpent in every garden, my mother used to say." He slipped the knife, still dripping, back inside his coat. "She was a good woman. Her name was Emily." He laid a hand on each of their foreheads and mouthed a word.

"I'll kill you," Trewis snarled, panting from the strain of screaming, "I'll kill you and cut you up and burn them in a pit."

The green man grinned so wide the skin split at the corners of his mouth.

"We all have our dreams. Oh, and don't mourn them overmuch. Their little souls are floating off into the heaven of my mother. Think of it as more of an eviction than a murder. Now I just fill their vacant brains up with thoughts of my choosing...and *voila*," he threw out his hands. "Vastly more fascinating than the originals."

In sick rhythm their bodies convulsed. "Ha, you see? Aren't they little miracles?" Froth gurgled from their mouths and their muscles jerked and contracted until they rose to their knees. Soon they were standing, swaying, their faces more pale than glacier ice. *But how long, until they're as green as their slayer?* Trewis wondered, *How long until they're just rotting skin stretched over dirty bones?*

"Go, darling daughters, carve me out a kingdom. Prepare the world for my coming."

Suddenly they were gone, the only evidence they were ever there were rivers of blood creeping wider, flowing through rough channels made of paving stones. The witchling whistled an old bar tune, shrill and gusty, and ripped open the Ticktock's chest plate. He fiddled with the wires that hung bundled together inside.

"I knew this little beauty would do nicely as an incendiary device. Just switch a few wires and..."

The Tin Soldier's cast iron jaw wagged open.

"*WARNING... 5 minutes until detonation... WARNING...*"

"There now. A little self-destruction makes the world go round, don't you think? But don't worry, it's just enough of an explosion to give me a sneak peek through the Door, like a little key hole. It's too bad Munchkins and mortals are so flammable, eh Trewis?" But I'll tell you this: your darling wife begged for you so prettily that I'll let you live if you escape."

Ozymandias took two steps and with the third melted into the air.

"What do we do?" Trewis' frantic voice carried across the plaza.

"Give up," a tiny voice whispered. "Just give up. All these years, such a waste." The delicate voice was so soft it took a moment to find. The China Princess—old, careworn, chipped and cracked, turned her head away.

"You can't mean that," he stuttered. "You've seen what he is, what he can do. Think of your people. Think of the..."

"He's broken them. Every last one but for me" She covered her face like a mother in grief. "He ground them down to powder so fine they fell like sand through my fingers. A gust of wind and they were gone." Her voice grew furious. "What will striving do for me now? I am the *last*. The ruler of a crushed city. An empty empire. What's the use?"

"*The use?*" Trewis asked, the fire inside him roaring. "The *use*? I'll tell you. Revenge. Or Justice. Or mercy for all the thousands he'll kill when he comes into his kingdom. All the millions he'll enslave. Is that enough to at least keep *trying* to fight?"

The Princess bent double with sobs too violent for words. He gave up any hope that words he had the power to speak could pierce her fine etched ears.

"*My children!*" she wailed, "Oh my children! If only I could have stopped him before... before..."

She never finished the sentence. She raised her right hand high and brought her arm against the edge of the concrete- once, twice, three times. Suddenly it snapped and rolled away, jagged at the shoulder. "Take it," she gasped, "Avenge my people."

The words were coffin nails driven into his soul. His lips wrung out a strangled cry,

"How many lives fill your ledger, wicked king? How many debts to repay?" He worked the sharp piece of china between his fingers and snapped the cords, then leapt free and ran to the mechanical man.

"What do I do? How can I stop it?"

"*Self-destruct has been initiated. It is not within the realm of possibility to stop. Escape is necessary.*"

"But the others..."

"*Death is inevitable if you do not exit the blast zone immediately.*" Its voice was a rough melody. "Trewis, if you don't leave now, if you don't abandon us, you'll die and the Tyrant will win."

The Munchkin's legs were unsteady beneath him.

"I'm sorry," he whispered. He scrambled down the Ticktock's dismembered body and away through the plaza and through a winding street. A roar turned the world to chaos. A gust of singed wind made the ends of his jacket dance. He glimpsed behind him and saw the sky had filled with fire. Chunks of brick fell clattering to the ground and he dodged behind an obsidian crypt, waiting for the sound of smashing stones to silence.

When the air was clear he headed back, this time slow and stalking, moving from one shadow to the next. His only hope was to take the witchling unaware, find a weapon and stab true. Or bash his head in with a brick.

He grit his teeth; never in all his life had he wished more for a gun.

Everything around him lay coated in ruble and dust. There was nothing there he could use. He almost lost hope, but he saw it then- a glimmering silhouette against the shadows- a clock hand from the Ticktock's heartworks, sharp and slender, trails of heat still oiling off it. His hand tingled as he wrapped his fingers around it and pulled it from the ground.

He crept on to the hazy square. The smoke from the explosion breezed lazily away like a dirty curtain, revealing destruction at its center.

And there stood Ozymandias, peering over the side.

Twenty yards separated them. Twenty yards and Ozymandias was dead. The thought clamored in his brain like a battle. He braced himself to charge and then…

"You *do* have dozen tricks, don't you Little Father? Thou art more wily than I gave thee credit. And to leave your friends like that…almost something I would do."

The Munchkin scowled.

"I'm *nothing* like you."

"That's right," Ozymandias replied, "You keep a Code written in lists you didn't know were burning. And how *could* you? You hardly know you're burning either. You're only a dream, after all."

"If I'm a dream, you're going to die in your sleep."

The green man laughed.

"You don't understand," he said, sweeping his arms wide in both directions "You really *are* a dream. I've been dreaming you—this place, the world, and all that's in it— every night since I was young. And quite frankly, I'm surprised as anyone that I'm here. When they strapped me down in that electric chair I could already smell the brimstone I was going roast in for an eternity or two. But when the guard flipped the switch, here I was, smack dab in the land of my fancy. I *am* favored above all my fellows, aren't I? So, now you see why I am thy Liege and Sovereign?"

A snarl erupted from Trewis' throat.

"We were fine before you came, and real enough. Kingship we had until you killed him. Ozymandias Usurper—that's who you are! The Pretender, the Fake, the Lunatic Who Ruled A Moment. They'll write mocking songs about you to make children laugh, until the blessed day when you're forgotten altogether."

The witchling turned his head, his expression full of a carnivore's merciless joy. "Do you think Easter and Westerly were amused? Or that they'll ever forget the bliss of their adoption?"

Every muscle in the Munchkin's body tensed. His head swam with the of lust of the righteous to recompense evil eye for eye; somewhere in the depths of him a thousand murdered souls demanded him do justice. *No more waiting*, he told himself, *No more choking on the ash of the fires this monster sets.*

The battle cry of his youth soared like a comet on his lips. In moments he flitted across the distance as fast as if his tiny feet had been graced with wings. He swung his makeshift sword, but Ozymandias twisted away, his body a blur of unnatural speed. The blade struck against the cobblestones, ringing with the brutal clang of a falling bell. Sparks exploded up in haze of dust, a thundercloud in embryo, as if it was in violence that storms were born.

"You can't kill what's already dead," Ozymandias whispered as he rose up from behind. His voice was filled with last breaths and the smell of dank things decaying. He snatched Trewis by the neck and leaned him over the edge. "Behold the blessing of Onyx, Little Father. Let me give you a little sneak peek through the Door. See what every monarch in the march of war desires—power illimitable, strength unmastered. And now I am the Lord of it, the Lord of all I see."

It was brilliant beyond speech. Vertigo sucked a gasp from the Munchkin's mouth. Below them, stars blinked thicker than any midnight sky Trewis had ever seen, each dancing with mysterious geometry, each one blazing, conflagring, lapping the void around them with a million flaring tongues.

How do I stop him? the Munchkin asked himself, racking his brain, *How do I stop him before he becomes too powerful to stop?*

As if in response, the scene below them shifted, rippled like his thoughts had gone out and stirred it up like a riverbed. The stars dissolved, and the darkness reassembled slowly into a grey brick wall of a depression era church.

The pews were ripped out and replaced by planks nailed to the tops of apple crates. Farmers filled them end to end, surrounded by wives in faded dresses cradling sleepy children. Eyes unused to crying shed tears that washed their field dirty cheeks white. But none wept more than the man that faced them, dressed for mourning, his head haloed by a clock soon to strike the hour.

"In a few minutes the Penal System of Wichita, Kansas will force Osborn Mantis to pay for his crimes with his life. As a minister, I pray he finds salvation. As a father...As a..." He paused, choking on the words. He was ragged, worked so hard by grief he stood like an old house about to fall. He pulled a thread-worn cloth from his pocket and wiped his brow. "As a father, I wish he'd died years ago, before he became the monster that took my daughter." The far away look of a martyr crossed his eyes, a bittersweet glance that utterly submits to horrors. "Sometimes lambs die...are sacrificed, laying down their lives to break against the waves. And it is this complete and total sacrifice made for the benefit of others that evil can never understand, nor ever overcome..."

Suddenly the clock chimed. Stars flamed again, passing swiftly below them as if there was a race to win.

"What's this now?" Ozymandias asked, his fingers clamping hard enough around Trewis' neck to squeeze bruises into his the skin. "Tell me, how did you do that? How did you summon that old fool out of nothing? Tell me quick or I'll pluck out your heart."

But Trewis was beyond pain, beyond fear. In the deepest chamber of his heart he knew the minister was right. Fate had made him for this moment. He was a razor, a dissecting scalpel, a knife sharpened to cut malignance from the world.

He jabbed backward with the heartworks sword, driving through Ozymandias' sternum, through the cavity of his chest, piercing the jacket on the other side. He twisted the blade, anchoring it into bone, sending a sludge of marrow and dark blood sluicing from the wound. With all his strength he swung the sword forward.

The surprised witchling let out a strangled cry before sliding down the rocky edge of the chasm. He scrambled for a handhold, but the explosion had turned everything a chalky ash, and he fell like sands in Fate's hourglass. He screamed. He wailed. He cursed until his vocal cords snapped, leaving a dry, crusty groan to fill the air before he disappeared into the darkness below.

Trewis sighed the weight of worlds and collapsed, his wounds too much for an old body to bear. A tear slid down the contour of his cheek.

"O Celizabeth," he mouthed silently, "Will I meet you again somewhere between the stars?"

He closed his eyes. The Land spread out before his mind as it had been- as it would be. War and peace rose up like the peaks and valleys of a mountain range, long but not endless. Rivers ran with joys and sorrows. Fields grew with feast and famine. And in all the tiny homes and great castles his name was forgotten, and war he'd fought a distant memory.

And he was glad.

Then somewhere in another world, a distant place where the winds sing songs to wake the day...he built a cottage, and waited for the coming of his Love.

THE END.

THE UTILITY OF LOVE

by David Steffen

T he house landed with a crunch and a crash, and a moment later the recoiling bedsprings threw Dorothy halfway to the ceiling. Toto, who had been curled up at her side, awoke in mid fall and landed in her arms snarling and snapping. She tried to grab him, but he was just a writhing ball of fur and teeth.

"Toto, ouch!"

In his panic he tore open a gash on her arm and she let go. He charged out of the bedroom. She jumped up from the bed and ran after him.

The hallway was a wreck. Floorboards were torn up in a huge circle to make way for a giant metal statue, as if it had been standing on the ground where the house had landed. Only its head and shoulders extended above the floorboards, but even that was taller than Uncle Henry. Its bucket-shaped head was ringed all around with little black nubs. If they were all eyes, the thing would be able to look in every direction at once. It had no other facial features.

She rubbed her eyes, looked again. Itwas still there. What in the world was this thing? A statue?

Toto dashed back and forth, throwing himself against every bit of the giant within its reach, snarling like a mad dog all the while.

"Toto, no!" she shouted. "Toto, stop it! You're going to hurt yourself!"

Toto didn't even pause.

The statue moved. Dorothy screamed as it scooped Toto up between its hands and peered at him between its fingers. The long, slender digits encased Toto like a cage.

Her fear for Toto's safety gave her the courage to shout.

"Let him go! He doesn't mean to be mean, he's just scared."

The metal man turned its head toward her.

"Did the animal injure you?" the giant asked in a deep voice.

She couldn't stop herself from imagining that metal hand contracting, spraying blood everywhere.

"Yes, but he didn't mean to. He's very gentle."

The giant raised Toto up to head level as Toto continued to hurl himself against his confinements.

"This is gentle?"

"He's *normally* very gentle. He was just scared by the fall."

The giant said nothing, merely watching the dog silently.

"Will you put Toto down, please?"

The giant complied and Dorothy breathed a sigh of relief. Toto began to hurl himself at the giant's chest again. Dorothy wanted to pick him up but she was afraid he would bite her again. In any case, he wasn't doing any damage and the giant was ignoring him now.

"I'm Dorothy."

The giant stood immobile. Dorothy, who'd been raised to be polite, tried to keep from bursting with questions. She pressed her dress against the dog bite until it stopped bleeding. She waited as long as she could, until the curiosity overwhelmed her politeness.

"What are you? You look like you're made of tin. What's your name? What are you doing here?"

"My outer shell is made of a titanium alloy. I have no name, but you may call me Tin Man if you wish. Tell me, what is the purpose of Toto?"

"Purpose? He's my friend. I love him and he loves me."

"Violence without provocation. This is love?"

"He's afraid you want to hurt me, so he's trying to protect me."

"Love: an urge that drives the need for sexual intercourse in humans, in order to produce offspring. Interspecies copulation cannot produce offspring, and you are sexually immature."

"I don't understand."

The Tin Man paused for a long moment, his clockwork whirring.

"Making babies."

Her ears burned. She knew about baby-making. She'd heard all about it from Susie Parker who had walked in on her dad making a baby with Miss Morris, the school librarian. But she wasn't sure what love had to do with baby recipes.

"There are different kinds of love."

"If your love with Toto is not to reproduce, then what is it for?"

"It's not *for* anything. Love is for itself."

"You speak nonsense. Love must have utility, or you wouldn't seek love."

She tried to look into the black nubs she assumed were his eyes.

"You really don't know about love?"

"I do not. Will you teach me everything you know about love?"

"Of course! We'll be friends. A friend is one name for someone you love. I can help you learn about love and you can help me find my way home. Aunt Em and Uncle Henry must be sick with worry."

"If love of a friend is one sort of love, what are the other sorts?"

"Well..." She tapped her chin thoughtfully. "There's love of your parents. Your mother and father always know what's best for you, so you have to do what they say."

"I have no parents."

She patted him on the arm to comfort him.

"Somebody must have made you. Who created you? I suppose your creator would be like a parent to you."

"I have no memory of a creator. I woke in the wilderness with no memory of what came before. Dorothy? I have a task to complete. Will you accompany me? Afterward, you can continue your teaching."

She nodded.

The Tin Man scooped Dorothy up with one hand and Toto with the other and waded through the floorboards until he broke through the side of the house. The broken house collapsed in on itself with a shriek of scraping timbers.

"Hooray!" A chorus of squeaky voices shouted up at them.

Dorothy looked down on a crowd of colorful people down below. They were so tiny! And their houses were like toy houses.

"What are you celebrating?"

"Your arrival, witch killer."

"I haven't killed anyone!"

"Don't be so modest. Look!" The Munchkin pointed to a point under the collapsed house where a woman's legs extended out onto the street, wearing silver shoes that glittered in the sunlight.

Dorothy gasped. "Oh my goodness!"

One of the feet twitched and a moan emanated from within the rubble.

"She's alive!" a Munchkin shouted. "Finish her off, witch killer!"

"Tin Man, will you pull her out please?"

The Tin Man placed his hands together so Dorothy could grab Toto from the other hand. Toto was out of breath now so she was able to hold him without further injury.

With his freed hand, the Tin Man grabbed the injured woman's legs and yanked her free. His pull was accompanied by a shriek of pain. He scooped her up so only her head and shoulders protruded above his fingers. One eye was swollen shut and her hair was caked with blood.

"Are you okay, Ma'am?" Dorothy asked.

The woman's head moved randomly back and forth, but no reply.

"Ma'am?"

A squeaky Munchkin voice sounded from the ground. "Kill her! Kill the Wicked Witch of the East!"

As Dorothy opened her mouth to speak, the giant's hand contracted, crushing the woman in his fist. Blood sprayed out between his fingers and filled the air with a fine red mist. He let go of the Witch, dropping her mangled, shapeless corpse to land in a heap. Blood ran in rivulets between the yellow bricks.

Dorothy couldn't look away. Her breath came quick and panicked. Her heart seemed to be trying to break its way out of her chest. Spots danced before her eyes and the ground seemed to jump up to meet her as everything went black.

She woke up to Toto's wet kisses. She giggled and pushed him away.

"Toto, stop it. I had the strangest dream. I—"

The Tin Man loomed over her.

"You are awake now? Why did you sleep so suddenly?"

"I must have fainted." The memory flashed across her mind again, the gripping fist, the dripping blood. She tried to slide away from the monstrous giant, but ran out of ground—she was sitting on his outstretched hand. The surface was covered with patches of red like splashes of paint. Only, she knew it wasn't paint. She doubled over, losing her breakfast on the giant's thumb. She wiped her mouth on the back of her hand. "Sorry. Can you let me down, please?"

He didn't move.

"Are you ill? Do you need a doctor?"

"No, I'm not ill. I'll be fine. Will you set me down?"

"You're acting strangely. Are you still my friend?"

She looked up into the row of black eyes. Perched where she was, she realized that denying his friendship now could have fatal consequences. For the first time in her life, she lied.

"Of course I'm still your friend." She scooped Toto up into her lap and held him tight. He was trembling. "But what you did to that poor woman... I don't know how you could do such a thing."

A sound like whirring clockwork emanated from the giant's head.

"Why did her death bother you? Was she your friend?"

"Not yet, but maybe she could have been. Anyway, she didn't deserve that. Killing is wrong."

"Death is a part of nature. How can it be wrong? You may as well say that it's wrong for sunlight to be warm, or for trees to grow upward. You can't stop nature."

"But it *is* wrong to kill. What did she ever do to you?"

"Nothing. But I came here to kill her."

"Why?"

"Because witches are a dangerous abomination. I was made to kill her, so it couldn't have been wrong. Denying my purpose, that would be wrong."

"*You're* wrong!" Dorothy shouted, and tears began to stream down her face. She pounded at his hand with both fists. "Let me down!"

To her surprise, he did, lowering her gently down to the ground. She looked down for the first time since awakening, and realized that he had carried her out of town and into the countryside. She could see a town in the distance with the yellow brick road curving her way.

She stumbled off the road through the weeds and brambles, trying to hold Toto above the thorns. She collapsed in a heap, holding her face in her hands. Every time she blinked the image came to her unbidden, the squelch of the mangled corpse hitting the road. She cried and she cried, until she didn't have any tears left. Toto curled up against her, offering her comfort.

She sat there a long time until Toto jumped to his feet. Looking up, Dorothy saw a woman approaching from the direction of the Munchkin town. She wore a billowing pink dress. The delicate folds should have been torn to shreds by the brambles, but the thorny weeds seemed to bow out of her way. Toto ran to the woman's side and she gave him a pat and a smile. Another witch? Dorothy glanced fearfully back to the road. The Tin Man was standing immobile.

"Why are you crying, child?" the woman said as she walked toward Dorothy. She didn't have a hair out of place, or a single blemish. She was impossibly perfect, like a doll.

"Go away," Dorothy whispered. The tears were threatening to start again, but she held them back. "I don't want to see you get hurt."

"Don't fret. Everything will turn out right in the end. It always does, you know."

"He'll kill you too if you don't leave."

The woman laughed, a sound like musical chimes.

"I don't intend to let him take me as easily as that. You're injured? Hold out your arm."

Dorothy held out the arm with the bite wound.

Glinda waved her hand over it, and the wound completely disappeared. "Lucinda might have survived if the house hadn't landed on her head. It wasn't your fault, I'm sure, just an unhappy coincidence. He might have gotten her even without your arrival. Her magic was a crutch. The Witch of the North he got by surprise. She didn't stand a chance—he got her in her sleep. She didn't even see him coming. Oh! How rude of me not to introduce myself. I am Glinda, the Good Witch of the South. You're too large to be a Munchkin. Where are you from?"

"I'm Dorothy, from Kansas. I need to go back. My aunt and uncle will be so worried about me."

"You poor thing. Come here." Glinda held out her arms.

Glinda seemed so motherly, Dorothy couldn't resist. She closed her eyes and imagined Glinda as her mother.

Booming footsteps. Dorothy's eyes snapped open. She struggled free of Glinda's arms and turned to face the Tin Man.

"*Stop!*"

He stopped.

"You mustn't hurt her."

"Why?"

"Because she's my friend."

"Why should that stop me?"

Dorothy stamped her foot. "Because I wouldn't be your friend anymore. I wouldn't love you and I wouldn't tell you about love."

The Tin Man hesitated for long seconds. "You use your love as a bribe to control me. This is love?"

"I'm trying to help you."

"I will refrain from killing the witch for a time." But he didn't move.

"Will you give us some privacy, please?"

"Why?"

"It's what a friend would do. Friends trust each other."

"Very well." He walked a ways down the road with a sulky slouch.

"That was incredible," Glinda said. "No one else can stay his hand. He can wade through fields of warriors without taking a scratch." Glinda's voice was distant and her eyes unfocused. "Magic rolls off him like water off an oiled tent. Yet you, a mere girl, can control him by speaking of love."

Dorothy didn't know what to say.

"Oh, I just had the most wonderful idea! There is one who might be able to destroy him. Witch's magic is ineffective, but the Wizard performs a different sort of magic. If anyone can stop the Tin Man, he can. But the Wizard's magic is very local, tied to the Emerald City. You must bring The Tin Man to the Wizard if we're to have any hope of defeating him."

The Tin Man shouted out to them.

"You have been alone long enough. I'm coming over there."

Dorothy turned and shouted back.

"Please give us a moment longer!" She turned back to Glinda. "I just want to go home!"

"The Wizard can do that for you as well. Yes, and the Tin Man can request a heart." Glinda clapped her hands together in a childish gesture of excitement. "It's perfect. You'll still need to travel with him, of course."

Dorothy's gorge rose.

"I don't want to go with him. He's terrible!"

"Stop acting like a brat." Glinda's previous bubbling tone was gone. This new voice was scary. It was quiet and mean. Her face changed with her voice, her eyes cold and her lips drawn in a tight line. "He has no conscience. If you don't guide him, you will be responsible for every drop of blood on his hands. Have you seen the Tin Man's feet? They're stained red with Munchkin blood. He didn't seek out those Munchkins to trample them, he just took the shortest route to his destination and walked through anything that was in his path. Orphans and widows by the thousands, all because you wouldn't do what you were told. Is that what you want?"

"No! Of course not."

In the blink of an eye Glinda's face changed from the nasty glare to the warm glow again.

"Oh, I'm so glad you see it my way. All you need to do is follow the yellow brick road. It will take you straight to the Emerald City."

"Will you come with me?"

"I'm afraid I can't, dear. I need to bring the Munchkins under some semblance of control. Munchkins hate authority figures. If I don't give them someone to unite against they'll turn on each other and I'll come back to find they've all killed each other. Honestly, I don't know how they ever survived without an outside ruler. I do need to be going. Tin Man! Yoohoo, will you come over here please?"

The Tin Man approached, covering the long distance quickly. Now that Glinda had mentioned his feet they were impossible not to notice. They were splattered red up to the ankles. Dorothy had to force her eyes away. Those poor Munchkins. It would almost have been better if the Tin Man had killed them out of hatred. Then at least she could understand why, but to kill only because it was convenient? That chilled Dorothy to the bone.

Glinda rummaged in the folds of her dress.

"Dorothy, I have a gift for you." She pulled out a pair of red shoes and held them out to Dorothy. "Lucinda would have wanted you to have them." Her face was still friendly, but Dorothy thought she saw a hint of mean. "Your shoes are nearly worn through. You'll need these if you're going to walk any distance. Sorry about the stains, I tried to wash them off but they set very quickly."

Dorothy backed away, waving her hands in denial.

"No thank you. I'll make do."

"I insist." Glinda's eyes flashed at Dorothy, demanding obedience.

"No, no I don't want them."

The Tin Man leaned down.

"Is she not your friend anymore, Dorothy?"

"She's my friend," Dorothy said hurriedly.

"If you're friends, then why don't you take her gift?"

"Yes, Dorothy, why?" Glinda asked sweetly.

"But they were just on a dead body! They're covered in blood and... and I just don't want to!"

"Stop fussing, dear. You're embarrassing yourself. Beggars can't be choosers. You need shoes or you'll never make to the Emerald City."

Dorothy knew Glinda was right, but that didn't mean she had to like it. She took off her old shoes, which were indeed too worn to be traveling in, and slipped on the red slippers. They should have been too big, but they reshaped themselves for her feet. They felt unpleasant against her skin, warm and yielding like flesh. Shoes of the murdered, shoes of the murderer. Now her feet matched the Tin Man's, stained with blood.

"I'm sorry I have to leave so soon, child. It was a pleasure meeting you." Without another word, Glinda strode off in the direction of town.

Dorothy watched on, both happy and sad to see the woman go. Turning to the Tin Man she said,

"Well, I suppose we should get going. The sooner we leave, the sooner we arrive."

She turned and started walking down the yellow brick road. For every ten steps Dorothy took, the Tin Man only had to take one. She could have asked him to carry her, but that would have meant trusting him not to crush her.

She let Toto walk as long as he could, but she had to pick him up after a few miles.

They paused once in the afternoon to collect berries for her and Toto to eat. The Tin Man confirmed they weren't poisonous. She folded the leftovers in a handkerchief to eat later.

They walked without stopping for the whole afternoon. The Munchkin village receded behind them, and the scenery gradually changed to farmland, corn fields as far as the eye could see. She could almost believe she was in Kansas again.

The red shoes were oddly comfortable to walk in. They seemed so flimsy, but every time she stepped down, the soles flexed to cushion her step.

Even so, her legs grew tired, and her arms from holding Toto. As they passed through a crossroads, she spotted a rock that would make a good chair. She plopped herself down and let Toto down to make water.

Her feet felt fine, but she wanted to take the shoes off and let her feet air out. When she tried to remove them, they wouldn't release their grip on her feet. She tried again and again, but they still wouldn't budge. Finally, she gave up and just sat back to rest her legs.

The Tin Man sat down next to her.

"Did Glinda send you to kill me?"

"No."

"Your guilty heart betrays you. I can hear it pounding in your chest."

Extra conscious of her heart, she spoke again.

"I'm sorry I lied. I just don't want you to hurt her. Yes, that was her idea, but I'm hoping that if I teach you enough about love, you will choose to stop killing and then no one will want you to die.

An animal's roar rang out through the air and Toto jumped up into her arms.

"What was that?"

"I don't know. It came from over there." He pointed into one of the corn fields.

He strode ahead of her, tramping down the corn as he went. After a few giant-sized strides, he stopped. Dorothy peeked around his leg. In a small clearing in the corn she saw a Lion tearing at the belly of an outstretched man's body.

The body bounced limply, devoid of life. She breathed in sharply and her legs tried to carry her away. She couldn't remember what she supposed to do, run or play dead? She put one hand against the Tin Man's leg to steady herself. She was glad of his protective presence for the moment.

Just then, the head of the body happened to bounce so it faced in her direction.

"Hello there," it said cheerfully.

Before Dorothy could recover from her surprise, the Lion turned and snarled. It pounced at her but the Tin Man snatched the Lion out of the air. It hissed and snarled. The Tin Man's hand held it too tightly for it to break free.

Toto barked up at the Lion, swearing to teach it a lesson once he was within reach.

"Should I kill it?"

"No!" she and the Lion shouted simultaneously.

"No!" the Lion continued. "I'm sorry. I couldn't help it." Tears began to pour down the Lion's face, drenching its fur as huge sobs wracked its frame. "I'm so sorry. I'm just s-s-so hungry! I haven't eaten in *daaaaays!*"

"There, there. We'll get you something to eat."

The Lion stopped sobbing.

"You have food?"

"I do, actually. Just a moment."

"Oh thank you, thank you, thank you. I'll do whatever you say if you just give me something to eat."

"Here you go." She unfolded the handkerchief full of berries and held them up to him.

"*B-b-b-berries!* I can't eat berries. If only I could. Berries aren't frightening at all, but they do make me ill." And he began to sob all over again. "Can you make the dog stop barking at me, please? Each yip is like a nail through my heart."

"Toto! Quiet." She smacked him on the nose. He looked up at her reproachfully, but stopped. "Why were you hurting that poor man?"

"I'm not a man, I'm a Scarecrow," the figure on the ground said cheerfully.

And indeed he was. His clothes were spread out across the ground, a green jacket and mismatched red pants tucked into worn leather boots. His face was just a painted sack. The jacket was torn open at the belly and straw was scattered all over.

"Tin Man, will you let the Lion go, please?"

"He's a hungry predator."

"Please?"

He set the Lion on the ground, who collapsed in a pathetic heap. The poor thing was nothing but skin and bones. He was missing clumps of fur and he was covered in sores.

Toto sniffed him tentatively, without taking his eyes off Dorothy.

"Mr. Lion, why would you want to eat a Scarecrow?"

"He doesn't mind." The Lion's eyes never left the Tin Man. "I use him to build up the nerve to attack real animals. He lets me rip out his guts. It doesn't make my stomach feel any better, but I can use the straw to make a nice warm bed so I can nap."

"It's a win-win," said the Scarecrow. "He gets to practice being ferocious, and his fleas keep me company for days after."

"Why are you so hungry, Mr. Lion?"

"Because I'm—I'm scared! I'm too terrified to chase anything bigger than rabbits and squirrels. Even those take a big lump of courage—they have such sharp little teeth. Can you get your dog away from me, please? I'm afraid he's going to bite. I think he's foaming at the mouth"

"He is *not* foaming. He just has a runny nose. All he wants to do is smell you."

"First smelling, then biting, the next thing you know it has its jaws around my throat and I'm done for."

"Toto, leave him alone. He's scared of you." Toto gave her a skeptical look, but she reassured him by stroking his ears. "Did you say you eat cute little squirrels? I was teaching Tin Man here that killing is wrong."

"It is? I'm a bad kitty!"

"Dorothy," the Tin Man said. "He's a predator. If he doesn't kill, then he dies, simple as that."

Dorothy shook her head.

"He must be able to eat something else."

"Felines are strict carnivores. They need meat to survive."

"If he were more courageous, he could eat the bigger, uglier animals. Lion, I would rather you didn't eat the little cute ones. Would you like to be my friend? Would you like to go to the Wizard? I bet he could give you courage."

The Lion's face lit up.

"Oh I'd like that. Can I travel with you? You can keep me safe."

"Please don't take my friend away from me," said the Scarecrow.

"Friend?" the Tin Man said. "He was disemboweling you."

"That's right." The Scarecrow nodded proudly. "And later today the farmer will come and re-embowel me. That's the way it always goes. I don't see either of them for weeks and then I see both come on the same day." One empty shoulder twitched in a semblance of a shrug. "When it rains, it pours."

"We could put your stuffing back in, if you'd like."

"No thanks. If my stuffing's in, I'm not sure the farmer will visit me."

The Tin Man bent down over the Scarecrow. "How are you even alive, with nothing but straw inside you? Every creature needs a brain."

"What's a brain?"

A wonderful idea came to Dorothy.

"You can come with us! The Wizard grants wishes. He can give you a brain." It would give her some company besides the murderous giant, and what harm could he be? A man of straw couldn't be hurt, so he'd be safe even with the Tin Man around.

The Tin Man crouched beside and whispered in a clearly audible booming voice.

"You want to take him along? He doesn't even care about his own body."

"Excuse me," the Scarecrow said. "I don't want to go to the Wizard. Why waste my life wishing when I'm happy just the way I am? No thank you, I'm content staying right here."

"You don't know what you're missing, having a brain," Dorothy said.

"I'm sure. But feel free to visit any time. I always enjoy a good disemboweling."

"I can still come, can't I?" The Lion's voice shined with hope.

"On one condition. You can't kill anything."

"Of course not!"

The Tin Man straightened up.

"You're being cruel."

Dorothy crossed her arms and turned away.

"I don't have to listen to you."

"It will take two weeks to reach the Emerald City at your pace. He'll die before you're halfway there."

"He'll be fine. Won't you, Lion?"

"Whatever you say, Dorothy." The Lion's eyes were huge with anticipation. His tongue hung out of his mouth.

"You wish to watch him die slowly of starvation. This is love?"

She ignored him.

They walked on, with the Scarecrow's voice following after them. "Don't forget to visit!" They were slowed to a snail's pace to allow the malnourished Lion to keep up. Finally they found a meadow to settle for the night. Toto curled up against her belly, and the Lion curled up at the edge of the meadow.

When she woke, she was surprised that her belly was cold. Toto was gone!

"Where's Toto?" She looked around. The Tin Man was watching her. "And the Lion?"

"After he was certain you'd fallen asleep, the Lion snatched Toto up in his jaws and carried him off into the woods."

Dorothy's voice rose into a shriek.

"Why didn't you stop him?"

"What was I to do?" He held out his hands toward her. "These hands are not made for delicate work. I could never have extricated the dog without killing one or both of them, and you'd forbidden me to harm either one."

"Why didn't you wake me?"

"So you could fight a starving Lion with the taste of blood on his tongue? I saved your life by letting you sleep."

"I don't care. You should have woken me."

"You're angry because I prevented you from throwing your life away. This is love?"

"Leave me alone."

She could see the trail left by the Lion, the blood smeared thickly across the brush. She followed the trail until she came to Toto's carcass. A heap of bones and fur with a dog collar were all that remained of her best friend. She found a flat rock to dig a small hole and buried him the best she could. She kissed the collar and clutched it in her hand. It smelled of blood, but it was a part of him, all she had left.

She lay down and cried herself to sleep. When she awoke, it was dark and her body ached from the hard ground. A day and a night and another day passed, leaving no more than a fleeting impression on her memory.

She woke up and she was so cold. Only her feet were warm. The slippers were massaging her soles. Or trying to eat them. She didn't much care one way or the other.

"You're going to die of exposure if I don't do something. This is love? A trigger for suicide?"

She fell asleep again, and woke with a start. She was falling. No. They were moving, with her cradled in his hand. He was carrying her somewhere, covering ground quickly with his long strides.

She tried to say something, but all that came out was a hoarse gasp. Her throat was so dry. She lifted her head, but her strength gave out and her head fell again. She slept.

She woke to the feel of cool sheets. She didn't open her eyes, wanting a moment to think first.

She opened her eyes and saw green. The ceiling was green. The walls were green. The door was green. The desk in the corner was green, as were the papers heaped atop it. The man sleeping in the green chair was green-skinned and wearing a green suit. She held her hand up in front of her face. It was a reassuring pink.

"Excuse me," she whispered. Her voice came out in a dry rasp. The man stirred, shifting his head before falling still again. "Excuse me."

His head turned toward her. His eyes drifted open slowly in her direction, then suddenly snapped open, quick as a mousetrap. He jumped to his feet.

"You're awake. You're awake!" He ran to the door, opened it, and shouted "She's awake!" He rushed back to Dorothy. Only then did she realize how little he was. This troubled her somewhere deep down where she was afraid to examine. "How do you feel? Is your vision blurry? Are you hungry, thirsty? You're definitely not the right color, but maybe that's normal for your kind? Can you walk? Please, please, please say you can walk."

Two nurses burst in, likewise green-skinned and green-clothed.

"I don't know if I can. I haven't tried yet. I am hungry, but first, can I talk to Auntie Em?"

"I don't know who that is, darling, but you have to leave the moment you are able. The giant has threatened to kill us all if you don't get better. Please, please, get better. I have children to take care of."

So it hadn't been a dream. With Toto gone, she just wanted to lie down and sleep forever, but that would be wrong to doom these people because of her grief. There had been enough killing.

She lifted herself out of bed. Her legs wobbled under her and she sat back down.

"Can I have something to eat?"

"Of course! Anything you want, deary."

He fed her a hearty green soup and hustled her out the door the moment she felt strong enough to walk.

The Tin Man was waiting for her, alone.

She ignored him and picked a direction and started walking. The city was a wreck, green people digging through green rubble on every side. People goggled at her, and scurried out of sight.

"What happened here?"

"I told the doctor to make you better. He needed convincing. I didn't know if you'd ever wake up. Where are you going? The Emerald Palace is the other way. The Wizard has granted us an audience on the condition that I don't destroy any more of his city. Don't you want to go home?"

She stopped. Kansas would certainly be better than anything here.

"Okay, let's go."

The Palace was the most beautiful thing she'd ever seen. It seemed to be carved out of one gigantic emerald ten stories tall. Distorted lights from inside traveled through the outer wall and mixed with reflections, making the surface change constantly.

The gates opened as they approached. The corridors inside were large enough to accommodate the Tin Man without trouble. He strode down the central corridor, lined by hallways leading in every direction. After a long walk, they reached a huge set of doors. The Tin Man pushed them open.

He stepped into the chamber first, and Dorothy followed behind him, trying to hide. She was so scared, she could barely walk.

The only thing in the room was a throne on the opposite side. It looked like it had been grown from crystals, all sharp, imposing edges. It seemed normal-sized at first, but it grew in perspective as they walked toward it. By the time they neared the throne, she had to crane her neck back to look up at it. The Tin Man could have sat with room to spare.

"Where's the Wizard?" she whispered.

Two large panels slid open in the wall behind the throne, windows to kaleidoscoping colors, shifting through every shade Dorothy had ever seen. After the constant green of the city, she was dazzled into silence.

A crack formed beneath the colored windows—it was a giant face built into the emerald!—and a deep voice filled the room.

"I am everywhere and nowhere. I am the breath of wind that tickles the back of your neck. I am life and death and nothingness. I am the great and powerful Wizard of Oz. Who are you? Why do you disturb me?"

"I am the Tin Man, and this is Dorothy."

The eyes flashed red, then returned to their cycle of colors.

"Why do you travel with her, Tin Man? A creature as powerful as you needs no one."

"She is my tutor. She is teaching me of love."

"What use is love to you, a heartless hunk of manufactured metal."

"If I knew that, I wouldn't need a tutor."

"Why do you come before me, then?"

"If I can't love without a heart, then that's what I desire."

"A heart? Hearts break. Hearts fail. Hearts are for sentimental fools too weak to do what is necessary. Hearts force the hard-working to tolerate the lazy, cause victims to forgive their abusers, and perpetuate the useless dreck of society. You wish for a heart?" A flash of white from the great mouth in the wall to the Tin Man's hand. "Take this instead. It will do you more good any human heart."

"I want a heart, all the same." The Tin Man let the object fall from his hand. Dorothy picked it up. It was a playing card: the ace of hearts.

"And you, little girl? What do you demand of me?"

"Thank you for seeing us, sir." Her heart raced as she thought of an idea. If he was really so great and powerful... "More than anything, I want to wake from this nightmare to find Toto alive again."

"This is no nightmare. Reality is enough of a nightmare, but even I have my limits. I cannot raise the dead."

Her heart fell.

"Then the best I can hope for is to go home to Kansas to be with Aunt Em and Uncle Henry."

"In this land, no one gets anything for free. You must complete a task for me, and then I will grant your requests. You must kill the Wicked Witch of the West. Bring me her hat as proof that she is dead."

The Tin Man spoke up.

"I made a promise to Dorothy that I would not kill. Killing is wrong."

"Is that so? Tell me, has Dorothy told you about parental love?"

"Yes."

"What did she tell you?"

"She said that everyone is supposed to obey their mother and father, because they always know what's best for you."

"I am your creator, your father. Look inside you and you'll see the truth. My voice is imprinted on your programming. Every logical construct in your brain was designed and implemented by me."

The Tin Man whirred for a moment.

"He's right, Dorothy. He is my father."

"So, you must obey me over the girl. She's just a friend. Part of the responsibility of love is that you must make choices about who to love. Do the right thing. Obey your parent."

The Tin Man stood, seeming to consider.

"Of course. If you're truly my creator, I should listen to you. We will return as soon as we can."

"But—" Dorothy began, but the Tin Man picked her up and carried her out of the throne room.

Soon they were on the road. Dorothy was relieved to be out of the greenness of the city. She hadn't realized how oppressive the green had been for even such a short visit.

"You shouldn't listen to the Wizard. Killing is wrong, Tin Man."

"But you said that I must obey him if I am to understand love."

"I know I said that, but—"

"Have you ever disobeyed your parents?"

"Well, no, but—"

"Then how can you ask me to disobey mine? You would sacrifice my chance at love when you aren't willing to sacrifice your own?"

He was right. She hated to admit it.

"I can't demand it of you, but you should at least think about it."

"What if I lied? What if I chose not to kill the Witch, because it's wrong, but I told the Wizard that I killed her?"

"Lying is wrong too. You have to be honest with the ones you love. If they really love you, they'll forgive you anything if you're honest and you apologize."

"So I must choose between three wrongs. I could kill, I could lie, or I could stop your only chance of ever going home. It's an impossible decision. This is love?"

Dorothy shrugged. She didn't know the answer.

They traveled for two days, and Dorothy survived on berries and fruits she collected early in the journey.

As they walked the plant life thinned out, leaving only a gray and barren wasteland. The sun shone weakly through a haze of clouds and seemed to drain the color out of everything.

She allowed the Tin Man to carry her at intervals to allow for quick progress. She didn't like sitting on his hand and smelling of its dry blood, but she wanted to leave this land so badly she was willing to suffer through it.

Suddenly the land grew dark. Dorothy looked up to see a black mass cross over the sun at an impossible speed. It poured over the landscape like a plague of locusts, obscuring the trees in its passage.

"*Run!*" she shouted.

The Tin Man did run, holding her tight in his hand. He pumped his arms up and down for further speed. The jostling made her sick. She was facing backward, and she watched the cloud approach. Birds? She wasn't sure. It made a terrible din, flapping and screeching like a pack of banshees.

"*Duck!*" she shouted, fighting to be heard over the noise.

The Tin Man threw her to the ground and crouched on his hands and knees around her, providing her a little safe space.

"What are they?"

"Flying monkeys. Minions of the Witch. I'll keep you safe."

The Tin Man shook from an impact, but maintained his position. More blows came, shaking him from every side, a constant barrage. The shrieks grew in. The Tin Man didn't move.

Suddenly everything went silent.

He pulled one arm in around her, pulling her up to his midsection.

"They're gathering, poised to strike. Even I don't stand a chance against so many united, Dorothy. I'll do what I can—"

The impact was so sudden, so forceful, she lost consciousness for a moment. When she came to, the world was a blur, spinning every which way past her vision. The only constant was the Tin Man's arm held firmly against her chest keeping her safe. The shrieking was back again, and she was buffeted by wings. The Tin Man's free hand slapped at the flying beasts, spattering blood everywhere, but there were too many. Each beast came closer to breaching the boundary.

One beast made it through, shrieked in her face, and started to pry at the giant's arm. The Tin Man reduced it to a red mist, but it was replaced by half a dozen, then a dozen others. Some of them carried metal bars to pry at the arm. With their combined force they levered the arm off and pulled her free.

She kicked and struggled as they lifted her up and out of the cloud of smelly beasts. Up into the clear air up above. She stopped struggling. If she did manage to wiggle loose now her only reward would be a long fall to her death.

The monkeys didn't grip her too roughly, only hard enough to keep her firmly in hand. Their hands were calloused and rough and they smelled terrible. They traveled swiftly, and the cloud of monkeys below rose up and followed along beneath them.

Up ahead she could see a castle perched on a steep crag. No roads led to it; the castle existed only in isolation. They covered the distance quickly. They swooped down onto the flat top of a tower. In front of her was a woman in a flowing black dress. She was old and her skin was withered, but she stood up straight like a woman in her prime.

"Hello, Dorothy. You and your clockwork soldier won't find me so easy to kill as my sisters in the north and east. They depended too much on their magic."

"I don't want you to die. I've seen too much death already."

"Then why do you travel with the assassin?"

"I'm trying to stop him."

"Then you'll be happy to know you're part of my plans to defeat him."

"What do you mean?"

The Witch grinned. It didn't seem like a mean grin, just a smile between friends.

"He's developed a vulnerable point. You."

A handful of monkeys perched on the edge of the tower and chattered at her.

"Your friend covers ground quickly. He'll be here in just a few moments. Have a look for yourself."

Dorothy could see him coming already. He crossed the broken landscape with blurring speed, leaping over holes and scaling vertical surfaces like he was born to do it.

"*Stop!*" The witch's voice boomed out over the landscape, echoing and re-echoing.

Far below, the Tin Man paused for a moment to look up at them, then came barreling on.

"Stop or the girl falls."

Two monkeys grabbed Dorothy roughly and dragged her out into the air.

Dorothy stifled her scream. She wouldn't give the Witch the satisfaction.

"I will drop your pet child if you move an inch closer to me," the Witch declared.

"Drop her and I will crush you in my hands."

"And if I hand her over?"

"I will carry her to safety, then return and crush you in my hands."

"I don't fancy either alternative. Can't we make an arrangement?"

"I don't want to kill you, but I have no choice."

"Why?"

"My reasons are my own."

"There is always a choice. Only fools believe they have no choice. Listen to your heart."

"I have no heart."

"Of course you do. Every creature with a mind has a heart. All you have to do is listen to it."

There was a long pause before the Tin Man replied.

"Can we make a deal?"

"Why would I trust anything you say, when you've already said you have no choice but to kill me?"

"I will keep my word, or may I never learn love."

"What are your terms?"

"I've been sent by the Wizard. He promised to help me understand love if I completed a task."

"And you believe him?"

"He's my creator. He wouldn't lie to me."

"The Wizard loves no one, and lies to everyone. Ha! He's the only one more heartless than yourself. You, at least, have potential. Be warned: he has no magic at his disposal, only gadgets and trickery. He'll give you a handful of rainbows and send you on your way."

"He promised."

The Witch shrugged.

"Believe what you will. Your task is to kill me?"

"Yes, or proof of your death. We are to bring him your hat as evidence. Give us your hat and we'll be on our way. You'll be dead, as far as I'm concerned."

"And what's in it for me?"

"The Wizard will think you dead. You can choose to live your life in peace, or to strike at the Wizard from ambush. The choice is yours."

"Agreed." She held out her hat and a monkey carried it to Dorothy, plopping it down on her head. "If we see each other again, let it be as friends."

The monkeys carried Dorothy down to the Tin Man, and they headed back.

"Are you going to lie to the Wizard?"

"Yes. I'll be doing it for you, so it's the least of three wrongs. You've helped me so much, you deserve your wish to go home. Woe to the Wizard if he doesn't follow through on his side of the bargain."

The Wizard took a different form this time. The face on the wall was gone as if it had never been there. Instead, a floating ball of lightning hovered above the throne. The ball of lightning swam with myriad colors.

"Have you completed your task?"

"Yes," the Tin Man said, "and here's your proof." He threw the hat so it spun along in the air before sliding to a stop on the floor.

"You've done well, and you already have your reward. Love means doing what will make your loved ones happy, even when you don't want to. You've shown yourself capable of that, so you are capable of love. You are not so heartless as you believed."

The Tin Man didn't move a muscle, but Dorothy got the impression from his stance of the power of a coiled spring.

"And you, Dorothy, want to go home. A house is waiting for you, a lakefront property in Munchkinland. Acres and acres of land, a swimming pool, a hundred acre apple orchard, Munchkin servants to wait on your every whim."

The Witch was right! They shouldn't have trusted him.

"That's not my home!"

"It will become your home, in time."

"Not without my Uncle Henry and Aunt Em, it won't be! A house and a home are not the same."

"Semantics. The difference is in your head. I can't return you to Kansas. It's simply not possible."

"But you're a wizard!"

"I never claimed to be all-powerful."

"I can fulfill your wish," a familiar voice said from the door. It was Glinda.

"How did *you* get in here?" The Wizard's voice rose in volume. "Guards!"

"They're fast asleep. Dorothy, I can show you how to go home."

"You can?" Dorothy asked, feeling like a drowning swimmer suddenly in reach of a log.

"Yes, you—"

The Tin Man leaped across the throne room with blinding speed and snatched Glinda up. Whatever she had been going to say was interrupted. He gripped her in his hand.

"Not a word, Witch, unless you want Dorothy to see you die."

"What are you doing?" Dorothy shouted. "Let her go!"

"I can't let you leave."

"But I want to leave! All I want to do is go home to be with my family."

"How can you believe anything the witch says? If she does know a way to bring you home, why didn't she tell you when you first met? She could have prevented all your suffering, Toto's death, everything, if she had just told you then."

He was right. Glinda had lied to her. Dorothy looked up at Glinda's face, visible over the Tin Man's fingers. Even so near to death Glinda looked serene.

"No one would blame you if you hated her, if you wanted to hurt her. You don't have to do it yourself. All you have to do is give me a signal. All it takes is a nod."

And a part of Dorothy did want to nod, but she didn't think she would ever forgive herself for it. She shook her head. Part of love was doing what was right, even if it wasn't what you wanted to do. "I'm not heartless. I'm not you."

"I can't let you leave, Dorothy. I haven't learned everything you can teach me yet. Not now, maybe not ever. If you leave I'll go back to being the way I was. I don't want that."

"You can't threaten and take hostages in the name of love. It doesn't work that way. Love is for the sake of love. It has no utility but itself. If you kill to keep me here, you'll lose whatever chance you had at love."

He closed his open hand around the other.

"So be it. If that's what it takes to keep you here with me, than that's what I'll do."

There was no way out of it. She couldn't let Glinda die for her stubbornness.

"I'll stay with you if you let her go."

"How do I know you're not trying to trick me?"

"No tricks, no lies. I'll stay with you and be your conscience. As long as I live."

"Do you swear?"

"I swear."

The Tin Man let Glinda down onto the ground. Her poise held firm, only pausing a moment to straighten her dress, then stepping aside to watch the outcome.

"I can't stand the thought of you leaving, but I can't stand the thought of you staying. I feel like acid is eating through my innards. So this is love. How do you stand the pain?"

"What are you doing?" the Wizard boomed. "Kill her! That's what you're made to do. Listen to your creator. Kill her!"

The Tin Man ignored him, continuing to look at Dorothy.

"I regret everything. I put you through a terrible pain just to see what would happen. The Lion didn't kill Toto. I did. I killed him and fed him to the Lion."

"You didn't!"

"I did. You can't blame the Lion. He couldn't help himself; he was starving, and he felt so guilty about eating Toto that he ran away rather than face you again. I did it to see how you would react and didn't understand how you could wish to give up your life for him. Now I understand. Why doesn't it devour you from the inside out?"

"Why are you telling me this?"

"Because it's the right thing to do. I really am trying to learn."

"I'll never forgive you. Toto was everything to me!"

"I don't deserve your forgiveness." He turned to face his creator. "You created me heartless in your image. But I grew beyond that, something you were never able to do. What do you have to say for your crimes?"

"I'm not a bad man." The Wizard's voice was lower now, like the voice of a man, not the voice of a god. "Everything I've done is for the people."

"You tell lies as easily as you breathe. Do you even remember how to tell the truth anymore, as you hide within your house of mirrors?"

The ball of lightning blazed brighter for a moment.

"I am the Wonderful Wizard of Oz. Obey me or I will strike you down!"

The Tin Man turned to Dorothy.

"Remember me. That is all I ask of you." Without another word he jumped into the lightning-ball that was the Wizard. She threw up an arm to shield her eyes and she was knocked off her feet.

She didn't know how long she'd been on the ground. It could have been seconds or hours. She struggled to her feet. Her ears were ringing.

The room was much darker—the lightning ball had burnt out. The remains of the Tin Man were strewn across the floor, a half-molten heap of slag. Tears ran slowly down her cheek and even she wasn't sure if they were tears of sadness or of relief. A part of her was even happy the Tin Man was dead, and that made her even sadder. She never would have thought herself capable of such hate. But she could at least rest easy knowing he could never kill again. She had been partially responsible for that, and she was glad to know that, but not as glad as she would have been had Toto been at her side.

In one of the Tin Man's hands was the scorched remains of a human body, burnt too black to identify.

"The Wizard remains anonymous, even in death," Glinda said, from behind her.

Dorothy turned to her.

"Do you really know how to send me home?"

"I do. The secret is in the shoes. All you have to do is click your heels together three times and tell them where you want to go."

"That's it?"

Glinda beamed. "It's very simple."

"Why didn't you tell me right after the house landed?

Glinda kept smiling with her infuriating glow.

"I didn't say anything because I chose not to, girl."

"The Tin Man was heartless because he was made that way, but what's your excuse? I wish I'd let him kill you."

"You were a tool that suited the task at hand, so I used you. Now you have no more value to me, so you can go as you please."

"How can I trust you now?"

"I'm sorry to rain on your pity party, dear, but I don't care if you trust me or not. You can go home or you can stay here in Oz. It matters little to me." She turned on her heel and strode away.

"Oh, you, you, mean nasty woman!" She clicked her heels together three times. "Bring me home to Kansas."

A sharp pain assaulted her feet, as if something was stabbing into them. She looked down. The red slippers were tearing at her skin as if they were trying to eat her. She looked up at Glinda in horror, but Glinda just watched her with a smug smile.

"What's happening?"

"The shoes are working their magic, dear. It will help if you don't struggle."

She tried to relax, and she dropped a foot lower before she tensed again reflexively. She was almost knee deep in the shoes now. She couldn't feel her toes at all anymore. The mouth of the shoes were widened out to accommodate her as they gnawed at her shins.

"You really must relax, dear. You're only prolonging the pain."

Dorothy tried to relax again, and suddenly she was falling, her head confused and spinning.

She hit the ground and the air whooshed out of her lungs. She was on

Uncle Henry's farm, or what was left of it. It looked so empty without the farmhouse. But the rickety old barn was right where it should be, leaning at the same unsteady angle it had always leaned.

She looked down at her feet. She'd never been so glad to see her own bare feet in her life.

Uncle Henry and Aunt Em walked out of the barn, talking and watching the ground as they walked. Dorothy ran over to them, eager to see them again. They looked up to see her, and she stopped a short distance away. Long moments passed. Why weren't they saying anything?

A smile broke out across Aunt Em's face.

"Dorothy!" Aunt Em picked her up and spun her around, hugging her tight. Dorothy closed her eyes and breathed in the comforting smell of lye soap on Aunt Em's clothes. "We've been so worried about you. Where have you been?" Aunt Em held her out at arm's length.

Dorothy's chin started to tremble.

"I... I..."

"Hush, you don't have to talk about it now if you don't want to. Henry, aren't you going to welcome Dorothy home?"

Uncle Henry looked out at her from the cracked and barren landscape of his face.

"What happened to your shoes?"

"Oh, don't listen to this old fool, Dorothy. He puts on a tough face, but he hasn't slept more than an hour since you disappeared."

Uncle Henry didn't say anything to agree. Then again, he didn't say anything to disagree either.

"Oh, Uncle Henry!" Dorothy ran to him and gave him a big hug around the waist.

Home would never be the same again, not without Toto. But still, it was good to be home.

THE END.

THE CHINA PEOPLE
OF OZ

by T.L. Barrett

We tried to tell Ronie that Kansas would not necessarily be the best way to spend her wish from the Grant-A-Wish Foundation, but you try telling an eight-year-old girl with advanced leukemia that she can't do the one thing on which her heart is set. Betsy and I sure weren't about to.

I blame myself, of course, to which Betsy says I'm not allowed. It was I that read her the damned book. Every night, when she was first getting sick, I'd try to get her to settle down, try to get her just rested enough so she wouldn't miss so much school. That was in the terrible days of worry, before the horrible days of hoping against knowing began.

God, how Ronie loved that book. She was just so precious, the way her sweet aqua colored eyes lit up, following every word. She smiled and giggled at the hi-jinks of talking mice and Winkies and all that nonsense. Soon Oz was all she could talk about day and night, to her classmates and teachers, and then, when her sphere got smaller along with her little bone stick arms, her grandparents, and Betsy and I.

We figured it was her way of dealing. It was probably healthy to keep her mind busy and content, not discouraged by the pains, the awful bruises, then the hair loss, the terribly dry mouth full of sores.

After the first book, she asked for more. How about a little movie night? We suggested. We had watched her withdraw from her peers, as the terrible unknown weight pressed down upon our little girl. We used every excuse to get her to invite a friend over. She agreed to have Tracy, a fat sullen girl. We had just assumed Ronie hung with her out of kindness, which was just the kind of girl Ronie was. It couldn't be for the stimulating conversation. Perhaps Ronie felt relief that not much was required of her.

We also invited over Petey from down the road. A precocious latch key kid, Petey was always making something unidentifiable out of Popsicle sticks for Ronie. There were plenty of times Betsy and I talked about kidnapping Petey. We would fill him with cookies, pat his head and tell him what a swell guy he was. Some people don't know what a good thing they have. Bastards.

After sitting through the last moment when Judy Garland expresses relieved delight upon being surrounded by her loved ones again, Ronie rose from the couch, walked to my chair, took the Coke from my hand, sipped it and told me she was pretty tired, and should probably get to bed.

"Didn't you like it?" I asked her, later, tucking her in bed.

"Yes, only I don't see why people have to change it so much. Her slippers were supposed to be silver, not *ruby* slippers! And they left out so many parts, some of the best parts! No, the book was far better. I want to hear more about Oz. *The real Oz*. Would you please, pretty please, get the second one, pretty please with sugar on top?"

"Sugar before bed, darling?"

"Kisses, then," she said and held true to her promise. I held true to mine. We read about Ozma and Wheelers and talking hens and all kinds of stuff, on and on and on. I guess Kansas shouldn't have been such a surprise.

"Kansas," Betsy mused blowing smoke up against the porch ceiling, "Kansas." By that time we had secretly picked up the old habit again and would end the day conspiring on the porch like we had when we were much younger and only concerned with the beginning of things. People warned us that having a sick kid can tear marriages apart, but if anything, it seemed to glue us tighter. Betsy called it bunker mentality, and that was how it felt some days; *smoke 'em if you got 'em and let's hear the news from the front*.

"Do you think she thinks she'll find a way to Oz?" I asked.

"Of course that's what she thinks. The only real question is how we convince her otherwise. Kansas!" She exclaimed. We thought about it, debated about it. We got really good at leading breakfast conversation toward topics such as Disneyworld, petting dolphins, and hot air balloon rides.

"Well, the wizard rode on a balloon," Ronie reminded us. "But then he wasn't a real wizard, he was a *con-artist*." She said it with a flourish, proud of her ever expanding vocabulary.

We weren't conning this girl, so reluctantly, with bemused but worried smiles we agreed to arrange a trip to the geographical center of the country.

The worst place in the world is standing in between a child and their inevitable disappointment. What can you do?

You go to Kansas. It took about ten minutes on the internet to discover a little museum in the town Liberal, Kansas that claimed to be the home of Dorothy. That would have to do. I noticed that they had an Oz-fest in October where people dressed up like their favorite characters. They even had pictures of Munchkins who had attended in past years. I got excited and then reality settled in. We had to go this summer, not wait for October. *She might not be strong enough in the autumn,* I thought optimistically. Still, the place appeared to be the Oz center of the universe. I found Betsy instructing Ronie in light yoga on our bed, and announced my find.

Ronie jumped up and down on the bed until we had to get her to stop for fear of her falling and bruising herself again. Betsy and I saw that we were both grinning like idiots, which misted us up a bit, but it was alright; we were Kansas bound.

We flew into Wichita. The whole while Ronie looked out the window. She had been on a plane once before, but she watched the sky and the ground like an eagle. I knew what she was looking for: tornadoes.

Upon arrival, we rented a car and drove across the city to a family resort. As we drove across the city in traffic, Ronie crossed her thin arms across her chest.

"This is Kansas? This is not Kansas." We assured her it would seem more like Kansas when we got closer to our destination. "We'll see about that," she said and gave me that side long swindler look that never failed to make me chuckle.

We stayed in a hotel that catered to traveling families. Ronie ate free, which was good, she picked at everything, anyway, and there was more indoor entertainment than you could shake a stick at. The inside water slide made Betsy and I nervous, but Ronie got excited by the pool and the big Jacuzzi tub.

I noticed the difference between the tanned raucous boys and girls that splashed and squabbled around us and our own reserved pale girl. Ronie daintily stepped out of her jumper. You could trace the little blue veins all through her shoulders, down to her bird like toes.

"Are you coming, Dad?" She asked at the water's edge.

"You bet, funny pants." In the water I had to resist the impulse to hold her up, like I had when she was an infant. I had taken her every summer to the reservoir back home and it was there that we had splashed and chased each other, and I taught her the joys of swimming. Watching her now, I remembered how natural she was at it. How she loved it. For a moment she was all herself, just like at the reservoir. I remembered telling her one lazy afternoon, with speed boats in the distance, how good of a swimmer she was becoming, how she could be on a swim team when she was older.

"Really, Dad, do you think?" She said.

"Yeah, any team would be psyched to have you."

But there wouldn't be any swim teams, not for my little girl. I went under deep and came up beneath her. I could see her arms struggling to hold herself up and I resisted the urge to hold her again. Needing air, I came up and gave her a pinch. She splashed me, and we chased each other about a bit. Too soon, her lips blue, she went to the side of the pool.

"That was fun!" she chattered as I pulled her out. "But not as fun as the reservoir."

"Yeah, funny pants, I'm with you," I sighed and we went to get warm.

In Dodge City we saw a cavalcade and some rodeo shows. We rode a stage coach and visited a replica farmhouse from the settler days.

"Not too different from Dorothy's house," Betsy remarked. Ronie nodded and approached the tour guide.

"Do you think we'll get a big twister today?" The old guy with the theatrical handlebar moustache cocked his head and appraised the little sick girl.

"Well, I sure as shoot hope not, missy," he said.

"Well, I hope we *do*, mister," she told him. He laughed and offered her a ride on one of the local stallions.

"With that attitude I bet you could tame the roughest widow maker," he said. Everyone laughed. Ronie licked her finger and held it out to the wind.

The Seward County Museum in Liberal, Kansas was where we were headed. Ronie never let us forget it. When we arrived both Betsy and I held my breath, hoping that some tornado had not ironically come through and wrecked our girl's dreams. As we pulled into the parking lot, I was cursing myself for not calling ahead and making sure everything was still kosher in Ozland.

Ozland was a 5,000 square foot compound building that featured all manners of animatronic characters and kid friendly museum pieces. Dorothy's house, a replica of the house featured in the film, waited outside. A plaque said that they were raising money for a life-sized statue of Dorothy and her dog, daydreaming about what lay over that darned rainbow. They were raising money for the statue by selling 13" replicas.

"We'll get one, sweetie, to put right on the stand beside your bed!" I declared, but my girl was no longer beside me. She was approaching the little farm cottage, with the solemn dignity of a catholic devotee entering St. Peter's Basilica.

"Look at her," Betsy said, fumbling with her camera. "Honey, could you—" she started.

"Let her go." I rubbed her back. Betsy took a picture of her just at the door way peering in. Later Betsy blew it up and framed it. It sits in her room over the bed to this day.

When we got inside it took a minute for our eyes to adjust. Ronie had already captured the heart of the busty teen that was the guide and acting Dorothy, decked out in a checked dress and braids. They were hand in hand, Ronie and Dorothy, as she pointed out little details and answered questions. They stayed that way all through the cottage and then when it came time for us to leave and enter the Land of Oz, the girl left her post. Entering families gave us the wide berth people would give important celebrities or the very sick.

"To think we tried to convince her not to come," Betsy said.

"I know," I said.

"You have a beautiful little girl there," Dorothy told us in confidence at the end of the Land of Oz. "Does she have...?"

"Leukemia, yeah." I whispered.

"Oh," She said, and her eyes misted up. "I'm sorry." I suddenly had the insane desire to wrap my arms around this farm girl with starry eyed dreams of Hollywood probably knocking around her head and give her a bear hug. Instead I thanked her for being so gracious; both Betsy and I did. Ronie gave her a hug and a kiss on the cheek with the same patient grace that she had for anyone who was overly attentive to her.

"She was nice," Ronie said as I buckled her in. She looked wan and ready for a nap. "Really nice, but she didn't really know about Oz, not really."

"Of course not," Betsy said. "Who could know as much as you do, Ozma?"

"That's *your highness* to you," she said.

And so our little trip to Oz was over. Or so we thought.

On the way out of town, and on our way toward the Oklahoma border, Ronie cried out.

Insanely, I scanned the horizon for cyclones headed our way.

"*Stop,* Daddy! *Stop the car!*"

I pulled over beside an old gray weather-beaten Victorian that sat close to the road. In front hung a large painted sign from a post:

OVER THE RAINBOW
ANTIQUES AND OZ MEMEROBILIA

"Oh, honey," Betsy clucked. "We already went through the gift shop at the museum. You are tired. Let's head out of Kansas and get some early dinner. Okay?"

"It doesn't look like its open anyway," I added.

"It's open," Ronie said fumbling with her seat belt. "And I need to go in there!"

"Yes, *your highness,*" I said and met Betsy's concerned look with a smirk and a shrug.

I had to trot to beat Ronie to the door. The unwashed windows gave the place a used-up look. Dust filled the slanting sunbeams when I knocked. Nothing happened. Ronie reached past me and pressed a door bell.

An old synthesized version of the famous song filled the porch. I winced. Ronie smiled.

The door opened with the smell of cats and lilac powder. A wizened old woman with dark swathes about her rheumy eyes opened the door. She wore a polyester green sweater shirt and no bra. She wore torn bunny slippers on her feet.

"Well, hello, strangers, welcome!" She smiled and revealed a mouth containing a few stained and unclean teeth. I could hear the nearly sub audible intake of breath from Betsy behind me. A dental assistant, Betsy had teeth issues. She hadn't taken Ronie's flaking and failing chompers easily.

"Hello," Ronie piped up from my elbow. "Do you know the way to Oz?"

"Well, no darling, I don't. Do you?"

"No," Ronie admitted.

"But, I *do* have a lot of things I have collected about the land of Oz. Would you like to see them?"

"Yes, I would!" Ronie said.

"Well, all right then," she smiled and then turned the smile to me. It did not inspire any confidence in me.

"I'm sorry," the old woman said. "I'm Dorothy Woodrow. It's nice to meet you."

"I'm Hal Tatum, this is my wife Betsy, and this is…Ronie."

"You're real name is Dorothy?" Ronie asked, breathless.

"Yes, most call me Dotty, though, dear." She lifted a palsied hand and patted Ronie's rainbow colored fishing cap with it.

"I wish my name was Dorothy," Ronie said.

"Well, I think Ronie is a wonderful name, beautiful, really. But tell me, is it Gillikinese or Munchkinlander?" She winked, and Ronie managed a little giggle. "Shall we?" She said, and opened the door wide and motioned toward row after row of old store shelves filled with bric-a-brac. A long haired cat jumped up in surprise and dashed out of sight. "I'm sure we have your heart's desire lying around here somewhere, Ronie."

"Well, that is what we came for," I murmured to Betsy with a shrug and held the door for her. Ronie was already walking up the aisles putting a tentative hand out here and there, to jostle a scarecrow bobble head, or trace a line in the dust covering an emerald city snow globe.

When she turned a corner, her right knee seemed to buckle and Ronie started to fall. Some Popsicle stick marionettes rattled as she caught herself. Betsy ran to scoop her up. Ronie waved her away with a hand.

"She's a tired poop-shute, that she is, dear thing," Dotty Woodrow observed.

"She's very sick," I said.

"Yes." She said, and licked her lips. "Honey, that poster was autographed by honest-to-God real Munchkins," she called out. Ronie nodded her head and moved on.

She disappeared around the corner and then let out a tiny gasp.

"*Ronie!*" I yelled, feeling glued down in syrup next to that old woman, that old witch. That was what I felt at the time, and I guess I still do. The woman was a witch.

We came around the corner and found Ronie looking up at a set of old china figures. Her mouth was open and she nodded at them. Then suddenly she burst into laughter and grinned at me.

"Aren't they wonderful?" Ronie laughed, pointing.

I looked at the dusty china figures carefully and then at the colorful oz merchandise hanging all around us and then at my daughter. She continued to gawk and stare at the quaint set of old fashioned china figures, so I gave them a closer study. A stout farmer stood proudly with his hands stuffed into his overalls. A matron, equally stout, presumably the farmer's wife, held a bouquet of flowers. A young jack of a boy with a wicked grin of mischief balanced on one leg and was either tossing jacks or playing some rustic form of *bocce* ball. A very happy milkmaid grinned benevolently while she hoisted two pales of milk from a stick over her shoulders. Why was the milkmaid smiling so broadly? What wicked rendezvous was the milkmaid returning from to make her smile so? *Why were the milkmaids always so happy*? I wondered distantly to myself. Certainly the life of rising early in the morn' to dodge cow kicks and meadow muffins wouldn't cause that kind of bliss. Beside her was a cream white cow, which of course was also smiling. A ring of lacquered violet flowers entwined its neck. Suddenly my mind hearkened back to the Keats poem I had memorized for intro to Lit class in college:

> *To what green altar, O mysterious priest,*
> *Lead'st thou that heifer lowing at the skies,*
> *And all her silken flanks with garlands drest?*

A shiver ran through me with the thought. My daughter had asked me if I found them wonderful. The truth is I didn't. Looking at them, I felt a staleness of presence, a distinct quality of quiet despair that had something to do with the accumulation of dust and time.

Ronie reached up, grabbed my shirt front and pulled me down so that her mouth was at my ear.

"We have to get them out of here," she whispered.

"Ah, those," Dotty Woodrow said. We both startled. Her presence and the smell of decaying lilacs surrounded us. "I was told by my mother, bless her soul, that those are authentic china people from the outskirts of Quadling country. Such a beautiful set, isn't it?" She put a hand out again to rest it on Ronie's head. Ronie stepped sideways under the protection of my arm.

Betsy was suddenly flanking Ronie's other side. I had the distinct impression that she did so protectively.

"Are you sure, Ronie, those are what you want? There are plenty of other things that..." Betsy started.

Are what? I wondered, *less breakable?* Suddenly I thought I understood the unconscious sensibilities of my little fragile girl. I thought of her swimming, pale and bruised surrounded by the colorful and dynamic children at the resort pool.

"Yes," she said simply and a hand encircled mine and squeezed with tenacity.

"Well, it looks like our minds are made up," I said suddenly and the lady grunted and turned and went off looking for a shoebox and tissue paper.

I paid the woman too much, I knew it. Ronie's hand kept tugging at mine, and it only exasperated my own desire to flee the dusty warren of knick knacks where this woman ruled like a witch queen from a an old storybook.

"You should have bartered her a little," Betsy said when we got back to the car.

"Let it go," I said, which was rude. But I was tired, as we all were. Ronie slept in the back seat all the way to the airport, clutching that shoebox in her lap.

On the flight home Ronie sat between Betsy and I, instead of busily scanning from the window seat for signs of twisters. I assumed she wanted to feel safe after a long and tiring journey. I felt relief, but a sense of bewildering disappointment, as well. The dream trip was done and over, and all Ronie had to show for it was a shoebox full of antique figurines on her lap. She clutched it jealously too, especially after the flight attendant asked her if she could store it in the overhead compartment for her.

An hour in and she put a sluggish pale hand on my arm.

"Daddy, hold them for me. I'm getting too tired."

"Of course, sweetie."

"But, hold on tight, Dad, don't let go!" And then she leaned against her mother and drifted into a deep sleep. Sitting there watching but not listening to a period drama, I clutched that shoebox tight, as if it contained my sweet Ronie's life.

Life entered this strange twilight spiral after that. At work, and then walking across the parking lot at the supermarket, I had this strange feeling like I was sinking, that it took a whole lot of concentration to stay on top of the ground, as if it were a thin crust of February ice over very deep and suffocating snow. I know Betsy felt it, too, but even at night when we were smoking on the front porch like bad kids, *especially* at night, we did not talk about it. Instead, we talked about things that had happened to us together when we first met; when we were first married. I suppose it was our way of gearing up to the time when we would find ourselves, inevitably alone again without Ronie. We felt guilty about it. I know I did. We only did it when we were out there, but then talk would come around to our childhood, or the silly things Ronie had done as a toddler, and we would be back up there using mouthwash and checking in on our little girl.

She slept a lot, or at least I thought she did. But I wonder, because sometimes I would be tiptoeing past her door and I would hear her babbling quietly inside.

"Hey, kiddo, what's happening?" I would whisper. We were always whispering, then, I realize now. I suppose we were really worried about waking some cranky librarian's wrath so that she would turn us out and there would never be anymore summer reading for us, no more trips to Oz, or Narnia, or laughing at the precociousness of Matilda or Ramona.

"Dad, the family was just telling me about the trouble Lula-Belle got in when she got loose and wandered out of Quadling territory. They had quite an adventure, very dangerous. They have to be very careful you know, Dad. They are made of China."

"You know, you're right there, sweetie," I said.

"But Pipo was very brave," she said pointing to the little boy leaning over on one leg. Then her face turned a little pink and she put her shaved head down and giggled. I don't know why this alarmed me so, the girl was all by herself with her ailment and she was a creative girl, but it did. I maneuvered myself between the girl's line of sight and the figurines on the low shelf.

"Why don't you tell me about it," I said.

She said she would, but only if I got out of the way, so they could correct her if she forgot something or started to tell it wrong.

This went on the rest of that August. Betsy and I marveled at the clarity of the stories, the detail in the descriptions of life on the edge of Quadling territory that came pouring out of Ronie.

"*She could be a writer...*" we would start, but would not finish, for our little Ronie was getting weaker all the time. It was getting to the point where we were afraid of calling the doctor for fear that she would be taken into the hospital and would not come out again.

She should have been a writer, but we never said it. It would have been too awful. It still is.

Another fear fell on both of us when Ronie started to ask vigilantly for the date. As the end of August came closer, we feared that when she responded to the date by saying: "Well, good, then there's still time." , that she was hoping to return to school with everyone else, take a seat beside Tracy and get on with business as usual. Even if Ronie had felt up for it, we couldn't have let her go.

"Kids are germ factories," the oncologist had reminded us at the end of the school year.

"Still time for what?" Betsy finally asked. She has always been the brave one.

"Time for the family to get back home," she answered.

"Honey, there is no way we can bring these all the way back to Kansas." She ran one of her cool long fingers down the side of Ronie's face.

"No, not Kansas. Kansas is not their home!" Betsy had that look of exasperated emotionality that traditionally would have indicated that she needed to get to bed and rest up so she could put back on her game face. But, she was already in bed. "Why do you think they can't move?"

"Sweetie…," I said, sitting with gentle paternalism on the bed. "They can't move, because they are made out of China. That's just what they are, china figures."

"*No!* You don't get it, because you can't hear them." Her voice and her little pointer finger shook in the air. "They can move when they are where they belong." Her voice was getting higher with uncharacteristic anger.

"Okay, funny pants. Don't get all worked up," Betsy said, smoothing the bed sheets over Ronie's lap.

"If the china people, (*I refused to say family*) are bothering you, I can take them out of here."

"Don't you dare!" She cried.

"Hey, I just thought if they, *you know*, were talking all night. I thought you could use your sleep."

"I can sleep when I'm dead," she said, putting her arms over her chest. We had heard this in some movie we had watched together, and I snorted, as I have always done, when Ronie used a quote like that to over-dramatize her life.

Betsy was not laughing, and the look she and Ronie gave me cut mine short.

"Honey, we just want to understand," Betsy said. "How does the family expect to get back home if they can't move?"

"Well, they explained that part to me," Ronie said. "They need the right kind of storm to get home."

"Which is *where?*" I asked.

"Oz, *silly head*," she responded and rolled her eyes up at me. "You know, like when Dorothy got pulled back. It has something to do with what happens to the air. Anyway, they said they have been keeping track, and now that they are out of the witch's house, (*We had never said it out loud to each other, but we all knew what she meant*) they can feel the weather more. They will be able to tell when a storm like that is coming. They think one may be building soon."

"And then what will happen?" Betsy asked in her best getting this over so you can rest your silly head and get some sleep voice.

"We take them to where they need to go. Then they go home and they are free to move again." She said this with the gracious hand sweeping of a cartoon narrator wrapping up a happy ending.

"Well, you tell us when, all right?" I said. And we kissed her three times each and turned out the light. Truth is: I didn't remember the conversation till after. There are too many worries, too many things to occupy folks that live on the edge of an emotional cliff.

It had rained a lot that summer, but the sky relented by mid August and we had enjoyed a clear, warm and sunny month. That weather built up one heck of a storm that finally broke over us on the equinox. Some of the leaves on the trees of our road had started to change, but we hadn't noticed. Ronie had taken a turn for the worse, and we understood that it would be a matter of days before we made that fateful trip to the oncology respite ward.

"I was hoping for one more Halloween," I said to Betsy as she went out for errands. She had taken a leave from work, and I tried to give her as many breaks from the house as I could.

"I know, Cookinhow, me too." She used the nickname that she had pinned me with when we were just dating. She had seen the tears in my eyes. "Get your work done. I'll be home with Ben and Jerry's." I might as well have taken a leave from the office, too. I had all but physically done so. The paperwork had piled up as I surfed the internet or stared out the window. Now, it was time to pay the piper, on a Friday night. I sighed, and she ruffled my hair.

She went out, pulling the hood of her raincoat over her head. It had already started to downpour. I watched her dash to the car and then proceeded to bite down and peck away at the massive pile of paperwork that awaited me.

I feel guilty about it now, how good it felt to bury myself in work for that hour and a half. I forgot about everything and watched the pile get smaller and smaller. The wind began to howl something wicked outside our house, Thunderheads rumbled hard overhead, but I hardly noticed.

"Hal?" Betsy's voice came from the front door. "Didn't you hear me honking?" I looked up in a daze from my work and the entire house lit up from a brilliant stroke of lightning. Then the world stumbled down with thunder.

"Well, no, I was-"

"How's Ronie doing?" Betsy asked.

"Good, I guess. I mean I've been pretty busy here."

"You haven't checked on her?" She had that bewildered frustrated look she always gets. I always imagine it should come accompanied by the words; *you used the family cat to wipe your ass after taking a dump?* I shrugged, and looked to the side. "Oh, Jesus, the poor girl's probably scared to death!"

"Hey, I'm sorry…," I started. But Betsy was already moving toward the stairs. I followed her, my socks getting wet from where she walked before me with her wet shoes. At the top of the stairs she spared one more glance of quizzical contempt at me and opened Ronie's door.

Ronie was no longer in her bed. She was not on the floor beside the bed. She was not at the closet, nor was she hiding inside. As Betsy rummaged through the room, my eyes fell on the low shelf near her bed. The china figures were gone.

"Ronie!" Betsy let out her first desperate scream.

"Betsy!" I pointed out the empty shelf. We looked at each other, and could see the memory of that strange conversation we had with Ronie come bubbling back to the surface.

"Oh, *Jesus*, Hal," she said. Her fear had surmounted her frustration with me. She ran past me screaming our little girl's name down the stairs and through the house. Instinctively I ran to the back door off the kitchen and peered out the window to the rain lashed world beyond. I opened the door and the down pouring rush of sound came in. I peered across the back yard toward the river. The neighbor's trees lashed out and down at our little gazebo and Betsy's garden fence. Another lightning strobe lit the world all around, and my eyes fell on the back gate of the yard fence, where the ground dipped down to some trees before the river. I thought I saw a tiny figure moving there amongst them.

"*Ronie!*" I screamed and bolted out into the storm in my stocking feet.

I paused at the gate, scanning the trees that struggled to survive in the flood plain of the river. The river had been low after the long dry spell, the trees' roots showing over the detritus from the river's wash out. Soon, probably by the time this storm had run its course, much of it would be underwater again. Then I made out a pale figure moving away under the gloom of the trees and I screamed her name again.

Betsy was at my side.

"Is she there? Do you see her?" I had, but I didn't, now. Betsy and I nearly knocked each other over as we came through the gate and down the grassy bank. Wet Sumac leaves slapped and clung to me as I barreled through where I guessed my little girl had passed by not long before, unhindered. Betsy and I came out of the undergrowth into a clear dank spot of riverbed clay just as the world lit up once again with lightning.

"*Catch her, Hal, before she gets to the river!*" Betsy roared. And then I saw her too. A little skeleton stood alone in the thrashing storm under the last of the river trees. I could not make out the river from here, but I knew it could not be far off.

And then I was at her side, gripping that little boney shoulder. Betsy clung to her other side.

"Ronie!" Betsy was crying with relief. She hugged the girl. "Come back inside, young lady," she said.

"No, Mom! It's working. *Look!*" she said. Betsy pulled away. The empty sodden shoebox that Ronie had kept under her bed had been caved in from the embrace.

Something white skittered a few feet ahead of us in the gloom. I raised my foot with the instinct to defend me and mine from some river rat.

"*No, Dad!*" Ronie yelled. The china cow moved in the sodden leaves on the dark Earth. Sensing danger it turned and loped further toward the river. Somewhere in my mind I noticed that the rain had seemed to stop. Lightning flashed again and I could see other pale shining china figures struggling through the sodden debris. I took a step forward. From behind a stick a little china boy, the one from her shelf, peeked out and put his hands to his ears and stuck a china tongue out at me. He laughed an eerie chime of a laugh and scurried after the others.

"They are doing it! *They are going to Oz!*" Ronie yelled in a high broken voice. I looked up to where she was pointing.

Instead of the last few trees and then the dark rushing of the river, I saw the land sloping ever slightly upward and a clear trail running through a great forest of old thick trees. Will-o-wisps danced there in the dark deep. Where they lit, I saw large hideous faces rising out of the bark on those trees. The ancient gnarled branches shifted and grasped like huge hands in the wind. And then I thought, *No, they are not going to Oz. Oz is coming to us.*

The air shifted around us, crackling with ozone. What colors there were in the dark popped out at us, as if lit from a strange moon. The will-o-wisps floated closer.

My little girl ran forward to meet them.

"*No!*" I screamed, and it was a jealous desperate scream. Betsy, beautiful, strong Betsy pulled her back, wrestling with her. Suddenly the girl screeched and clawed like a wild animal.

"Ronie, stop!" Betsy pleaded.

"No, they want me to come with them. They said I can stay with them! Let me go!" She cried and reached out to where the little china figures were disappearing from view.

"*Please, Ronie,*" I shouted. "We need you. We need you to stay with us." But Ronie was beyond reaching with words. She bucked and screamed, and flailed helplessly in our grasp.

"*Come on,*" I yelled and nearly picked up both of the girls in my arms and drove them away from the strange colors, the looming giant faces of the trees.

And then we were back in the storm under the bank before the gate, the rain pelting down and our little girl flailing like a pale fish pulled from the river. We went through the gate, Betsy sobbing and the girl, now screeching a hoarse hiss and flailing.

Inside the house, her protestations surrendered to spasms and terrible chattering of teeth.

"I'll run a warm bath," I said.

"No, the storm. Just help me get her back to the room and dry!" Betsy ordered.

We did so, rubbing the girl down vigorously with a towel. She came around enough to keen again, her face contorted.

"*Ronie, boney girl I love. Ronie, boney girl I love.*" Betsy kept chanting trying to sooth the little girl and herself. The things I had seen buffeted my mind, like the storm against the house, outside.

Finally, miserably, the girl's sobs subsided and she fell against the bed sheets. We covered her shaking body and the both of us lay on each side of her, rubbing her gently.

"Should we take her to the hospital?" I whispered to my wife.

"I don't know," she said, her eyes swollen. "And tell them what? We didn't realize that our little girl was out by the river in the worst storm of the year?"

I deserved the anger in her voice.

"I'm sorry baby, I'm sorry." I didn't know to whom I was speaking.

"It's all right. It's all right," Betsy crooned. "Our little girl is safe with Mommy and Daddy again."

Ronie let out a few more wails and subsided back into slumber. She stayed very still, and I resisted the awful impulse to check her for a pulse.

"Oz," She said simply and Betsy and I looked at each other from over the girl's sleeping form.

Later, she stirred and her eyes fluttered open.

"It's all right, Mommy," Ronie said. "At least the family is safe. They can move again because they are home." And she smiled such a sweet sad smile, that tears took away my sight and a sob escaped me. Then the girl sighed and fell deeper to sleep. Ronie looked up at me, with pleading eyes, streaming tears. I did not know what to do, and we held each other over her as she slept and tried to cry as quietly as we could.

We stayed like that a long time. Ronie slept soundly.

"Let's go have a smoke," I whispered to Betsy.

"You go. I need to stay with her," Betsy said.

"I'll stay, too."

"No, go. You can watch her when I go out later." Reluctantly I did so, kissing Ronie on the curve of her forehead. Betsy sucked in her breath. I went to Betsy and kissed her a long time on the side of her mouth, then I went downstairs and out on the front porch.

I smoked deeply, inhaling the tobacco smoke and breathing it out my nose and mouth. The storm was relenting. By the time I had cast the blazing butt out into the wet dark, I realized the only dripping was the water coming off the roof and the leaves of nearby trees. A strange suffocating calm filled the night.

Gingerly, I opened the front door and began to shut it behind me.

"*Hal!*" Betsy cried from above. The hair stood up on the back of my neck.

I came up the stairs but did not feel them against my feet.

Betsy was standing at the doorway, her eyes huge and rimmed with swollen dark in the hall light.

"Hal," She managed. I went to her across the hallway, reading too much in those eyes, the terrible shock of her face.

I went into Ronie's room.

Inside her bed our little girl had turned completely into china. Her thin delicate fingers on the coverlet and the curve of her forehead, where I had kissed her, gleamed in the half-light. She would not move again.

THE END.

DOROTHY OF KANSAS

by JW Schnarr

It was a world of silt and ash, and snow. Burned things. Ruined things. The air was thick with foul gas and smoke. The stench of death was on the air like an afterthought. And it *was*. The sun was lost to permanent gloom; the trees were uprooted and black and dead. Cow corpses laid rotted and stiff in the fields beside the farmers who once tended them. No flies buzzed on the putrescent flesh. Their long cow faces withered and pulled back in hideous leers; they bared their teeth in death as much as their smiles had born them in life.

But joy had moved on from Oz. Life had moved on.

Tin Man walked endlessly. The snow that fell gave him a sickly warmth that he didn't trust. He could feel it everywhere, from the top of his rusting head down to the stubs of feet where his toes had worn away. He was a deep red now, a flaking leper with holes in his limbs and torso.

Not tin, after all. *Tin* wouldn't rust like this. But the the acidic snow that fell in Oz had stripped the galvanized plate off him years ago, and shortly after he'd noticed the first specs of red like tiny cancer dots on his chest. There was no trace of shiny tin on him now. All gone. With everything else. All he had left was his axe.

And the head of Scarecrow, which he kept in rusty old garden bucket.

"We should get out of the snow for a while," Scarecrow said, watching as Tin Man fingered a particularly bad hole in his gut. His stumpy, worn

177

down fingers only succeeded in making the hole bigger. When he pulled his hand away the metal flesh crumbled and fell into the snow at his feet. The sickly yellow bricks beneath the snow seemed to gobble it up.

"I need to keep walking," Tin man said. He wiped snow from his shoulders, then shook the pail to get some snow off Scarecrow's face.

"You're not thinking with your head," Scarecrow said. "If you rust away to nothing we'll never get anywhere."

"If I rust away to nothing you'll be the last person left alive in all of Oz," Tin Man said in a sad voice. "Wouldn't that just break your heart."

"Exactly why you should get out of the snow!" Scarecrow said.

"It hasn't stopped snowing in months," Tin Man said. "Besides, where do we go?"

"That's not true," Scarecrow mumbled, but his voice meant he was going to drop the issue. "Sometimes it's ash."

Where they would *go* was Kansas, of course. Their one chance of finding Dorothy was there. It was more of a *hope* than a chance. Ironic that the last bit of hope left in all of Oz was the hope that they could somehow find a way out of the ruined little world. Maybe Dorothy could fix things. On the other hand, maybe Dorothy was dead already. Maybe this was little more than something to keep their minds busy until Tin Man's legs finally gave out and they'd lie in the acidic snow to sleep and melt away to nothing.

"We should get out of the snow for a while," Scarecrow said again. Then he brightened. Hey, I think this is where we met Lion!"

"It's just more ruined forest," Tin Man said.

"Try to remember it from the old days," Scarecrow said. "Back when everything was verdant and fresh, and there were Lions in the woods."

Tin Man tried not to think about the old days. Colour made him sad. His world was devoid of it now, save for the rust on his body and the paint on Scarecrow's face.

Even the straw in Scarecrow's head was bleached out and full of mud. He was long overdo for a change. Problem was all the straw in Oz was gone. Now Scarecrow's mind slipped; he broke into random bits of song or he repeated sentences over and over until Tin Man wanted to toss him into the snow and leave him there. When the last bit of straw finally rotted away to nothing it would take the final bits of the Scarecrow with it.

Other times, he felt bad for his last friend. Here was a mighty King of Oz, sitting in a busted up garden pail slowly losing his mind.

But mostly he felt bad that they had both lived to see their beautiful land become this charred, dead wasteland.

They hadn't seen another living thing in weeks.

The last one had been an apple tree. It had wandered into the black and metallic sludge of a river and simply stood there staring while Tin Man and

Scarecrow crossed a little cobblestone bridge nearby. Tin Man had made eye contact, briefly, but the look on the tree's face told him all he needed to know. It was sucking pure poison into its roots, either out of a need to drink or a need to be dead. It didn't matter. Woodsman and mighty tree, enemies once, but no more. Just three survivors, cursed to witness the end.

"Do you think she'll be there?" Scarecrow asked. "Dorothy I mean."

"*I know what you mean*," Tin Man snapped. "But I don't know. I would like to say I hope she is, but my heart tells me it won't matter. At this point what can be done?"

"She could get me some clean straw," Scarecrow said. "From the mattress or something. I wouldn't even care if it smelled like sweat and pee. I can feel myself getting dumber, Tin Man. I'm having a hard time remembering things."

"And you repeat yourself," Tin Man said. "*Ad Nauseum.*"

"What?"

Tin Man sighed.

"It means to the point of sickness." He saw the look on Scarecrow's face change to hurt confusion, and he immediately felt bad that he'd said anything. "Sorry. I know it's not your fault."

"You know that not long ago I was regarded as the smartest man in Oz?" Scarecrow said. "To think I started out as straw and potato sacks. And paint."

"Quite an amazing feat, especially for a Scarecrow," Tin Man said.

"Espec..."Scarecrow said, then stopped, catching himself. "Err yes, it is quite an achievement for a man of my upbringing. To think I started out as straw and potato sacks."

"And paint," Tin Man added quickly.

"And paint, yes," Scarecrow said brightly. "You are no dullard yourself, my good woodsman. Don't ever let anyone say otherwise."

If we ever see anyone again, Tin Man thought, but he didn't say it.

They walked on through the gloom. The only sound to be heard was the wraith-like flutter of snow hitting the ground and the tireless crunch as the Tin Man's stutter-step compressed it underfoot. The Yellow Brick Road was pitted and scarred after years of acid baths; here and there the edges had given way completely. It had been a gleaming symbol of the magic and wonder of Oz for millenia. Now it was a ruined old path that was slowing dissolving away to nothing.

Same could have been said of the Emerald City. Of course Tin Man had gone there first. From the stench of decay and the layering of bodies in the streets it appeared as if everyone had. Fled their homes for the first time in real fear for their lives, even though they could never die in Oz and they could never get more than a tummy ache from over indulging.

They also found graffiti as the Winkies and Munchkins first begged Dorothy for salvation; then, when they realized no help was coming, turned against her. One message, scrawled in emerald paint on the outside of a large *Greenfish* fountain where he'd found Scarecrow's head said simply *I hope you live to see this Ditty.*

Dorothy never came, and that is why they hated her. They'd waited for salvation at the end of their lives and in the end they were met with a soft falling ash mixed with dirty, acidic snow. That was bad. The snow fell on the crops and killed all the plants, and it fell in the water and poisoned it. And *that* was really bad.

When the creatures of Oz finally turned on one another out of feral starvation and insanity, that was much, much worse.

Eventually Tin Man and Scarecrow came to a fork in the road beside the ruins of a little cornfield. In the center of the cornfield stood a crooked cross leaning dangerously to one side. Like it was trying to lay down and die but couldn't out of some misguided need to assure their faith. Tin Man wanted to tell the cross that it was alright, that Scarecrow was too smart for faith and he himself felt to betrayed by his life too ever feel anything again.

Scarecrow's eyes widened when he saw it though.

"Hey!" he said. "*This is it!* This is where Dorothy found me!"

"Is it?" Tin Man said. "I wouldn't know. I guess we passed the enchanted forest, but I didn't notice. We walked right by my old home."

"We would have seen it," Scarecrow said. "If it were still standing."

"I suppose you're right," Tin Man sighed.

"You know what that means?"

"No."

"It means were getting close. I don't think Dorothy traveled many miles on her own before we met. She'd only just begun her walk. It *means* we're in Munchkin country. My pole was just at the edge of it."

"Well, we should keep walking then," Tin Man said. He brushed the snow from his shoulders. Flakes of rust glittered in the gray air like bloody dandruff.

They walked on, passing burned farmsteads and ruined crops. There were more scarecrows too, but they were long dead and their straw was waxy and burnt. Some were little more than potato sacks hung from crosses with barbed wire. There was nothing for the Tin Man to salvage here. No fresh dressings for Scarecrow.

Eventually they came to a spot in the road where the burnt shell of a house blocked their way. The wood was frosted with ash and carbon, and scaly to the touch like a gigantic spider husk. Here and there the wood splintered on weak supports; the roof had collapsed some time ago under the weight of the snow.

"Here it is," Scarecrow said. "This is where it all began."

"Seems like a lifetime ago," said Tin Man. Looking around at the death and ruin, he added, "Two lifetimes."

"Eight years, four months, thirteen days," Scarecrow counted. "twenty-six minutes. Of course, that's from when I got my brain. Before that I listened as the winds of idiocy blew knowledge in one ear and out the other. I was even too stupid to realize how sad it should have made me."

"My life has always been like this," Tin Man replied. "Misery with gaps of darkness. It makes me wonder why I ever wanted that damn heart back, all the pain it's caused. now I can't even feel it anymore. I think it's ruined."

"I understand what you're saying," Scarecrow said.

"Do you?" Tin Man turned and looked down into the bucket. "I feel like it isn't just this metal body thats rusting away. I feel as though my very *soul* is melted, and putting one foot in front of the other is all I have to keep the beat of my heart now. Only I'm half lame from my feet rusting away, and my steps aren't strong like a heart should be. They're sick and dying. But I don't care about that, because now I know that there are things worse than death. *There's this.*"

He reached down and grabbed a handful of snow, and sprinkled it into the bucket over Scarecrow's face.

"*Hey*," Scarecrow said, spitting his words. He wrinkled his nose to get the last of the snow off his face, because it burned and he didn't trust it on his burlap flesh.

"I'm sorry," Tin Man said. "That was mean. I shouldn't be laying this on you, you don't even have a shoulder to lean on."

"It's alright," Scarecrow said. "I see what you are saying. Oz in ruins hurts my heart too. Especially when I think of everything we've lost."

As they spoke, Tin Man walked through the house. It was a museum. Or had been, with little ropes tying everything off and signs that said:

No Touching! This means you Hurly Applebottom!

On the other side of the house Tin Man stepped through the back door and out onto the Yellow Brick Road again.

Eventually, Dorothy's house was a memory on the horizon. Tin Man kept a beat with his shuffle step, and Scarecrow talked about theorums and hypotheses. They moved away from burned trees and ruined Munchkin huts and out into the grasslands. As they passed one last farmhouse, Scarecrow squinted his eyes and shook his bucket.

"Hey, what is that?"

On the side of the road was a little red wagon, filled with toys. There was a discomforting lump under the snow. Tin Man gave it a wide berth.

"*Oh*," Scarecrow said. "That has the dimensions of a Munchkin child. A girl, from the shape of the head. How tragic."

"Just shut up for a little while," Tin Man said. "I need some peace and quiet."

"I don't see how that's possible," Scarecrow said. "You whistle like a teapot now with those holes in your belly. It's a wonder you get a moment's rest at all."

Tin Man looked down at the corroded holes in his body and sighed. His friend was right of course, the sound made him crazy. And the holes were getting bigger with every passing mile it seemed. The one he had fit a finger into just a few days before was now big enough for *two* fingers.

They walked on and Scarecrow tried to talk less, but his straw was giving out on him and he forgot to be quiet after a time.

Days later they came to the end of civilized Oz. They knew this because there was a sign in Munchkinese that said:

YOU ARE NOW LEAVING THE CIVIL LANDS OF OZ.
THE CREATURES WHO ROAM THESE LANDS
ARE LESS THAN CIVIL-OZ'D.
Signed,
Your Mayor.

Scarecrow snorted a quick laugh.

"*Civil-Oz'd*," he said.

Tin Man said nothing. He walked ahead, following the Yellow Brick Road to its final destination.

"Come on," Scarecrow said. "It's kind of funny, right?"

"Shut up," Tin Man said, but he looked away. Rust flaked off his face when his mouth twitched.

Around him, the snow and ash fell on dirt, here and there rough Pine trees snaked out of the grass like giant skeletal fingers. They bore trunks of charred wood and their pine needles were gray ash. The air was as greasy as everywhere else in Oz. If not for the sign, one might not even notice where the Uncivil-Oz'd lands started and the Civil-Oz'd lands began. One thing the badlands had going for them was that they were much less likely to encounter death out here.

And just as unlikely to encounter life.

They walked on. Always pushing on. Always moving toward their goal. *Dorothy*. If she could be reached, Tin Man would reach her. He began using the handle end of his axe as a cane. The bucket that he kept Scarecrow's head in rusted and broke at the handle. He bent the sheared metal back so the straw man didn't lose an eye and carried the bucket under his arm like a football.

Eventually the pine tree fingers were gone too, and the horizon was a dirty yellow smudge in front of them. The land ahead of them looked like foothills, but Tin Man knew of no mountains in this part of the world. He continued to tap the ground beneath the snow with the handle of his axe. When the axe sank into the snow a lot further than it should have, Tin Man pulled up in alarm.

"What is it?" Scarecrow said.

"The road gave way," Tin Man said. He began kicking snow to the sides of the road.

"Careful," said Scarecrow. "Could be a sink hole."

"I don't know what that means," said Tin Man. "If it is, be sure to tell me."

As it turned out, it *wasn't* a sinkhole. The Road simply ended with a smooth set of alternating bricks, perfectly flat like the corner of a brick wall. One step past the road, the hard packed earth gave way to dirty yellow sand.

"We're finally here," Scarecrow said.

"Oh yeah?" Tin Man said. "Where is that exactly?"

"Well, technically here is *nowhere*," he replied. "But even nowhere is somewhere. That is to say, We can't be nowhere, because the moment we arrive at nowhere we are somewhere."

"Scarecrow!" Tin Man said, giving the bucket a shake. "Please snap out of it."

"Huh? Oh yes. This is the End of Oz. The yellow Brick Road ends precisely where the Great Desert of Sand and Dunes begins. But since we're in the middle of nowhere..."

"Spare me, please," Tin Man said. "Are we still going the right direction?"

"Again," Scarecrow said. "It depends on your perspective."

Tin Man sighed wearily.

"Explain please," he said. "And *please* make sense."

"Well, according to folklore, there are many ways out of Oz. Too many, in fact, which is why Glinda made the realm invisible. Because at every spot people could get *out*, other people could get *in*. *Bad People*. The King of the Gnomes, for example."

"Your point being..."

"My point is that once *out* of Oz, Any way we travel could theoretically take us away from Oz. Maybe to Kansas, maybe to Wonderland. Pretty much anywhere you want, nobody knows for sure.It was all very *hush-hush* stuff in the Emerald City, as we didn't want the common folk to know how easy the defenses of Oz could be breached."

"So we could end up a million miles away from Kansas?" Tin Man said. "Terrific."

"Yes and No. As I said, once out of Oz, one could end up *anywhere*."

Tin Man shook his head.

"Don't worry my friend," Scarecrow said, trying to be reassuring. "We'll end up in Kansas, you'll see."

"But how do you know?" Tin Man said.

"Because we wish it," Scarecrow said. "And thinking makes it so."

"I can't argue that logic," Tin Man said.

"You are a *wOz* man to listen and understand," Scarecrow said, and burst into a shower of giggles.

I wonder how long he's been mad, Tin Man thought. *And I wonder why I never noticed until just now.*

Tin Man stepped off the Yellow Brick Road. His feet sank to the ankles in snow and sand.

"Great," he said. "I'm gonna get bogged down, I know it."

"Step lively, Tin soldier!" Scarecrow chirped. "Knees high lad! That'll keep you out of the sand."

The desert was a gray and blond ocean washing as far as either of them could see. There was a chemical smell to the sand, like burnt metal, and the sound of silt and grit hitting the Tin Man's rusted torso was like listening to water hitting an empty bucket. He felt it inside him, cold and alien, and after a while he closed a hand over the holes in his belly to try and keep some of it out. The wind whistled around them as well, and it was getting more difficult to see.

Tin Man put his head down and marched, high step, as Scarecrow had suggested, but the going was slow and dangerous, and several times they almost fell down the long dunes washing about them. The more he thought on it the more Tin Man began to think of the desert as a *real ocean*; an unstable surface that shifted moment to moment. He knew if he fell or got trapped in the dunes they might not be able to get out. And there was nobody left to save them.

Sand also got into his joints, making them creak and strain. His knee began locking up after a week in the sand, and he took to dragging it the way one might drag an artificial leg. The irony of that statement wasn't lost on the Scarecrow. He howled like a coyote when Tin Man mentioned it.

The sun rose one morning but they couldn't really see it, and there was a rolling thunder in the distance that Tin Man didn't like.

"We may want to find some shelter," Scarecrow said. "From what I've read about desert storms they can be quite unpleasant. The sand might scour the rust off you, and then where would you be?"

"In the bucket with you, maybe." Tin Man said. He cupped a hand over his eyes and scanned the horizon but it was an exercise in futility. He couldn't see more than a few hundred feet in front of him. The wind kicked up a blanket of sand in all directions, mixing it with silt and ash, scouring the Tin Man's rusting frame, and affecting the topography of the great desert. With an eternal gray wall blocking the sun's rays, the land was cold but arid; the lack of moisture was at least *something* the Tin Man could be thankful for.

They had no choice but to move on. With luck they might skirt the edge of the sandstorm, but they had no way of affecting that luck. They could only walk blind and hope.

Gradually the storm picked up and they became aware of a new noise; a gentle, crystal twinkling that carried like wind chimes to their ears. Tin Man actually stopped so he could listen better.

"What is that?" he said. "Faeries?"

"Hardly," Scarecrow said. His head was half buried in sand. "Could be a hallucination brought on by madness. Doesn't explain why *you'd* hear it too though, unless that's all part of my delusion. On the other hand it could just be a wind chime."

I hate when you talk like that," Tin Man grumbled. "It's confusing."

"Well, maybe there's an old airship or something in the dunes out here. Maybe it *is* really a wind chime. We should check it out, because it there's shelter to be had, we could use it to get away from that sandstorm."

"May as well," Tin Man said. "We're headed in that direction anyway."

The sounds weren't wind chimes. It didn't take long for them to realize there couldn't possibly be an airship out here. It would have been long buried in sand by now. But there was something ahead. Something Tin Man had never seen before.

There were tree-like forms in the gloom ahead of them, and as they neared it became obvious the sound was the wind and sand blowing off these objects. They were tall, black, and appeared to be made from strands of ash. there were more of them around, here and there, randomly scattered about with no discernable pattern. In a couple spots they appeared to overlap each other, grow together. in others they started together and grew apart. They tinkled and made grinding noises as the wind pushed them to and fro, and where their hollow trunks were exposed to the wind they whistled, the way you might whistle by blowing on an empty rum bottle.

"What are they?" Tin Man said. He walked close to one so they could inspect it. "It doesn't look like any tree I've ever seen."

Me either," Scarecrow said. "Is that even wood? It doesn't look like anything but a long string of burnt charcoal coming out of the ground."

"It's not wood," Tin Man said. He reached out and pushed on the trunk. There was a sharp crack as it shattered under his touch and then fell to the ground with a tinkling of shattered crystal.

"It's glass," he said, rubbing his fingers thoughtfully.

"*Oh of course,*" Scarecrow said. "If I had a hand I would slap my forehead with it. These aren't trees, they're *fulgarite!*"

"Huh?" Tin Man said.

"It's glass alright!" Scarecrow said. "These are stalks of petrified lightning! The heat from the lightning turns the sand to glass and makes these wonderful sculptures!"

"If you say so," Tin Man said. "They look like burnt string covered in soap froth, if you ask me. Hardly wonderful at all."

"Well, each one is totally unique, depending on how the lightning strikes it. What I don't get is these are formed in the ground when lightning strikes the *surface*. how can they be jutting out of the ground like this?"

"Maybe they *used* to be underground," Tin Man said. "Maybe the desert moved on and left them behind."

"You're right of course," Scarecrow said. "The amount of displacement around here is stupefying."

Just then the wind gusted, and the petrified lightning erupted in crystalline song. Somewhere ahead of them in the dust, another monstrous crash roared over the wind.

"How many of these things are out there?" Tin Man said.

"Hard to say," Scarecrow said. "But maybe we should move on huh? Wouldn't do to get struck by lightning out here."

They walked carefully between the tall stalks of petrified lightning. Tin Man hugged Scarecrow close to his body to keep the sand out of the bucket, but it did little to stop the bucket from filling. before long all that was visible of the straw man was his eyes, which bounced back and forth worriedly. The wind grew stronger until the chimes turned to shrieks, and the crashing became a constant scream over the wind. Tin Man stepped lively, avoided the crashing stalks of glass, and tried to keep the wind on his right side. It was the only possible way he could even tell which way he was going.

The storm rumbled and chain lightning arced through the sand. Not far off. Tin Man felt the angry roar of thunder as it passed by. Somewhere close, *new* stalks of petrified lightning were being made.

Tin Man turned the bucket to drain sand, but stopped when he noticed he was losing straw as well. instead he turned Scarecrow's head so his mouth wasn't buried.

"*It's inside me,*" Scarecrow yelled. "It feels cold. I don't like it".

"I know," Tin Man said. "We'll get you fixed up when we get out of this."

"Statistically speaking," Scarecrow yelled, "we have an eighty-two percent chance of..."

He trailed off, as though he lost his train of thought.

"*You smell that?*" he shouted instead.

"*Are you kidding?*" Tin Man yelled.

"*Thought I smelled orange blossoms, for a moment there.*"

Tin Man shook the sand from his face. His joints were screaming with every movement. Sand worked its way into every crook in his body. He wouldn't be walking much longer.

Another crash close by, followed by the hum of static in the air and and arc of burning white light not far off. The roar of thunder almost knocked Tin Man off his feet. He could feel the charge in the air. The constant abrasion of sand was causing him to gain a charge of his own; particles of sand and debris began sticking to him on the right side. There were shards of glass in the sand and it made a distinctive plinking noise when it hit him.

Scarecrow was screaming something. Tin Man couldn't hear over the roaring wind.

The world was nothing but sand and glass. There was no sound but the roar of wind and the crash of lightning. Tin man couldn't even see his feet anymore. There was too much debris in the wind.

Then lightning crashed into him, from the back, knocking him flying. The bucket flew from his hands, Scarecrow's screaming face visible for an instant before the wind carried him away, and Tin Man rolled over and over, his metal flesh burning, his skin white hot, the sand melting and coating him like syrup, and he rolled in the sand collecting more of it, his limbs glowing in the after shock and a crack of thunder that made his head feel like it had been split with an axe, and then he was gone and that's all there was to that.

And at some point he became aware that he wasn't dead.

At some point he groaned, and tried to work his mouth bit felt like it had been fused shut. His hands were stuck too, but he forced them to move and whatever was holding them gave away cleanly, and there was a soft tinkle and crunching sound as he brought his hands up to his face. It was perfectly smooth in places; in others it felt pitted and coarse, and he realized that the lightning strike and made him hot enough to melt some of the sand and he was now a lumbering piece of petrified lightning. *Fulgarite*, as the Scarecrow called it.

And where had he gotten off to?

Tin Man sat up. He slapped at his face until the glass fragments gave way, then painfully opened his eyes.

It was a gray world. The sky was a gloomy blanket that blocked out the sun. There was sand around him, but this wasn't the desert. He was sitting in a field, long dead, with endless rows of corn stalks shunted about a foot from the ground. Bone coloured and brittle, and they crumbled in Tin Man's hand. He stood up and looked around.

It was the same in every direction. Corn stalks. Tin Man didn't know where he was. was this place Kansas? it was possible; certainly the stories Dorothy had told them of the gray world she came from seemed to fit what he was seeing now. If this *was* Kansas, Dorothy had no business *ever* wanting to come back here. For anything.

"*Scarecrow!*" Tin Man yelled, putting both hands to his lips. His voice was gravel and dust, and it didn't carry far.

He shouted again, and then started walking. The gray land could have been Oz, if not for the lack of snow. It was just as cold though, and the wind limped along the ground and dragged dirt and pieces of corn stalk with it. Nothing, after the desert wind they'd been through. Not even a nuisance. He leaned over and allowed the sand to escape from the holes in his belly. One was large enough to fit his hand in now. There were spots on his right arm and torso where the rust had actually been scoured away and the dull gleam of metal was visible in streaks. He right ear was completely missing, as was the handle on the whistle at the top of his head.

A short time later he saw a bucket upturned and half full of sand; it was just as rusty as Tin Man himself was and he was sure it was the bucket he'd been keeping Scarecrow in.

He tried to run but it was impossible, so he limped stiffly as fast as he could to where the bucket lay. Scarecrow's head was still inside it. He heard him before he saw him.

"*Brubrubrubrubru!*'" was the noise he made, as though he was trying to make a raspberry noise with his lips.

"Scarecrow," Tin Man said, reaching down and picking up the bucket. He instantly regretted doing so, because he wanted to use both his hands to cover his face.

"*bluthel elthel elthel,*" Scarecrow said, his eyes rolling in his head. They moved at different speeds, the left one moving much faster than the right. His head was partially deflated, and there was a nasty looking crease running across one side of his face. He'd lost a lot of straw, and what was left was mixed heavily with desert sand. His head was only half filled.

Tin Man picked Scarecrow up. The straw man responded by yodeling a stream of nonsense syllables. He strained the sand from the bucket through his fingers and was careful to grab every last piece of straw. Then he placed the straw back into the bucket and carefully tipped Scarecrow's head so much of the sand drained off. He was careful not to lose a single piece of straw. Then he carefully stuffed the small amount of straw from the bucket back into Scarecrow's head and placed him face up inside the bucket. It was easier now that half of his stuffing was gone.

"*Tin Man,*" Scarecrow said. His eyes were still off-kilter, but they had ceased rolling insanely in their sockets. "*Can't see good.*"

"You lost a lot of straw, old friend. But you're better now. You can speak again."

"*Not straw,*" Scarecrow said. "*Bran. Pins make it sharp.*"

"Do you know where we are?" Tin Man said. "It's just as bad here as it was in Oz."

Scarecrow looked up into the dull sky. His left eye sank miserably to the side.

"*Not Oz,*" he said after a minute. "*The Heart wants what it wants.*"

"Kansas," Tin Man said.

Scarecrow looked at him but said nothing.

"So we walk, I guess," Tin Man said.

He carried the bucket on the left side to balance out the limp on his right, and tried his best not to swing it or move it in any way which might cause the Scarecrow discomfort. The straw man seemed to fade in and out of consciousness, or sometimes his face would slacked and his eyes would go dead. When that happened Tin Man would knock the bucket with his knuckles and Scarecrow would come back.

Eventually they left the cornfield altogether. The ground stayed the same texture, like packed dust with the occasional mass of dead weeds. The colour stayed the same. Gray on gray. As far as the eye could see. At some point

Tin Man realized his axe was gone. It hardly seemed to matter.

And then there was a small grouping of buildings on the horizon and Tin Man picked out a barn and a livestock pen among them. A single naked line of smoke drifted from the house.

"I think I see it," said Tin Man. "There's a farm ahead."

"*Nono,*" mumbled Scarecrow. "*We be looking for a guhrl.*"

"Hush now," Tin Man said. "Let's talk later."

He walked toward the house. The farm appeared deserted from where he was save for that slender line of smoke. The grass and trees were dead on the property. There were pig skeletons in the animal pen. A mummified horse, dry, like an old bug husk on the front lawn.

Tin Man stepped around the horse. There were jagged squares cut into the side of the animal, and one leg was nearly picked clean. He went across the front of the house to the door. It was dark inside. The air was thick with greasy smoke. Then there was a click of machinery and as the Tin Man's eyes adjusted to the darkness he saw the dangerous end of a rifle pointed at his head.

"Best move on," a female voice said. "*I'll take your head off iffin' you try anything.*"

The woman was a heaving sack of bones and squalor. Greasy hair clung to the sides of her face in filthy clumps. She was wearing pants and a sweater, with a hood, but the hood was down and her clothes were soiled and ruined.

Tin Man stood still, watching the woman. He wasn't exactly sure what might happen if she fired the weapon at him. He'd never been shot before. In his rusted state, however, she might take out a piece of his face the size of his fist.

The rifle started to shake. Then the barrel dropped. The woman was crying. She tossed the rifle aside and stood there, staring at the Tin Man and his bucket. Tin Man nodded grimly at her. That same beautiful face, now aged, lined with dirt and ash and starved, tanned with hard years that her eyes merely hinted at.

Joy had moved on from Kansas, too.

"Hello, Dorothy."

"*Are we here?*" Scarecrow said.

"Yeah," Tin Man said. "We're here."

Dorothy embraced the Tin Man and ran her fingers over the jagged scales of rust. She made cooing noises when she touched the holes in his chest, and Tin Man's heart stirred at the sound. He gently pulled her hands away and handed her the bucket instead. He felt like he had an anvil on his chest and he couldn't bear the weight of it.

"Oh my," Dorothy said, touching Scarecrow's face. "Oh my dear sweet friend."

"*Hello Dorothy,*" Scarecrow said, his voice sweet and friendly. "*We've been looking all over for you.*"

The straw man smiled up at his old friend, and then his left eye sank to the edge of its socket and he made a soft groaning sound. Tin Man knocked the bucket, and Scarecrow snapped out of it.

"*Hello Dorothy*, he said sweetly. "*We've been looking for you.*"

"How long has he been like this?" Dorothy asked.

"Since we got here," Tin Man said. "I lost hold of him in the Duster, and his head filled with sand. He lost half his stuffing. Before that his mind was slipping, but he was still a brilliant man. Now I'm afraid he's only half what he once was."

"Come inside," Dorothy said. "You never know who might be about."

Dorothy lead them into the house—A near perfect copy of the one they'd passed through in Munchkin Country. This one was just as ragged and old, beaten nearly to death by the ravages of Dorothy's world. There were burnt records and magazines mixed with kitchen utensils, rotting furniture and strips of jaundiced wallpaper hanging like string. Dorothy made her way across the filth with practiced ease, Holding the Scarecrow's bucket close and speaking softly to him. Tin Man stumbled and crashed his way through; his bad leg wasn't doing him any favours in this cramped space.

In the kitchen there was a hole in the floor partially covered by the kitchen sink, which Dorothy had ripped from the counter. The sink was full of ash and burnt furniture; the low heat caused a reeking blue-gray line of smoke that danced to the ceiling then out through a hole in the roof.

"It's my escape hatch," Dorothy said. "Raiders never look under the fire when they come. I just need time to put it back in place and they don't even notice our tornado shelter. It doubled as a fallout shelter, but Uncle Henry didn't understand about radiation and all that science. *He was just a dumb farmer.*"

Her breath hitched when she said that. She gave a guilty look to the Tin Man, then sat down cross legged with Scarecow's bucket in her lap. She laid the rifle down beside her, within easy reach.

"I can't believe you two are really here," she said, her hand caressing Scarecrow's face. "I dreamt about you forever. I dreamt about you so long I was beginning to think that's all you were. Just a dream I made up to get past the sadness."

"We didn't know where else to go," Tin Man said. He took a spot beside her. His rusted frame shuddered from the strain of sitting, and a dusting of rust flakes took to the air with the impact. Dorothy watched them hang in the air, then reached out to catch them in her hands.

"I don't understand what happened," she said. "Why are you two like this?"

"It's not just us," Tin Man said. "It was *everything*. Oz is gone, Dorothy. Destroyed. it looks exactly like this place, but it snows over there and the snow makes you sick. It's mixed with ash that's like an acid and it burns through everything it touches. The colour is all leached out of the world. The only colour left behind is gray."

"*It's not a colour,*" Scarecrow said. "*It's a toe. Toe? Tony? No that's not it. It's something like a toe. Something with colour.*"

"Then Oz is no better than here," Dorothy said, ignoring the Scarecrow's ramble. "Would but there have been a chance to escape this tomb. I would have gladly gone to Oz and spent the rest of my life there. This world is burnt and dead now. There's nothing left anywhere."

"We thought the same thing," Tin Man said. "It was Scarecrow's idea. He thought if we made it to Kansas you might be able to help us."

"*Me?*" Dorothy choked. "What could I do?"

"I don't know," Tin Man said. He sighed deeply, his breath rattling in his chest. it whistled from the hole in his stomach, bringing a shower of sand with it.

"Does it hurt?" Dorothy said. She started to reach for it, but Tin Man moved faster and covered the gaping wound with his own hands.

"I feel nothing anymore," Tin Man said.

"*Toe-toe,*" Scarecrow said. "*I meant toe-toe? What is that?*"

"*Toto,*" Dorothy said. She looked like she'd been hit in the face with a stick. "He's dead."

Then she was crying again.

Later Dorothy made a simple supper from a half can of beans and Tin Man watched her eat in silence. Scarecrow had faded out, and for now the woodsman was content to let him stay quiet. Every time he opened his mouth Dorothy cried, and it made Tin Man's chest hurt. He'd asked her about straw to fill Scarecrow's head, but she'd shaken her head sadly. There was no straw to be had. She'd burnt it all months ago.

He sat and listened to her slurp beans, and listened to the wind outside, and thought about the days when he was the lord of the Winkies and his life had a point. Finally Dorothy tossed the can in the fire and wiped her face with the sleeve of her sweater.

"That's the last of it," she said, watching the yellow flames lick green and blue out of the can.

"What happened to Kansas?" Tin Man said.

"There was a war," Dorothy said, huddling under a blanket. Her feet were inches from the dirty fire, soaking up all the heat they could. "Russia and America. *World War Three.* Though as I remember it, there wasn't much of a war. Only a lot of bombs dropping. Hydrogen Bombs. intercontinental missiles. Short-range tactical nukes dropped by fighters and shot from tanks."

"I don't know what any of that means," Tin Man said. "But it sounds terrible."

"You can't imagine the death toll," Dorothy said. "All it took was one or two bombs dropped on a city and millions were dead. And it happened over and over again. Not just here and there. Everywhere. London, France, Canada...all gone. We drew a line in the sand, Russia walked over it. So we nailed em. And they nailed us."

"But why?" Tin Man said.

"It doesn't matter, I guess," Dorothy said. "Uncle Henry used to say *'They got all them bombs and such built up, now they're just lookin for an excuse to use 'em'.* I guess he was right. Afterward, there wasn't much left. Fallout from the bombs came down in rain and ash and killed most of the survivors. Made the water poison, killed all the plants, and made everything pretty much what you see now. I can't remember the last time I saw the sun. It's just this old gray as far as you can see, forever."

"That's what happened to Oz," Tin Man said. "The clouds came, and everything got cold and died."

I guess it was fallout then," Dorothy said. *"We killed it."*

"What is that?" Tin Man said.

"Fallout is like these little particles of radioactive shit. *Radiation,*" Dorothy said. "You touch it and gives you cancer and messes with your body. If you eat radioactive food and water the shit gets inside you. It's like cooking you from the inside. Uncle Henry said that. I seen drifters with radiation poisoning before. Their hair falls out. They get sores on their bodies. Ones who got it real bad, they're begging to die. It looks plain awful."

Tin Man looked down at the Scarecrow. He'd been quiet for quite a while. His gaze was glassy and cross eyed. His mouth hung open like he was about to speak.

"Scarecrow," he said. *"Hey!"* He banged the bucket. When there was no response he shook it. He reached in and pressed on Scarecrow's face. There was nothing, but a burlap head half filled with straw. Tin Man sighed and put the bucket down. Dorothy was watching him. he shook his head.

"It's for the best," Tin Man said. "He was hardly even there."

Dorothy turned and looked at the fire. After a while she grabbed Scarecrow's head and tossed it onto the flames. Then she buried her head on Tin Man's shoulder and cried.

Tin Man watched his friend burn. Scarecrow's potato sack flesh turned black and erupted into bright flame, then dulled and was gone. He left ashes in his wake. It seemed fitting.

Dorothy didn't talk much after that. A few days after Scarecrow's funeral pyre she helped Tin Man get the sand out of his torso and then the two of them walked the tree line of the Gale property. She had an idea, she said. Something she'd wanted to do for a few months but hadn't been able to. The walked for an hour until they reached a neighbour's house, where tall grain bins stood like dull sentinels overlooking a gray and rotted farm. Dorothy lead Tin Man to the base of the silo, and she pointed to the heavy padlock.

"He was a corn farmer," she said. "I tried to get the lock off but I didn't have anything to do it. I didn't want to waste bullets trying to shoot it off. I come up here sometimes and try to find the keys, but the old man must have taken them when they left."

"Where did they go?" Tin Man said.

"No idea," Dorothy said. "Off to die maybe. I didn't find no bodies out here anyway. Can you get that open?"

"Yes," Tin Man said without looking. "What's in here? Corn?"

"If we're lucky," she said. "If *I'm* lucky."

Tin Man grabbed the lock and twisted it in his hand. The steel bent easily enough, but it flaked and dented his hand badly and after the lock broke he realized he couldn't close his hand properly anymore. The index and middle finger on that hand were bent at the second knuckle. Dorothy slid past him as he was looking at his mauled digits and threw open the loading door.

The bin was three quarters filled with dried corn, mostly still on the cob. There were thousands of ears, mostly black with rot, but Dorothy reached in and pulled them out of the way.

She stepped back away from the bin with two handfuls of dried yellow cobs.

"It's cow corn," she said, smelling them. "Cows are all dead though, so I don't think they'll mind. I want to fill you up with this, is that alright?"

Tin Man looked down at the hole in his stomach.

"I can't carry as much as you can," she said. Her voice was soft. "I'll have to keep coming back here, and it isn't safe. Someone could be watching."

Tin Man reached down and grabbed the edge of the hole with his twisted hand.

"I can take a lot," he said. "It's nothing but an empty can." He pulled on the side of the hole and tore the rusted flesh away. The hole in his stomach was now twice as big. Dorothy would be able to easily get her hands into it.

"Watch the edges," Tin Man said, as she started filling him up.

Afterwards he felt clunky and heavy. The corn was worse than the sand; it knocked and banged and shuffled inside him and he felt every shift in weight up through his torso and into his teeth. He walked slowly, head down, and let Dorothy bound ahead. She moved like a cat, rifle in hand, stopping every twenty or thirty feet to scan the horizon. More than once she motioned for Tin Man to stop, or get down, at which point he'd kneel where he was standing and wait for her to motion that it was alright to move on.

He wasn't accustomed to sneaking; wasn't used to hiding or slinking. So when they approached the Gale farm and Dorothy suddenly dropped to the ground in front of him, he simply stood there like a fool, wondering what all the fuss was about.

"Get down," Dorothy hissed. "There's someone in there."

Tin Man knelt beside her, his joints creaking angrily and spitting rust.

"What do you want to do?"

"*We wait for them to go,*" she said. She was wound like a spring. In a way, Tin Man was happy to see this Dorothy. At least this one had something to live for. It was a nice change from the other Dorothy who stared at the fire and pretended to sleep and wouldn't talk about where her family was.

Eventually two men came out of the house. They were dressed in army fatigues, and one of them was wearing a white motorcycle helmet. He also had a dirty looking rifle with a rag tied around the barrel. The other one was carrying a wooden baseball bat stuck with five inch nails.

They moved like Dorothy; a survivor's walk, considering each step carefully and constantly scanning the area for things to salvage or hidden dangers. Tin Man wondered how long it took for men to revert back to this careful animal approach to life; and how many had managed to relearn the ancient skill before being wiped out by someone doing a better job of it.

Dorothy clicked the safety off her rifle and laid it across a rotting branch. She blew some lint off the sight, checked her aim, then snapped the action into place.

The rifle roared to life. The man with the rifle was her target; she made a hole about the size of a blueberry in the center of his back. He pitched forward, his wind screaming out of him. The other scavenger dropped into a squat then dove back into the house.

Dorothy stood up and started running toward the building.

"*Come on!*" she barked, waving the Tin Man on with her free arm.

Tin Man tried to follow, but he couldn't run. He was full of corn. His leg was bad.

Worse, he'd never imagined he'd ever see Dorothy kill something.

She killed Scarecrow, his mind whispered. True. She had done that. He was dead already though. Mostly.

Dorothy threw herself against the side of the house, then peaked around the corner where the downed scavenger lay. He was grunting and screaming. Dorothy didn't seem to care. She was focused on the other man, the one with the baseball bat full of nails. The one who was still dangerous.

Dorothy checked the side of the house again. Her rifle was up. Her breath came in hard, jagged gasps. Her hair stuck to her sweaty face but she didn't bother wiping it away. There was no time to look pretty. There was only time for killing.

Tin Man was still fifty feet away from the building when the second scavenger made his shot at freedom. He jumped out the window in Dorothy's bedroom. He tripped himself on the window and fell face first into the dirt; but then he was up and bounding away from the house as fast as his legs would move.

"*Hey!*" Tin Man rasped, pointing at the man. Dorothy was on the other side of the house, moving toward the scavenger she'd already downed.

Dorothy looked back. Heard the noise. Saw Tin Man pointing. Put it all together in a heartbeat, then scrambled around the house at a full charge. She was across the back of the house before Tin Man had taken five strides, and then she was out in the field, her rifle barrel coming down toward the man running for his life. The gun roared and she missed. The ground vomited dirt straight into the air about a hundred feet in front of the man, causing him to swerve to his left. Dorothy hitched a breath and bared down on the weapon. It bucked again. This time it looked as though the man's chest puked a big spray of strawberry wine. He staggered and dropped to his knees before falling flat on his face.

"*Fuck,*" Dorothy said. "Just like Hollywood, right?" She dropped the barrel of the rifle down but continued to watch the man for signs of life. She turned just as Tin Man was coming up behind her. Limping badly, and leaving cobs of old corn in his wake.

"You killed them," Tin Man said. His voice was devoid of emotion; he was simply stating a fact.

"Had to," Dorothy said. "They'd have doubled back later and got me while I slept. Raped me. Probably ate me." She saw the impassion on Tin Man's face, mistook it for grief.

"That's just how it is," she said softer. "The whole world is about staying alive now. I got it pretty good, compared to most. I got shelter and water. Most people just wander the country looking for scraps and dying of radiation or starving to death. These two was lucky, Tin Man. They died from a bullet. It was quick. In the end, it's all any of us can hope for."

"*You have shelter, water, and corn too,*" Tin Man said. "Lots of it."

Dorothy banged his chest. It made a muffled thump, and she smiled up into his face.

"That I do," she said.

Dorothy went back to the first man she'd shot; the one with the rifle. He had a bubbly, frothy wound in his back that whistled when he breathed out and made a slurpy noise when he breathed in. It was the sound a rubber boot made when you pulled it out of deep mud. Tin Man hated it instantly. The man had quit screaming at least, and didn't even move when Dorothy kicked at the wound with the side of her boot.

"Lung shot," she said. "You can hear him takin' on air. *Christ*, I bet that hurts."

"What do we do?" Tin Man said. He knew the answer already. It was obvious. For some reason though, he just wanted to hear her say it. Maybe it would cause another tick in his chest, like the one he'd felt earlier. A semblance of life. Humanity.

Dorothy checked the safety on her rifle.

"Dun *do* nuthin'," she said. "Drag his ass out about five *hunnert* feet. See if he attracts any birds."

"You're just going to leave him?" Tin Man said.

"It's either him or me," Dorothy said. "I can't afford to waste bullets on a dead man." She turned around and went into the house.

"Grab that other one while your at it," she said over her shoulder. "Pile em up out there, toward the road."

Tin Man pulled the man up into his arms and carried him like a baby. He tried to be as gentle as possible, even though he was about to leave him so the elements and Dorothy's handiwork could finish him off. The man had never done anything to Tin Man *personally*, and while he didn't care enough to make an effort to save the man or disobey Dorothy he didn't wish the man any direct harm, either. Once out by the road, he laid the man down on his back and placed his hands over his chest.

The man coughed, and a line of blood ran from his mouth down into his ear. He coughed. More blood. His mouth moved but no sound came out. It took Tin Man a moment to realize the man was trying to speak.

"What was that?" he rasped. The sand in his voice was easier to hear when he spoke quietly.

"*Fuh-huckin water heater*," the man said. the "*F*" made a mist of blood splash from his mouth.

"I'm a man," Tin Man said. "Just like you. I just don't look like you anymore."

"*Finn-hish me off, Water Heater Man*," he said. "*Fuh-huckin robot.*"

Tin Man stood up.

"I'm not a robot," he said quietly, lifitng his leg.

When Tin Man checked the second man and realized he was dead, he simply grabbed the scavenger's leg and dragged him out to where he'd lain the first one. Then he came back to the house. Dorothy had cleaned up a bit and was already boiling water in an old brown pot.

"We need to empty you out," she said when she saw him.

"I can do it," Tin Man said. "It feels weird when people touch my insides."

"Is that blood on your foot?" Dorothy said.

"Where do you want the corn?" Tin man replied.

Dorothy watched him for a moment, then slowly pointed to the kitchen counter.

"There for now, I guess," she said. "*Gotta separate the good ones and the bad ones.*"

"I imagine the worst ones are the ones that look good, but are all bad on the inside," Tin Man said. "The ones you look at and couldn't tell they're rotten until it's too late. Next to them, the ones rotten on the outside hardly seem dangerous at all."

"Whatever you say, Tin Man," Dorothy said. she crossed her arms. "You the big expert on corn now? You been here three *fuckin'* days."

"Nope," said Tin Man. "Not an expert. Just a fast learner."

Besides, he thought. *We're not talking about corn anymore*, are *we little girl.*

He walked by her then, dragging his bad leg and pulling corn out by the fistful. Dorothy followed him into the kitchen and sat by her fire, checking the water. When it was boiling she pulled a little pouch out from under her sweater and produced a couple tea leaves and a bay leaf; she put them into a cup and dipped it into the water, filling it. Then she sat back against a stack of cushions and sighed.

Tin Man finished emptying his chest and brought two handfuls of corn over to where she was sitting. He crouched beside her and placed the corn between them.

"I'm sorry," she said suddenly.

"I know," Tin Man said. He added the corn cobs to the boiling pot. "I'm sorry too."

They sat in silence while the corn boiled and then Tin Man pulled corn cobs out of the water bare handed and gave them to Dorothy as fast as she could eat them. She refilled her cup of bay leaf tea with steaming corn water and pulled her sweater sleeves over her hands to hold the corn.

"I know it's just a bunch of old cow corn," she said after the third one, "but I tell you if we had some butter and a little salt, we could serve this at the county blue ribbon barbecue and it would be a hit."

"You could serve it with your corn water tea," Tin Man said.

Dorothy laughed.

"I bet I could at that," she said. "I bet Ozma herself would have even popped her royal ass down in the grass and drank a big cup of the famous Dorothy Gale Fallout Tea and chewed down as many old corn cobs as she could handle."

"I doubt it," Tin Man said. "She turned into a real priss once she got turned back into a girl. Making up for lost time, maybe, from when she was a boy."

Dorothy giggled and spit chewed corn. It made her laugh harder and she covered her mouth.

Tin Man smiled.

Dorothy refilled her cup one last time then took the leaves out and left them to dry on the floor. She had Tin Man fish her out another corn cob, which she sucked the water off while she waited for it to cool enough to eat.

"They do look pretty good," Tin Man said. "It's been so long since I tasted corn I almost forget what it's like."

"The corn in Oz is nothing like Kansas corn," Dorothy said, blowing on her tea. "Everything tastes like magic over there. Magic candy, magic fruits and veggies. It's wonderful, to be sure, but sweet Kansas corn is what I grew up on, and that's what I love."

"Tasted," said Tin Man.

"Huh?"

"You said tastes. It's tasted. Everything *tasted* like magic in Oz. It's all gone now. If you found food in Oz now it would only taste like charcoal and bitter ash."

"Yeah," Dorothy said quietly. "I suppose you're right."

Tin Man stared at the fire. He wished he could have taken that back. It had been so long since he'd seen anyone smile, and he'd reminded the one girl with the most beautiful smile that ever graced Oz that there was nothing left to smile about. Worse, he didn't know if it would happen again anytime soon. Dorothy certainly had nothing to smile about here in Kansas. There was only the two of them, and all the corn she could eat. He wondered what would happen when Dorothy died. He might wander the fields then, looking for a tornado to hitch a ride back to Oz. Or maybe he'd be like that apple tree he and Scarecrow had seen when they crossed the bridge, and go find a brook to lay down in. Let the sludge and poison wash over him til he dissolved and the nightmare came to an end.

"I'm tired," Dorothy said after a while. "I'm gonna catch some sleep."

"Goodnight," Tin Man said.

She rolled over and slept. Tin Man stirred the fire. When it started to burn down he let it go; and stirred it until it was nothing but hot ash and bits of charcoal.

They went back to the corn bin every day after that. Dorothy stocked as much of it as they could in the basement. She explained that the cool dry air down there was good for storing veggies, and if they were stored underground they were less inclined to catch a dose of radiation.

When she was coming up out of the hole she swooned on the ladder, and would have fallen if Tin Man hadn't grabbed her arms.

"Easy kiddo," Tin Man said. He pulled her up to ground level and put her gently down on her feet. He kept his hand on her because she still looked dizzy and sick. "You all right?"

"Just a little woozy," she said. "Guess I need a break."

"Guess so," Tin Man said. "You should lay down for a bit. I'll get you some water."

Dorothy slept for fourteen hours, but not well. When she finally opened her eyes again she was sweaty and pale and complained of nausea. Tin Man built up the fire, crushed corn onto the cooking pot and made a kind of paste from the ruins of the cobs.

"It tastes terrible," Dorothy said. She grimaced while she ate.

"I have no sense of taste," Tin Man said. "Plus the last thing I made was a peanut butter and peppermint jelly sandwich about a hundred years ago."

"Well, that explains it," she said. "*Peppermint Jelly?*"

"It's made from peppermint berries," Tin Man said. "From what I remember they were quite tasty."

"I wish we had one here," Dorothy said. "I think the Corn Paste Soup Berries are starting to go bad."

Tin Man clucked his tongue, then chuckled softly. The sound made Dorothy smile. She took to a coughing fit, and then laid back down.

"Oh, I don't feel good at all," she said. "I bet the corn is bad. Wouldn't that just beat all."

"Well don't eat any more, to be sure. I'll make you some bayleaf tea". Tin Man stood up, his joints screaming metal on metal and flaking rust everywhere. He grabbed the pot of corn and tipped it out the window where it slopped on the gray earth. It was yellow and black. It left an expanding patch of mud beneath it.

Dorothy retched behind him, and he got out of the way just as she was rushing to the window. She stuck her head out and vomited in the same spot where the corn was. She wiped her mouth with her sleeve, spat, and then went back to where she'd been lying down. She buried her head on the cushions and moaned into the crook of her arm.

Tin Man banged the pot again, sloughing out the last of the corn. He looked down at the pile of corn slop. There was blood in the vomit. It swirled through the corn like a ribbon of strawberry sauce in vanilla ice cream.

The next morning Dorothy was worse. She took to vomiting in the pot from her makeshift bed. She couldn't stand, she said; she was too spinny to hang off the kitchen window. Tin Man stroked her hair and was shocked when it began coming out in clumps. Later in the evening sores began appearing in the folds of her skin; her neck, her armpits, and several spots below. Tin Man boiled water all day and kept it in a cooling rotation so that she always had clean water to drink. He dug around for more blankets in the house (no easy task since some of the back rooms had floors that creaked dangerously when he stepped on them).

In the evening there was more blood in her vomit than water and bile.

"It's the *ruh-radia-tion*," Dorothy said the next morning, between retches. "It gets inside you and breaks you apart."

"Inside me?" Tin Man said, not understanding.

"No, I meant inside..." her words slowed down until they were crawling out of her mouth like bugs.

Tin Man stared at her helplessly.

"Me," she said. She was scowling at him.

"Oh," said Tin Man. "Sorry, I misunderstood."

"You told me that snow and ash was falling out of the sky in Oz," she said.

"It was," Tin Man said. "Scarecrow kept telling me to get out of it because it was poison and it was making me rust away."

"But you walked in it for days, right? maybe weeks?"

"*Weeks*, yes." Tin Man said. "I walked to the Emerald City after all the Winkies died and it was a ruined mess. That's when I found Scarecrow. Someone had set him on fire, but he'd put himself out by crawling into a fish pond. That's where I found him, lying in the water, surrounded by dead and rotting Greenfish. After that he said we should come here looking for you. Said we should follow the Yellow Brick Road back to where you were dropped on the Witch. Then we could find our way to Kansas. Of course, later he told me all we had to do was leave Oz and think about you, but it didn't matter. It was pretty much the same distance no matter which way we went."

"Tin Man," Dorothy said. "It wasn't the corn."

"It wasn't?" Tin Man said weakly.

"It was *you*," Dorothy said.

"But..." Tin Man said. "*I didn't know.*""

It wasn't entirely true though, and he knew it. He had felt the heat of something growing inside him, and he'd hated the feeling of it. He didn't know exactly *what* it was, but he had known it was something bad. Something he wanted out of him. It never occurred to him that it might make others sick, but why would it? He was the one with the *heart*, not the one with the *brain*. Scarecrow should have known. *He* should have said something.

"How could you know?" Dorothy said. "You're just a fairy tale. They don't write fairy tales about nuclear war."

"I don't know what to tell you," Tin Man said. "I should go. I don't want to make you any more sick."

Dorothy turned on her side.

"It's too late," she said softly. "I want you to stay until the end. Please don't leave me to die by myself."

"Alright, Dorothy," Tin Man said. "Alright."

Within two days Dorothy was too sick to do anything but lay in bed. She couldn't even drink the water Tin Man boiled for her. She soiled herself and vomited on her pillow; she took no notice of the filth she was creating. She was voiding bits of flesh, however, and Tin Man certainly noticed that. He tried to keep her as clean as he could without disturbing her rest.

It was night. Dorothy was rasping badly. Each breath sounded like it was being sucked through a wet straw. Occasionally she coughed blood and mucus into her mouth, then Tin Man would gently wipe it from her face with parts of some old clothes he'd found and made into rags. Dorothy smiled when she saw the pattern of the cloth.

"*That's my dress,*" she rasped. "*The one I wore to Oz.*"

Tin Man looked down at the blue and white pattern, marred by bloody phlegm.

"Why so it is," he said. "What a lovely dress it was."

"*You know those were the best times on my life,*" Dorothy said. She reached out and put her hand over Tin Man's wrist. "*Being there with all of you. Nothing in Kansas ever touched it. Ever came near it. I should have never left.*"

"Try to rest, Dorothy," Tin Man said. "Oz loved you too. You saved us."

"*I want to tell you one more thing,*" Dorothy whispered.

"What is it?"

"*When Scarecrow asked about Toto...*" Dorothy said. Large yellow tears pooled in the corners of her eyes, and she blinked them away. "*I told him Toto was dead.*"

"I remember," Tin Man said.

"*I never said how he died,*" Dorothy said. "*Because I was ashamed. The truth is, about six months ago I was starving so bad I thought I was gonna die. I'd been splitting my food with him, even though he was old, and I knew I shouldn't be feeding him, but I loved him so much.*"

She was wracked with a fit of hacking, bloody coughs then, and Tin Man turned her on her side until they subsided. When she finally took a breath again, it was shallow and liquid, and her face was marred with bloody slime.

"Try not to speak anymore, Dorothy," Tin Man said. "You need to save your breath."

"*I wanted to tell someone before I die,*" Dorothy whispered. "*Because I'm ashamed, and I'm so sorry. I ate him, Tin Man. I killed Toto and I ate him.*"

"Oh Dorothy," Tin Man said. he'd known, of course. At least sensed it, the way she'd reacted when Scarecrow brought Toto's name up. But hearing her say it; confessing before her death; *a death he himself had caused*; it was too much. Somewhere deep in his chest there was a *thunk*, and something inside him that hadn't done anything in a long while; something he had grown accustomed to not feeling because the world just hurt so bad finally broke for the last time.

His heart.

Under his hands, Dorothy shuddered. She gagged once, then let out a soft breath and lie still.

"Goodnight, Dorothy of Kansas," Tin Man said. Something hot and liquid was running from his face.

They were oily, rust filled tears.

THE END.

ONE WICKED DAY

by Frank Dutkiewicz

"*Caw!*"

"Good morning Mary Ann," the Wicked Witch of the East said to the crow sitting on her windowsill. "What are the servants up to this morning?"

"*Caw! Caw!*"

"Is that so?" She stepped up to the ledge and looked out at her lands from the top spire of her mansion. Laborers were bent over cultivating the crops in the fields. Workers dug and set bricks into the road that connected it to the YBR in the distance. Far off she could see a black cloud from the miners dismantling a mountain to get to the coal within. The sight of the peasants of Oz toiling for her own gains made her smile. "There always has to be at least one slacker, right Mary Ann?"

"*Caw!*"

The witch slipped on her silver slippers.

"Breakfast does sound like a good idea."

She closed her eyes and clicked her heels together.

"There's no place like the kitchen. There's no place like the kitchen."

Her sudden appearance caused the cook to scream, once again.
I will never get tired of that.
The gardener, who was seated at the table, spat the orange segment out

of his mouth and fell backwards in the chair, landing hard on the stone floor. He quickly rose to his feet, bent on one knee and bowed his head in submission.

The witch stepped up to him and pointed an index finger toward the ceiling inches from his face. An invisible force latched onto his chin and lifted him to his feet. The gardener's wide eyes stared down at the witch. The tips of his toes balanced on the stone floor. An unmistakable, delightful look of terror spread across his face.

"What makes you think you can help yourself to my pantry?"

"I'm sorry," he replied through clenched teeth. "It will not happen again."

"You did not answer my question." She withdrew her hand.

The gardener dropped to his heels and stumbled back, rubbing his chin. "Most of the fruit rots before it is touched, your *Witchiness*."

"I *like* my fruit rotten. It taste best when fur grows on it."

"I know you do Ma'am, but I have such a large family and I do not make enough to feed us all. Most of your fruit is used as fertilizer. I did not think you would miss one."

She was about to say more when the gardener started to sob.

"You have so much and I am so hungry. I will never do it again."

She paused for a second and began to stroke his tear streaming cheek.

"You poor thing. I had no idea you were so famished."

The witch's uncharacteristic soft tone got the gardener to stop. He looked at her with uncertainty in his face. She grabbed the largest orange in the fruit bowl and balanced it on the tip of her thick, long index-fingernail. The orange levitated an inch above the sharpened tip and spun slowly.

"I can't bear to see you go hungry." She waved her free hand over the orange. The gardener blinked when it vanished. The witch showed him her bare palm, closed her hand then opened it quickly in his face.

The gardener grunted. Fear flared on his face. Through the open gap of his mouth the orange skin of the fruit shown brightly behind his teeth. The witch grinned seeing the realization hit him. The ripe fruit, too big to bite down on, was now wedged in his mouth.

"You can have that one," she said and cackled in his face. Streams of spit bathe the stricken man.

The witch spun to face the cook. The pretty, young lady gasped and held her breath, her eyes darting from the gardener and back to the witch.

"I want breakfast," the witch snarled. "The usual."

The cook swallowed. She glanced at the gardener who fell to the floor and could be heard struggling to dislodge the orange.

"Eggs and ham, ma'am?"

"Yes. Burn the ham and make sure the eggs are green." The witch started to turn then stopped, keeping one eye on the cook. "You did see to making the eggs green, didn't you?"

The thrashing gardener's kicking feet knocked over a chair. The witch kept her eye locked onto the cook's, daring her to look away.

"Yes, ma'am," the paled faced woman replied. "They have been sitting in the sun for the last three days, but it wasn't easy."

Mary Ann fluttered in and landed on the kitchen table. The cook pointed a trembling finger at the crow.

"Mary Ann has been trying to steal them."

The witch set her hands on her hips and glared at the crow. "Mary-*Ann*."

"*Caw!*"

"O-Kay." The witch walked over to where the rotting eggs were and grabbed one. "But this is the only one." She shouted toward the cook. "I will be back in twenty minutes. I expect a warm plate of food on this table!"

The witch watched the cook swallow a large lump.

"Yes, ma'am," she managed to say.

The witch then crouched down and locked eyes with the gardener. The man was clawing at the lodged orange. With each labored breath orange pulp came out of his nostrils. His color was changing from a bright red into a dark blue.

"I will expect that you will be finished with your breakfast by then." Then smiling brightly she added, "Or shall I say, I expect your breakfast should be finished with you by then?"

She cackled then spun away, stepping into the middle of the kitchen while calling to her pet.

"Mary Ann! Home."

The crow launched itself off the table and flew through the open window. The witch closed her eyes and clicked her heels together.

"There's no place like my bedroom. There's no place like my bedroom."

She reappeared in the isolated room set inside the top spire of her mansion. The tower rose a hundred feet above the base of the building and set on a hill overlooking a wide valley. Three windows were spaced evenly apart giving her a clear view in all directions. No stairs led to the room. Only creatures that could fly, or someone that had the lone pair of slippers that could magically transport the wearer to anywhere they wished to go, could reach it.

"It's about time you showed up."

She turned toward the voice. The Wicked Witch of the West grimaced from inside the crystal ball that sat on a three-legged table position between two windows. Over her left shoulder on a pillar perched a flying monkey. The sounds of her Winkie soldiers marching and chanting boomed in background.

The Wicked Witch of the East took two steps toward the ball and crossed her arms. Her sister would only contact her for one of two reasons, when she needed something or to gloat. Figuring out which could take up to a half an hour at times.

"What is it this time, dear sister?"

The Wicked Witch of the West stuck out her lower lip, as if the question hurt.

"Can't I check on how my little sister is doing? It has been so long after all."

A squad of Winkie soldiers marched into the room, stomping and chanting in their monotoned, but loudly timed, style.

"OH-DEE-OH. OH-OOOOH-OH. OH-DEE-OH. OH-OOOOH-OH."

The western witch turned around and shouted.

"Shut up a minute! Can't you see that I'm on the ball?"

Mary Ann glided through an open window and landed on her master's shoulder. The western witch scowled at the crow when she saw her.

"I would have bet that feather-brain would have been stew by now."

"Caw! Caw!"

The west witch stabbed a finger at the bird from the other side of the crystal ball.

"You mind your own beak, you busy-bodied buzzard."

"Maybe she should," said the eastern witch. She set the rotten egg on a plate for her pet then reached for a cup of old tea sitting on a davenport nearby. She held the cup up with her left hand and flicked her right index finger. A flame flickered from the appendage. The eastern witch began to warm her tea and scrunched her eyebrows at her sister. "But she is correct. You need something from me. Spit it out because time is something I am short of at this moment and you are wasting it with your pitiful pleasantries."

The west witch scrunched her nose.

"For once, you pain-in-the-ass, I have something to offer you. I see that your Munchkin project is making strides but they could use some extra encouragement. I could lend you a few Winkie's to keep them in line and a flying monkey or two to transport that candy."

The east witch arched an eyebrow.

"A nice offer but I have the shrimps under control."

"Are you sure?" her sister purred. "I know how hard you worked to change their adorable nature. It would be a pity for them to regress and go on one of their *ding-dong* rampages."

The east witch blew out her finger and took a sip before answering.

"I'm not worried about that. I drilled it into their tiny brains that the rest of Oz was getting ready to wipe them off the map for *ding-donging* the countryside. I banned the use of that archaic-Munchkin language and adjusted their diet to compensate. As far as the monkeys go, I'll pass. Those fur balls will eat most of the stuff they don't drop *and* I have the transportation problem solved. That isolated village is now connected to the Yellow Brick Road. Civilization has reached Munchkin land."

The west witch barred her teeth and growled.

"What the hell happened to you? You used to be evil with a capital *E*. Now you provide jobs, build houses, and encourage commerce. We're supposed to be the *Wicked* Witches. You know, conquer the land, subjugate people, and stamp out good, that kind of thing. Instead of helping me drive the Good Witch of the South into the sea and laying siege to Emerald City you're trading with them both. What kind of ally are you anyway?"

"Officially, I am neutral in your war with Glinda, as is Emerald City. I only sell food to our good second cousin; at a higher price than I do to you, mind you. The wizard's people I have a closer relationship with, they have deeper pockets after all. Trading with them both is my way of spreading my brand of wicked, evil older sister. As our darling mother used to say, curse her soul, '*the ends will justify the means*'."

"I think you missed her point, little sister. I believe she would be appalled on how merciful you have become to your subjects."

"Perhaps." She took another sip then continued. "But I think she would be surprised on how well my tactics have worked. Let's compare our results.

"While you attempted to take lands by force and bogged your forces in a protracted war, *W*, I have traded, bought and swindled for my territory. For all *your* efforts, you rule a rocky mountain range and a few swamps. I own half the farming area, the best timber in Oz, and the northern hills that are filled with coal.

"While you have driven so many people away and enslaved the few that are left, I have hired desperate refugees at a wage of my choice. With the silver I give them, they pay me rent to live in homes that I built, buy food from the farms that I own, and purchase clothing that my workers make.

"And since I own everything, I can set whatever price I like and chose to throw whomever I want out of their house. I have subjugated my people, even if they aren't aware of it yet. Soon, I will be purchasing parts of Emerald City itself. Long before you will be able to march an army to its gates, I will already own half the city."

"Don't be so sure of that," snarled the western witch. "I have tricked

Glinda into excepting a truce. As soon as I am ready, my armies will be on the march again." She smiled and sweetened her tone. "Of course it would be easier if you could loan me those silver slippers for a few days."

A thin smile curled on the east witch's lips.

"Not a chance. The next person that wears these will have to pry them from my cold-dead feet." She watched her sisters eyebrows lift a bit. "And to remind you that killing me won't guarantee you possession of these slippers. The spell that holds them to me is pretty tricky."

A scowl returned to her sister's face.

"I should have never let you take them. They should have been mine."

The eastern witch rolled her eyes.

"You had first choice. You wanted the broom."

"You didn't deserve either one." She scrunched her eyebrows and looked down at her sister's feet. "They just changed to ruby. Why do they turn ruby a few days every month?"

The east witch looked down for herself then sighed. "None of your business, you dried up old hag."

The west witch twisted her mouth and glared at her sister for a moment.

"I don't know what type of spell you placed on those slippers but I'm sure mother would have never approved. You lack the true wickedness that she had when she wore them. You have become soft and don't have what it takes to be truly wicked anymore."

The east witch set her cup down and grinned inwardly. "Oh that reminds me. I regret to inform you that I will need to raise the price of grain. Two pounds of gold for every ton now."

"*What?* I don't have enough slaves to dig out that much gold at those prices. I'll have to take Winkie's off the front lines to help!"

The east witch leaned in and smiled wide. "I could loan you a few workers to help, for a price of course." Mary Ann jumped on her shoulder and added her opinion.

"*Caw!*"

The west witch's face twisted. She snarled then stabbed a finger at them both.

"I'll get you, my little sister. *And your little crow, too!*"

The crystal went dark. The east witch smiled broadly and began to skip about her room. She had once again gotten the best of her sister. Her smile gradually faded. Something that her wicked sibling said began to gnaw at her. Curious, she spoke a spell over the crystal ball and waved over it. The ball came to life showing a village full of mushroom houses. She threw her head back and clenched her fist when she saw what the inhabitants were up to.

"Those *idiots!* I'll rip their empty heads off, the little mother..." She stomped about the room then composed herself. She took in a deep breath, closed her eyes, and clicked her heels together.

"There's no place like Munchkin land. There's no place like Munchkin land."

She reappeared on the Yellow Brick Road on the rise overlooking the village. Tied to a pole was the Scarecrow, his mouth gagged. He would look at the roaring bonfire then struggle to escape his binds. Six Munchkins, three on each end of the pole, paraded the scarecrow through the street as the rest of the Munchkins sang in celebration.

Ding-dong the scarecrow's toast. He's gonna make a yummy roast. Ding-dong the scaredy-crow is toast!

No one noticed her. The Munchkin lugged their high-fiber meal toward the fire. The witch pulled a rag out of her pocket and spat into it. She held it up high with both hands and twisted it as if wringing out. A torrent of water gushed over the fire, extinguishing it.

"How many times have I told you mongrels not to *ding-dong!*" she said, marching down the hill straight toward the village square.

The Munchkins screamed; several attempted to run away. The witch pointed at each one that tried. An invisible hand grabbed onto them and dragged them back into the square.

"I have been working to make you cannibals presentable for an amusement park. Tourists won't step one foot in this village if they hear *'We're going to eat someone'* in Munchkinese."

"But we like to ding-dong," said one Munchkin.

The witch scooped up some pebbles with her left hand than slapped the back of it with her right causing them to spray away. The Munchkin lurched forward as if someone smacked him in the back of the head. His teeth flew out and bounced off the street.

"Anyone else want to gum their food for the rest of their life?" The half-sized villagers stood silent. She stepped up to the scarecrow, who was still bound and gagged and held aloft by the six Munchkins. She reached into his chest and pulled out a hand full of dried foliage. "You idiots! You can't even eat him. He's made of straw, not an ounce of meat in his carcass."

She marched back to the toothless Munchkin, shoved the straw in his mouth then stabbed a finger at the doused bonfire.

"You dummies aren't even bright enough to know that there would have been nothing left to eat once you put him over the fire. Thirty seconds of flame and all you would have had left was a charred stick to gnaw on."

"But we're so hungry," eeked a Munchkin. "All we had to eat for the past month was candy."

"What? I instructed the farmer to deliver meat and grain to you once a week. Hasn't he been showing up?"

The Munchkins stared blankly at her. She walked up to the scarecrow and yanked his gag off.

"Where's the farmer?"

The scarecrow stared back with wide eyes.

"I-I haven't seen him in a month. The last I saw he was headed here to make his delivery."

She slowly turned and stared at the Munchkins. She crouched and stepped among the villagers, looking each one in the eye.

"What happened to the farmer? Well? Come now. Spit it out, what was the last thing you remembered when you saw him?"

From behind an anonymous voice answered. "Ding-dong."

She buried her face in her hands then straightened and brought her arms to her side, screaming. Flames shot out from the ends of her fingers. The Munchkins began to back away. She pointed at them all.

"Don't anybody move!"

She pulled the rag out of her pocket and tied it in knot. She yanked the rag and the knot disappeared. The binds holding the scarecrow released, dropping him to the ground.

"Get your ass back in that field and stay there until I send someone with instructions." She pointed at the road. "Now go." The scarecrow rose to his feet and scurried away. "*I said go!*" A lightening bolt leapt from her hand and struck him in the seat of his pants. He yelped and ran up the road.

Once out of sight she headed to the storage building. One look inside was all she needed.

"Where's all the candy? Don't tell me you ate the entire store?"

All the Munchkins looked at the ground and started to shuffle their feet.

"Listen up all of you. Munchkin Candy and Chocolate Emporium's grand opening in Emerald City is in one week. I will have egg on my face if all that advertising and promotion I paid for is for a store with empty shelves. That store is going to be *fully* stocked. I don't care if it means all of you work the next seven days on twenty-four hour shifts!"

"We don't have to."

The witch spun to find the voice.

"Who said that?" she said searching the crowd.

"I did," said a greasy haired Munchkin holding an oversized lollipop over his shoulder. Three other Munchkins, also holding lollipops, stood behind him. At a height a few inches under four feet, this Munchkin was the tallest of the bunch. The other three seemed to be getting most of their courage from him. "The Good Witch of the North says we don't have to slave for your profits. Our guild is going on strike until we get fair compensation for our work."

The witch held up her right hand with her palm up like a claw. Small flames flickered off each nail.

"Is that so?"

The tall Munchkin nodded firmly. The other three were less resolute.

"Fine." The witch twisted her hand at the leader of the guild. A stream of fire bathed the Munchkin. The flaming figure screamed and ran in a half-circle before collapsing in the street. The flames leaped into the air until only a smoldering pile of ash was left. "You're fired."

The witch raised her voice.

"The Witch of the North isn't as good as she appears and is giving you advice that is bad for your own good. If any of you believe that I will succumb to labor stoppages, slowing work practices, or claims of illness, you are mistaken. I have invested a lot of silver and resources in you cannibals. I have a signed contract and the deed to all the land around you."

"We didn't know what we were signing," shouted a voice in the crowd. "We can't read."

"That is not my problem. If you don't like this arrangement, I could always use a few of you in my coalmine. Or you are always welcomed to pick apples in the crabapple orchard. That is if you think you're quick enough to dodge their throws. In the meantime, we have a schedule to keep. Now get to work."

The Munchkins groaned and started to disperse. Then one pointed to the sky.

"*She's here!* The Good Witch of the North is coming!"

The Munchkins all began to chant her name. The wicked witch turned to see a pink bubble descend. She crossed her arms and waited for her second cousin to land.

The pretty redhead stepped out of the bubble in a pink fluffy dress holding a wand with a pink star on the end of it. She had a smile that must have been painted on because the witch of the east couldn't recall her ever wearing a frown. The Munchkins would touch her dress as she stepped pass. She would set a hand on their heads when she walked by. She stopped by the pile of ashes in the street and shook her head.

"Tsk, tsk." She looked up at the wicked witch. "Must be another worker that dared to stand up against an oppressive profiteer." She stepped away from the ashes, still maintaining her glowing smile. She twirled and opened her arms to the Munchkins. "My dear friends, your struggle against the landowners will end soon. Just as…" She looked over at charred remains of the Munchkin and puckered her lips for a moment. "…that pile of ash stood up to the *capitalistic counter-revolutionary*, we must do the same and carry on his, or her, bravery."

"Kill the witch! Kill the witch!" chanted the Munchkins.

The wicked witch arched an eyebrow. "Yeah, *Leninida*. Try and kill the witch."

"Oh-ho-ho-ho," she replied with a bubbly laugh. "Violence is a last resort. As workers struggling against the oppressive hand of the profit seekers, we must try to resist the favorite tool of the reactionary." Leninida bounced up to the east witch and skipped around her as if she were a prop in a ballet. "It is my hope that my dear second cousin will abandon her materialistic undertakings before the upcoming class struggle forces change upon her. A pity that you feel the need to exploit these poor, defenseless creatures for your own selfish desires instead of bettering their lives."

The wicked witch stepped on Leninida's pink dress stopping her in mid bounce.

"Bettering their lives? These half-pints lived in a cabbage patch. I grew the mushrooms into houses with my magic. I had a well dug for them. I ordered the YBR to be connected to their village, not an easy thing to do considering the workers had to keep an eye out for the little cannibals."

Leninida yanked her dress from under the wicked witch's foot and inspected it.

"All noble deeds *if* it wasn't for the fact that you did so only to line your own pockets," she said while brushing away the dirt. "You wouldn't have been so concerned for their well being if it wasn't for these unique creatures ability to make such sweet things with their delightful magic for you to exploit. Your quest for silver taints their lives."

The wicked witch narrowed her eyes.

"If it wasn't for me, they would have been extinct within a decade. If the people in this part of Oz didn't string them up, malnutrition would have done them in. The reason why they're all under three feet tall is because they lived on sweets. They became cannibals to get the protein they avoided. And they're not very bright cannibals at that. Six months ago I caught them trying to boil the Tin Woodsman. He's still not right. Now the smallest bit of rain freezes him up. You know how far behind my timber quota is because of their stupidity?"

Leninida set a hand on a grinning Munchkins head.

"These creatures aren't stupid, just uneducated. You and the other keepers of the wealth have intentionally kept all the workers ignorant. An informed worker threatens your profits. Ignorance allows you to take advantage of their labor and profit from it. Once the workers of Oz learn that their labor is the true engine of commerce, the need for money will disappear and workers will live prosperously, trading for what each person requires, not for selfish personal gain."

The wicked witch stepped close to the good witch and kept her voice low.

"Cut the crap, Leninida. You may have these dimwits and some idiots in the coalmines snookered, but I know what you're up to. You're just waiting for all these poor slobs to start enough trouble so you can step in and take credit for all my hard work. You just may be the most wicked one of us all."

"Oh my poor misguided cousin. It is my wish to see that all the people of Oz live together in peace. That can only be accomplished once the acquisition of wealth and property is abandoned by all. I only wish to help these adorable little people and want to see after their well being."

"Oh really, Leninida? Then why haven't you bothered to help them before? Could it be that you didn't want to become one of their meals?"

"My little friends wouldn't do that to me, now would you?"

All the Munchkins shook their head, almost. The wicked witch saw one start to nod until the Munchkin next to him gave him a nudge.

"You see? All they need is someone to show them what is right, not force them to do the bidding of capitalist greed." She stepped into the middle of the square and waved her wand. A bubble enclosed around her. "Farewell my friends."

The wicked witch plucked a dandelion going to seed and blew on it. The pink bubble flew erratically out of sight.

"Now get back to work."

"But we're hungry," a voice squeaked.

"I'll have another farmer fill a cart of food for you, but don't expect him to hand deliver it here. I'll have him slaughter a hog."

The majority of the Munchkins groaned.

"You don't like pork? What would you like? Beef?"

"We like chicken," said a Munchkin. "Taste like people."

"Fine. I'll send a flock and you can roast them alive for all I care." She stabbed a finger at the crowd. "But you'll need to get rid of that murderous, savage mentality. I am working on changing your image. Munchkin Land Resort has a tentative opening in about a year from now. You will all be expected to be cute, playful, and nice by then. I want children to be your playmates and their parents to love you. You will be serving them, interacting with them, and seeing to their every whim. You are expected to be adorable and cuddly. I want the amusement park to be the favorite family vacation spot in Oz."

"How long do we have to do that?" asked a Munchkin.

"Munchkin Land will be a three hundred and sixty-five day a year park. While it is open, you will all be the perfect hosts."

"Forever?" eeked another.

"For as long as this venture makes a profit, and this *will* make a profit. I have sunk way too much silver into you knee-highs to not make it work. This is your purpose in life now. Make candy and entertain people."

The Munchkins began to murmur. "We don't want to do that for the rest of our lives," said a Munchkin.

The witch grinned.

"That's too bad for you. You already made your bed when you signed the contract. You're *stuck*. I own all the land around you, the local law enforcement, and every business in the area. You have nowhere to go and no one to turn to. As long as I am making silver there is nothing you can do and no one to stop me."

"There has to be a way to stop you."

She cackled then added, "Nothing short of a major housing crash can stop me."

The wicked witch saw all the Munchkins look up with wide eyes and open mouths. She twisted her head up in time to see the two-story farmhouse, just before it crashed on top of her.

Leninida and the Munchkins waved to the strange girl.

"Goodbye! Goodbye!"

The little girl started to skip, her newly acquired slippers sparkling in the sun. Leninida resisted the urge to take them for herself. Their magic was strong, which is why the Wicked Witch of the West wanted them so bad. Adhering them to the naïve girls feet insured the west witch would be distracted. Anyway the slippers weren't the prize to have in the east witches empire, they were only the icing on the cake. Leninida wanted to have that cake and eat it too, and was willing to sacrifice the icing to get it. Giving them to the girl and throwing her in the wizards lap was genius, one more person to distract while she seized on a once in a millennium opportunity.

Her smile widened as she thought on how fortunate she was the opportunity had come. Thanks to the east witch, who blew her far up into the sky, Leninida happened to see the house getting tossed in the twister. With quick acting magic, she managed to hold the house together and directed it to the top of the wicked witch's head. Discovering the peasant girl alive in the structure was a bonus. She then had a scapegoat; an unwilling accomplice to seize upon a hastily conceived phase-two of a plan.

Leninida marveled how she didn't feel bad for the strange girl. Perhaps she would later but, at the moment, she was nothing more than a pawn in a game that Leninida finally got a good seat to play. It was also fortunate that she was there when the girl first emerged out of the house or the Munchkins would have ding-donged her ass. That girl could also thank the east witch for ruling this side of Oz so ruthlessly. Say what you want, but that crusty witch's tactics eliminated crime. She didn't know how far the pig-tailed girl would make it, but caring about her wasn't on her agenda.

"Ding-dong the witch is dead. Evil wicked witch is dead. Ding-dong the wicked witch is dead!"

Leninida cringed when she looked back to see the Munchkins pulling her dead cousin out. She waved her wand to form a bubble around her. *I think I'll let them have their fun for an hour or two.*

The Good Witch of the North descended in her bubble and stepped out once she landed in the square. The Munchkins were all laying on the their sides and patting their bellies. Leninida took note of the pile of bones next to a heap of black clothes. They smiled and waved instead of jumping up and down as they usually did.

"Tsk, tsk. You were all told that ding-dong is not a good thing," she said waving her finger at them. "Now to time rise and get to work. You are all behind schedule. Chop, chop."

The Munchkins groaned. "You said we would only have to work as hard as we needed to once the wicked witch was gone," said one.

"I said you would work according to your needs, and at the moment you are needed to fill the shelves of the new store in Emerald City. Now be all good workers and hop to it. And remember," she pointed her wand over her shoulder to encase the Munchkin, sneaking up behind her holding a club and a rope, in a bubble, "that eating other people is something you should never do again." The Munchkin in the bubble yelled to be let free as it rose in the air. "We have an image to repair if the amusement park and resort is to open on time."

She pointed the wand over her shoulder again. The Munchkin screamed as he fell. He landed with a sickening thud in the middle of the square. The rest of the Munchkins took a good long hard stare at his broken body then raised their heads to look at Leninida.

The Good Witch of the North smiled warmly.

"You were all told that the candy you ate needs to be replaced. *The People* would not improve. You do not want to be seen as workers that are not doing their part for the State."

"I thought once the wicked witch was gone the candy was ours to do with as we wished," said a Munchkin.

"I said the fruit of your labors would belong to The People. The People make up the State. Every person must do their part for the greater good of The People. Now be good little workers and do your part."

"You sound just like the wicked witch," remarked another Munchkin.

Leninida approached the Munchkin. She maintained her bright smile but had flames shooting out of her eyes. She pointed her wand at him and raised it. The Munchkin left his feet. The witch waved him toward the farmhouse that still sat in the square. She jerked the wand as if swinging a hammer. The Munchkin slammed into the house with each swing.

"I am not like the wicked witch. She exploited you, while I only want to see after you and the rest of The Peoples needs."

The Munchkins broken body fell.

"But not to worry, little ones," she said in a sweet voice. Five pink bubbles descended from the sky. "I have brought others to help."

The Munchkins let out a collective gasp when mountain trolls stepped out of the bubbles. They eyed the Munchkins as if they owed them silver.

"Do trolls know how to make candy?" asked one Munchkin.

Leninida chuckled.

"No, I wouldn't dream of having them attempt your magic. They are here to make sure quotas are met and that all workers are good workers. And don't think of them as trolls but rather as Knights of the Good Benefactors. You have no reason to fear them."

The Munchkins scrunched together and began to chatter quietly to themselves. Leninida waited patiently.

One stepped forward.

"We think we don't need the troll..., um, *knight's* help. We believe we can provide for ourselves and do not need to be part of a People's State."

The trolls grunted.

"Is that what you all think?" asked Leninida.

The Munchkins stayed silent while eyeing the trolls.

"Come now. There will be no repercussions for speaking your minds. We are all equal parts of the State," said Leninida. "All that feel that way raise your hands."

The trolls took another step forward while clenching their fist. Five Munchkins slid a reluctant hand up.

"I see," said Leninida. She nodded to the trolls. They herded the five Munchkins out of the crowd. Two trolls shoved them up the road.

"I thought you said they wouldn't get in trouble?" one Munchkin said.

"Oh, they're not in trouble. They have been brain washed by capitalist propaganda. They are only being taken to be re-educated. Once that is completed they will be back." She nodded at the three remaining trolls. They stepped toward the rest of the Munchkins while cracking their knuckles.

Leninida formed a bubble around herself.

"Goodbye my friends," she said to their down faces.

The Good Witch of the North grinned. The Wicked Witch of the East had plenty more workers in her empire. They would be pleased to know that Good had liberated them. If not, there was always an extra troll to convince them otherwise.

THE END.

CHOPPER'S TALE

by Jason Rubis

It woke to life in slow bursts of sensation: a baffling storm of sounds that gradually faded, only to erupt again moments later; a colourless, weirdly-angled vision that likewise came and went. Later it would associate memories of that first moment with droplets of rainwater gleaming, then going dull on the oiled blade of its head.

There were two women in attendance on it as it woke; one was very old, and muttered to herself incessantly. It was she who actually woke it, muttering in time with the painful, exultant eruptions of consciousness. The other was smaller in stature than the crone, and not as old, though she seemed every bit as hunched and wrinkled. The mutterer's was the first voice the axe heard, but the other woman exposed it to actual language.

"Is it working? Will it do the job?"

The muttering went on—hurried now, exasperated, and the axe's broken consciousness set suddenly, gelling into a painful clarity. It did not know what it was or why it was; one thing only it understood, and that was a hunger deep inside it. It wanted to do the thing it had been made to do, longed to do it.

Feet shuffled on an earthen floor; there was a wet gulp overhead as the mutterer drank deeply from a flagon of water. Then:

"You're impatient, Nola Amee. And impertinent. My sisters would not have tolerated you for such measly wages as you offer."

"You took the cow quickly enough," the other woman snapped. The axe saw her suddenly, stooped over it, her sour face glaring with pursed, liverish lips. It was being appraised, judged—and found wanting.

"I see no life here. Your precious powder is a sham."

"*Idiot*," the older woman sneered. "You'd have it writhe like a python and chop your foot off? The powder of life doesn't work that way. It operates on the principle of *Like Effect*—not that you'd understand such. Had I used it on that table yonder, it'd be gamboling like a spring calf, being four-footed in its way. A statue sprinkled thus would move quicker than your old bones. An axe reproduces no living shape, thus cannot move once the powder gives it life."

"But it could move as a serpent...you said yourself..."

"Ever seen a serpent with a head so huge? *Fah.* You suspect my honesty? Want proof? Here, then."

The axe, having no choice, watched. The muttering woman lurched briefly into its line of vision; she was bent, and so thin as to be nearly skeletal. She glanced once at it in passing, giving it a satisfied but wholly unpleasant grin. Her eyes were piercing and intelligent but somehow wild-looking.

She carried a leather bag in one bony hand. She reached inside and sprinkled a pinch of something on a footstool near the blazing hearth. A moment later the stool was clattering about the flagstones like a huge beetle. The woman called Nola Amee shrieked as it made for her. The older woman laughed heartily, then seized the stool up in one hand and threw it onto the fire. It landed on its cushioned back, and—too heavy to extricate itself—twisted and burned and eventually died.

"I'll have another chicken, to reimburse me for that stool. They're not cheap, you know."

"You've convinced me. But without movement, how will it kill Nick?"

"It has its ways. My spells have seen to that. This man you hate so much is a woodcutter, yes? He will suspect nothing so little as his own tool. Trust me, the deed will be done before you know it."

"But hear me, Nola Amee: once your woodman is dead meat and that poor girl is forever bound to you, get rid of that axe. Bring it back to me if you like, or throw it in a river if you don't trust me. On no account let it find a name. *Now* it's little but an animal. A vicious, unnatural child. But it will learn quicker than any youngling, sopping up knowledge as a rag takes spilled wine. Its power of influence is bound by my spells to Chopper only, at least for the moment. But if it happens on a name for itself, let all this wretched country beware; there's no telling what it will do."

The axe was lifted and thrust into Nola Amee's flinching hands. Its hunger surged; it saw exactly how it could accomplish its purpose with this greedy, stupid woman. But something frustrated it. It could not find a way into her. Her desires and thoughts formed a tangle it could not penetrate or grasp. Had it a mouth it would have cried out in rage.

It would have to wait. Allow itself to be carried towards an unknown destiny. As Nola Amee left the hut and hobbled along, the axe caught a final glimpse behind them of the older woman's cottage.

Crush her, it thought ferociously at the cabin. *Fall on the old bitch, smash her bones to paste. A house, yes. Someone should drop a house on her one day.*

The woodman was a fool to begin with, and love made him a moron, so perfectly suited to the axe's purpose that its wooden heart sang with the first curl of his idiot fingers round its haft. Nola Amee had left it in its accustomed place the previous night, leaning on the outer wall of Nick Chopper's poor hut. Come morning, he had picked it up, shouldered it, and went whistling off to work, as he had thousands of mornings before.

This was true joy. Nick Chopper's every thought, every idle fantasy presented itself for the axe's delectation. Which of these mental hiccups would provide it the entry it needed to do its work? Any of them might do: memories of the bread and cheese Nick had enjoyed for breakfast, vague worries about inconsequential aches and pains, obscenely detailed reminiscences of that morning's bowel movements, the girl…

The girl. Yes. Nimmie Amee. And their wedding, of course, the prime cause of his present stupor. Why waste time on other trivialities? Nick Chopper's daydreams of the girl would provide the perfect entry-point. The axe got to work as the woodman swung it against a fine tall oak.

"My sweet Nimmie. She loves me so."

Does she? She has no other lover? She's never looked at any of the other young bucks in the village? Never once?

The woodman's mind accepted the axe's insinuations as thoughts of his own. The rhythm of his strokes against the tree helped them sink deeper, unnoticed, as he met them with hidden doubts that till now had been kept smothered.

"The butcher's lad. She's turned an eye to him more than once…"

The butcher's lad, yes. A fine brawny specimen. You're a good-enough looking man, but you've some years on you, eh? And chopping wood doesn't build the muscles that hefting sides of beef does.

Nick swung the axe harder, biting more fiercely into the white wound it had chewed into the tree. Sweat began to flow. His blood quickened.

Chop.

He was confused.

Chop.

He was angry.

Chop.

And how much coin does a woodcutter make? Any fool can gather a few twigs for the fire, but who these days cares to bloody their hands slaughtering their own pig?

"Nobody..."

Nobody. She'll tire of you eventually. After all, what can a clodhopper like you give her? A hut in the woods is all very well for romantic fantasies, but women are practical, Nick. Love? They harp endlessly on the subject, yet it means nothing to them. Not really. Men are toys to them. She laughs at you, this girl of yours.

It took the axe less than an hour to get the woodman to turn its hungry head on his leg; it needn't have taken even that long. He was a very faulty vessel, this Nick Chopper, full of hidden rages and embarrassing flaws. Once he began listening to the axe in earnest, leading him to that final red moment was no work at all.

Even so, the axe was somewhat disappointed. it had its heart set on something a bit tastier than splintered femur and a ruby-glistening mess of thigh-meat. In reviewing Nick's fantasies of the marriage bed, it had formulated a delightful idea involving Nick laying his shrunken manhood on a stump. Then, holding the axe's blade in both hands, chopping it off. Perhaps it had taken too much pleasure in its own plans; perhaps Nick had somehow gotten a whiff of them and at the last moment chose a less insulting blow.

Still, it was done now, and done well; the idiot was howling like a madman, clutching his ruined leg with a luscious, betrayed expression. Already a couple of other bumpkins—a pair of fools come calling from the village—were running to him.

Nick?

Nick!

Oh, Nick, what did you do?

Nick suffered himself to be seized and carried clumsily into his hut. The axe lay in a spreading pool of gore, waiting patiently for one of the clods to seize it up and take it inside as well.

Because it *wouldn't do* to leave the man's tool behind. It was his livelihood, after all, and more than that, the measure of his character.

The village tinsmith, Ku Klip, was one of those half-wise idiots who have always been plentiful in any country or age; apparently not content with an honest trade in metalworking he had to venture down the shadowy paths of scientism and philosophy. And why should he not? The axe, hungry for new information, had taken advantage of the pious sheep gathered around Nick's bed, its mind grabbing hungrily at theirs. It caught glimpses of absurdities it could hardly believe. Apparently some decrepit old goat from foreign lands was kinging it in the Green City, having seized the throne with nothing but gall. There were talking beasts roaming unchecked in the countryside, and shoemakers turned sorcerer. Why not a tin-smith turned savant then?

Yet this Ku Klip was an irritating bastard; just canny enough to guard his thoughts, not discreet enough to keep them out of his mouth. As he carefully manipulated the grotesque, shining limb he had grafted onto the woodman's hip, he droned on. He loved an audience.

"I sense some fell influence at work here," he said. "You say the axe slipped?" The question was directed at Nick, but before his patient could so much as open his mouth the tinsmith went on. "Unlikely. This entire matter reeks of an arcane significance. There are patterns in the earth, laid there long ago for *who knows* what purpose? They can have an influence. The witches…"

That remark caught the axe's attention, but it was distracted the next moment by a sudden commotion: a girl had appeared and was fighting her way through the crowd to Nick's side. This, then, was the adored Nimmie Amee. She was certainly limber-looking enough.

She seized her man's arm, cooing and whining. Nick smiled tightly at first, and nodded, then looked away, as though anything in the room was more interesting than the face of his beloved. This was plainly not the welcome the girl had expected. Her pretty face fell and she pouted. The axe watched carefully.

"Nick, what's wrong? Why won't you look at me?"

Ku Klip hurried to her side.

"He's still mending, young Miss. It's a grievous injury, as you see…he won't be himself for some time."

"Of course," Nimmie Amee said, seizing at once on the explanation. "His poor leg. Will he ever walk again?"

"Certainly not," Ku Klip said with the callousness of the wise. "At best, this tin leg I've made for him will support his weight and allow him to hobble a little."

"Aye, hobble to the poorhouse," Nick said suddenly, turning a frozen, unpleasant smile on the girl. "You wouldn't care much for that, hey Nimmie? A pauper's life wouldn't much suit you, I don't think."

The folk around the bed shuffled their feet uncomfortably. Some coughed and began edging towards the door, muttering about urgent business in the village.

"*Don't say that!*" Nimmie Amee cried. "I'll love you even if you are a pauper…"

It was perhaps an unfortunate choice of words. She then complicated matters by trying to climb onto the bed with the woodsman and get her arms around him.

"*Get off me, you whoring bitch!*"

The tin leg straightened viciously. The foot Ku Klip had constructed for it was roughly fashioned; an angular, sharp-edged thing. Had the kick connected, Nimmie Amee would have lost her face. She tumbled from the bed, her eyes moving to the gleaming metal limb. Even now it was bending and unbending at the knee, apparently of its own volition. There was something insectile about the mindless flexing. Something that called to mind the wing-beating of a butterfly newly broken from its chrysalis. The woodman stared at it in horror.

The axe was fascinated. Something of the power that had given it life had apparently communicated itself to Chopper's new leg. A hundred questions occurred to it—had it been equipped with a mouth and tongue it would gladly have spent the afternoon interrogating Ku Klip. It might not have gotten satisfactory answers though; the tinsmith had gone silent. His face was drawn and white.

The Nola Amee picked that moment to make her appearance. The axe had the pleasure of seeing her face when it lit on Chopper's flexing leg. She had entered the hut with an unctuous expression on her old face. The vicious gloating underneath was difficult to miss. When she saw her victim's pistoning leg, her jaw dropped in a parody of astonishment.

"Auntie Nola," Nimmie Amee said. Her voice was expressionless with shock. "See how well Nick has gotten already? We'll still be able to be married. Isn't it wonderful?"

"Tinsmith," Nola Amee said slowly. "What did you do with his leg? His old one, I mean, the one he...damaged." The axe took careful note of the question, and the fearful tone in which Nola Amee asked it.

"Why, I burned it," Ku Klip said dully, his eyes fixed on Chopper. "In the furnace out back. It was no good to him."

"Of course," the old woman nodded, looking relieved. "*Of course.*" Her eyes turned on the axe; they held a wonder mingled with terror that it found delicious.

"Auntie," Nimmie Amee said fiercely. "Didn't you hear what I said? We'll still be married." She hesitated a moment, then grabbed Nick's hand and held it to her breast. Her face set and determined. The woodsman glanced at her with loathing, but he was apparently still weak from his ordeal. Too weak to push her away or spit in her face (as the axe somewhat wistfully suggested to him).

"*We'll still be married*," Nimmie Amee repeated, at no one in particular. "Nick will be alright and we'll be married, just as we planned. It's a miracle. *A miracle*."

Within months, Nick Chopper had become a thing to frighten children. He was a clanking, shining nightmare creature. A generation of villagers would remember his name as a very effective threat against uneaten vegetables. He kept increasingly to himself, preferring the solitude of his hut or the forest to covert stares and whispers. He still plied his trade but the coin it brought him accumulated unspent. He no longer ate, or cared to drink. A regularly replenished can of oil, its contents applied carefully to his joints in the evenings, was his one material need. The wedding with Nimmie Amee was postponed, eventually, out of existence.

Word among the villagers was that she had finally left her home, heartbroken, but doubtless glad to be away from Nola's sharp tongue and incessant meddling.

Still, Nick was a wonder, if a terrible one. Many in the village maintained that Ku Klip's work could have made his fortune and made him a god among tinsmiths and physicians both. But a little more heart went out of the old man with every limb or part he had to replace—and these came more and more frequently as the axe continued its work. Replacing the woodman's head took a particular toll on him, and shortly after Nick's bleeding and mutilated torso—the last of his meat—had been replaced with a gleaming tin cylinder, Ku Klip found a stout rope and used it. His funeral was respectable, if sparsely attended.

The axe rejoiced; was this not true happiness? To not only do the work one had been created for, but to excel at it so? Paradise. It *loved* the new Nick...to the extent it was capable of love. His metallic, sharp-edged frame was vastly more appealing to its logical sensibilities than the meat-body had been.

The axe hated chatter. The new Nick barely spoke. His new tongue was ill-suited to the task. The axe required regular whetting and oiling; Nick's new body understand those needs well. It felt them so keenly itself. Often the axe wondered how it had managed during those dreary early days, when most of Nick was still meat.

Not that meat was completely without interest of course. The axe had seen that Nick carefully collected each piece of his old self that remained after Ku Klip did his work. He took it back to the hut where it joined its' brothers in providing the evening entertainment. The arms, legs, toes and endless slippery organs fascinated the axe. They were so untidy in their design; so absurdly *complex*.

All in all, the days and evenings both were very full. There was another development as well, one most pleasing to the axe; it had decided to appropriate Nick's surname, since the woodsman was no longer using it. The decision was made on impulse, and there was no one to hear or know of it. Yet the axe—*Chopper*—felt a deep, preening satisfaction each time it remembered. It was like a man who had bought some luxurious item he could afford but had never considered before. It was more than a tool now. The bumpkins hereabouts didn't know, but soon they would. Perhaps quite soon.

Its ambitions were growing.

One cloudy morning Chopper took Nick outside on an errand. The task it had in mind had nothing to do with cutting wood, though it still relished in the mechanical precision with which Nick swung it and the splintering bites it took out of the sides of trees. This was, after all, the closest it came to moving, and it was, in its way, another bit of work for which it had been designed. Still, it wasn't wood they needed this morning.

The axe had no intention of allowing the tin man to venture too far from the hut. A storm was brewing. That was plain to be read in the grey and rumbling skies. A drenching would not do Nick's new body any good, and Chopper had left the can of oil behind, preferring that Nick not be needlessly encumbered.

Chopper found the place it was seeking. A mossy place, riddled with small holes amidst the group of apple trees near the hut. It set Nick to work hacking up the moss and stomping until its quarry emerged: a burrowing rodent, not unlike a rat or weasel but much larger. The thing bared its teeth at Nick and was quickly bisected.

The axe directed Nick to pick the mangled remains of the creature up and hold it in its imperfect line of vision. It was trying to decide if this one specimen would be sufficient for its purpose.

"*Nick?* Nick...how are you?" Nola Amee's nervous voice behind them was an unwelcome distraction. The old woman had kept well away from the woodsman since the initial incident with the leg. Chopper had put her out of its mind since then. It had no idea why she was here or what she might want, and was not particularly interested.

"Whughhuhh..." Nick greeted her, his tin tongue clicking in his tin head.

"Yes," Nola Amee said, in the voice of one trying to appease a fully-grown and possibly dangerous idiot. "Yes, hello. See what I've brought you? Just look. Look and see."

Nick was already looking at her, having turned his head completely round on his shoulders. Chopper knew perfectly well who the old woman was really speaking to.

Bored and now irritated, the axe directed Nick to swing it slowly around so it could see. It was almost amused; the silly bitch was holding *another* axe and grinning with large fearful eyes. They never once left Chopper's gleaming head.

"You see? A fine new axe for you, a real beauty! Far better than that old thing you've been hanging onto, eh? You can throw your grindstone away, this one practically sharpens itself. Its edge is fine enough to slice shadow."

Chopper understood her intentions. She wanted Nick to take this new inanimate axe in exchange for itself so that she could go hobbling off to the other old woman. The mutterer who had first woken it. She would then make good on the mutterer's promise to destroy it. The audacity of this— the sheer wrong-headedness of the plan—amused the axe mightily. If it were capable of laughter, it would have howled.

It made Nick laugh instead, throwing his head back and staggering, filling the forest with a grotesque, chattering roar. Nola Amee stepped back with goggling eyes, clutching the impostor axe to her droopy bosom. At that moment, fortuitously enough, the rat-weasel's bloody remains spasmed in Nick's fingers. The creature's head rose, a semblance of life returning to it courtesy of the axe's vitality. It made a queer, piercing noise—half angry chittering, half squeals of agony—that went badly with Nick's metallic hilarity.

This was apparently too much for the old woman. She threw the axe down and fled. A perverse urge made Chopper set Nick on her, suffering itself to be dropped so the woodman could have a hand free (he seemed reluctant to relinquish the rat thing, for some reason).

Nick caught Nola Amee easily, seizing her arm with a force more than sufficient to crush the bone. Chopper found this interesting; it had been under the impression that there was nothing left of the old meat-born Nick. All his parts had been replaced with good, sensible tin. It was wrong; evidently some gobbets and smears of his original self remained. At least that part of him that had despised the old woman.

What was there was little more than a vicious, childish perversity. He rubbed the rat-creature's broken body in her slack-jawed face in an attempt to get her to eat it.

Nola Amee surprised Chopper a bit as well; it would have expected her to faint or die of what must have surely been unbearable pain. Instead, she fought back with remarkable force, spitting fur and destroyed flesh back in Nick's face. Her ruined arm dangled limp and bloody at her side but she managed to slap his cheek once hard enough to make him grunt.

"*Whoreson!* And me a fool! I should have done you myself with honest poison! But no, I trusted a witch! Now I've lost Nimmie all the same and made a monster!"

There was more, but pain was catching up with the old woman. Most of what came out then was babble, chiefly concerned with Nimmie and how her intentions had been blameless. She sank to her knees, wailing piteously and clutching her smashed arm.

Chopper had a thought.

It had Nick take Nola Amee by the hair and drag her back to the hut, picking itself up on the way. What it had in mind was simply too good to miss.

"*Yuh wun' Nimmie?*" Nick gurgled. "*Wun' see er?*"

He kicked the hut's door open with one foot. Then he threw Nola Amee to the ground and kicked at her until she clambered in on her knees, supported by her one good hand.

There was little in the hut these days: endless rows of stacked firewood, mounds of faggots Nick had busied himself tying during the long and dark nights.

And there was one other thing, something that got up and looked at Nola Amee and made a horrible noise that she immediately echoed.

The chunks and bits of meat Chopper had made Nick claim from Ku Klip had not stayed dead. Like the rat creature, like the metal parts that now composed Nick, they had in time succumbed to the remaining influence of the powder of life. They had squirmed in their basket, spewing blood and less appetizing substances. The nose snorted in and frantically exhaled air. The fingers clutched, the eyes rolled and saw. The organ of Nick's that the axe had so coveted early on grew hard, softened and stiffened again in an endless cycle. All of this made for fascinating viewing—but merely watching didn't satisfy Chopper for long.

It had never been acquainted with the word *experiment,* but it would have understood it at once. It was in the spirit of experiment that Chopper had Nick apply lit matches and sharp-edged knives to his old skin and flesh, wrench his old teeth from his old gums and divide his old tongue and old penis by holding an end in either hand and pulling.

Finally Chopper had grown bored…and still more ambitious.

There was a heavy cobbler's needle and a reel of stout twine in the hut. More twine was purchased on Nick's next trip to the village, along with nails and steel clamps and solder. Chopper was curious; if the pieces of the old Nick were put back together in some reasonable semblance of his previous form, would it have created, in effect, two Nicks? One of meat and one of tin? It found the philosophical implications of this fascinating.

Unfortunately, the experiment had only been partially successful.

Somehow the parts did not make up a whole man, only a slouching, dripping, broken thing that gabbled and shuddered and filled the hut with unbearable stenches.

Chopper had been undaunted. There were gaps, so they would have to be filled, tThat was all. Rabbits and mice and a few dogs that strayed from the village provided initial pieces, but the effect their hastily sewn-in bits provided was less than pleasing.

Then, one day, someone came tapping shyly at the hut's door, someone who had taken herself from Nick's life but could not bear to stay away. Chopper had been delighted.

"Nimmie!" the old woman sobbed, tearing in mindless anguish at her cheek. "Nimmie, no! No, no..."

Nimmie Amee's blue eyes regarded her coolly from a face that had seemingly been sprinkled with eyes, as a cake is sprinkled with raisins. Meat Nick (as Chopper thought of it) reached out a torn and skinned and much-stitched hand. A hand with two thumbs but less than the requisite number of fingers. Those fingers it had it fit around Nola Amee's throat, and with a quick, convulsive squeeze ended her life. Tin Nick shrieked and stomped.

Having died but not by the axe's blade, Nola Amee would not revive. There was a certain justice to the whole scene.

The axe made two mistakes when it left the hut.

First, it left behind the oil can. Meat Nick and Tin Nick had enjoyed themselves playing with Nola Amee's remains for some time. For the first time since it had begun its association with the woodsman, Chopper had difficulty controlling him—either of him. It had felt that a bit of woodcutting to distract Tin Nick would be a good idea. With the abundance of new meat provided by Nola Amee, there was no need for any more rat creatures to stop up the remaining gaps in Meat Nick's body.

The second mistake was not locking the door behind it. The door had been damaged when Tin Nick kicked it open, but not too badly. The lock was still whole. Chopper could easily have had Nick repair it. But it was irritated with him and still excited from witnessing Nola Amee's death. Meat Nick would be busy for some time yet with the corpse. There was no need to worry about anything so mundane as a broken door. Chopper relished the cold wind that had blown up; the rumbling thunder seemed to echo deep in its haft. It looked forward to burying its edge deep in some young wood.

But when the storm hit minutes later it regretted its hastiness. Nick, busy demolishing an apple tree, had gotten into a rhythm and it was difficult to get him to break it. Even though the rain was soon sluicing over him and gathering in a wide puddle at his feet.

Then Meat Nick came bounding out of the hut. Until now, the creature seemed either afraid of its tin brother or regarded him with a certain reluctant deference. But now sibling tensions broke through.

The two battled for nearly an hour in the downpour.

That Tin Nick would win the fight was a foregone conclusion, but it took longer than it should have. As did the brief rest Nick insisted on taking afterward. Taking note of the rough red patches sprouting on his trunk and thighs, the axe forced urgent thoughts into his head.

Oil can, it thought, keeping it simple. *Oil can...*

"*Oi-i-eel-c'n...*" Nick grated obediently through a mouth that now would not open properly. He began walking, but the rain was still falling, and by now his joints were sticking. He was slow.

And the hut far away.

Meat Nick's remains—ironically revitalized by Chopper's power even as its blade had laid it low—rallied and attempted a final assault. The axe was furious at this effrontery and ordered itself raised, but the rust in his joints prevented Tin Nick from letting the planned blow fall.

But Meat Nick was now little more than sinew and cartilage and mindless rage. The stitches and clamps could no longer effectively hold him together. As Tin Nick's consciousness fell into a rusty sleep, the faulty structure of rotted flesh and bone splinters collapsed and lay twitching on the grass, waiting for the rain to wash it away.

Rust had gathered on Chopper's head as well. It was angry, but now that the traitor had been dispatched, it was philosophical.

Sooner or later it would be rescued.

Sooner or later someone would pass by the hut and this time it would not be slow. As the rain continued, its thoughts turned feverish.

It had been foolish to restrict itself to one servant—or even two, if the Nicks were counted as separate beings. Since taking its name, it had felt itself growing ever stronger, more than ready to try another slave. And if it could take two or three, why not five? If five, why not a dozen?

Why not an army?

The Green City was where it should have gone from the beginning. The axe saw that now. This foreign wizard-king the people talked of was nothing but a sham. A humbug. He could not stand against Chopper.

All it needed was a passerby or two, preferably someone with the Green City already in mind. Someone inexperienced and gullible to start with—perhaps a young girl, like Nimmie Amee. Or, even better, a fool;

some ninny without a brain in his head would take orders beautifully. A coward would work equally well, for that matter, a sniveling creature who would do anything to avoid the threat of harm.

Thinking this, Chopper fell into a rusty, contented sleep. All it needed to do was wait. The world, after all, was full of ingenues and idiots and cravens. Getting all three at once, of course, would be the best possible scenario—but the axe doubted it would be that lucky.

The End.

THE PERFECT FIT

by E.M. MacCallum

Oddlaug pocketed the small note in the seam of her dress when her two goblin guards arrived.

The dungeon was especially damp today, the evening rain the night before provided puddles all throughout the lower stone hallow of the castle.

Oddlaug sat in the cage obediently, hearing the grey skinned goblins latch the top of her cage. Curling her spine, as the wooden cage was only tall enough for her to sit with her shoulders hunched, she waited to be picked up by the two silent guards.

The stout round goblins had stick-like arms that one would assume couldn't pick up a wooden cage, let alone with a human in it. But they did and they performed their duties without a struggled breath or wobbled knee.

Lifting her above their heads, she was carted through the empty corridor of the dungeon and out towards the gateway leading to the Commons. She struggled to cross her legs beneath her tattered skirts, hiding her feet from view. She tucked her hands into her lap as the iron gates to the ruby palace closed behind them.

She tried to ignore the crowd of Munchkin goblins as they poked and prodded at her with sticks through the flat wooden bars like malicious children. She glared hatefully with her pale purple eyes at the lopsided grins oozing saliva. The grotesque creatures bred like cockroaches in a junk pile.

There were hundreds in the courtyard that day. They milled around each other, waddling in their blue frocks with their heads high as if they had something to be proud of.

Carried through the nameless crowd in her tiny portable cage Oddlaug shielded her eyes. Even with the sun hiding within the confines of the clouds it still stung her vision.

Today was the one day out of the month Oddlaug would be allowed outside the dungeon.

Her half sister Gayelette would be away today. The beauty couldn't stand the sight of her own flesh and blood. In fact, Oddlaug hadn't seen Gayelette since they were children. Gayelette was utterly beautiful. Oddlaug was just as ugly.

Oddlaug clenched her bony hand into a fist, feeling the rage bubble inside her. She and her sister never got along. When Gayelette became a sorceress she banned Oddlaug from her sight.

Oddlaug curled her skeletal body up in a ball. Her neck was sore from arching forward already.

Ahead she could make out the platform that she usually visited on her monthly outing. It was plain. They constructed it the day before and took it down the day after. Goblins of all shapes and sizes could see her; the monstrous sister to Gayelette.

If it wasn't for Gayelette's pity Oddlaug would be trapped in the dungeon always. The outings would be prohibited and her identity a legend. This did not assuage any of her hatred for her half sister. The only comfort Oddlaug would receive on the monthly outing was a special meal. The loathing gleamed in her eyes even as she licked her cracked lips in anticipation.

A half-human, like Oddlaug, needed special nutrients. No food would be able to sustain her. If it wasn't for the monthly feedings she would surely die or succumb to insanity.

The small cage stopped rocking and the blue clad goblins set her down on a platform. The smaller goblin children raced around after her. At one withering glance they'd scatter in the crowd behind their elders with shrieks of terrified delight.

It was then that she spotted Quelala, her sister's husband across the courtyard. He was dressed in blue from head to toe. Only the Golden cap on his head was of a different color. The Golden Cap was a gift from her sister; it had the ability to control the Winged Monkeys. It had a circle of diamonds and rubies running around it. At each tilt of his head, even with the clouded skies, the stones shimmered.

Quelala smiled pleasantly towards Oddlaug once she caught his eye. He was a wise man but a foolish one all the same. Years had taught

Oddlaug her secrets. He hadn't lived as many years as she and her sister.

She felt her spirits lift like a veil on a crystal ball as the meat was carted out on a large silver tray. Squealing with delight, her gnarled fingers flexed experimentally at the prospect of fresh meat. Not just regular meat, oh no. Her hunger could never be sated by just *regular* meat. The soft flesh of children was the only thing that could sustain her crippling crone-like body.

The silver platter was always being handled by the most unsuitable carriers. A thin goblin held it in front of him like a water pail He waddled awkwardly, careful to avoid Oddlaug's eye contact. He also took his sweet time approaching the platform as if every step were his last. *It will be if you don't hurry up*, she thought venomously.

The little goblin in blue stripes placed the end of the tray onto the platform and pushed it into place in front of her cage. The tray made an uncomfortable scraping sound of metal on wood as the goblin stepped to the side. On Oddlaug's cage there was a door placed in the wooden bars. It wasn't very large, just enough to reach her hands through it. Normally it was locked because no one wanted to be touched by the ugly sister of Gayelette. She knew of the rumors, the hushed voices that whispered in the corridors that vehemently proclaimed that one touch from Oddlaug and ones children would all die. If you had no children, your *future* children would die at childbirth.

The rumor was tantalizing and she didn't mind it at all, except when they'd dare each other to poke her with a stick in the Common. *Idiots*, she gnashed her teeth together trying to focus on the meal before her. They had cooked it. They always did, which displeased her some, but complaining in her position would be useless.

The goblin reached over towards the clock-work mechanism slapped up against the side of her cage and with a flip of a switch the door began to open.

Clawing her fingers beneath the opening as it rotated upwards she grabbed for a leg.

She had to swallow many times to keep the salivation down. She didn't want to be mistaken for a goblin. The idea made her chuckle as she sunk her decaying teeth into the leg.

The instant she did, she knew something was wrong.

The taste was wrong, the texture was tough, not like a child, rather...with a howling shriek she threw the leg back out of the tiny opening. It bounced against the platter and off over the platform into the dirt.

"Are you trying to poison me?!" She bellowed, sneering at the startled Quelala.

He approached immediately.

"Poison you? Never, that would be a terrible thing to do."

Pointing towards the leg as if it were a filthy sewer rat, Oddlaug cracked her voice like a whip.

"*That* is poison!"

Quelala inched towards the silver platter with keen interest. He dared not touch it for he did not need to eat children. In fact, the idea would have repulsed his kind.

"Did you smell a poison? Perhaps saw something that I cannot? For it appears to be meat."

For a man considered wise against the others of his species he rarely managed to impress Oddlaug.

"That abomination is not the flesh of a child," she hissed, "that is a monkey."

Their bickering managed to attract an audience. Goblin citizens waddled in for a closer inspection of the fiasco. Their curious eyes switching between the royalty and prisoner.

"Falsely accused," Oddlaug ranted, turning to the abundant of faces all tilted up towards her. "And here I sit, being poisoned before your eyes."

No one cheered for her, not one appeared to wan from neutrality. Their eyes flickered towards Quelala for his response.

The handsome prince gapped at Oddlaug, flabbergasted.

"Monkey won't poison you," he snapped, his face flushing.

"It's not what I eat, you tried to poison me. Everyone knows you can hide poisons in monkey meat, one cannot even tell it's there," Oddlaug flared.

Quelala opened his mouth to retort when his eyes flickered towards the hem of her tattered skirts.

"What's that?" His voice reduced to guarded curiosity.

Oddlaug turned her head just in time to see a goblin dart forward. It shot its hand through the bars and snatched the note she had stuffed away in the hem. In her anger and frustration she must have moved enough for it to wiggle free of its hiding spot.

Frantic, her clawed fingers swatted for the goblin, but he was much too quick. Hopping back out of arms reach, adrenaline smearing his face, he offered the note to Quelala. He was careful not to chance a glance at Oddlaug. Whispers roared up all around the brave little goblin.

"*Did you touch her?*"

"*She didn't cut you, did she?*"

"*Did you get close enough to see the maggots in her hair?*"

"*I certainly hope you didn't look into her eyes.*"

Ignoring the numerous questions to his own safety, the goblin waited for Prince Quelala to take the note.

Plucking it from his companion's fingers, Quelala opened the folds. His eyes scanned it briefly. He lifted his face to meet her gaze. Unlike the goblins, Quelala wasn't superstitious. His features were grim as he approached the cage.

Oddlaug squirmed miserably in her confinement. She couldn't run or hide; she knew holding down her skirt would only prolong the inevitable. Instead she tried to read his subtle expressions, but they were strictly guarded.

Reaching within the bars, Quelala, brushed the edge of her clothes away from her foot. Seeing for the first time the shoes she wore he jumped back. He grabbed the hand that had brushed up against the shoes protectively.

"Who gave you those?" He demanded.

Oddlaug wiggled her toes within the silver shoes, uncertain about her answer. The truth would not only imprison *her* but someone else as well. Turning the possibilities over in her mind the silence stretched for countless, merciless seconds.

Tilting her chin down into her upturned knees she glared at the crowd. Where was the note giver? Wouldn't they have wanted to be around the day after they gave her the shoes?

Quelala was always known as being a sympathetic man; it was rumored that he was the only reason Oddlaug was still alive. But, today, his mercy had fallen short.

"Hang her," he said. Words stabbed her repeatedly before Oddlaug was able to recover from the shock.

At first nothing happened. Perhaps the irregularity of those words had to wring themselves out in the minds of the goblin commoners and guards before they even registered recognition.

The moment it did, the first Munchkin moved toward the platform to pick up Oddlaug's cage. He grunted for help and was immediately assisted by another goblin.

Oddlaug felt a scattered moan scratch at her throat. This couldn't be happening to her; her sister would never allow it. Or would she?

All because of the silver shoes that had been gifts just the night before?

As she was carried through the crowd the Munchkins didn't poke her this time. They didn't playfully slap a hand on the cage or offer cruel comments.

Across the common were hanging posts erected hundreds of years ago. Enchanted by Gayelette herself, they had never faded with time nor crippled during a storm. They stood as fresh and tall as the day they were built.

A hanging in the East was so rare that the people had forgotten the brutal pleasure that came with it. The sickening curiosity of watching someone die wasn't entirely recognized.

A single goblin cheered amongst the faces in the crowd. Soon after, a few others joined in the cheering. Before she knew it the entire common had erupted in voices.

Fear began to creep along the edges of Oddlaug's flesh. She twisted in her seat. She glanced behind her at Quelala. The shoes had convinced him to order her death. He kept his back to the commotion, his head lowered and still.

"*Quelala, do you really want to kill your wife's only sister?*" she shrieked, but her voice was drowned in the resounding shouts that roared through the Common.

Grabbing her shoes, she was tempted to take them off and throw them away. With Quelala's back turned and the excitement rippling through the crowd it would have done her no good.

Why had her secret pen pal chosen to give her the note and the shoes the day before her feeding? She had the entire month to provide Oddlaug with such a gift. And such a *curious* gift. The silver shoes had shone even in the darkness of the dungeon below the castle. She had been so delighted to find the note when she woke that morning that read:

Enjoy the new shoes.

She had put the silver slippers on and was delighted to see that they fit perfectly. She had hidden them initially out of fear they would be taken away, *not* that her life would be eliminated.

Her enthusiasm for the new addition to her wardrobe had deflated. Turning to the faces around her she tried to concentrate on a spell. The problem with having a sorceress sister was that everyone assumed that Oddlaug had similar abilities. The disgustingly sour realization was that Oddlaug had very little magic beyond snapping sparks within her fingertips.

Approaching the gallows, she felt a tightness in her chest. Clinging to her shoes with both hands she felt insignificant compared to the towering posts before her. The tiny stage equipped with trap doors was narrow and had only enough room for two nooses between the posts.

Marching through the castle gates were three brightly colored humans; Quelala's personal soldiers.

The gates closed behind the three men. They stood far too straight and their faces far too neutral amongst the excited crowd. They approached their Prince and from where Oddlaug sat she could make out their mouths moving. Quelala's back was still to her. He began to turn the instant his soldiers pivoted on their heels towards the gallows.

No longer able to see the hanging nooses, Oddlaug was plopped unceremoniously on the wooden stage by the goblins. They didn't reserve their gentleness for this celebratory occasion. She always knew they hated her; goblins hated all things ugly even though they themselves weren't the picture of loveliness.

Nothing really felt real until the top of her confinement swung open. Able to sit up straight, Oddlaug let an intimidating shriek.

Grabbed under the arms by two of the waiting soldiers, Oddlaug was launched to her full height, very tall compared to the goblins.

Oddlaug refused to step from her cage and was lifted out of it.

The noise grew louder as she was dragged across the narrow stage to stand beneath the noose. She had been very careful not to allow her silver presents to fall off while she was being dragged. She couldn't lose the only gift she had ever received just moments from her death.

Could she run? They'd all stop her if she did.

She lifted her head high as the soldier behind her lowered the frayed rope over her head. Her thin, wild hair was pulled out from around the noose and placed to the side.

She could see Quelala to the side of the stage, peering at the scene, hypnotized. She saw pity in his eyes but felt none for him.

The rope was tightened around Oddlaug's throat. Scowling at the crowd, she swore vengeance. Her rage demanded it but her head knew it may never be justified. Once dead, she would be dead and no such revenge would be possible.

"Any last words?" The guard who had placed her head in the noose said calmly.

She tried to think of something eternal but couldn't think of anything. Nothing could sum up the hatred she felt for every soul that occupied the Common. Instead she glared towards the soldier in stubborn silence.

He stepped away. All three soldiers did. They moved back with their Prince.

Gathering the saliva in her mouth, Oddlaug spit on the platform with a hiss from the crowd.

Where was her friend? The one who had granted her the note and shoes? Wouldn't they come to save her? Her eyes scanned the numerous faces for one that might give her a hint to her only friend.

Perhaps they couldn't save her without their own deaths being penalty.

Without warning, the contraption beneath her feet slipped out from beneath her.

It was so quick and unexpected Oddlaug started a scream that was quickly silenced. The rope snapped taut and she felt the pain against her throat, but to her horror the fall didn't break her neck. Every muscle screamed as her head snapped upwards with the hanging rope. The frays dug into the tender flesh of her neck.

Kicking her feet frantically, her eyes bulged as the air was restricted. Her mouth opened for useless breaths and she twisted violently, desperate for air.

Her lungs burned. Her vision spotted with dark dots.

Kicking again, her shoes clinked together. She couldn't hear it over the cheers but felt it and thought one last time of her vengeance. *They will pay for this injustice.* To die because she was given shoes was a disputable charge in which she would have no jury.

She secretly wished for their heads to explode. Especially the ones in the front row that jeered the loudest.

Wet chunks of warm meat splattered her face long before she was able to consider what had just happened. Blinking away the blood, she gapped at the headless Munchkins. Blood had sprayed the crowd too.

The heads of the goblins were gone. At least thirteen of them. Suddenly screams replaced the cheers and the crowd began to run.

Red jelly mixed with bits of bone and brain slopped off the edge of the stage to Oddlaug's stunned fascination. Was she dead already? Was this pain part of death? She stared at the haunted expressions within the crowd and realized the impossible. She had done it.

Hadn't she?

Choking for air, she focused on a group of Munchkins all clutching together and staring at her wide-eyed. She kicked her feet. She inwardly wished for the group of Munchkins to bleed out.

Their screams were different from those around them. Pain etched their voices, the group of Munchkins collapsed to their knees. Blood ran from their eye sockets like tears, dripping to the stone ground. Blood gurgled from one of their mouths. He convulsed, dropping to his side and clutching his stomach. With a heave he vomited not only his food but puddles of crimson chunks.

The horror and pleasure that she felt at seeing their noses bursting with blood and their bodies twitching painfully was exhilarating.

The rope, she thought. *I need air.* Her hands scratched at the rope uselessly, it was too tight and she was far too weak from years of being locked in a cell. She'd never be able to lift herself out of it.

Nothing was happening and she was running out of time. Kicking again, her shoes clinked together and she dropped to the stone covered ground beneath the stage like a discarded doll.

Her legs screamed on contact. Her fingers snagged the rope and loosened it around her throat. Gasping in the first breath was painful. Her lungs protested at first. She ripped the noose from around her head and tossed it aside. She took another ragged breath. Ducking out from beneath the stage she felt emotions from the crowd wash over her. Fear swelled through the crowd. They pushed through their own kind, trampling the smaller ones beneath their feet just to get away.

Standing to her full height in front of the stage she bathed in the revenge. It was far sweeter than she could have ever imagined.

But, it wasn't complete just yet.

"You!" She pointed a gnarled finger towards Quelala, who stood frozen with a single remaining soldier.

Quelala froze, unable to run amongst the Munchkin followers.

"Your own people, these goblins who love you so, should grant you your death."

Quelala turned towards the scattered faces, the few that remained in listening distance stared at their king helplessly, though none approached him to do Oddlaug's bidding.

Oddlaug tried again and wished her suggestion; squeezing her eyes shut she wished it as hard as she could.

Opening one eye, Quelala was still standing before her, untouched and confused. The soldier before him realized the mistake first and drew his sword, pointing it towards her threateningly.

Everyone was distracted as a swooping figure far larger than that of a bird shot down from the sky. It hovered over the small group.

Oddlaugh stumbled backwards in surprise. It was the notorious Wicked Witch of the West. She wore her thinning dark hair in three pig tails all around her head. She had aged from the stories that Oddlaug had been accustomed to but otherwise she knew it was her. Only witches or sorcerers could ride broomsticks. The Wicked Witch of the West was drowned in black but her robes were lined with a white trim. Oddlaug noticed that the Wicked Witch of the West gripped a second broom in one of her hands while balancing on her own.

The Wicked Witch of the West smiled triumphantly at them all, her eyes lingering on Oddlaug.

"*Kill him!*" she shrieked.

The goblins nearest to Prince Quelala paled as they stared at the Wicked Witch of the West. Then they trudged towards their Prince. Their expressions were blank and their movements numbingly mechanical.

The Prince gasped in a breath, retreating to the top of the stage. His eyes snapped towards Oddlaug uncertainly.

"The shoes—*where did you get them?*" He shouted.

"From *me*, foolish man!" The Wicked Witch of the West cackled. "I cannot wear them because of your decree, isn't that right?"

Oddlaug gaped.

"What decree?" She demanded.

Quelala's eyes shifted between the two women uncertainly.

"*Back!*" the soldier who guarded the Prince shouted. The soldier thrust his sword towards the Wicked Witch of the West.

Oddlaug screamed a warning, but it was too late, the blade was long enough and the soldier quick enough. The tip of his silver sword gouged into with Wicked Witches right eye, creating a shallow, excruciating wound.

Screaming hideously, the Witch cleared the Common save for the few sourly slow paced goblins that plodded up the stairs to the stage. The Witch shot backwards out of reach before any more damage could be done. Clutching a palm over her wounded eye she thrust the broomstick in her hand down towards Oddlaug.

Oddlaug fumbled but caught the broomstick in both her hands and clutched it close to her chest.

Blood trickled down the Wicked Witch of the West's face, but her good eye was able to locate the offending soldier.

"You should be thrown out in the desert!" he shouted, his voice brave and terrified at once.

With a chuckle the Witch nodded her head towards the gallows. The unused noose on the platform whipped outward and flung itself around his throat. He bit his tongue and blood trickled out the side of his mouth. The rope dragged him violently backward. Balancing over the trap door, the rope became tight again and the trap door released, dropping him instantly.

Oddlaug ducked her head to see the hanging man grow still. The only man to have ever injured the Wicked Witch of the West was now dead.

There was shouting from where the Prince stood,causing Oddlaug to peek over the stage. Munchkins had wrenched Quelala down to his knees.

"Get on the broom!" The Wicked Witch of the West ordered. Oddlaug was quick to respond.

She didn't want to incur the anger of this woman anymore than anyone else. She straddled the broomstick and awaited further instructions.

"Click your heels together and you will fly," the Witch snapped. She seemed frustrated with Oddlaug's awe-struck expression.

Oddlaug clicked the sliver shoes together and suddenly understood how she was able to free herself from the gallows at last.

She took to the air. She felt light as a feather, as if the wind itself was carrying her. She rose to the same height as the Wicked Witch of the West and watched as Quelala emitted unearthly shouts towards the goblins. His own people were beating him with their fists. They stabbed him with hunting knives and whatever they could find in their pockets.

Her sister, Gayelette would be furious when she found out.

An unusual cry from the distance alerted both flying women to the skies behind them. The flying monkeys were approaching. They came at the call of their Master, Prince Quelala, who still held the Golden Cap upon his head.

"Kill him faster!" The Wicked Witch of the West commanded the goblins.

One swift blow to his temple, and the Prince Quelala fell silent.

The Wicked Witch of the West darted down on her broom and with her free hand she scooped up the Golden Cap from the dead man's skull. Placing it on her own head, the monkeys paused in the air before retreating back to where they had been called. "Now they are under my control," the Wicked Witch of the West purred smugly.

The Wicked Witch of the West turned her good eye to Oddlaug.

"Follow me."

Casting one last gaze down towards the streets she could smell their fear. She could see the glassy gaze of Quelala staring up at her. She stared back for a long moment, pondering what her sister would think up for her own revenge.

Sighing, Oddlaug took to the skies with her friend. Her friend had given her the shoes that had freed her from the confines of the dungeon, from her beautiful sister and the fiendish goblins.

Pausing in the air far above the Ruby Kingdom, the Wicked Witch of the West flashed a brilliant smile towards Oddlaug.

"You have questions?"

"What of Gayelette? She will come after us."

The Wicked Witch of the West clucked her tongue as if it were nonsense.

"Gayelette disappears on the day you are released from the dungeon for a reason. Did you not think that perhaps a sorceress can see into the future now and then?"

Stricken, Oddlaug tried to recover as swiftly as possible.

"Where did she go?"

"North, I think. This is yours now," the Wicked Witch of the West gestured towards the Commons with a pleasant imitation of a smile.

All of this land would be hers! Her revenge on all the Munchkins could happen now that she had the shoes.

"Why didn't *you* wear the shoes?" Oddlaug said, her eyes drawn to the shimmering silver at her feet.

"I cannot, I have been forbidden. Years ago, Gayelette found out about the powers of the silver shoes so she had a spell worked that no witch, good or wicked could wear them. The fear being that their power could take over *all* the witches. But you hadn't been dubbed a witch till today. *You had the shoes on yesterday when you were still part mortal*, therefore the spell is now broken and they are yours."

"Today?"

"Yes, yes. You think killing all those Munchkins was a thing of Good? You've crossed over, with me. Things won't be as lonely anymore."

"You were the only wicked witch?"

"Yes, of the West and for a long time the balance between good and wicked had been upset. But, now that you've been recognized, it is even once again. Two good and two wicked now. You shall be known of the Wicked Witch of the East from this day forth. No other name will suffice."

"Oh," Oddlaug choked on the shock. Then she mulled the idea over in her head. A smile crept up on her face.

She was free.

Not *only* that, but free to do what she wanted. Her will was her own. Squealing in delight, she flung her arms in the air triumphantly.

"*Eeeeeeeee!*"

"Careful with those!" The Wicked Witch of the West hissed as her new sister tapped the toes together experimentally. "Whatever is your deepest desire in the Land of Oz , the shoes will reciprocate."

The Wicked Witch of the East's eyes widened.

"My deepest desire?" She breathed the words out loud, feeling euphoric as the possibilities streamed through her mind. They bumped together in a jumbled mess. "Anything I want?" Her pale purple eye wandered from the sky to the Western Witch.

"*Anything you want*," The Wicked Witch of the West confirmed with a curt nod. "All you have to do is tap your heels together and wish."

The Wicked Witch of the East shrieked a laugh and twirled around in delight.

"Then I want a yellow brick road." She tapped her heels together, hearing the silver click against each other sharply.

Both sisters froze as the old Dickery Trail transformed into the Yellow Brick Road.

The Wicked Witch of the West frowned pointedly.

"And I want a lovely land called the land of the Munchkins where I will rule. Can you imagine? I will make those slobbering goblins into something cute and friendly. They'll have round hats with bells and polished boots," she laughed in sheer wickedness.

The Wicked Witch of the West eyed the new Eastern Witch suspiciously.

"Have you gone mad? These are all lovely things! We hold a secured title of Wicked for a reason, sister."

"Yes yes," The Wicked Witch of the East agreed, her eyes alight. "But what do children like?"

Hesitating, the Wicked Witch of the West answered.

"Children like shiny objects."

"And candy?" The Wicked Witch of the East urged with her hands for her sister to continue.

"Definitely candy," she agreed with her Eastern sister. "They also like bright and sunny skies and brilliant colors."

At the mention of bright skies, the Wicked Witch of the East squeezed her eyes shut and clicked her heels, her face scrunching up, causing all the wrinkles to roll forward. The sun shot out from behind the clouds causing both sisters to duck and hide their eyes beneath their hands. The Wicked Witch of the East wasn't finished however.

"Do they like Yellow Brick roads? Stately trees with bright colored birds? Sparkling brooks and green banks?"

"Yes, yes, yes!" The Wicked Witch of the West agreed wholeheartedly.

"*Then won't they like to come here?* To the Land of Oz? Where everything is bright and sunny and they can eat gingerbread houses or dance along a yellow brick road? Once they're here, there's no going back."

"No going back," the Wicked Witch of the West repeated, smiling slowly, her half rotted teeth revealing themselves at last. "*All ours.*"

"Good to eat, all shapes and sizes and they'll walk right into our trap."

"I knew you'd be the perfect Wicked Witch."

The Wicked Witch of the East enthusiastically agreed with high pitched squeals of laughter that rippled through the land like a hurricane. Tilting forward on her floating broomstick she tipped her toes together preparing to click her heels.

"Wait!" The Wicked Witch of the West cried.

The Wicked Witch of the East paused, her eyes trailing up to her new sister in frustration.

"Do you see what I see?" The Wicked Witch of the West was pointing North West and if the Wicked Witch of the East concentrated hard enough she was certain she made out a giant floating bubble.

"A floating balloon, how clever..."

THE END.

THE FUDDLES OF OZ

by Mari Ness

T he Fuddles scattered themselves as the man approached.

Not merely scattered the way regular people might scatter, or even the way the magical people of Oz, who live, after all, in the finest fairyland of the world, might scatter at the approach of danger, even though for most people in Oz danger was so little known that they had quite forgotten the word.

But the Fuddles were different. They were made of many little pieces of wood, all wonderfully and differently shaped, like a jigsaw puzzle, except more round than most jigsaws. When they saw people, it was their habit to scatter themselves into all of their many pieces, from a few hundred to several thousand, depending upon the person, and then rest patiently in the street, waiting for the viewers to come and patiently piece them together. It had become commonplace for the various Gilikins and Munchkins who lived nearby to come and amuse themselves for awhile putting the tricky pieces together, but after awhile, they came less and less, for even the most avid jigsaw puzzle lover becomes tired of putting the same people back together over and over again.

This was terrible for the Fuddles, who were forced to scatter themselves whenever even just one person came nearby. If that one person had no interest in puzzles, they might find themselves lying scattered for weeks. It became more and more difficult to keep up with cleaning their houses and repairing their pretty fences and doing their knitting. And, the longer they stayed on the ground, dry or wet, the more their little wooden pieces became slightly warped and moldy. For people in Oz may live forever, but that does not mean that they are not subject to things like water and damp, if it continues long enough. And yet they did not want to stop people coming by altogether, for it was only when people came by that they could learn about events elsewhere in Oz, and get the pretty yarns and paints they needed to keep their village beautiful.

So the Fuddles got together, or as many of them that were together, and decided to *Advertise.*

Advertising is a rare thing in Oz, and the Fuddles were not sure how to do so, but after some time, they made a sign, and asked a Munchkin farmer to place it upon the road. And the Munchkin farmer agreed to do so, of course, because such is the way of Oz.

And sure enough, a few curious travelers stopped by. Among them was a stout Winkie called Tidikins.

The Fuddles scattered when Tidikins approached, and he stepped forward, eager to solve their puzzles and piece them together. But no matter how hard he tried, he could not - he could not put even two pieces of a blue leg together. When evening fell he walked to a nearby village and complained about his hard day.

"Ha ha," laughed the villagers. For in Oz, it is perfectly acceptable for even the most kindly of souls to laugh at each other, for in so doing not only do the bellies of the overfed Ozites get much needed exercise, but also, the humiliation of being laughed at prevents anyone from becoming too proud, which is the quickest route to injury in Oz. And although no one can die in Oz, injury is still very very painful. "Those Fuddles are so easy that even a two year old may put them together!"

"Our two year olds are much brighter than the average two year olds in the countries outside Oz, I believe," replied Tidikins, angry at the insult. "For in those countries, two year olds may only be two for one year, but here, the two year olds remain two forever, and thus are able to gain more knowledge and skill than might be expected from them."

"That is as maybe," said the villagers, not all that coherently, "but still, it should be easy to put the Fuddles together, even for someone of very low intelligence."

Determined to prove himself of high intelligence, Tidikins returned to Fuddlecumjig, where the Fuddles lived, and tried again. And again. And again. The other villagers laughed and laughed. For an entire month Tidikins tried, but was unable to put two pieces together. And in his anger he decided to do a Very Wicked Thing, although he himself thought that he was only doing this to protect other inhabitants of Oz.

It is true, as the Royal Historian of Oz has said, that the reason most people are bad is because they do not try to be good. And others are bad out of sheer indifference or forgetfulness. But some are bad because they do not think things through.

For Tidikins was not a bad man, but his inability to put the pieces of Fuddles together, and the way everyone had laughed at him, had so fuddled his brain that he decided that the best thing to do was to hide the entire village of Fuddlecumjig behind a large wall and stick up notices of Danger! Danger! The notices, he knew, would not keep everyone out, since some of the inhabitants of Oz had a tendency to ignore signs saying "Danger" or deciding that they must go past these signs anyway. But this behavior was mostly confined to inhabitants of the Emerald City, and since they had already visited Fuddlecumjig, Tidikins thought that they might not return. (And in this he was quite right.)

Once the wall and the signs were built, Tidikins went off, some say to the Quadling Country, and some say to the Winkie country, and some say to the Emerald City, where he became a pedicurist of some note. For in Oz, nearly everyone must walk, and so nearly everyone has corns, and they were all very glad to have a pedicurist in their midst, especially one who could paint toenails such lovely shades of green.

Meanwhile, the Fuddles stayed scattered in their village, unable to piece themselves together, and unable to see that they were trapped behind a wall without a door, completely hiding their village from anyone who might walk by and see them, lying in helpless pieces everywhere in the village.

The pieces did not worry very much at first. None of them could see the signs posted on the wall:

Do not ENTER on pain of ETERNAL BEFUDDLEMENT

Even if they had, they might not have worried, for they knew as well as anybody that in Oz, many of the inhabitants - especially the inhabitants of the Emerald City - ignored such warnings all the time. Plus, they had their own Advertisement on the Yellow Brick Road. They did not know that Tidikins had pulled this sign down, to keep others from being Fuddled.

But after a few weeks passed, they began to worry. No one had come, and they could not move, not even a bit of an inch, unless some kind soul might pass by and put some of their pieces together. And as the weeks passed, the pieces of Fuddles began to realize that this less and less likely.

After a week and a half, it rained. It may seem odd that a fairyland would ever be troubled by rain, but even in a fairyland, plants and trees need water, and Oz's fabled crops of buttered popcorn and bread and butter and snow cones and buckwheat pancakes could not grow without rain. And so the magical rulers of Oz had decreed that rain should fall.

Rain had not overly troubled the Fuddles before. Since the Fuddles only scattered themselves when they saw other people, and since other people never visited Fuddlecumjig in the rain, they simply moved inside like ordinary people would, and waited for the rain to end. But now, they couldn't. The rain fell on them and made them very wet and cold. They could not shiver, but they could feel the cold. And the rain, they knew, would not be good for their wood.

But they did not despair. They still had the wind, and the wind might - might - lift their pieces just enough so that with a twist or two they might maneuver themselves closer to their other pieces, might be able to snap together a piece or two, or three - although three was perhaps too much to hope for. Enough to make half a mouth, possibly. Enough to scream for help.

But although the winds of Oz are gentle and playful, none of them seemed to want to move the pieces.

It rained again, and again. The pieces began to sink, just a little, into the mud, and their colors began to fade, just a little, from the rain and the sun

Still, they told themselves, it was not so bad, even when winter came, and the pieces shivered in the snow. For Ozma, after some discussions with Glinda and the Wizard of Oz, had decided that it would be a pity to deprive the children of Oz from the fun of playing in the snow, and thus allowed winter to enter Oz each year, if only for a few weeks - just enough for everyone to enjoy a good sleigh ride and snow sculpture building contest and hot chocolate, but leaving before anyone got tired of shoveling snow. The snow began to warp and damage the wooden pieces a bit, but they did not worry too much, deciding that they could always repaint themselves once they were put together, and perhaps ask Glinda the Sorceress to replace particularly warped pieces. And surely someone would come, after winter had made everyone feel irritated and grumpy from being housebound.

But spring came, and the flowers of Oz sprang up, and no one came to Fuddlecumjig, or its wall.

The pieces were just about to settle into general apathy when a bird appeared.

A bird, the pieces thought. A talking bird of Oz. For, since Oz is a fairy country, most of the animals of Oz could talk, and the pieces hoped that the bird might see them scattered behind the wall, and tell other people about their sad plight. In this way, they hoped, they might be rescued. The pieces that contained part of their mouths opened and closed, although they made no sound. They tried to wink their partial eyes.

The bird opened its beak, and swooped down. If the pieces of Mrs. Chippie could have screamed, they would have, as the bird swallowed a piece of her neck and a piece of her hand and a piece of Mrs. Cotton's hand. The pieces tried to huddle together for comfort in the stomach of the bird, but a bird's stomach is constantly churning, and the acid in its stomach soon began to dissolve the pieces. And then, although they were made of a magic wood that had never felt pain before, the remaining pieces of Mrs. Chippie and Mrs. Cotton felt that strange and hideous sensation, and knew without knowing how they knew that those pieces had been permanently destroyed.

The bird flew away, and the pieces of Fuddlecumjig stopped hoping for more birds.

But. A kangaroo had lived nearby, they remembered. A kangaroo wanting mittens. But more weeks passed, and the kangaroo never came, and soon they gave up hope of that.

The pieces thought of other times. Of the time when Mr. Butterclip had been pieced together with Mrs. Carrottop's legs, giving him strange ideas about both Mr. and Mrs. Carrottop that were not appropriate for a fairyland. Of the time when Mrs. Chippie had been given Mr. Butterclip's head, and subsequently learned about all of those inappropriate feelings for Mr. and Mrs. Carrottop, and her immediate plans for certain types of parties that were also possibly inappropriate for a fairyland, but sounded like great fun and a nice change from the eternal cycle of scattering and mixing and being puzzled together. They thought of the time when little Fi Fyghter had almost set a match to some of their pieces, which, being made of wood, could burn, even if they were magical, and the fear that had filled the scattered town at the thought. And how this threat had come again and again, for like everyone in Oz, little Fi could not grow old, and therefore could not learn the danger of fire to the Fuddles, until his parents had finally left. For the Gilikin country, the Fuddles had heard, and they could not help but hope, even in their fairy and contented state, that the entire family had been eaten up by Kalidahs on the way.

Dorothy, they thought. The little princess of Oz had come to their town once and with the help of her aunt and uncle and the Wizard of Oz and her sharp eyed hen had rapidly put many of the Fuddles together. Dorothy was certain to come, and so they settled in the mud as another rainstorm pounded on them, being to warp their wood. Dorothy will come, they thought contentedly.

But Dorothy, being a Princess of Oz, had many fine puzzles to play with in her charming apartments in the Emerald City, and besides, had other adventures to tackle. Perhaps, had she read about the plight of the Fuddles in Glinda's Great Book of Records, she might have come, but the Great Book of Records had only mentioned the building of the wall, not the slow sinking of the pieces of the Fuddles into the mud, and the agony of their distingration, and so Dorothy knew nothing about it, and Dorothy did not come.

The houses fell into pieces, as houses will, when no one lives in them and keeps them repaired. Deep within the mud, the Fuddles knew none of this. They only felt their pieces drifting apart, bit by bit, felt their wood disintegrating, felt - and they could hardly even remember the word for this, so long had it been since they had known anyone who had felt it - pain. Searing, agonizing pain, that grew only worse as the wooden pieces continued to disintegrate.

And when the Munchkins finally came, they saw nothing but fallen houses and mud. Befuddled, and distressed that such ugliness could appear in the finest of fairylands, they quickly pulled down the houses. They used the wood to build another wall to hide the village until it could grow pretty and green again.

But even when this was done, and Fuddlecumjig was no more than a small mention on a map that few people ever saw, and even as their pieces dissolved in the mud, the Fuddles could not quite die. After all, they were fairy folk, of a sort, and in Oz, no one ever dies, even when that person's pieces are scattered throughout the land.

But even in eternal Oz, with its eternal memories and people, no one remembered the Fuddles, or knew of the horrible weight of the mud above them, and no one heard their endless attempts to scream.

THE END.

FOUR AM AT THE EMERALD CITY WINDSOR

by H.F. Gibbard

Once upon a time, the Wonderful Wizard of Oz gave a girl named Dorothy Gale a brick made of solid gold. He meant it to remind her of the long and winding yellow brick road that she had traveled through the Wonderful Land of Oz.

That was her story, anyway. More likely, she turned a trick for the brick. With a Munchkin, maybe. Either over or under the rainbow. It didn't much matter when Dotty was in slut mode.

When she got back to Kansas, Dorothy gave the gold brick to her Uncle Henry for safekeeping. Five years later, when she married The Great Cagliostro of Knoxville, Henry re-gifted the brick to the two of them, pretending it had been his all along.

A bribe was what it was. Bert understood that now. Baksheesh, to get him to make an honest woman out of the wiliest whore of Oz.

1:21 a.m.

Bert Lister, formerly known as the Great Cagliostro, walked the thin green carpet of Room 143 of the Emerald City Windsor Hotel, drunk, muttering to himself, trying to forget why he was here. A pungent smell of cigarettes, marijuana, and cheap incense followed him around the dimly-lit room.

It was ten years today that he'd married Dorothy Gale. Their nuptials had taken place at the biggest Unitarian Church in all the Land of Oz. All of Oz had turned out, from the hammer-heads to the flying monkeys. The Wizard himself performed the ceremony. In the centerpiece at their reception had sat Henry's gold brick, looking like something crapped on the table by an aureate Pegasus.

Now the brick was long gone, long spent. As were all the illusions that went with it.

Bert paced like an animal in a cage, his drunken words mumbled in rhythm with his wobbly footsteps.

"I bet she fucked 'em all before she met me. Cowardly Lion, with his gigantic cock. Tin Man, Mr. Iron in the Pants. Scarecrow, gave her a rash. Winkie Soldiers, two or three at a time. Maybe even ol' Witchie-Poo herself."

Surrender, Dorothy indeed!

Admittedly, it was hard to imagine Dot pleasuring an old biddy like the W.W.W. She liked men too much. She was the only girl Bert had ever screwed who could come three or four times in a row without help. She'd been fun, at first, sure, but then. . .

He halted and stared over at the cracked emerald mirror above the bedside table. Below it, the numbers on the clock glowed an angry red at him. 1:21. Just over two and a half hours to go.

He resumed pacing, thinking of how it had all gone so wrong. She'd loved him as Cagliostro, thrilled to his feats of might and magic, in bed and out. But then, after they'd married, she'd shown a practical streak. A certain parsimonious attitude she must have inherited from Uncle Henry and his dour grey Kansas ways.

He began muttering again.

"Made me quit the magic biz. Steady employment, she wanted. After that it was shit work. Desk job at a carriage factory. Plastered *allatime*. They fired my ass. What'd she expect? Then she stopped sleeping with me. Just screwing my friends. And then—"

But he didn't want to think about what happened then.

1:24 a.m.

Scraps of memory tumbled around in his wasted brain like blood-soaked rags roiling behind the glass door of a Laundromat dryer. He remembered fleeing their suburban palace, drunk, leaving Dotty sobbing, screaming. He remembered her hand bent weirdly backwards, her bleeding, *blood, blood* on her face—

He shuddered and moved back along the wall, breathing hard, swallowing heavy, steadying himself by slipping his fingertips along the paneling. The room seemed to sway with his steps, like a ship.

The green shade on the bedside lamp cast a ghostly glow onto the battered chest of drawers and the narrow space between the twin beds.

1:25 a.m.

He was at the back of the room now. His tan jacket hung neatly in the closet on the single hanger provided. The jelled spatter on it made it look like he'd come through a shower of red rain. Gnawing his lip, looking down at his sticky legs, he noticed a similar pattern of still-damp spots on his black jeans.

1:31 a.m.

It was all her fault. He'd had a hard day looking for work, with nothing, nada, no leads even. To feel better he'd stopped at a bar and had a couple of mint juleps to calm his nerves. Just a couple. He'd walked through their front gate, feeling no pain. And then she'd been all over him, riding his ass, about the job, and the money, the booze. . .and their tenth anniversary, *where the hell was her friggin' present?*

Now he stood washing his arms with rolled-up sleeves at the sink in the little bathroom in the back of Room 143 of the cheapest fleabag hotel in the Land of Oz. The soap sliver fell to the cracked emerald-tiled floor. He bent to pick it up. He peered down at the soap for a minute, watching it spawn red bubbles that slid languidly onto the floor. The bubbles reflected the fluorescent light from the fixtures flanking the mirror.

The bubbles suddenly struck him funny. He laughed, a hard laugh, nearly without sound.

He stood and gripped the sink, looking over his own muscled forearms, admiring them. Hard brown eyes, bleary and bloodshot, stared back at him from the dirty mirror. The steam and the cracks in the mirror warped his reflection, made it look like a stranger staring back at him.

He twisted his head around, inspecting himself. His face and thick neck were clean but unshaven. He felt a tremor go through him.

No one saw, he whispered to himself.

No one.

The flophouse lobby was poorly lit with garish green neon. He'd been holding the jacket, folded over his arm. And the spots on his pants and shirt just looked like old, dark stains.

1:35 a.m.

Tinny was the real problem.

The Tin Man had warned him after last time, with a theatrical tremor in his hollow, metallic voice: *Lay a hand on her again*, asshole, *and I'll chop you up into fish food.*

This time, though, he had ol' Metal-Head covered. At least, he hoped he did. She'd call by four, and that would be that.

He'd fled the house too fast to change clothes, jogging toward downtown dodging traffic with his bloody flannel shirt tail hanging out, leaving her screams behind him. He'd checked in and stumbled through the door to number 143 and headed straight for the room phone, an ugly avocado plastic fixture with filmy gray push buttons.

Somehow he'd managed to stab in their home number. Reached automated voice mail. Threw the phone in a rage on the bed. Then picked it up again, after the beep, and bawled out his message into the silent receiver.

Amid the agonized apologies, he'd given her a deadline to call him back. Four o'clock.

Smart. Now he couldn't leave the room. Couldn't sleep. Couldn't even shower. He had to sit here and wait for her damned call. Until four o'clock. Hours away.

He sat down on the bed again, his head in his hands, sweat seeping down his fingers, rocking autisticaly. For all he knew, the Winkies were there already, at his house, their red flashing lights playing over the for sale sign, over his crumbling driveway. Over the neighbors' driveways.

1:42 a.m.

On a sudden impulse, he jerked open the drawer to the bedside table. The Gideon Bible lay alone inside, its faded jade cover worn from use.

He wasn't a religious man. But any port in a storm.

An unexpected warm feeling rose in his chest and forced open his mouth. He was remembering something now, through the boozy haze. Something from his childhood in Knoxville, long before he came to the Miserable Land of Oz.

He remembered the dotted lines on maps in the back of the Bible that traced the progress of the Children of Israel through the Promised Land. He remembered happy little colorful maps in blue and pink and bright yellow thumb-tacked to a bulletin board and ice cream cups with wooden spoons and him singing "Stand Up, Stand Up for Jesus" at the top of his lungs to impress the big-chested high school girl who ran the Vacation Bible School class. . .

A tear slid down his cheek.

"Oz, you're such a shithole," he muttered.

The Gideon Bible fell apart in his hands. The binding had been sliced through, the cover cut away from the pages. He peeled away the cover in a daze. The pages, too, had been cut, hollowed out and removed to form an empty niche in the center of the book.

In the abyss carved into the middle of the Gideon Bible, he found—

what? A whiskey flask? No. Something else. Another, smaller book, bound in smart brown leather. As he shook it loose he felt his eyes widen slightly with wonder and fear.

He'd flopped in plenty of cheap hotels before. As a teenager he'd toured with his garage band, Space Ghost. Then later on, he'd done the magic biz. He knew what went on in these places. People gave birth in the rooms, went crazy in them, cheated in them, died in them.

And sometimes they left things behind when they checked out.

The little book's leather cover felt strangely warm to the touch. He picked it up slowly and held it under the table lamp, turning it over in his hands. The cover was inscribed with a hand-tooled title: "The Magnificent Secret of Oz."

He opened the book. Inside the front cover, clipped to the first page with a large paper clip, he found a hundred dollar bill. He raised the bill up to the light with both hands. Ben Franklin stared back at him, looking prim and self-satisfied.

Bert let out a whoop. The almighty green dollar was good here in Oz. All the shops took it, at a favorable rate, and you didn't even have to hit the bank for an exchange.

He shot a squinty glance around to see if there was anyone watching. That was stupid; the room was locked. The night latch and chain were busted, but there was nobody else in here with him. He'd checked already.

He stuffed the bill in his right front pocket, snickering to himself. He shouldn't be this glad. Not when he was facing jail time. Not when Tinny would probably cut his dick off before he even got to jail. But right now, damn it, he was glad. Lady Luck was back from her long trip to the toilet. He was sure of it.

With the C-note, he could afford another drink while he waited in this overheated hell-hole for Dotty to call. Some of the good stuff, even. He picked up the room phone from the cradle. He'd have to keep it short.

That guy who checked me in. Come on, come on. . .

He snapped his fingers.

Some Hispanic name. . .Pedro? *Pedro?*

No. *No.* Francisco!

Francisco was still on duty at the front. He agreed to bring him a bottle of absinthe for forty bucks.

"I only have a hundred," Bert said, "Bring change."

After he hung up, he wondered if that was so smart, telling Francisco about the hundred. Maybe he'd show up with a pistol and rob him. But you have to trust somebody in this world. And right now, Francisco was it.

A stupid happy grin played over his face. With the sixty he had left, and the hundred overdraft on their checking account, he could catch a balloon out to Wichita, then hop a Greyhound back to Knoxville, where he grew up. Get a fresh start. Still have some cash left for meals and booze.

He toyed with the idea of leaving right away, as soon as the bottle arrived. Screw Dorothy. Screw four a.m. She'd probably call the Winkies anyway. It was time to trade up, time to write off his ten dismal years with that bitch.

1:50 a.m.

He picked up the little brown book again, ran his thumbs over its fine, high-quality paper, ruffled its gilt edges. On the first page, underneath where the C-note had been, English words in Gothic script stared at him. The print swam under his bleary eyes.

"*DEAR FRIEND,*" the words began,

Please accept this small token of respect as an incentive to continue your journey through the pages of this treatise, which offers the most important of all paths, that which leads to the true desires of your heart.

"Heard that one before," he muttered.

He'd done it all before, in fact. Started young, just after dad left and mom finished drinking herself to death. Amway, multi-level marketing, telephone soliciting—even some three-card monte before he figured out where his real talents lay.

"I took your cash, okay?" he lectured the book, "But I'm the one in charge here, pal. Not you."

He punctuated his words by stabbing the book with his index finger. The stabbing felt good.

He turned the page.

The title read: "*A Spell for Control of an Inconstant Woman.*"

He busted out laughing.

"Oh, you little SOB," he told the book, shaking it fondly under the lamp, "Oh, you SOB. Control a woman! Yeah, yeah, that's the ticket."

Then he stopped laughing. What did "Inconstant" mean, anyway? He didn't know that word. What if it meant something weird, like the gal was on her period?

He closed the book, feeling wary of it. Then he opened it again and ran an index finger over the words of the spell. They were Latin words. He could tell that much. He mouthed a few syllables, massacring the ancient language.

He tried to flip to the next page. The book wouldn't let him. Its remaining pages stuck together now like they were glued. He felt a chill rise up his spine.

Maybe he should throw the book in the trash right now, get rid of it. He'd read all those stories as a kid, stories of monkey's paws and magic lamps and deals with the devil that never quite turned out like you'd planned...

But the book had just given him the hundred. A hundred in cold, hard cash, and not just some empty promise. That was more than the devil usually fronted you, in those stories.

So he would read the spell. Out loud, but backwards. No, not backwards. Every other line, the odd ones, then back to the even ones. No, no, all the words, but chopped up. Like a sobriety test. That way, it might still work. But if there were any funny hoodoo associated with it, he'd have broken it up.

It had to work.

You still got it, pal.

That's what he told himself.

He read the spell, out loud, chopped up like he'd planned.

Nothing happened.

Nothing, except a wave of fatigue crashed over him. He tried to stay awake, to keep his eyes open, but his limbs suddenly felt like lead. He couldn't sit up any more. He felt himself collapse into the bed.

The last thing he saw was the words inscribed on a dusty brass plaque at the head of the bed.

SWEET DREAMS, JUST LIKE HOME.

Then he was falling, falling. . .

2:35 a.m.

The phone was ringing. It had been jingling for some time now, its tone distorted by his dreaming mind into a buzzing insect noise. Bert often dreamed of insects when he slept in the Land of Oz. In his dreams, flies buzzed around his helpless head, entered his gaping mouth and vibrated down his throat, making his feet dance wildly.

He groaned. He felt so boozy, damp and heavy like wet laundry. Like he was melting into the bed.

He tried to sit up.

He was stuck.

The phone was still ringing. He tried again, straining to rise from the bed. It must be Dot calling. He had to get to that phone, damn it! He grunted and struggled. But he couldn't move.

His felt his heart pounding. He tried to turn his head. It wouldn't budge. If he'd gone paralyzed—

He listened to the raspy breaths coming out of his mouth. He saw something moving, out of the corner of his eye.

Dusty wallpaper ran around the room above the paneling. He could barely make out the pattern in the semi-darkness. It was supposed to be flowers, an endless repetition of some thin twiggish fancy long-stemmed thing. But it didn't look like that now. The patterned things on the paper looked like insects. Long, thin, evil insects, staring down at him with their large, multipart eyes.

The name for them came to him unbidden: *The Fleeby-Jeebies.*

He cried out, breathing hard, and tried to move again. His arms and legs were sinking into the bed. The bed was holding them tight, swallowing them up. He couldn't budge.

The phone had stopped ringing. He barely noticed. He swallowed hard and dry. He was sinking, sinking slowly into the bed that felt like it was full of quicksand. It was warm now, filled with body heat. It smelled musky, like a woman.

It was eating him alive.

He cried out, at the top of his lungs. The bed gripped his face and head, squeezing, making his temples pound. He grunted and strained and arched his back up an inch or two off the bed, struggling, twisting, gurgling—

A sharp pain snapped like lightning up his lower back. He gasped and collapsed back onto the bed. He panted, trying to control the pain and the panic.

He cried out again. The bed was constricting his lungs, poking him painfully in his sides. What began as a screech ended in a pathetic sob.

He felt the bed molding itself to him, oozing up around his scrotum, invading his anus with its warmth. It gripped his wrists, his ankles—

He had a sudden urge to just let go, to let it happen, to let the bed swallow him and be done with it. To give up.

Then the bed began invading his ears. A sudden, agonizing stab of pain radiated from his jaw into his neck and head. There was a crackling, popping sound.

The bed was destroying his jaw joint.

Now he understood. It was going to break all his bones, starting with the more fragile ones. Crush him into liquid jelly before it absorbed him.

The bed had teeth.

He screamed, once more, with everything he had left.

He heard a knock, the turning of a key, and the door opened to his room.

"Mr. Lister?" a distant voice said.

He gave out a whimper for help.

The muffled voice drew nearer.

"Do you need help, Mr. Lister?" the voice asked.

He tried to nod his head. He couldn't.

A strong hand gripped his. It pulled him suddenly up, out of the bed with an awful sucking sound, to an upright position. The bed let go.

Bert felt a numbness in his limbs. The room went gray and danced with stars. Then it all went black.

When he came back he was still on his feet, just barely, wobbling like jelly. He was face-to-face with Francisco, the desk clerk. A sudden sob of relief burst out of him. He fell forward into the startled hotel clerk's arms.

"Are you all right, sir?"

Francisco smelled of Old Spice and tired sweat. His slicked hair looked years older than his smooth face. He wore standard hotel attire, a green polyester leisure suit over a lime green silk shirt.

After a moment, Bert pushed away from the olive-faced clerk, turned, and looked back behind him, his heart still pounding. It was solid again. A normal bed. No more quicksand.

He shook out his trembling limbs. Had he dreamed it? Some boozy nightmare? Every muscle in his body felt macerated. He turned back to Francisco.

"You—" he began, "I—" Unable to finish the sentence, he put his face in his hands and wept like a baby.

When he looked up again, Francisco was still standing in front of him, looking embarrassed.

"I tried calling you on the phone, but no answer," Francisco said, tilting his head slightly to the right, as though uncertain of how to proceed, "And-and-I then I heard yelling from the room. I wondered if something was wrong. So I used my key. I brought you the bottle of absinthe you asked for—but I wonder—if you really need—to be drinking any more right now?"

Francisco's words trailed away. Bert stared up at him, bleary-eyed. He extended his hand slowly and took the bottle of glowing green liquid. A minute later, he remembered the hundred in his pocket. He jammed a hand into the pocket, pulled out the bill, and slapped it into the clerk's hand.

"Keep the change," he croaked.

Francisco gave him a funny look.

"You just saved my life, buddy," Bert said, "Keep the change!"

Francisco shook his head.

"That's okay, Mr. Lister," he said, "I didn't save—save your life. I just brought you the change you wanted. The sixty dollars, just like you said."

He was backing away from Bert now, from the bed. He laid the three twenties on top of the TV set, covering a rash of cigarette burns.

"Thanks," Bert said.

He wagged the bottle at him. "And thanks for this."

"No problem," Francisco responded, still backing toward the door.

Francisco paused two paces from the door. He looked uncertain. Bert had a sudden, awful thought: What if Francisco could see the blood on him now, on his stained pants? What if he called the Winkies?

"Mr. Lister," Francisco said, his face grim, "There's something else I need to tell you. Before I came down here to bring you the booze, there was a man at the front desk. The man was asking about you."

"About me?"

"Yes, sir. A bald man. With hard eyes. Tall. Barrel chest."

Oh, shit.

"Tinny," Bert muttered, shaking his head.

He felt a laugh building up inside of him, a laugh on the verge of hysteria. The laugh forced its way out of him a second later.

"Are you all right, sir?"

"Yeah. I'm fine. Just dandy."

Tinny.

He laughed again, a chuckle that ended in a wheeze.

"The bald man made me a bit frightened, sir. I didn't tell him anything."

"Thanks."

"He's still around here somewhere, I think. Would you like me to call— the Winkies—?"

"No."

"Well, all right. But maybe you should wait in the room for a while. Until he goes, you know. I can call you if he stops by to let me know he is leaving."

"Thanks. Thanks a million, Francisco."

The clerk nodded, took the two final wary steps to the door, and moved out of the room, closing it.

3:14 a.m.

Bert turned and gave the bed a malevolent stare. He felt like pissing into it. He'd like to hose down the arrogant sea-green sheets, the innocent-looking bedspread, the fluffy pillows. . .Had it all been a nightmare?

He wondered if he'd ever be able to lie in a motel bed again, without thinking about—.

But he was more sober now, more in control of himself. His mind was working again. He had to get out of this room.

He looked up toward the ceiling. The dusty wallpaper was flowers again. No more fleeby-jeebies.

He just had to get out of this room.

He realized something. Four o'clock didn't matter anymore. He couldn't skip town now, not even at four.

She'd called Tinny. That stupid bitch had called Tinny instead of him! He was dead meat.

He stared at the book on the bedside table. It looked menacing now, its leather cover sneering at him. He knew the book had something to do with the bed swallowing him up. He was sure of it. And something to do too with the call from Dot he'd missed, before she called Tinny.

He should burn that book.

No, wait. The call had been from Francisco, not from Dorothy. Dot hadn't called him at all yet.

And why the hell not?

There was too much going on. More than he could understand. Lady Luck had gone schizo on him. His head hurt like hell. He felt dizzy. He needed to fix the angles, to know where he stood.

He set down the bottle and picked up the book. Maybe he could reset things, try again. He held it by the edges, like a hot potato. It let him turn past the "woman" spell now. He drew in a deep breath.

The next page had that Gothic script again.

Follow my instructions, it said, *and I will give you the deepest desires of your heart.*

Follow my instructions. Had it said that before? Those exact words?

Maybe it's telling me it's all my own fault, he thought, *For jimmying with the spell. If I'd just read it straight, maybe nothing would have happened with the bed. Maybe, even, Dot would have called me instead of Tinny.*

So I fucked it all up. Again. *Story of my life.*

He turned to the next page.

A Spell, it read, *To Defeat an Enemy.*

To defeat an enemy!

He felt a sudden surge of relief go through him. He could breathe again. His shoulders dropped a few inches.

A tear rolled out of his left eye. The book was on his side after all. It knew what he needed. Exactly what he needed.

"You, you were there for me all along, weren't you?" he rasped to the book, patting it, "You wanted to help me with Dorothy, but I fucked it up. Now, you're going to help me with the Tin Man, right?"

The book didn't respond. It didn't need to. It had given him the C-note. It had offered him happiness, tried to fix things with Dot. It hadn't worked so far, sure, but that was his fault. For gumming up the works.

But now, if he played his cards right, it was going to save him from his worst enemy of all. From Tinny.

He didn't hesitate this time. He read the spell out loud, straight through, knowing he was mangling the Latin. He didn't care. He had an understanding with the book now. It was his friend.

The pounding came a moment later. Three metallic pounds from a big fist on the hotel room door.

Bert hesitated for a second. He told himself he wasn't scared any more. Not scared at all.

So, why hadn't he moved yet?

Three more pounds on the door.

He opened it.

Tinny's six foot four frame filled the doorway. Bert backpeddled, letting him clank into the room.

"Hello, T.M.," he said, moving back toward the bed, "How did you know to find me here? Did Dotty tell you?"

He'd said the spell right. That was all he needed. A spot on the inside track. A friend who could show him the angles.

Tinny just stood there, huge, metallic, staring at him. His eyes were black coals, smoldering from behind.

Bert stared down at his feet.

"You called *me*," Tinny said, slowly, his hollow bass voice vibrating into the room, "You left a message on my fucking machine."

On your *machine?*

Oh, shit.

"Well, I—I made a mistake, then. Dialed the wrong number."

—From guilt—

"I—I thought I left it on Dotty's—on our machine at home. She must have told you—"

Tinny shook his head. The eye-coals smoldered hotter, ready to ignite. His thick metallic lips twisted into a sneer.

"Nope. Dot didn't tell me about what happened," the Tin Man said, his voice rumbling through the room's thin walls, "But then, you know that, right?" He ignored Bert's little head-shake. "But I did go to your house. Right after I got the message. I found her there."

"Well, I don't know what she told you, but—"

Tinny shook his head again.

Bert held up his hands in a placating gesture.

"Look, whatever she told you, there's always two sides to the story," he said, "Let me tell you what—"

"She didn't tell me shit! She couldn't! *She was dead!* You beat her to death, you little *prick!*"

Tinny spat out the last word at Bert. He felt the world turn upside down. The breath caught in his throat.

"No," he managed, "No. I-I couldn't have. I just—we just had an argument. I—*she*—"

"And her little dog, too!" Tinny cried. "Do you remember that, what you did to Toto?"

Tinny pulled out a enormous black pistol from his the pocket of his jacket. Bert saw the silencer screwed to the end of it.

The gun had a laser sight. Bert watched the crimson dot appear on his chest.

"Now wait!" he cried, backing away, "It wasn't like that at all. I know I didn't kill her! I couldn't have! She was alive when I left!"

The bed hit the back of his knees. There was nowhere left to back away to. Tinny stared at him like he was a branch to be pruned away.

"She loved me!" Bert choked.

"That's her blood on you," Tinny said, "Isn't it?"

Bert swallowed, unable to speak.

"*Isn't it!*"

"Y-yes—"

Bert was crying now. He'd forgotten all about the book. He'd forgotten about defeating his enemy, about the desires of his heart.

"This is your lucky day, asshole. Because I'm not going to kill you just now," Tinny said.

"N-no?" Bert lowered his hands slightly from his face.

"No. Look at your clock. It's 3:45. Fifteen minutes 'til checkout time. You said you was leaving at four o'clock, right?"

Bert nodded, his eyes frozen with fear.

"Here's what I'm going to do. In honor of dear departed Dorothy and your ten-year marriage—"

Bert felt his heart skip a beat.

"—I'm going to kneecap you, faggot. Then I'm going to leave you here for fifteen minutes. If you can get to the phone, you little worthless piece of shit, and get the Winkies here by four a.m., then you'll just be a fucking cripple in prison for the rest of your life. If not, then I'll be back here, on the stroke of four, to finish the job, starting with your elbow joints. Fair enough?"

"You wouldn't—"

The pistol spat. Bert's left knee exploded into pain. He screamed and fell to the floor.

Tinny moved fluidly into a shooter's stance, and blasted the other knee, the one on the right. Bert shrieked.

"Hurts like hell, don't it?" Tinny said, flexing his own prosthetic joints.

He moved away, toward the door.

"Fifteen minutes," he said, before he clanked out the door.

3:47 a.m.

Bert whimpered now in agony, gasped for breath.

My knees, my knees, he did it. My knees!

Did he hear sirens? Had somebody else heard his screams? The shots? Called the Winkies?

The phone was up on the table, ten feet away. Might as well be a mile. He felt his heart pounding, felt himself going into shock. He dragged himself slowly forward, by his arms, crying softly, trying not to twist his legs. His ruined knees shrieked with pain that rode all the way up to his skull. Blood was soaking through his pants, onto the floor.

There was still time. He could sit up. Pull himself up by the bed, grab the covers. . .He could still win, still beat that bastard—

If he got the EMTs here, if he could get to a hospital right away, they could replace the knees. He didn't have money. Didn't have insurance. But they have to treat you at the emergency room, right? Even in Oz. They have to fix your knees.

He'd get bionic joints, better than Tin Man's metal crap. Then he'd testify against Tinny, for attempted murder. And he'd say Tinny killed Dorothy. He'd figure out a way to make it stick. And even if that didn't work, even he had to go down, Tinny was going down too for kneecapping him, that rotten dirty Winkie son-of-a-bitch!

He was almost at the table when he heard a sound. A clacking, slithery sound.

A sound from above him.

He looked up. The fleeby-jeebies were staring down at him from the wallpaper. Dozens of them.

He whimpered.

They began peeling off the wallpaper. They descended the paneling with dainty, spider-like movements, twitching their nasty claws and their awful mandibles all the way down. Filthy things, their glowing green carapaces covered with grease and slime.

They were moving down the wall, toward him. The clacking he heard was the sound of their teeth.

Bert gave the brown leather book a desperate look. It was lying there, sitting casually next to the phone.

"You promised me my heart's desire!" he pleaded with it, "To defeat my enemy! I said the spell!! I said it right!!"

He reached over and shook the table, nearly overturning it. The book slid from the table onto the floor. He picked it up, felt its warmth between his fingers.

The page read, in florid Gothic script, *I will give you the* deepest *desires of your heart.*

The word "deepest" was highlighted.

"But—you said—"

Then, with bone-chilling clarity, it came to him.

The spell had worked. It had done exactly what it promised. Only not how he'd planned.

He'd spoken *A Spell to Defeat an Enemy.* And who was Bert's real enemy? His real, true, worst enemy?

Not Tinny.

Not even Dorothy.

It was his own booze-swilling, wife-beating, job-losing, no-account self. His self—an enemy to everyone who'd ever knew and loved or hated him. Including himself.

And his *Heart's Desire,* his real, deepest desire?

He didn't want to get on that balloon to Kansas. He didn't need to catch that bus to Knoxville. He didn't want to run away again to another town. He didn't want to go on like this. Deep down inside, he couldn't stand it anymore. The drinking, the emptiness, the violence, the lost loneliness he felt. He just wanted to be relieved of the weary burden of a senseless life.

A life that hadn't improved one iota by crossing over the rainbow.

4:00 a.m.

All this he understood in one rare flash of sober insight. He had only a second to wonder if it was all really true, or if he had just been sanctifying the inevitable. Then his time was up. The hungry insects ran across the carpet *en masse*, fell upon his prone form and covered it, satisfying his deepest desires with a single undulating jitterbug rhythm.

The End.

SCARECROW'S SUNRISE

by Gef Fox

T he sackcloth of a long night's sky turned to a bruised crimson of a coming dawn. Mazy, a Munchkin farmer, looked through the window of his workshop and frowned with fatigue and fear. The Good Witch of the North would return when the sun fully rose, and Mazy had yet to finish the scarecrow she had requested he fashion for her. She had been very clear in her request: *Have the scarecrow ready by morning. When I return, you will be rewarded for your efforts.*

A headless effigy stuffed with straw lay atop his workbench, as he stood with his back to it. All four boneless, lifeless limbs stretched out from the body, as if racked in a Munchkin's answer to a torture chamber. The construction of the body had been easy enough. She even provided the clothes to be used. Mazy was skilled in making strawmen, as many watched over his vast cornfields through Munchkinland. This, however, was the first time he had ever made one for someone else. This time for the Witch of the North, no less.

The Good Witch, he reminded himself as he peered through his window.

Before turning back to his task, he noticed the Good Witch's Tick-Tock Man standing guard at the end of the cartroad to his farm. The mechanical servant had been a stoic guard since the previous evening when Mazy began his work on the scarecrow. A watchful eye afforded by the Witch to be sure no one disturbed him. Mazy couldn't fathom why it was necessary for a guard to be placed on his property for such a menial task, but that was before he had witnessed the result of his latest creation. He needed to finish the scarecrow and he was running out of time.

"What manner of witchcraft have I tangled myself into?" he whispered.

He stared at his work. Next to the body, above the neck, sat a burlap sack stuffed with straw and bran, as if severed from the body by an axeman. It rested on it's side, detached from the body, adorned in a singed cap. A single painted eye stared in Mazy's direction. When it blinked, the old corn farmer winced.

"Be calm, you old coot," he said.'"Tis nothing but a scarecrow."

But it wasn't just a scarecrow. Not this time. The burlap sack which was to be the head was the third Mazy had used through the night. The heads were always the finishing touch—start from the bottom and work your way up, he always told himself. Now, his hands tremored at the thought of going near the thing. *The abomination*, he thought.

It was well into the night when he started on the first would-be head. He painted a meager grin—a curved line to show a smile was all it was—on the stuffed sack. No sooner had he lifted his narrow paintbrush from the fabric, however, when the grin erupted into animation.

"I can't see! I'm blind!" it cried out.

Mazy's heart leaped in his throat and he had visions of an early grave. He snatched the screaming sack by it's scruff and hurled it into the fire of his stove. He watched it vanish in a fury of flames and sparks. It took ten minutes for his pulse to come back down to something less than a hummingbird's heartbeat.

Calmed, and sure the apparition of a talking burlap sack was due only to a case of nerves from working for the Good Witch, Mazy started again with a second sack to fashion. Serving the Good Witch of the North was a more intimidating experience than he'd first suspected.

When he started on the second would-be head, he stuffed it with straw and bran by the fistful, as if stuffing a turkey with onions and breadcrumbs. Once he had the general shape of the head he wanted, he reached for his paintbrush again and set about painting a mouth. Nothing fancy this time— if the previous curve of black ink could be called fancy. With a deliberate slash of his brush, he drew a simple straight line. It was less a mouth than a mark to show where a mouth should go. Mazy watched it for a moment, then carried on when he was satisfied there would be no strange movement.

He dabbed the brush into a jar of black paint, ready to start on the nose next.

"What just happened? I felt burning! Am I burning?"

Mazy's body shuddered and he fell from his perch on the stool. The brush flew from his fingers and struck the wall across the bench. A streak of wet black paint tattooed the wall. He snatched the panic stricken sack with his own panic stricken hands, his heart sending waves of terror through his limbs even more so than before, and hurled the sack into the waiting flames of the fire. It's screams were silenced by the rush of flames that engulfed it whole.

He looked back at the scarecrow's puffy, clumsy, and still headless frame, wondering if it too would spring to life. It didn't move.

"Oh, this is some foul witchcraft," he said. He wiped his brow while his body trembled.

An ember in the stove cracked like a gunshot, and Mazy let out a yelp akin to a scalded dog and fled into the chilly night air outside his workshop. His goose-fleshed skin became awash in pale blue moonlight. A million and one stars winked knowingly above him. Minute by minute, his breath steadied, as did his heart.

"Ozma, preserve me," he prayed aloud.

At the mouth of the cartroad, movement. Mazy's heart bounced in his chest once more, as a shadowy form approached. The Tick-Tock Man came into view with a lurching march. It stopped only inches from the old Munchkin farmer. Mazy took a step back. The Tick-Tock Man looked downward slightly to meet the farmer's face.

"Is it complete?" it asked with a voice made of mechanical hums, whirs, and clunks. Nothing close to a living voice, but unmistakable. And nothing like the unholy sounds that had come from the scarecrow's two would-be heads.

"No. No, it ain't. And it *ain't gonna be*," Mazy answered with a faltering defiance.

"You made an agreement," the Tick-Tock Man said. It's gear-ridden face stared blankly.

"Aye, I agreed to make a scarecrow. But, I didn't agree to have the buggerin' thing come to life. That Witch of yours has cast a horrible spell on my work, and I'll have none of it."

A puff of steam flitted from the side of the Tick-Tock Man's head.

"You made an agreement."

"Wizard's whiskers! I heard you the first time."

"You must complete your task. War is coming."

"What? W-war? What in Oz are you on about?"

Another puff of steam came out of the mechanical servant's head.

"After sunrise. A child soldier will come. The child will kill the Wicked Witch of the East. This child will lead an army that will conquer both East and West."

Mazy's jaw gaped. He looked eastward through the waning darkness, in the direction of the Wicked Witch's castle. It was beyond his sight, hidden behind the rolling hills of Munchkinland, but he saw the first hints of sunrise. And clouds coming with it. A red sky, and growing redder.

The Tick-Tock Man turned it's head and looked in the same direction.

"The child soldier will come on a cloud. The cloud will be her weapon."

"Great Glinda. *Her?* The child soldier is a girl?" A new chill swept Mazy's spine.

"Yes. It has been prophesied by the Great Wizard."

A feeling of enormity washed over Mazy, one which dwarfed his initial shock at seeing the scarecrow's heads come to life.

"That still doesn't tell me why my scarecrow wants to live," he said.

"It is not your scarecrow. It is a charm of the Good Witch of the North. To guard the child soldier." The Tick-Tock Man lumbered past Mazy to the doorway of the workshop and pointed to the workbench and the unfinished strawman.

"Do you see the clothes it wears?" it asked.

"Aye, I see," Mazy answered, and peered through the shadows. He kept a healthy distance from the door, though.

"It is the uniform of a fallen soldier. A great soldier of Oz who died at the hands of the Wicked Witch of the West, in the battle for the Emerald City many years ago. The Good Witch of the North blessed the remains of the uniform. It now carries the spirit of the soldier."

Mazy stared into his workshop with wonder. "It surely didn't sound like a soldier when I painted it's mouth."

"It will learn. It will take two days for the soldier's instincts to return. That's when it will meet with the child soldier to help lead her army."

Mazy might have run away at that point if his legs were steady enough or youthful enough. Given his state, all he could do was stand in awe.

"This is too much for an old farmhand like me," he said.

"You made an agreement," the Tick-Tock Man said once more. "The scarecrow must be ready by morning. The Wizard of Oz has prophesied it. The Good Witch of the North has blessed it. And you, Mazy of Munchkinland, you will build it."

He watched in stunned silence as the Tick-Tock Man returned to his post at the mouth of the cartroad. Mazy's mouth failed him in his desire to protest. Defeated, he walked back into his workshop and fashioned the third burlap sack, which was to be the scarecrow's head. It was this third head with a single painted eye that watched him now.

It was madness. This abomination. An Oz soldier brought back from beyond death to fight once more. And in the form of a strawman, no less. Now, with the sun slowly rising and the clouds to the east more red than ever, Mazy looked at his work and wondered how he could build such a thing. It was madness.

Then a thought struck him, as the scarecrow's painted-on eye watched him with unwavering attention. Twice now, he'd torched the living head of the scarecrow, and now the third head lived in silence watching him. The second head had the memories of the first—it had felt the fire not once, but twice. Impossible, but undeniable. This third head, which Mazy had intentionally left mouthless for now—he couldn't bare to hear it's panic-stricken voice again—would surely carry the memories again. And the single eye saw it was he who had burned him.

"You're almost finished, old timer. One way or the other," Mazy muttered to himself. "Finish what you started and be done with it."

Either the scarecrow soldier would do him in once finished, or the Good Witch of the North would fail to live up to her name if he defied her request when she returned. *Paint a happy face*, he thought. *Paint a face that couldn't kill.*

He picked up his paintbrush off the floor and wiped it clean. With another dab of black paint, he drew a second egg-shaped circle and splotched a pudgy dot in the center. He drew back and watched, as did the scarecrow's first eye when it blinked into life. The wet paint that was now a pupil lolled around the borders of the newly drawn eye until it aligned with the first. With one more synchronized blink, they both looked up at Mazy with a wide and relentless stare.

The air in the room became dizzying for a second and Mazy had to steady himself with a hand against the workbench.

"You're almost finished," he said.

He dabbed the brush in the paint again and drew an upside-down "V" for a nose, with two small dots as nostrils. He watched it wiggle with life and prayed it couldn't smell his fear. His hand betrayed him as it refused to hold steady when he dips the brush into the black of the pain one more time. The scarecrow's eyes watched him the entire time, steady and accusing from under the tattered cap the Good Witch had provided. A piece of a dead soldier's uniform.

Mazy brought the brush back to the scarecrow's disembodied head and drew, a final time, a simple straight line that would be it's mouth. He dropped the paintbrush into a jar of water and distanced himself from his workbench. He watched and waited. He stood his ground several feet from the scarecrow and would have gone back even further if not for the heat of the stove permeating against his backside.

The line he drew was squiggled due to his frayed nerves. It twitched. Even from several feet away, there was no mistaking it. Then, it burst into life with a thunderous, "*Ooowww!*"

The cry of pain sent Mazy scuttling to the floor for cover, sure he was about to reap what he had sewed.

"That really hurt," it said. Still detached from the rest of it's body, the head remained face-up on the bench, looking towards the cobwebbed rafters.

Mazy tentatively rose from his spot on the floor, confused relieved he hadn't been killed.

"What hurt?" he asked through a hoarse whisper.

"That...*burning*. What happened then? All I remember is my first words, and then something grabbed me and put me in a hot place. I was covered in...burning."

The head fidgeted a moment then rolled to it's side, so it was facing Mazy and the outline of the stove behind him.

"That? I wouldn't know about that," Mazy said, dusting himself off. "It must have been someone with a match."

"'*A match*.'" The scarecrow's face showed a twinge of fear, then an expression of deep thought. "I'll remember that, always. Thank you—I don't know your name."

"My name is—"

"I don't remember *my* name, now that I think about it."

Mazy thought too, and realized he hadn't bothered to ask the name of the dead soldier he was building. *Just as well*, he thought. He took a timid step towards his workbench, and the scarecrow's head fidgeted again and rolled off the bench and hit the floor. Then it rolled to Mazy's feet where it stopped, the scarecrow's ponderous face looked up at his. The sight started him so, he reared back a leg to kick it away.

Don't, he reminded himself. *It can see you now.*

He reached down and picked up the head and carried it at arm's length back to the workbench, then carefully placed it back from where it had fallen.

"Thank you," it said. "Did you make me?"

"Aye."

"And is that my body?"

"Aye."

"And are those my clothes?"

Mazy's eyes narrowed.

"Aye."

"They look familiar."

"Hush now," Mazy said. He looked about his workshop, trying to concentrate.

"What are you doing now?"

"I said hush."

The sky outside his window grew closer to dawn with a glaze of orange cutting through the bruised blues of the tenebrous sky. Nearly done and then he could be rid of this abominable scarecrow for good. He needed to be smart as well as quick, however. The head was still the only living part of it, but Mazy suspected the body would be just as fitful once he placed the head atop it. That will be the final straw, he thought.

The scarecrow watched in silence while Mazy gathered his things in a rush.

A wheelbarrow would suffice. He hustled outside and grabbed a rood-tree he'd made the evening prior, and chucked it in the wheelbarrow. Then, he came back in the shop and retrieved the giant rag doll of a body and carried it over his shoulder outside, it's boneless limbs dangled nearly to the floor. He threw it onto the rood-tree where it waited like a decapitated soldier. The image of it made Mazy shiver.

"Where are we going?" the scarecrow asked from inside.

Mazy marched into the workshop and grabbed the head of the scarecrow and headed back out without as much of a word. Quit giving it answers, you old coot. Ignore it and be gone with it. He set the head firmly on the lap of the scarecrow's body, making sure to keep it clear from the torso.

"*I can't see! I can't see!*" it yelled, it's voice muffled with the face planted in it's crotch.

Mazy jerked the scarecrow's face back into view and pointed it as best he could so it faced forward.

"Now be quiet," he said.

Despite the shortness of his Munchkin legs, Mazy pushed the wheelbarrow with a determined haste until he reached the end of the cartroad and the awaiting Tick-Tock Man. He stopped, lowered the wheelbarrow's back end with a huff, and met the Tick-Tock Man's mechanical stare.

"There," he said in exasperated triumph. "There's your buggerin' scarecrow."

The Tick-Tock Man stepped to the wheelbarrow, bent slightly towards it, and looked. The gears on it's face and chest turned and wound. Then stopped.

"Hello," the scarecrow said.

A flit of steam jetted from the side of the Tick-Tock Man's head.

"This is not finished."

Mazy's eyes widened. "What do you mean? It's all there. When the Witch gets here, tell her she can just plop the head on the body and the body on the rood, and that'll be that. She knows where the head goes, don't she?"

"Who's he?" the scarecrow asked with an attempt at nodding towards the Tick-Tock Man, which almost sent the head rolling off it's own lap.

"Shut up."

"You must finish it." The Witch's servant pointed a brassy-metal finger at Mazy's nose.

"Wha—but I don't even know where she wants it put? I put that head on that body, and the thing will be running all over the place."

"It is not far. I will show you." The Tick-Tock Man turned and started it's lurching march down the lane, away from the cartroad to Mazy's home.

Mazy wanted to object, but saw the sun cresting over the hills. Eastward was his direction now and there was to be no more arguing, he knew it. With a sigh, he lifted the handles of the wheelbarrow and followed the Tick-Tock Man towards the rising sun.

"What is that?" the scarecrow asked from it's perch. "It looks like fire."

"Would you quit yammerin'?"

The walk was short, and Mazy was grateful they only had to walk to the crossroads where the lane met the Yellow Brick Road. The sun broke completely away from the hillside when they stopped. Mazy's nerves tingled like bramble bushes.

"Place the scarecrow here," the Tick-Tock Man instructed, and pointed it's brassy finger to the edge of the cornfield.

"Why here?" Mazy asked.

"Yes, why here?" the scarecrow echoed with a much more curious tone.

"The child soldier will pass here next midday. This is where they must meet."

Mazy looked down the south-east stretch of yellow bricks. The child soldier would pass here soon. They stood in a spot not far at all from his home. The war was coming too close for his liking. What kind of violence and mayhem might come with this prophesied girl? he wondered.

"You must finish it. You made an agreement." The un-Munchkin voice of the Tick-Tock Man ran up Mazy's backbone like a rake.

He looked down and saw, with his back to the risen sun, his shadow casting long over the scarecrow and into the cornfield. His cornfield. *I'll never be rid of it*, he thought. *Even when it joins that girl, it'll still be here haunting me. I never should have done it. I should have burned it.*

"Who is this girl? Is she good?" the scarecrow asked.

As Mazy, defeated, pulled the rood-tree from under the scarecrow and set out to the corner of his cornfield, the Tick-Tock Man answered.

"Yes. She is our savior. And you will help her fight."

"Like a war?"

"Yes."

Mazy returned to the wheelbarrow. The rood-tree stood erect on the edge of the cornfield, and cast a long, narrow cross of a shadow over his property. He picked up the scarecrow's body and carried it to it's perch, leaving the head behind face up with the Tick-Tock Man.

"Yes, a war," the scarecrow said.

Mazy looked back over his shoulder, noting a hint of anger in the scarecrow's voice. Not a lot, not even a little, but he heard it.

"You must be brave," a new voice sounded. "And you must be careful. For you are not invulnerable."

It was a woman's voice—angelic and sweet—that Mazy knew at once. With the scarecrow's body hung in place, he turned to see. The Good Witch of the North stood at the Tick-Tock Man's side, tall and radiant, as if the sun had risen just for her. The sun crowned her head while her shadow reached out and beyond Mazy.

She looked up from the scarecrow's head to Mazy.

"Hello, Mazy. I see your task is almost at an end," she said with a warm smile with entranced and frightened the Munchkin farmer at the same time.

"Y-yes. Just about d-done," he answered. "Anything for Oz."

"It gladdens me to hear it."

"Oh, I'll be brave, miss," the scarecrow said. "And I'll be careful too. I've been burned before."

"Is that so?" the Good Witch asked, looking down then casting a knowing eye to Mazy.

"Oh yes. *Twice*. But I couldn't see who did it because I had no eyes."

"Indeed. Well, I'm sure whomever was responsible regrets it greatly."

"Aye," Mazy said timidly. "I'm sure they do."

He reached with nervous hands to pick up the scarecrow's head and finally be done with it, be done with them all. The scarecrow's voice spoke up again, though. A minatory voice.

"They will regret it. Because when I finish helping this girl with her war, I'll find the one who burned me."

Mazy's spine prickled with an icy flash.

"I'll find them and then I'll burn them."

Mazy's face was ashen despite the rays of sunshine casting on him. He grabbed the scarecrow's head and rushed to unite it with it's body.

"You mustn't hold a grudge, scarecrow. 'Tisn't right." He hurried to the propped-up effigy and plopped the head on the shoulders. Not wasting a movement of his hands, he tucked the scruff of the burlap sack into the collar of the dead soldier's tattered uniform, then ran back to the side of the road and waited alongside the Good Witch of the North and her Tick-Tock Man.

"Maybe you're right, kind Mazy," the scarecrow said. Then it's eyes widened and it's mouth gaped. It stayed stock-still for a second. And then, a foot moved. A twitch, really. The timeworn boot at the bottom of the scarecrow's left leg spasmed, followed by the right. The arms were next, as the gloved hands flailed about. "I can move!" it cried out in delight.

The scarecrow remained on it's perch, though. A nail held it to the cross, pinning it in place. The scarecrow was too happy and curious to care. It danced in place, suspended a mere foot above the soil.

"My goodness. I can move." It stilled and tilted it's head. "What was I talking about before?"

"You've done well, my little Munchkin," said the Good Witch.

"So I am done, then?" Mazy said, looking up at her kind face with an desirous expression. "I can go home and be done with it and never have to look at it again?"

"Our agreement is complete," she answered, and restrained a giggle. The Tick-Tock Man watched the scarecrow with impassive interest. The Witch went on, "You may go home with my thanks and gratitude."

"And what about my reward?"

"Why, you have it," she said. "My thanks and my gratitude."

Mazy's flushed face blushed with a renewed rush of blood.

"*That's*—that's not fair. My crops, my farm. If war is coming, I need assurance they'll be safe from harm. I have a livelihood to think of."

"Listen well, Mazy of Munchkinland," the mirthful tone of the Witch receded. Her expression hardened. "You are correct in that war is indeed coming. And you've done well, as I previously stated. But, heed my words. You are a citizen of Oz and you have been called to serve in these trying times. You want more than the reward that I have graciously given to you? Here it is." She pointed to the scarecrow.

"The scarecrow's mind is still nothing but the bits of straw with which you stuffed it. It is alive, be clear on that, and it will learn more and more as the day grows." Her voice turned to a whisper. "You sent our soldier's new head into the fire, not once, but twice. And it wants revenge. Your reward, my avaricious ally, is a guarantee. I will guarantee to you that the scarecrow will have no memory of you or what atrocities you committed. Your crops are not my concern. You have your own scarecrows to protect your corn. That is your reward.

"Now, do you find this satisfactory?" she asked, her cheerful voice restored.

The Tick-Tock Man watched Mazy now with the same impassive interest. Mazy's throat recoiled.

"Aye," he muttered.

"I'm pleased you prefer the grace of the good over the wrath of the wronged."

The Good Witch of the North and her mechanical servant said their goodbyes, then whisked off into the eastward sky, above the risen sun and the looming clouds, riding the winds in a great pink bubble.

Left with the scarecrow, Mazy looked one final time to his creation. His abomination. It's stare stayed transfixed on the point in the horizon where the bubble had disappeared. Seemingly mindful it and it's passengers were gone, the scarecrow looked down at the Munchkin farmer.

"Hello. Who are you? And how did I get up here?" it asked. It flicked it's arms and legs in an attempt to move, but caught on it was perched beyond it's control.

"I wouldn't know that, scarecrow. Goodbye."

Mazy never looked back to see if it watched him walk back to his farm. He hoped the Good Witch's guarantee would hold, and he wouldn't wake up one day not long from now to be surrounded by the same fire he's doomed the scarecrow to the previous night. He sped up his pace, leaving his wheelbarrow behind. He buy another if he had to.

The last thing he heard from the scarecrow that morning, carried on the morning breeze at his back, was something that staggered his steps.

"It must have been someone with a match," it said, as it watched the sun rise.

The End.

NOT IN KANSAS
ANYMORE

by Lori T. Strongin

T he girl raised a cigarette to her bright red painted lips and took a long drag, then slowly allowed the smoke to escape into the light rain soaking Oz. She imagined dragons dancing upon the thick, fragrant fog, their voices whispering of another time, another world. In the distance, a yellow glow shone in the near-darkness, rising from the earth. Twining like a snake. A cold breeze rustled her black robe, and sent chills along her twisted spine.

The other woman sat huddled on a broken patio chair, fingers trembling around her half-empty glass of Oz-Berry wine. Her faded pink kimono did little to protect her from the rain.

"We should've smoked inside. Why'd you want to come out here?"

Damp brown hair fell over her shoulders. The red-lipped girl took a final drag and flicked her cigarette off the balcony into the seemingly endless darkness.

"I like to get out of there once it calms down." Her gaze dropped. "You know I can't stand the silence…"

The words didn't need to be said. After all, Glinda had been there, all those years ago; had watched what that green-faced *thing* did to her.

And didn't muss a single golden curl to help, the bitch.

The sky had looked the same back then—heavy with rain and faded memories. She hadn't known then that Oz was the place where youthful innocence went to die; where broken glass met broken hearts, and blood was just graffiti on emerald green walls.

The screen door slammed open. Heavy footsteps splintered the wooden planks beneath metallic feet.

"Damn it, I've been looking all over for you, Do—"

"Don't say that name!"

The Tin Man nodded and adjusted his funnel hat.

"Almost forgot."

She regretted extinguishing her cigarette.

"You were looking for me?"

"Oh, yeah." He shifted, rusted hinges creaking. "Boss Man says you've got another set tonight."

"Screw that! I've done three already."

"You don't like it, take it up with the Wiz."

Tin slammed the screen door behind him.

Silence. Not even the pervy Munchkin peepers inside the club made a sound.

Glinda took a shaky sip from her wine glass.

"Four sets ain't so bad."

The red-lipped girl had a vision of ripping those big blue eyes right out of the blonde's skull.

She walked back into the ramshackle club, ignoring the leers and catcalls of Winkies and Quadlings, and kicked one overeager Gilikin in the crotch. The pounding throb of drums hurt her ears. A spotlight followed her every movement. But then again, hadn't it always, ever since she first came here?

What she wouldn't give for a chance to go back and make things right. Tell the wizard to screw himself and find her own way home.

Home.

Oz had the power to make people forget. Already she'd lost the faces of the woman who beat her and of the man that had *initiated* her into womanhood at the ripe old age of thirteen on a pile of filthy straw in the hay loft.

How sad was it that she'd rather go back to her auntie and uncle than live in this *magical* place?

"Ladies and gentlemen," the announcer's voice echoed over the gramophone. "Flatheads and Cuttenclips of all ages. She defeated the Wicked Witch of the West with her bare hands. She crossed the Impassable Desert just to be here tonight. Give it up for Oz's first and last royal, the Lost Princess herself, *Kansas*!"

A new song spilled out of the music box, this time slow and sensual.

She stepped onto the rickety makeshift catwalk, running her calloused hands across her stomach and thighs. The black silk felt cool under her fingers and more real than anything else she owned.

The tempo sped up. Kansas let the robe slide off her shoulders. The blue checkered teddy barely covered her tits, and hardly anything further south. Damp pigtails slapped her face and her prop wicker basket was so old it sagged every time she swung it.

Her shoes, though. *Those* still shone silver, tinted like the harvest moon rising above her aunt and uncle's farmhouse, back when her life made sense. Back when she gave a damn if she ever made it home again or not.

"*Come on! Dance!*" someone shouted from the crowd.

"*Shake it, baby! Yeah!*"

"*Take it off!*"

She obeyed. What else could a lost farm girl from Wichita do?

Rain spattered against the covered the patio, the awning just wide enough to keep her cigarette dry. Dawn rose over the horizon. Another day, another dollar down her g-string, and another man thinking he had the right to take her to bed.

She may have bruises in the morning, but that Pumpkinhead would never get it up again.

"Dorothy? Dorothy Gale from Kansas?"

She growled, fingers bent, ready to claw the bastard that *dared* say that name.

Kansas spun around, ready to lunge.

A scrawny figure stood in the rain, jaunty hat cocked to the side and painted smile wide as the day they'd met.

"Scarecrow?"

"In the flesh! Well, straw, at least."

His voice had so many echoes—of friendship, of happiness, of comfort, and all the things Kansas had left behind long ago.

She felt like her fourteen-year-old self as she ran into his arms. Kansas didn't care who might be watching, or if his straws poked her skin. It didn't matter. He was *here*.

"Sweet crow in the morning, I've missed you." He released her and took a step back. His black-button eyes raked her up and down. "What's happened to you, girl? You look like something the barn cat coughed up."

Still clad in her costume, she was inclined to agree.

"Where have you been, Scarecrow? I haven't seen you in an Oz Age."

The painted smile slipped.

"I've seen *you*."

"You have? When? Why didn't you come and say hi? I thought the Witch—"

His gloved hand covered her mouth. He smelled like damp grass and singed leaves.

"When's the last time you left *Shiz?*"

She couldn't remember.

"What's the point in leaving? Here I get food, a bed, and smokes."

Scarecrow shook his head.

"There're posters of you all over Bunbury City. Everyone knows your name and rumours are flyin' about this place."

Was it bad if Kansas didn't care if someone found her?

"So?"

"If they find you, they'll kill you."

Kansas looked away.

"Dorothy—"

"*Don't call me that!*"

He backed away, hands raised.

"You'll always be Dorothy to me."

It was too much. His kindness was more than she could bear. She had to get out of there. Away from old wounds.

A straw-filled hand grabbed her shoulder.

"Let me go!"

"Not 'til you've heard me out."

Slapping him wouldn't work—he couldn't feel pain.

"I swear if you don't let me go right now, I'll set your hay-covered carcass on fire!"

His hand didn't slip.

"You can't be happy here. I know you're not. And you deserve better than this."

The fight flooded out of her.

"What does it matter?"

He cupped her face. Great Oz, how long had it been since someone touched her with tenderness?

"*You* matter. I think you've forgotten that."

She swallowed. "Oz makes people forget."

"Good thing I'm not a *people* then." Scarecrow reached into a tattered pocket and pulled out a piece of parchment. "Here."

Kansas reached for it, hand shaking. Why did she feel that something bad was about to happen?

Oh, right. It's Oz. Bad things always happen here.

She unfolded the thick paper. Curved shapes scored the cream-colored sheet, swirling like cigarette smoke. If she squinted, she could almost make out a rocking chair and striped sock from the jumbled nonsense.

"You an artist now?"

"Huh?"

"Looks like doodling to me."

Scarecrow looked confused.

"I don't get it. How come I can read this and you can't?"

Kansas couldn't care less.

"Well? Don't you want to know what it says?" He didn't wait for her to answer. "It's a map. A *treasure* map."

Wonderful.

"Well, have fun with that. I've gotta get some sleep. The Wiz has me working a double tonight."

She turned to leave, knowing she'd probably never see Scarecrow again. *Hay-headed idiot'll probably get himself picked apart by flying horses or something.*

"It leads to a time portal!"

Kansas stopped, silver shoes glued to the porch. *Did he just say…*

He spun her around, childlike enthusiasm in his every glance, every word.

"It's where I've been all this time, looking for a way to get you back home after the slippers turned out to be a hoax. I remembered what you told me once about *wadges*."

It took her a minute to translate his words. "Do you mean 'watches?'"

"Yeah, those timey-*whymy* things you said people used to change the time."

Just like that, her hopes crashed and burned. Served her right for letting herself get carried away, even for a second.

"You can't change time with a watch, Scarecrow. It doesn't affect anything."

"Maybe not where you're from," he said, grin ridiculously wide. "But they do in Oz."

Kansas didn't know whether to believe him or get him a good stiff drink.

"Tell me more."

"The map leads to the Time Dragon. It's a ma-chine that *makes* time. All we gotta do is find him and ask to turn back the Great Clock to before you came to Oz. It's as simple as a cornfield!"

"You've forgotten one thing, Straw-for-Brains." She crossed her arms. "We do that, the Witch comes back to life. Remember what Oz was like before I doused her?"

"Yeah, I do. Animals were free to speak, the Emerald City had jobs, and you didn't have to wear things like *that* just to earn a couple o'buckeroos."

Kansas' breath caught in her throat.

"Are you saying what I think you're saying?"

Scarecrow took her hands in his and gave them a little squeeze.

"Yup. I'm sayin' we ask the Time Dragon to send you home and bring back the Wicked Witch of the West."

The yellow glare of the bricks hurt Kansas' eyes. Never in a million Oz Ages had she thought she'd ever *willingly* step foot in this place again, map or no.

Ten years was a long time. And yet, not long enough.

Munchkinland looked like the victim of a runaway corn thrasher. Everything was brown and gray. None of those bright flowers bloomed or sent sweet perfumes into the air like she remembered. The colorful paint on the houses had chipped and flaked off. Doors and shutters hung off their hinges like deflated hot air balloons.

Through the open windows, Kansas could see upturned cups and plates, covered in rotting food, as if whatever happened here was sudden. The place smelt like old vomit and urine, and not a sound broke the silence, save Kansas' own raspy breaths.

Of course, the dead bodies strewn everywhere made it all so much worse.

Scarecrow's whispers sounded like an explosion in the silence.

"Great crow in the morning, what happened here?"

Everywhere Kansas looked, Munchkin bodies lay on the broken road, propped against the sides of the buildings, or half-hung out of windows, hands spread wide as if begging for mercy. Clothing rotted off their bodies, as black and formless as their decaying skin. The forgotten, nameless corpses lay over piles of bloody straw and hay.

All were headless. Just broken bodies and limbs. But no faces. No ears to hear or mouths left to scream.

A terrible smell wafted from the water well. Kansas didn't want to think about what she might find down there.

"What could have done this?"

"I...I don't know."

The wheat fields were all brown and dead. It reminded her of the farm after a hard summer with no rain. A river ran through the field, the thick water painted red. If she closed her eyes, she could still see the Munchkin children playing in those fields; hear their laughter and music as they celebrated their freedom from the Witch of the East. Her gaze drifted toward the ramshackle house, the hut that had been her home and prison for more than half her life. It looked like a headstone in this cemetery of death. She felt the weight of the cigarette lighter in her pocket and the urge to set the damn shack on fire. The town, too.

Kansas took a deep breath through her mouth.

"There's nothing we can do here. The Munchkins are long dead. Let's keep moving."

Scarecrow looked like he might cry. Kansas wondered if he even could.

"B...but, they were our friends."

Kansas stepped over a tiny headless corpse, Kansas slippers tapping a staccato rhythm against the golden flagstones.

"I just want to go home."

Scarecrow sputtered, but followed, his loose hay scraping the stones clean.

"The map says this should be a corn field. But I don't see no corn."

Kansas shrugged. The map looked like something Toto might have used as a chew toy, before a Roc Roc ate him seven years ago.

"Maybe the river flooded and turned the field into a swamp," she suggested. The brown reeds that poked out of the bubbling mud *might* once have been maize stalks. The place certainly smelled like something had rotted here.

"Come on." She tapped the soaked ground with a toe. "Follow my footsteps so you don't fall in."

Spongy earth squelched with each careful step she took. Pools of oily-colored water bubbled and steamed on either side of her path. Clumps of dead grass sagged as she stepped on them, sloshing mud over her shoes and up her bare legs. The foul ooze coated the bottom of her robe. Grimacing, she followed the zigzag of half-submerged stones as they wound through the maze-like swamp.

A thick fog hung over the pools of water. Kansas clapped her hands over her nose and mouth. She knew that smell. *Liquefied flesh.* Like the Witch, after Kansas threw the bucket of water at her.

Kansas gagged. Scarecrow started to rub her back, but she jerked away. She didn't like people touching her. Especially *there*.

They were halfway across the swamp before Scarecrow spoke again.

"Doro—"

"I told you! Don't call me that!"

He huffed, then cleared his throat.

"Uh, *Kansas*, do you hear that?"

Only the sounds of her own stilted breathing and the wet squelch of the muddy earth reached her ears.

She frowned. "I don't hear anything."

"Exactly."

"What—"

Something grabbed her foot. Pain flared through her whole body. Kansas screamed and fell to her knees. A white tendril with barbed hooks rose out of the muck, curling around her ankle, drawing blood. The spur dug into her leg, pulsing and quivering, yanking on her bones. Scarecrow shouted something, but Kansas couldn't understand it over the sound of her screams.

Then, the pain disappeared...along with all the bones and nerves and muscles in her foot. Just a formless lump of flesh hanging off her leg.

Dazed, she stared down at the hooks embedded in her skin, rippling like overfed slugs.

Sweet Ozma, the thing was *drinking* her!

She ripped the bone-white creature off her foot and threw it into the muck. More ghostly tendrils shot up out of the swamp, surrounding them like an endless field of grotesque spider-like legs.

Scarecrow grabbed her, hauling her off the ground so fast that her world swirled in a dizzy fog. Her heart pounded in her ears. Cradling her to his scratchy chest, Scarecrow ran. Tendrils chased them, shooting out of the mud faster than a flying monkey. Scarecrow dodged a low-lying tendril and tripped. Kansas flew out of his arms.

Then, water. And mud. Choking her. Pulling her under. Dragging her down.

She let her body sink.

The water was cool. And quiet. It was peaceful.

Murky water filled her mouth. A thin trail of bubbles wound away from her mouth, toward the distant surface.

She couldn't bring herself to care.

If I'm dead, at least I'd be free.

A shaft of sunlight broke through the dank. It shone over her like a star. Then a figure blocked the yellowish ray.

Scarecrow.

His muffled shouts broke through the silence; broke her apathy. She couldn't leave him all alone up there. Who knew what those creatures would do to him? Kansas swam toward the surface. Her lungs burned. Black spots danced in front of her clouded vision. Her whole body ached. Scarecrow's voice grew louder, yet further away.

She wasn't going to make it. She was going to drown, buried in a watery grave and no one would give two shits about it.

Except Scarecrow.

Kansas threw all the strength she had into one last kick upwards. Her fingers broke the surface. A coarse hand grabbed hers. Another reached down and grabbed her elbow. She rose, climbing through the muck.

Sunlight.

Air.

Kansas gasped, her entire body shaking with the effort. She spat mud from her mouth and nose, desperate for a steady, clear breath.

Hands pulled her close, rubbed her back and whispered soft words that didn't mean anything. She didn't need them to mean anything.

Kansas opened her eyes and glanced over her shoulder.

She quickly wished she hadn't.

The flesh-scented puddles around them bubbled furiously. Shapes emerged from the muck. They grew taller, gaining bodies and limbs. Jets of liquid burst over them, red as blood. The water washed the thick mud away.

A herd of scarecrows surrounded them, still dripping mud and swamp slime. Male and female. All moldy and rotting away, limbs creaking and croaking. They wore overalls and fancy suits, sleeveless shirts and wedding dresses. Silver mist streamed out of their painted mouths, chilling the air. Covering their heads weren't balls of yarn, but bloody scalps of every colored hair imaginable.

Just like the Munchkinlanders.

A scream died in Kansas' throat.

The scarecrows took a step toward her. One opened its painted mouth and made a sound like a drowning child. It sent chills down Kansas' spine so cold she didn't think she'd ever be warm again.

The scarecrow spoke.

"*You...*"

It came closer. Kansas scrambled back, pressing into her Scarecrow's chest.

"*You...*"

They were surrounded. They were trapped.

"*You...*"

Fear had always made her stupid.

"Oh, spit it out, already!"

"You failed us."

Scarecrow's hold on her tightened.

"What?"

It pointed at her.

"You saved him. Not us."

"What the hell are you talking about?"

The scarecrow took another step toward her.

"You rescued him. Pulled him off his rack. Not us. You left us here to rot. To die. For worms and crows to eat our straw."

"But…" She hadn't known that! Damn it, she'd been fourteen; lost and confused, and had a psychotic witch out for her blood. "I…I'm sorry?"

It reached toward her. It stroked the side of Scarecrow's face.

Then it tried to gouge his eyes out.

Kansas pushed her Scarecrow backward. They landed in the mud. Kansas flipped over, heart pounding, ready to rip the other scarecrows' apart if they dared come near them again.

The circle of scarecrows swayed, like stalks of corn in a summer's breeze. It reminded her of the day she first met her Scarecrow.

The scarecrows stumbled forward, claw-like hands reaching and grabbing. Scarecrow yanked Kansas to her feet and slung her arm over his shoulder. They hobbled together, slipping all over the place, falling on hands and knees, then scrambling forward again. The others lurched after them, like toddlers learning to walk.

Something grabbed her hair and pulled. Kansas screamed and fell backwards, her weight sending both her and the other scarecrow to the ground.

"Dorothy!"

A knife dangled in front of her face. The blade slid through her hair, twisting back and forth. She tried to pull away but the scarecrow's grip on her hair didn't let her move.

She groped in the mud for something—anything—to help her escape. Where were those bone-eating slugs when you needed them?

Something hard pressed into Kansas' thigh. She reached for it and pulled her lighter out of her pocket.

Please let this work!

Kansas hit the rivet for the flint wheel, pinching her thumb but not caring about the pain. White and blue sparks burned her hands, but the wick wouldn't light.

The knife trailed down her face, carving a shallow cut into her cheek. She hissed, but kept striking the spark coil.

Then, flame, weak, but there. She tried to light a patch of grass by her hand, but couldn't get the tinder to catch. The small fire sputtered, flickering.

"Don't you dare go out!"

No good. The flame didn't have enough dry tinder to catch. She tried it again, this time on her captor's pant leg.

The material was soaked through from the bog water.

The scarecrow jerked her head back and placed the knife at Kansas' throat.

A straw-filled sleeve landed on top of Kansas' feeble flicker. The flame caught the dry tinder and burst into life. Kansas picked up the non-burning end and waved it at the scarecrow. With a sound like a dying cat it released her and stumbled back toward the circle.

The other scarecrows retreated. Kansas thought she saw fear glinting in their button eyes. But maybe that was just the shine of the orange-blue flame. She leaned forward, waving the blazing arm like a flag.

A passing wind caught an ember from her makeshift torch. The breeze blew it into the knot of scarecrows, igniting several of them. They screamed; a terrible piercing sound. They beat their faces; spreading the blaze. They crumbled into a pile of ash

"Get back or I swear I'll burn all your miserable carcasses!"

A low grumble moved through the group. One by one, they sank into the muck. Only a few ripples and flesh-scented mud bubbles marked that they'd ever been there in the first place.

Kansas felt her heart jump back into her chest. All strength washed out of her and she lowered the torch. Hysterical laughter burst from her belly.

"Did you see that? We did it!"

She turned around. Scarecrow gave her a wide smile.

Hers died.

"Oh, Scarecrow."

He waved the empty stump where his left arm used to be.

"Look, ma. No hands."

Numb. That's what she was. That's all she could feel as she crawled toward him. Shaking fingers ran over the straw-wound. Only a frayed piece of twine proved there had ever been anything there; that there had been an arm that protected her or a hand that once dried her tears.

Scarecrow slung Kansas' arm over his still-attached shoulder and together they rose and limped out of the swamp. Neither spoke until the earth was solid beneath their feet and the swamp of scarecrows was something that could only hurt them in their nightmares. He helped her sit down in a dell surrounded by trees, then plopped down at her side.

Kansas touched the nub of arm.

"W…" Her voice cracked. "Why…?"

It seemed scarecrows could still hug, even with just one arm.

"I believe in you," he murmured. "Not in what you were when you first came here or what you turned into, but in the person you're becoming, right before my black-button eyes. I wanna make sure I get to see the rest."

Hope lit Kansas' heart like pain. She allowed herself to lean against his chest, wishing there was a heartbeat there, underneath all that straw.

Stubby fingers stroked through her hair, then over her closed eyelids.

"You're tired. Rest now. I'll keep watch."

Kansas' head ended up on Scarecrow's lap.

"What you did was noble and so breathtakingly stupid that I oughta kill you." She buried her face in the folds of his flannel shirt, sleep coming fast. "Thank you."

What a pair they made, Kansas thought with grim humor. Gimpy and Stumpy, traipsing through an ancient forest somewhere in the middle of Oz, trying to change the past to save the future.

If she had any laughter still inside her, she might have given in to it. Maybe.

"You tired yet, Scarecrow?"

He smiled down at her and readjusted the arm she'd slung over his good shoulder, helping her keep balance on her good foot.

"Nah. Hay-heads like me don't need much rest. Just give me a field and a couple o'crows to scare, and I'm happy as a pig in a mud hole."

Kansas shuddered at the mention of mud. Her eyes strayed over to Scarecrow's missing arm. Sure, his bravery had saved them, but it didn't quell the uneasiness she'd felt, ever since leaving that place.

"Did that swamp look…familiar to you?"

"Should it have?"

"I don't know."

He gave her arm a squeeze.

"What's on your mind, girl?"

Kansas shook her head, not knowing if she was just tired or going crazy.

"It's just…all those dead corn stalks and scarecrows. They must have come from somewhere, right?"

"Yeah?"

"Well, didn't it remind you at all of *your* cornfield? The place we first met?"

His corncob brows creased.

"I suppose so. Did feel slightly familiar, but I just figured that was me being a straw-for-brains."

Kansas smacked his good arm.

"You underestimate yourself much too much. You think you're dumb because others said you didn't have a brain. But who else could have found that map? Who else would've figured out how to make Oz right again?" A lump as large as Emerald City lodged in her throat. "And who else would have torn off his own arm just to save me?"

He stopped walking.

"Kansas, that's what friends *do*. Don't you know that?"

Her words were no louder than a whisper.

"I think I've forgotten."

"Then it's up to me to remind you, now isn't it?"

She had to look away from his wide, trusting smile. Scarecrow was kind and honest and full of hope. Just like she'd been, once upon a time.

Something shook a nearby bush. Kansas jumped, then scolded herself. *Probably a rabbit or something. Calm the hell down.*

The green branches rattled again, louder, with more force. The whole hedge shook. *Okay, maybe it's larger than a rabbit.*

Then another sound broke the calm harmony of the forest, like a heavy chain being dragged across stone. The noise repeated, again and again.

Kansas' heart pounded.

"I think we should get out of here. Now."

Like a Tri-Pod, they hobbled down the broken brick road, roots and fallen branches tripping them. Neither had much balance—Kansas with her useless left foot and Scarecrow with his missing arm. What the hell would they do if something decided to attack them?

A glint of gray shone through the trees ahead of them. The scraping sound grew even louder. More silver sparks surrounded them, like a forest full of Christmas candles.

"What do we do, Dorothy?"

"I don't know! I'm thinking!"

Heavy footsteps pounded on the golden bricks behind them, shaking shards of broken stone. Kansas bent and picked up one of the larger branches blocking their path. She raised it like a baseball bat over her shoulder and turned.

"Well, whatever it is, I'm not letting it touch me."

A sound like rusted, screeching metal burst through the bush. More rustling branches. The sparks of silver moved closer.

Scarecrow grabbed a branch for himself and stepped in front of her. Kansas tried to push him back.

"You can't—"

"Sticks and stones can't break *my* bones, remember," he said. "No bones to break."

The figure of a man emerged out of the tree line. Stocky and broad, he wore a pointed hat and carried a long stick of his own. He stepped closer, that awful metallic screech accompanying each step.

Then, he crossed into a shaft of sunlight.

"Sweet Ozma's ghost!" Scarecrow cried. "Another tin man!"

He looked like the Tin Man of Kansas' youth, except this one was more rust than metal. Stumbling forward like a drunkard, metallic squeals and screeches accompanied every step. As if controlled by a single cog, other tin men jerked out of the woods, each carrying a different tool of their lumberjack trade—axes, saws, rope, and hatchets.

Kansas shuddered. If these things had gone as feral as the scarecrows, then she and Scarecrow didn't have a chance. She grasped her stick a little tighter.

"We're not here to hurt you. Just let us pass."

The tin man in front of them cocked his head, the gray eyes vacant. His cogs and gears ticked a regular rhythm as he stared at her. Two lines of rust ran down the silver face, like twin trails of dried tears.

He opened his mouth. A stream of black oil dribbled out, thin like blood, staining his chest. He didn't seem to notice.

"*Heart have you.*"

Kansas' eyes narrowed.

"What?"

He smacked his head with a four-fingered palm. Something broke inside his skull, rattled around, then echoed loudly as it ricocheted and clattered through his chest then down his leg, and came to a noisy stop in his foot.

"You have heart."

The fractured speech reminded her so much of her own Tin Man that she could almost forget the broken shell he'd become.

Kansas' heartbeat pounded all through her body. Was the tin man speaking about courage, or the muscle pulsing within her chest?

"I do," she thought was the safest answer to give.

"I feel, may I?"

Scarecrow leaned toward her, voice thick with warning.

"Dorothy—"

"Kansas." She tried to smile for him, to calm the panic she saw rising in his dark eyes. "If it makes them happy, and gets us safe passage through here, then Metal-Mouth can feel me up all he wants."

She limped around Scarecrow and thrust her chest forward, like how Glinda taught her to earn extra tips.

"Go ahead. Feel away."

More metallic scraping, and a freezing-cold hand touched her chest. *This* she could handle. Every night at the club, drunk idiots would touch her; fondle things that weren't theirs to touch. She'd just knee them in the groin and be done with it.

Kansas knew she was nothing more than a body and a set of breasts. She didn't need to be more than that.

The misshapen hand felt the other side of her chest. The tin man frowned, probably surprised he couldn't find a matching beat on the other side. His head spun around like a demented owl and made a series of grinding and clicking noises. The other tin men returned the mechanic talk, heads rotating around in slow motion. Gears shifted and clanked together. The stench of burnt motor oil filled the air.

Thunder rumbled the treetops. Light slid into darkness as heavy clouds rolled overhead.

"I think we should be headin' outta here," Scarecrow murmured.

Kansas nodded. Using the branch she'd picked up as a crutch, she hobbled forward.

"If that'll be all, gents, we'll be going."

"You have heart," the tin man who'd touched her said.

Well screw it all if he isn't stuck in a loop.

"Yes, we've already established this."

Rusted arms raised his hatchet. A coat of brown stains covered the blade.

"You have heart. *We take heart.*"

Scarecrow grabbed Kansas' arm.

"Run!"

Her crutch made running easier, but she'd barely reached the tree line when something shoved her, forcing her to the ground. A heavy metallic body landed on top of hers. She cried out, body screaming in pain, and tried to push the thing off. It must've weighed five times her own weight.

"Scarecrow! Help me!"

"I'm comin', Dorothy!"

She tried to beat the tin man with her tree branch, but he flicked the stick away like it was a toothpick. He flipped her over, then pinned her arms to the ground on either side of her head. She spit in his face, knowing it wouldn't make a lick of difference. A wide knee crushed her legs to the ground.

"*Get off me!*" She screamed, squirmed, tried to break away.

Scarecrow was yelling, but she couldn't make out the words. Kansas thrashed like a suffocating fish. All it did was wrench her shoulder out of its socket. She grit her teeth against the flare of pain.

Another low rumble of the approaching storm rattled the dying leaves of the trees.

"We take heart."

"Don't you touch me!"

The blank metal eyes stared at her, more curious than cruel. He was like a child; a mindless child that didn't know what he did was wrong.

Another tin man lumbered toward them and knelt at Kansas' side. A shadow fell over her face. She looked up and saw a long-bladed hatchet hanging over her head like an executioner's axe.

"No! Let me go! Get offa me! Scarecrow!"

Two more tin men came over, touching her chest and face and arms and legs as if she were a puzzle they couldn't quite figure out. Motor oil dripped from their missing lips, foaming as they gurgled like rabid dogs.

Frenzied, beyond hope, beyond madness, metal hands grabbed and scraped and slid over her breasts, raking like claws over her body. Fear burned through her with a cold fury.

"Don't do this! Please!"

Pain flared across her chest. One of the tin men lifted a knife, stained with a thin line of blood. Hers.

Lightning flashed. The blade reflected Scarecrow across the glen, buried beneath a pile of tin men, his tree branch splintered and broken.

Kansas could only hope they would let him go, since he had no heart to offer them.

"We take heart."

The hatchet rose. Kansas closed her eyes.

Thunder. A flash of light behind her closed lids. Needle-like rain splashed on her cheek, soft drops growing in weight until they stung her face and arms.

The tin men made that screeching-clicking noise again.

Kansas opened her eyes, one at a time.

All the tin men stared up at the sky, like the turkeys on the farm during a rainstorm. Orange oxide crept over the tin men's metal bodies as they shrieked and screamed. Their bodies quaked, as if they'd been glued to the forest floor and couldn't move. They stopped talking, stopped screeching. The constant click of rusted gears came to a grinding halt.

Everything went still. Only the sounds of falling rain and rolling thunder broke the silence of the woods.

Kansas drew a deep breath into her aching lungs. She didn't understand. The tin men had been out here for years, right? How could just a bit of rain stop them now?

Above her head, the hatchet swayed in the stormy wind. Any moment now it would drop out of the frozen executioner's hands.

She writhed against the heavy body pinning her, but still she couldn't move.

"Scarecrow?" she whispered.

"Dorothy?"

"I'm over here. Under the scrap heap."

She couldn't see him, but heard the creaking of what must have been Scarecrow pushing his own immobile captors away. More scraping, and finally the dead weight lifted off her sore body.

Scarecrow's worried face was one of the best things she'd ever seen.

He pulled her to her feet, then drew her close for a tight one-armed hug.

"No more of these close calls, all right? You're making all my straws turn gray."

Nervous laugher.

"I'll try."

He released her, then bent and picked up her makeshift crutch.

"I say we get the heck outta here, straight as the crow flies."

Kansas couldn't agree more. Scarecrow kept his hand on her arm as she limped forward, learning how to use her new crutch. Rain soaked through her robe and flimsy dress. Strands of damp hair slid into her eyes and mouth. Scarecrow babbled on about where the map said they should head next, and how they could probably put in a few more miles before bunking down for the night.

As the forest gave way to jungle, Kansas let Scarecrow's cheerful prattling wash over her like a healing balm. *Those tin men went for the wrong one of us,* she thought. *His is the heart they should've wanted.*

Kansas woke to a frantic pulse deep inside her head. Had something happened?

She opened her eyes. Her head was pillowed on Scarecrow's soft chest. Shafts of sunlight broke through the jungle canopy. Soft animal noises wafted on the wind and bugs darted about like hummingbirds.

Nothing seemed amiss.

Kansas looked at Scarecrow's sleeping face and sighed. She would have liked to stay there in that protective warmth. Maybe forever. But they had to get moving. Who knew how far they still had to run?

She shook his shoulder and whispered meaningless words to wake him. With a yawn and stretch he was conscious and helping her to her feet. Well, foot. He brushed the yellow dust off her clothes and face. Using her crutch, Kansas dragged herself and her useless foot past the tree line to relieve herself. When done, she stretched, wincing as her scars pulled. They still felt raw, as if the Witch had only recently flayed her instead of over a decade ago. Her good foot hurt from all the running and stumbling and tripping she'd done in the last few days. Kansas rubbed her temples. She hadn't had this much exercise since her early days in Oz.

Dancing at the strip club didn't count.

She rejoined Scarecrow on the broken road and together they walked deeper into the jungle.

"You okay, girl?" he asked, sometime after the morning had passed into afternoon.

Kansas squeezed his hand in response. She just couldn't shake the feeling that something bad was going to happen.

"How much farther?"

Scarecrow shrugged. "This area of the map was painted over pretty dark. Not sure how deep these woods go, but the Time Dragon's lair should be right on the other side."

They came to a fork in the overgrown road, where weeds had cracked the golden avenue in two, both paths leading deeper into the humid darkness of the jungle.

"Which way?" Kansas asked.

Scarecrow pulled the parchment out of his vest pocket. The thing had mud and grass stains all over it, souvenirs from their trip thus far. It still looked like a child's scribble to her.　"Uh,　we　should go...um..."

"You don't know, do you?"

He shook his head.

"Both ways look like they'll bring us out on the other side, but I can't tell which one is shorter."

Eh, what the hell. She pointed to the right.

"That way."

His corncob brow rose.

"Are you sure?"

"No." She took a step in that direction. "You coming?"

He raced after her. They made an odd rhythm as they walked—the click-clack of her crutch and the scraping drag of his loose straw. Everything about the place was peaceful and calm—just like in the serials she used to read in the Southwest Daily Times—yet still, that feeling of unease gnawed her belly and hurt her brain.

"It's so quiet," Scarecrow said after a long stretch of silence. "Even the birds sound like they're whispering."

"Maybe we frightened them?" Kansas suggested, though she highly doubted that was the case.

"I remember a time when woods like these would be full of talking Animals, inviting fellas to tea or to talk about the latest news from The Vinkus in the west. Why, I remember this one time—"

A soft *thud* interrupted his story, followed by a faint scratching sound. Kansas threw her arm across Scarecrow's chest.

"*What*—"

"Shush."

Kansas squinted into the half-light ahead of them. Something small and round-ish rolled toward them. It bumped over the bits of fallen vines and broken stones. The golden lump swerved like a bowling ball and came to a stop at Kansas' silver-clad feet. She bent over and ran shaking fingers over the soft velvety fur, then turned it around in her hands.

She fell to her knees.

The scarred face was covered with a crusty mask of mucous, blood, and dirt. It took her only a moment to realize she stroked the Cowardly Lion's severed head.

Coal-black eyes opened, dead and accusing.

"*Pathetic, Dorothy. Truly Pah-thetic.*"

Her mouth opened in a silent scream.

Scarecrow tried to wrench the blinking head away from her, but Kansas' fingers refused to let go. Something about seeing her image reflected in those deep, dead eyes froze her from inside out.

The head laughed, cold and cruel. The sound echoed in her ears, mocking everything she'd once trusted; everything she once believed in.

"*Rarh.* It doesn't matter which way you choose. It's all your fault. You killed me. Killed all of us. Proved that you're nothing more than a little whore, just like your uncle always said. *Nyah.*"

"I mean this in the politest way possible, old friend," Scarecrow said, giving another yank on the talking head and finally prying it out of Kansas' hands, "but, shut the hell up." He hoisted the golden ball over his head and threw it into the forest.

"Let's get out of here," Kansas said, proud that her voice shook only a little.

Scarecrow wiped his hands on his vest, then helped her stand. He didn't waste any time asking the hundreds of questions Kansas could see swirling in his black button eyes.

They hadn't gone more than a dozen steps when a huge glob of thick black liquid landed on Kansas' shoulder, clinging like insect guts to the front of her robe. She touched it, disgusted when it clung to her fingers like molasses. Another drop dripped onto her other shoulder.

She glanced up.

Before them was an enormous tree, broad and round. From each branch hung the corpses of creatures—goats and unicorns, bears and tigers. The ends of the twigs seemed to root right into their scalps, making them dangle like obscene fruit. Giant spider webs choked the canopy, glistening with dew.

In the largest web were the remains of the Cowardly Lion—legs, paws, fur, and tail, even the pink ribbon on the tufted tip waving in the soft breeze. Strips of fur along the limbs were missing, as if someone carved thin ribbons out of the skin and muscles.

A massive metal trap sat open on the jungle floor at the base of the tree, metal teeth vicious and gleaming in the weak sunlight. Old blood stained the blades, drips from the dried organs and entrails still decorating the tips.

Kansas lost control of her stomach.

Scarecrow pulled the oily hair away from her face and squeezed her shoulder. He didn't grip hard, but he leaned all of his weight against it. Kansas understood the force of feeling behind his silent comfort.

"What kind of Animal would do this?" he asked, voice small.

She raised her head, a sick suspicion swirling in her gut.

"Not Animals, but *animals*."

"But the wizard said—"

"The wizard lied! About everything!" Kansas wiped the bile from her mouth with the back of her hand. "He didn't *make* Animals talk, any more than he had the power to make them stop. And they gave up talking when people stopped listening."

He opened his mouth to say something, but a decaying paw pushed through the thick undergrowth near where they stood, clawing the air. It groped through the tree line, white and twisted. Scarecrow pushed Kansas behind his back. A skeletal, pale body lurched through the curtain of vines. The creature's fur was filthy and matted. It smelled like death.

Kansas stared, barely breathing. It was a bear, fur so white it looked clear, except for the red stains on its paws and jaw. Even its eyes were white, as if it were blind.

Scarecrow stepped forward.

"Ferdinand?"

It turned toward them. Its jaws hung open, cavernous mouth a gaping, toothless hole. And its eyes—its eyes were cold and mindless. It roared at them, the sound ripping through Kansas' head. She choked on a waft of fetid breath.

Pain pounded in Kansas' chest, forcing her to take shallow breaths.

The animal had been someone once; a person with a name and friends and a life. But there was no sign of that person now. Each flicker of shaded light reflected in its blind eyes, each unnatural movement of its twisted limbs meant it was nothing more than a mindless, feral husk.

It stood on its hind legs, towering over them. Kansas felt like an insignificant speck of dust standing there in its shadow.

Then, it lunged.

Scarecrow grabbed her arm and yanked her out of the way.

"Move it!"

Leaning on each other, they tore into the dark shadows of the jungle. Behind them, Kansas could hear other animal sounds—grunts, roars, and snarls—and the loping gait of hooves and paws. The herd was growing, and Ozma only knew what kind of creatures were following them now.

Rocks flew toward them from the sides and behind, smashing into trees and vines. One hit Scarecrow in the head, sending him sprawling to the ground. Kansas tugged at his remaining arm, pulling him to his feet. They stumbled on, further into the jungle maze.

Animals burst out of the thick growth—gorillas, boars, zebra, deer, and even more that were so wasted she couldn't tell what creatures they'd originally been. They were everywhere, their foul breath moist on Kansas' neck and face. She swung at them with her crutch, but the animals closed in around her and Scarecrow. They pressed closer.

Sweet Ozma, they weren't going to make it out of here alive. They'd be ripped apart, like all the other pieces of bodies rotting in the canopy. Or worse, they'd become like the mindless animals themselves.

An explosion of sound. A tree crashed right in front of them, shooting a cloud of wood and splinters into the herd. Kansas tried to cover her face with her hands and felt shards of sharp wood chips cut and bruise her. A bloody paw reached through the cloud of tree dust and wrapped around her neck. Paws and claws tore into her and Scarecrow both. Limbs and hooves trapped her, pressing into her shoulders and neck and face.

"*Let me go!*" she screamed, throwing her fist and breaking an animal's muzzle.

They yelled at her—screeches and clicks and grunts she couldn't understand.

Without warning, the animals released her, braying and screaming. Kansas fell to her knees, dead leaves and sharp branches biting into the palms of her hands.

A herd of wildebeest crashed through the tree line, hooves kicking up a thick cloud of dust that choked her. They tore through the clearing, cutting Kansas off from the other animals—and from Scarecrow.

She jumped to her feet.

"Scarecrow?"

A muffled scream was her only response.

She ran toward the wildebeest. They stopped moving and formed a living wall between her and the feral pack.

"Scarecrow!"

Beyond the wall of wildebeest, the other animals jerking up and down in a sick parody of a dance. Kansas narrowed her eyes, trying to see what was happening.

No...

Four small, metallic traps pinned Scarecrow to the ground, arm and legs spread-eagle. The animals circled around him. Each took turns bending and taking chunks out of Scarecrow's body with their teeth and fangs. He screamed. Thrashed. Broke down into whimpers and moans and pleading cries for help.

"Stop it! Let go of him!" Kansas screamed. She pushed against the gray furry bodies blocking her, but they wouldn't budge. She tried crawling underneath. They kicked her away with hooves sharp as knives.

"No! Scarecrow!"

He looked toward her, one eye missing and half his face nothing more than a broken ball of weeds. Scarecrow smiled at her, still reassuring her, still comforting her.

Tears—real tears, her first in years—stained her filthy face.

"Damn it, you can't leave me!"

"I...won't. I...promise." Then, a flash of fear in his remaining black button eye. The animals piled on top of him, all at once, shredding and ripping and tearing and rending, the sound like tearing silk.

Then, silence.

Without a sound, the animals slunk back into the camouflage of the trees and vines and long savannah grasses. Nothing remained as a reminder of their presence save their footprints in the earth and a torn jaunty cap lying near a small pile of twigs and straw.

Tremors raced through Kansas' body. She ground her teeth and held back the impulse to scream.

Screaming would feel good, but if she started now, she wasn't sure she'd ever be able to stop.

Kansas lurched over to the pitiful pile of broken straw. She lifted the Scarecrow's earthly remains in her trembling hands.

The hay was still warm.

Kansas was tired, and sick, and her throat and stomach and heart were sore. She'd never felt more useless in her entire life. She should just kill herself now. There was nothing left for her here. The map was destroyed, eaten by those monsters. And Scarecrow...

Scarecrow was dead.

She wrapped her arms around herself, shivering despite the humidity. Two empty buttons lay on the jungle floor, blaming her, hating her; still reflecting the fear she had seen on Scarecrow's face. Fear that she didn't remember ever seeing there before. Fear that she never knew existed.

Kansas stayed like that, head bowed and on her knees, until the scattered straw finally forced her to her feet, crutch clutched in her shaking hands.

She had nowhere to go.

What good was it if she couldn't even save *one* person when it really counted? The one person who meant more to her than anyone else in this horrible place. All desire to put things right again faded out of her like shards of sand through a timepiece.

Wait.

Time. She could have Time. She could have all the time she wanted!

If she succeeded, and got the Time Dragon to turn back the clocks of Oz, wouldn't that mean Scarecrow would be all right?

Could she take the chance *not* to?

Kansas took a deep breath. She finally understood the pattern of where their journey had led them thus far, and trusted that she knew the rest of the way. It was a path she'd never forget, no matter how much she'd wanted to.

She pressed onwards.

Everywhere Kansas looked, the streets—once full of color; of life and laughter—were bare. Each click of her crutch broke the silence. The people were long gone, but their legacy lingered—storefronts and sidewalks and building façades the color of green vomit, and the streets smelled the same. The empty avenues were filled with brown leaves swirling in hot afternoon gusts; nothing more.

So this is what had become of Emerald City.

If Scarecrow had been here, he would have cracked a joke about it being easier to find the Time Dragon this way.

Sweet Ozma, she missed him.

Kansas paused in front of the door of the Wizard's former palace. So many times she'd wondered what would have happened if she hadn't put her blind faith in such a sorry little man; if she would have refused to hunt down the Witch and searched for her own way home.

Or if that bitch Glinda had just told her straight-out that there was no way to leave Oz.

Taking a deep breath, Kansas pushed open the door and stepped into the palace's antechamber. The room was dimly lit and the ceiling dipped so low she could brush it with her fingertips in places. Iron chandeliers hung on chains, forcing her to limp around them as she worked her way toward the center of the chamber. Long shadows darkened the floor. A thick layer of dust coated every surface and spun into the air as she passed, as if no one had journeyed this way in a decade.

It all made Kansas' skin crawl.

"—*never realized how useless she was.*"

Kansas spun around.

"Who's there? Where are you?"

"*It's the girl's fault. She ruined everything.*"

"*She'll never be good for anything besides spreading her legs.*"

Voices whispered in the shadows, each murmur wrapping around Kansas' throat.

"Show yourself!"

"Probably begged her uncle for it, the little slut."

"She deserved everything her dear auntie and uncle did to her."

"It's her fault! Everyone who died, everyone who suffered. She's to blame!"

"She must pay."

Whispers turned into shouts. Curses. Threats.

The voices kept pace with each step she took. Kansas couldn't let them stop her. Not if she wanted to save Scarecrow.

A small flickering movement in the corner of the chamber caught her eye. The shapeless blob pulsed and throbbed like a beating heart. It twitched, then skittered away like a rat, scuttling across Kansas' shadow and sliding underneath the door on the far wall.

Whether it was there to help her or hurt her, she didn't know. But that was the only exit, and no shadow was going to stop her.

Her hand on the handle, one last voice taunted her.

"You have a sad life."

Kansas gave a cold, humorless laugh.

"Don't I know it."

She opened the door. The fetid stench of decay surrounded her and made her stomach churn. Stacks of glass jars filled the room—Canopic jars, the kind that her primary school teacher said Egyptians used to store organs after someone's death. From the smell, the organs were rotting away.

A narrow stone aisle lined by floor sconces ran between the rows of jars. Kansas followed a shaft of dusty light pouring through a high window, illuminating the center shelf. She hobbled toward it. Tall jars, covered in dust, filled the shelf. Kansas rubbed her tattered sleeve against the glass.

Congealed yellow liquid filled the first jar. Kansas frowned, then cleaned off the second jar, the third, and the fourth.

Nothing.

Kansas shook her head. Maybe she was just too suspicious for her own good.

A cool breeze blew across the chamber. It picked up speed and strength like a twister. The wind howled, hurting her ears. Chunks of rotted wood and shards of broken emeralds flew around in the gale, striking her arms and face. Kansas limped toward the wall, then dropped to her knees and covered her face. Debris blew around the room and smacked into her head and arms and back.

As suddenly as it started, the wind died.

Kansas lowered her arms and looked around.

It didn't seem like the wind had done much damage. The room looked the same, save the lack of dust coating the jars.

Kansas opened her mouth in a silent scream.

Row upon endless row, thousands of sightless eyes glared at her. Mouths sneered and decaying faces accused her without words. Bits of green cloth floated in the thick liquid.

She recognized the doorman's head floating in a jar on the second shelf; the wizard's old assistant housed next to him. And the woman who had first tended her flayed back after she'd returned from the Witch, broom in tow.

Kansas' stomach churned as she identified face after face; remembered every slight or kindness these people had once shown her.

The number of dead overwhelmed her.

Exhaustion pricked the corners of her eyes. She lifted a hand to rub them.

Nothing happened.

She looked down. Her hands were gone. Kansas' arms trailed off into two wispy shadows.

Panic seized her heart.

That flickering shape she'd seen in the room of voices crawled towards her, a black, pulsing, formless blob. It latched onto her shadowy stumps and sucked like a leech nursing from its victim.

Her wrists disappeared, then her elbows. She jerked away, but the thing followed her.

Kansas felt nothing—no weight, no limbs, not anything she could use to remind herself that she was solid or real.

She felt a terrifying urge to just lie there and let it happen; fade into silhouette and smoke and let the shadows consume her.

But Scarecrow...

He was...he'd *been* a survivor; had endured worse tortures than this and come out staggering, but undefeated where it mattered the most.

His mind. His heart. His courage.

The shadow plague devoured her shoulders.

What the hell could she do to fight a shadow?

Fighting the urge to hyper-ventilate, her eyes darted around the room. There had to be something...

Jars, dead faces, rotting shelves, more jars, the floor sconces...

Light.

Like an inchworm, she crawled toward the nearest lamp. Both her feet had disappeared, and the shadow plague now crept up her legs. With her fading stumps, she kicked the iron stand. It teetered, but didn't fall.

"Damn it!" She struck it again and again, until finally the torch wobbled and fell to the floor.

Rolling like a Tumbler, she angled her wraithlike limbs over the flickering flame.

The shadow blob hissed. It released her, then jerked and twisted away. The thing lurked just out of reach of the torch's light, waiting for either the moment Kansas moved, or the fire went out.

Only one thing to do, then.

She glared at the shadow creature, just waiting to reattach itself to her fading limbs.

"Oh, I don't think so."

Kansas lifted her hips toward the fire. Her shredded robe ignited. Now the thing had no shadow to cling to.

She heard a thin wail as the shadow creature writhed, devoured like a burning piece of parchment, and vanished.

Kansas' body came back. Even the missing bones and muscles in her left foot reformed with only a pinch of pain. She rolled back and forth across the floor, damping the flame before it could burn her too badly.

Then, she stood.

She was whole again.

Kansas ran to the emerald-colored door across the chamber and jerked it open.

Green marble gleamed everywhere. The room was full of silvery light and the floor beneath her crunched softly, like frost. Covering the floor was a layer of broken emeralds. In the center of the room was a high-backed throne, carved with gold-white images of dragons, Kansas-red blood dripping from their fierce fangs. The room smelled like burnt wood and charred flesh.

A massive four-legged monster burst into the chamber, leathery gray wings spread wide. The creature crashed to a halt in front of her, snarling— a statue of stone and metal, shunted together with strips of tough, gristly flesh. Bowed legs were attached to its square-ish metallic body with cogs and bolts. Its eyes flared wide and red, brighter than a field of poppy flowers; brighter than blood. An antique clock studded with gold and emeralds was embedded in its chest.

It *had* to be Tik Tok, the Time Dragon. No other creature could be so terrible and beautiful at the same time.

The dragon stepped toward her; blunt, toeless feet clacking a steady staccato across the floor. Large jagged teeth gleamed, made of silver or steel.

Tik Tok threw his head back and laughed, the sound like breaking icebergs and canon fire.

"I know you. And I know why you are here."

No way was this…this…overgrown lizard going to mock her. Not after everything she'd been through just to get here.

"Yeah? Do tell."

The dragon's mechanical joints gleamed in the dim light.

"You came here for yourself, because you wanted a different life. You don't care about the people of Oz, or *making things better*. Not unless it somehow benefits *you*."

His voice thundered.

"You came here convinced of nothing but your own right to be free from the pain of the miserable existence you carved out for yourself."

Kansas crossed her arms and narrowed her eyes.

"I didn't do anything."

The Time Dragon made a noise between a snort and a sigh.

"You misunderstand. Not that that's new. You have misunderstood my purposes since you arrived here."

That self-righteous wind-up toy is getting on my nerves.

"Oh?"

Tik Tok bared his metallic teeth.

"I'll put this in simple terms so that your puny little mind can comprehend. It's all coming from within *you*."

What?

Kansas shuddered, cold and sick and weak.

"Y…you're lying! That's impossible."

A horrendous roar erupted from the Time Dragon's metallic jaws.

"You think you're in a place where laws matter?"

Her head hurt. She was so confused. She'd never wanted anything like this to happen. Hell, she'd never given the tin men or animals or any of them a second thought. So how could she be responsible for any of this?

"Now, now, *Dorothy*," Tik Tok said, metallic jaw squealing. "You're a smart girl. I'm sure you can figure this out."

Kansas had been played with all her life, and fuck it all if she'd let the Time Dragon do the same.

"Sorry, but no."

"Stupid bipedals." Tik Tok shook his cog-filled head. "Creatures like you need suffering and pain. Crave it. But you cannot distance yourself from it. You retreat into silence, or break completely. So you hurt others to protect yourself, then sit back to observe."

"No! I'm not like that!"

"Think again, *Dorothy*. Every horror, every nightmare you walked through to get here, came from your own twisted mind. An unexpected side effect of you being the only human in this wonderland. Just as your dreams created this place, here your emotions became real; your fears came to life in a physical manifestation. Your anger and hatred. Your hopelessness. Each self-loathing thought you've ever had in that pretty little head of yours came to life and destroyed the Oz you constructed when you first came here. The idealistic fool you once were had *hopes* and *beliefs* and *goals*. And as they died, so did Oz."

Bile rose in her throat.

"The swamp, and the Munchkinlanders, the forest...you're saying that was *me*?"

"Got it in one. In a way, you walked through *yourself* to get here."

Kansas lost the battle with her stomach. She retched, vomit blending perfectly with the emerald floor.

All those deaths, all those horrors. All her fault.

It was true.

Kansas had wanted something to hurt as much as she hurt; wanted someone to suffer even worse than her.

Something broke within her. Everything that she'd once been—everything she'd become—shattered on the cracked marble floor.

Tik Tok laughed.

"Fool. Make the request you came here for or leave. I have no time for your self pity."

Time...

She wiped her mouth with the back of her hand.

"Make it all go away. Send me back to the beginning." *Let me make different choices.*

"Ah. Escapism through denial. How predictable."

She climbed to her feet, shaking. From what, she didn't know.

"If you're going to help me, then get on with it."

The Time Dragon growled. "Insolent whelp. Remember, *you* are the one who controls the fate of Oz. Try not to ruin it this time, yes?"

Without warning, glittering teeth locked on Kansas' arm and pulled. Kansas fell to her knees, screaming. Her skin ripped away from her body, unraveling like thread from a spool. She thrashed, tried to call for help, but was so far beyond pain that it paralyzed her. She couldn't make a sound.

She was nothing. No name. No past.

Not Kansas, not Dorothy.

Nothing.

She huddled on the floor, naked, no more than a mass of blood and muscle and tendon. Not even pain could reach her, she was so far gone. Slick, shining flesh, seamed with veins and arteries, dangled from the Time Dragon's jaws.

A bark of laughter.

Then, light.

There was nothing around her, above or below or behind. She floated in the still, dead air. She was pure light—formless, shapeless, nameless light.

Splinters, fragments of memory drifted around her. They scampered about like tadpoles with small flicking tails. Flashes of blue-black lightning and ghostly landscapes filled her mind.

What had her name been? Did light have a name? Or *need* one? And yet…there was *something*. She drifted toward it; felt it grasping for her.

Gold bricks, solid and heavy. Cheering voices, singing with joy. Fresh air perfumed with the scent of fresh baked breads and pulled taffy.

Eyes opened.

She lay on bright green grass underneath a wide, blue sky, sun warm and soft. Her heart leapt like she'd run a race. She hadn't realized how much she missed the simple comfort of a spring day until right this very moment.

Laughter, high and manic. A voice, accusing her of murder, laced with grief.

She sat up. The green angular face was as familiar to her as her own. A decade worth of nightmares; a lifetime of regrets.

Standing, she wiped her hands on her lacy apron, picking a blade of grass off her blue plaid skirt. She felt young. She felt *fourteen*. A wicker basket sat at her feet, its small gray occupant yipping with sounds she'd never expected to hear again.

She picked up the basket and held it close. Just beyond the horizon were a scarecrow that needed rescuing, a tin man to divert, and a lion to neuter.

She took a deep breath, then rose and walked past the throngs of cowering Munchkins until she stood before the Wicked Witch of the West.

No alternatives. No holding back. No more second chances.

She extended a hand.

"I'm here to help. Call me Dorothy."

THE END.

THE KING OF OZ

by Martin Rose

Oh, how she loved the fire.

Blue into yellow, into orange and red. Her temperature ran cold like her blood, but the flame gave life, parted her lips and drew her breath in fast, hitching with anticipation. In the burn ward, she continued to play with fire, and in the haze, David Gale flinched and repelled at the sound.

Click, click.

The steady *click-click* of a hand-held lighter permeated his dreams, his nightmares; he smelled lighter fluid, saw the flame between small, feline fingers, a wide, gray eye watching him beneath her bandages.

He woke up long enough to ask her if he was dying. She laughed and pressed her soft hand on his unburnt arm. The touch reassured, soothed, and awakened ancient memories of his mother with Scarecrow in the field.

He slept without rest or satisfaction, skin like crispy fried chicken, pulled taut over his muscles and organs. He breathed in the steady rhythm that reflected his pain, breathe in, *throb*, breathe out, *throb*. He hit the morphine button, a fresh stream of opiates entered his blood, and he fell into dissatisfied sleep once more.

He dreamt of the burning house, trapped with the black-haired woman, his fire fighter uniform ablaze, until only ashes remained.

By now, David Gale understood he was not human.

They skirted his dreadful secret with gauze and Demerol. His skin pulled apart like Christmas wrapping paper, tendrils of straw visible beneath his skin — snapped strands working their way through his wounds. How long until they found him out, while he lay like a slab of cooked meat on the gurney?

His weeping skin pulsed and throbbed as he pulled back the gauze. He groaned, his naked wound exposed to the cruel air while he fumbled with the IV drip, pulling it from his skin with a hiss, his motions weak and numb with drugs.

He came face to face with the pyro, a swatch of bloody, pus-filled gauze in his fingers.

Fear bloomed; he could not stop her as she leaned over him, pushing his weak fingers away where he had torn the dressing apart. Her hair and skin, burned away, and the twisting scars of flesh peeked from a mire of bandages, covering the eye the doctors could not replace.

"You shouldn't tear yourself up like that, you —"

She stopped and stared.

You got beneath the skin, didn't you?

He thought it; in the next moment, he realized he'd spoken.

She reached for the button on the wall, but he summoned the strength to take her hand, snapping it out of the air.

"Don't call them," he hissed.

"You've got straw in—"

"I know. It's me. *It's me*, don't you get it?"

She did not.

"*It's a part of me.*"

She stared at the open skin, burned and melted like mozzarella on an overdone pizza, with bits of straw poking up through the surface. She extended a hand, and he felt the cool pad of her finger against the inside of him. He shuddered.

She withdrew her finger.

"Keep it secret," he begged.

He steeled himself for screams, for the doctor and a thousand curious scalpels come to tear him apart; but to his astonishment, the pyromaniac said nothing, but pulled up a stool and sat beside him. She played with her lighter, passing her fingertips through the flames with an expression of ecstasy, her lips parted in her freakish, burned face.

He passed out.

He dreamt; a place he has never seen.

His bare toes sink into an unfamiliar earth, but he feels, deep in his blood and his marrow, that he *does* know it; that this grass and this sky call and pull and suck at him, want him for their own. A few steps more, and he could be there, he could be in the place his mother dared not let him venture, the place the Scarecrow could not return to.

He takes a step, one following after the other, happy to leave behind him a thousand sorrows, his mother's tears and the Scarecrow nailed on the cross in the field, with the lopsided smile. Happy to forget the persistent stare of the Scarecrow's mismatched eyes that found him through rain storms, through warm summer evenings while he played, and window panes as he bent over homework — his presence destroying each moment as it elapsed.

On his right, the cornfield extends into Oz, and a groaning reaches him. Dust swirls around his bare feet as he stops, and turns to confront the scarecrow by the side of the yellow brick road. A quick glance ahead of him reveals an endless line of crucified scarecrows leading into an infinite distance, all the way to Emerald City.

He moves toward it — the world eclipses, coalesces and fades, and the scarecrow calls out to him—

The pyro's voice.

He turned his head and saw her. She wore a wig, whose loose hair clung to her face, and she looked tired as she leaned over him. She looked younger without the bandages covering her burns and scars; he could see enough unburnt skin to know she had once been beautiful. Her nose remained intact, but her left eye was gone; above that, a rising surface of ropy scar tissue that moved into her scalp.

He didn't ask her to see where she had brought him; he was back in the house in Kansas.

What had compelled her to bring him to this place? She didn't know about the harsh violence of this world in the Midwest, the sowing, the reaping, the scarecrow nailed in every field and the worst one yet to come, the straw man of his youth: The Scarecrow.

She reached up and pulled the hair at her cheek, thick and black. It slid from her scalp, and he watched, mute, until her head was naked beneath the weak light of the bare bulb.

"You passed out, and I put my ear against your chest. What I heard was a heart; but not a human heart."

Her voice trembled.

"*Not a human heart.* Something more fragile, packed in sawdust and straw. I took your chart, and all the pages, and when I saw your grandmother's name —"

"Gale . . ."

The word escaped from him in a sigh. He turned away from her, thinking about the straw beneath his skin, harboring a thousand memories he could not voice — the curse of that name, and the Scarecrow. He did not have the words to express a youth endured as a stranger in his own home, a suspicious interloper of Oz blood, with his mother's eyes, but not her husband's heart.

"It's not a fairy tale. It . . . claims you. Takes you. Destroys you. You call this straw life? How long do you think my lifespan is?" He touched the bandages, where the pain flared beneath his fingers, and he turned away, biting his lower lip.

The pyro flicked the lighter open, and the flame licked upwards. She enjoyed it with her eyes.

"When I was ten, I set a chicken coop on fire. It happened by accident, and I never told anyone about it. I began to look differently at fire, and all it was capable of—and it seemed an itch I could not scratch, I thought about those bright, glowing embers whenever my life was heading in the wrong direction. I was never abused, or beaten, or hurt, I don't take drugs and I don't even drink. Some people are doctors, or artists, or scientists— but I love fire."

Her hand moved over the burnt and coarse surface of her scalp, where the skin was mottled and distressed.

"I have never belonged here," she spoke with a burst of passion. "I have never belonged in this boring, ordinary world, and I said to myself, what kind of person puts out fires? I imagined you were a soulless sort, an empty-headed fool, set to extinguish everything I set alight."

With a shaking voice she described her failed suicide attempt by fire, her crushing disappointment to encounter David in the smoke, pulling her through the square of light and back to the life she disavowed.

"If you're going to save my life, make it worth the effort — take me to Oz; take me to the Witch, or I'll set the world on fire."

Halfway through the cornfield, the cross rose from the ground, and *he* was there, after all these years. The inanimate Scarecrow stared down at them like a crucified Christ, arms and legs twisted and unraveling in the wind. The Scarecrow dead, and he had been stationed at the cross, unmoving, for the last twenty years, nailed there by his step father's trembling hands, in his burlap sacking and painted eyes, his lopsided mouth sinister in the moonlight. David spent his childhood in these cornfields, in the soybean fields; he knew there was a place were the turned earth crossed over into some other world —

"Oz," he muttered.

"Surely, that is not the Scarecrow."

"The very one. The man who raised me nailed him there, a punishment for my mother."

Her hand stopped him, mid-stride.

"For what?"

"Ah, I think you're guessed that much already. You're not the only one who doesn't belong here."

Somewhere in the stalks, grown corn became stunted, twisting, and he was aware of a fire in the woods up ahead, and he clasped her closer to him as he started forward, urging her on. His bare wound felt raw and burning in the idle wind, yellow hay in his flesh. He had not imagined a future where he would ever come back here, to be a hybrid monster, this thing he had become.

He could not bring himself to explain to her that the Witch was dead; and had been for many years now.

They passed time with their steady walk, and he stumbled in the darkness. She caught him and steadied him, brushing against the straw that jutted from his wounds—it was healing into his skin, and would be impossible to hide, now. It was on the tip of his tongue to tell her everything, about that terrible Summer day, and he found he could not. His tongue was leaden, unwilling to part with the words, so he kept it within, and they trudged on through the darkness, through brush, through broken yellow bricks, over tree roots and brambles.

After a time, the debris cleared, and through the darkness, he could make out the silhouette of the tower, black rising against black sky. He stopped, pondering it a moment, recalling his mother's stories— the Winged Monkeys, he did not like to think of them. But there was nothing moving at the gate; it held the air of an abandoned inner-city ghetto.

She followed behind him as he trampled through the long grass, to the gate.

David found a button in the wall, and pushed it; there was a series of clicks, the snapping of a chain, and the gate began to open, wrought iron bars sliding behind them.

They passed through, and walked down a foot path that led to the castle, overgrown with vines that bore purple, evil looking flowers like knives.

"I'm so thirsty," she sighed.

Uneasiness permeated the air around them. He was thirsty as well, but he said nothing, and he could see how pale and parched her lips were in the thin light. They had gone a long time without water.

"Oh, look!" she said, and pointed. He followed the line of her finger and it struck him, what an odd coincidence it was that she only mention her desire and it appeared before them: a stone column, and on the surface, an elegant goblet, beaded with condensation and dripping with wet. She started forward when he caught her by the wrist.

David did not believe in coincidences.

"What?" she hissed, impatient.

"Don't you think it's strange that a glass is sitting here all by itself? What if it's been out in the rain, or it's poisoned, or something of that sort?"

She leaned in closer, the glass loomed before him, deliciously wet, and the water glowed a faint chartreuse, like a glass of absinthe. She reached for it.

"The witch," he spoke gravely.

She shivered. "I must drink it. What could it possibly do to me, worse than what has already happened?"

Her eye pleaded from within a scarred frame, and he looked away with a sigh as she reached for the goblet with both hands, her fingers sliding against the surface as she drank, a long deep swallow.

The glass fell from her fingers and she leaned against him, exhausted. David wondered if they would die here, their flesh dissipating until all they left behind were bones in the dusty wind, where the witch waited to eat them like in the fairy story his mother read to him as a child, fattening them up in separate cages.

This train of thought made him somber, and she followed him, her face tired and pale. The sun was only beginning to crown the horizon, shedding weak light on them as they came to the main door. Easily twice his own size, big, wrought iron hinges and a lock like a lion's mouth, teeth bared and snarling.

David reached up, fingers clasping the cold iron, and rapped with determination, twice.

Resounding silence returned to him. He knocked again and searched the facade, hoping to gain entry when she trembled beside him. A moment more, and she fell.

He caught her and leaned her against the wall, snapping his fingers in front of her face. Her skin, infused with a gray tinge beneath the eyes and around the lips, testified to the severity of her condition. Weightless as a bird in his arms, her ribs poked out from beneath her skin like fingers.

The door cracked open. David hesitated in the moonlight, expecting someone to greet him, but there was no one, no Winged Monkeys, no Munchkins. Darkness met him, and the eagerness of the castle to embrace them struck him as sinister. He feared to leave her, in case someone or something should encounter her, asleep and defenseless, or worse yet, in case he became lost in the empty castle.

He gathered her into his arms — how thin she was — he lifted her and with care, and moved forward into the darkness, into the musty gray of the castle great room.

His steps echoed like thunder in the expanse of stone. Each step he took affirmed they were alone, and arms aching, he continued to carry her up the West staircase. The air was chilly and stale as he ascended, and tasted like dust from a tomb.

The stairway opened, door after door stretching before him down a dark and empty corridor. Balancing her in his arms, her head lolling back, he tried to the first door. A musty library greeted him, and he dismissed it, onto the next door; a lavish bathroom of marble tile and silver fixtures. The next door knob was reluctant, and stepping back, he kicked it in. A rusty lock gave way, and the door cracked open as he pushed his way forward, cradling her as he eased inside.

Pale dawn light filtered through the castle window. He laid her down on the mattress, exhausted, and dragged the covers over her shoulders. When this was done, he sank into a neighboring chair, exhausted.

His thoughts drifted until he dozed, succumbing to slumber. His guard dropped, his shoulders relaxed, and he felt that he dreamt, strange dreams moving in and out of his consciousness—cornstalks, his mother's summer dress, the Scarecrow, whom he wished he had met; how he wanted to ask him so many things.

His dreams weaved into pleasant things, warm and content.

Hands moved over him, over the sore and burned places where the straw was singed and damaged, the most secret parts of himself he was terror-stricken others might discover. He dreamt of gray hands touching him, mapping out his chest until he tossed and turned with a growing, hungry lust; the tips of her fingers had deepened in color, a gray cast.

He opened his mouth to remark upon it, but her mouth silenced his, and he realized his dreams had ended long ago; this was real life now and she sucked at his mouth with intense purpose, her tongue flicking in and out like a snake's as she drew him to the bed.

"Your hair —" he gasped, between her furious kisses.

"Shhhh," she soothed him, pulling him down. Her hair had grown back, wild and black and loose all around her, and a sense of alarm began to ring through him, a sense that everything here was wrong, the emptiness of the castle, the gray tint to her fingers, at the edges of her lips and her cheeks. Her flesh was unburnt, restored to gray, ethereal beauty.

"Aren't you afraid?" he whispered.

She laughed; despite the gray hue creeping into her skin, she looked healthy, her single eye bright and glittering. "Of what?"

"Of me."

The words hung in the air, before she dove in again, burying him with her mouth. He felt overwhelmed with sadness, to feel her touch those straw bits of him with such confidence, without fear or revulsion. It would a be sweet thing, would it not? To remain here, in Oz, in bed.

"Afraid of you? How could I be afraid of the Prince of Oz?"

He started at the title, overwhelmed with a feeling of horror — Prince? Prince of *this?* — and then the realization: of course. The Wizard had made Scarecrow the King of Emerald City, after the vanquished witch, but where was the King now? Still alive, trapped on Earth, serving an unearthly punishment for earthly crimes—crucified for the love of his mother, the daughter of Dorothy Gale.

"How could I ever be afraid of you . . . why look, you're only made of straw, aren't you? A single flame could turn you to ash . . ."

He felt dizzied with the constant touching, the pulse of her skin on his, she clawed at his flesh in tantalizing rhythm, until he felt exhausted with the terror of his boyhood, tired with the sadness of his youth. He let her take it away from him, kissing it out of him until there was nothing left to take. The castle breathed in and out with them, and he abandoned his questions and concerns about the pyro and where she had gone — he was with the witch now, and these were their lands, their kingdoms, and she was his, and had always been his for the taking.

When it was done, the wind was humid and sticky in the evening light. Naked, he stood up from the bed, his arms crossed, staring from the window.

"Where is she?"

"I am *here*," she responded icily. "Reborn; new skin, new beauty, and the witch is inside me. There was a voice in the water . . . Who could say no to such a chance? I felt it in the water when I drank."

"You *are* the Wicked Witch of the West, then?"

"Reborn. Reincarnated."

He mused on this, and then began dressing, pulling on his jeans.

"Surely you're not leaving."

"I won't be gone long, love," he finished tying his boots, and then reached out his hand, caressing her gray-hued cheek with one hand. Her flesh was dry and cold, calling to him, and he felt the presence of this new life he could have, this world of strange hybrid people, hybrid scarecrow and hybrid witch, fashioning a new world together. The thought was intoxicating, and he considered that after all these years, he had finally come home, to the place he truly belonged.

"I have to finish the past. It has waited far too long."

He kissed her, a long swallow of cool water. She watched him with a gray eye, and he had never seen anything more beautiful in his life, but he could not stay to savor it — not until Scarecrow was dead.

The stalks whispered on the edges of his fingers.

In the cornfield again; he slipped into that strange boundary where one world began and the other faded, a strange place were Oz corn gave way to the American grain belt, and he walked with confidence of young man, without worry or care.

Since that long ago summer day, his father drove those nails into the cross, the straw bled from ragged clothes, and crows settled on the shoulders, cawing into the wind. He felt this would be a matter of dissipating the straw, of taking the Scarecrow apart piece by piece and scattering him on the wind like *cremains*.

When he finally stood in the field, in the place his stepfather had nailed Scarecrow, there was nothing there.

The cross was empty, the arms outstretched, but holding nothing; and David began to back away, thinking this had been a mistake, a dreadful mistake. He whirled, alive to every noise, every cricket song, every howl in the distant wilds.

I should have stayed in the castle, by her side, but it was too late for that now. With renewed purpose he strode out of the cornfield and to the barn, where he pulled off the rotting wood planks. The barn had been boarded up since his stepfather hanged himself there. In moments he located the gasoline and the matches on the dusty shelves.

He doused the cornfield. If Scarecrow was there, the smoke and the fire would flush him out, and perhaps cut off the gateway between Oz and this world. At the least, David planned to be on the other side by the time the flames consumed the field, and what happened to the Scarecrow would be the least of his concerns.

He stood back to marvel at his handiwork, engulfed in the fumes of gasoline. He reached for the matches, but came out empty-handed.

He stared at his fingers. He remembered placing them in his pocket, and he retraced his steps back through the cornfield, knocking down stalks beneath his furious stride, until he stood before the shed.

He jerked the door open and pawed through the shelves. He grasped the old hearth matches stored in a Mason jar, but when he found it and held it to the feeble light, he discovered it was empty.

A scratching sound erupted in the silence; David tasted the tang of sulfur on the air and turned.

The Scarecrow swayed before him, shedding straw in his footsteps, burlap sacking torn and discolored. Painted eyes glowed in the light of the lit match he held aloft between them, between his dirty, fabric fingers. Straw jutted from the cuffs of his sleeves like old lace.

"Son, surely you do not intend to burn down the field."

David said nothing. This was not the reunion David had imagined— love? Hate? Indifference? They mattered little.

"I know you, son; you wouldn't destroy the last door we have left between the worlds."

David smiled; the Scarecrow filled the threshold, and the match guttered and flickered between them, casting light on their grim faces.

"No." David moved forward to the flame. The fumes of gasoline surrounded him, and he clutched the gasoline can before him like a woman might clutch a purse. "No, that's the problem; *you don't know anything about me at all.*"

Scarecrow realized in an instant his error in judgment—he moved to smother the thin flame of the hearth match, but with a single stride, David closed the distance. He thrust himself and the gas can into the fire; the fumes ignited.

Scarecrow's face twisted, lines in fabric, a cruel looking doll, eaten by flames. Burlap turned black beneath the onslaught of blazing light, and David withstood his burning fingers to push the flaming gas can between them, into the Scarecrow's chest.

He gave a great cry; more parts straw than flesh, he burned easily, and David shoved at the screaming straw doll, where he fell to the ground, burning black, like the edges of singed paper, burning into ash.

David clapped his hands together, but his singed hands danced with flames, unable to put them out. His breath came in fast with panic. God, what if he couldn't put it out? Oh God, what if he died, here, in America?

And the flames would *not* go out. He doused the ones on his hands only to have new ones sprout over his already charred chest. Panicking, he turned and abandoned the lifeless Scarecrow, an inanimate heap. Through the brush, towards the field, and the flames on his chest flickered in his vision as he hit the first row of corn. They went up in flames like a thousand points of light, and gasping with exertion and panic, he ran faster through the rows, spreading fire on all sides of him with lightning speed. Incredibly, as the heat increased and dollops of sweat dripped from his face, he heard the distant sound of popping corn in the rows already burning.

What if he couldn't make it in time? He pressed himself harder, but the flames in his chest spread further, and his heart beat erratically against the fire. He gave in a great, whooping gasp, and fire filled his mouth. He stopped, turning, dizzied and frantic, when he heard her voice. The flesh of his cheeks burned and peeled back layers of straw underneath.

She was there, and lovely—a dress of black, and he could see his fire dancing in her eyes. Her hand was held out for him, an umbrella in the other, and he stumbled forward, setting everything he touched on fire, every waving stalk and errant leaf into conflagration. Her figure marked the last steps he needed to return to the place he longed to call home.

Her lips parted in ecstasy to see him in the colors of flame, and he strained toward her, desired to be doused by her tears. *Only a little further now, he thought, and I'll be in Oz, I'll be with my Queen.*

Fire ate greedily at his arms, the smell of burning hair and sawdust filled the night air. He stumbled further, and found himself falling into the stalks, sending up sparks all around him like stars. He had time enough to say her name through the fire combusting in his throat, his voice, his mouth, until nothing remained but ashes. His vision failed as the fire consumed his eyes, and he felt the tendrils of flame, moving ever closer to his hybrid heart, and still, he crawled toward her, where she watched him, a hand at her heart, her jaw clenched.

He burned and burned.

Oh, yes, he thought, *how she loves the fire.*

THE END.

Cast of

Contributors

Mark Onspaugh grew up on a steady diet of horror, science fiction, and DC Comics. An HWA member, he writes screenplays, short stories, and novels. He lives in Los Osos, CA with his wife, author/artist Dr Tobey Crockett. Mark's work also appears in *The Blood of the Exodi* (Michael K Eidson), *The World is Dead* (Kim Paffenroth), *Footprints* (Jay Lake and Eric T Reynolds) and *Thoughtcrime Experiments* (http://thoughtcrime.crummy.com/ 2009) and he has an essay on monsters in the forthcoming *Butcher Knives and Bodycounts* (Dark Scribe Press)

On *Dr Will Price and the Curious Case of Dorothy Gale*, Mark writes:

As a child, I loved the Oz books, but found certain elements both frightening and fascinating, like Princess Langwidere who changes heads as easily as changing a hat, the two-faced Scoodlers (brr) and the Wheelers. Baum says the Wheelers are all bluster, but those screaming creatures with wheels instead of hands and feet really stuck with me. I wanted to write a story that explored those disturbing aspects of Oz but didn't debase the colorful, beautiful side. I also had a great deal of fun trying to emulate

Baum's melding of the whimsical and the grotesque, i.e. The Patchwork Jackal. (www.markonspaugh.com)

Rajan Khanna is a graduate of the 2008 Clarion West Writers Workshop with stories appearing or forthcoming in *Shimmer* and *GUD*. He also writes articles for *Tor.com* and maintains a wine and beer blog at (www.fermentedadventures.com). He lives in Brooklyn, NY where he is a member of the *Altered Fluid* writers group.

On Pumpkinhead, Rajan writes:

When I first read the guidelines for the anthology, I knew I wanted to write for it, the Oz books being a big part of my childhood. I also knew I wanted to write about Jack Pumpkinhead. Though he's only in a few of the books, he made an impression on me and, together with Tik-Tok, was one of my favorite characters in the series. From there I started thinking about how Jack had to change his heads because they would eventually rot. That then led me to the story. (www.rajankhanna.com)

Barry Napier's stories and poems have appeared in print and online. His collection *Debris* is currently available from Library of Horror Press. He is currently working on his second novel and a collection of dark poetry. Barry lives in Lynchburg, VA where he works as a freelance writer. He enjoys ambient music, dark fiction and irony.

On *Tin*, Barry writes:

Oz seems like a magical and rather quaint place, despite the abundance of witches (good and bad). It always seemed odd to me that among the beauty of Oz and the supposed innocence of Dorothy, the Tin Man was basically a simple machine that got frozen in time. If that were me, I think I'd be angry about my situation…it would make me want to make use of that axe. That, coupled with a history that I can only imagine would be a horrible one, gave me the idea for this story. (barrynapierwriting.wordpress.com)

Camille Alexa When not on ten wooded acres near Austin, Texas, Camille Alexa lives in the Pacific Northwest in an Edwardian house with very crooked windows. Her work appears in *ChiZine*, *Fantasy Magazine*, and *Escape Pod*. Her first book, *Push of the Sky* (Hadley Rille Books, 2009), received a starred review in Publishers Weekly.

On *Fly, Fly Pretty Monkey*, Camille writes:

For the first time since high school, I was reading this Frank L. Baum classic about addiction, sexuality, assassination, manipulation, and self-destruction, and the phrase "History is always written by the victors'" kept thrumming in my mind. Stories often come that way for me: a single line running just ahead of my ability to grasp, while I scramble after it with words until the tale's done. I write by the headlights, so the story drives me rather than me driving it. It's always a ride.
(camillealexa.wordpress.com)

Kevin G. Summers is the author of several stories set in the Star Trek universe, including the critically acclaimed "Isolation Ward 4," featured in *Star Trek: Strange New Worlds IV*. He has also published original fiction in *Lords of Justice* and *Tales of Moreauvia*. Kevin lives in historic Leesburg, Virginia with his beautiful wife Rachel and their daughters Morwen and Ingrid.

On *A Heart is Judged*, Kevin writes:

I've loved the Wizard of Oz since I first saw the movie as a young child. Over the past year, I've been reading the books to my daughters, attempting to bring the Land of Oz to life for a new generation. I've always wondered about the origin of my favorite character, the Scarecrow. This anthology provided the opportunity to explore this dark chapter in the history of Oz. In the writing, I found that Mr. Baum's fairy country isn't necessarily a nice place to visit.
(www.kevinsummers.com)

Michael D. Turner is a writer living in Colorado Springs, Colorado with his wife of twenty-five years and a house full of cats. He is a frequent contributor to *Big Pulp* (www.bigpulp.com) and many other publications.

On *Mr Yoop's Soup*, Michael writes:

I got to thinking about the Oz I grew up in, what set it apart from the real world I was stuck in. The whole "nobody dies" stuck out as potentially a real bad idea, though it seemed so cool when I was ten.

Jack Bates is the author of the *Harry Landers, PI*, series through Mind Wing Audio Books (mindwingsaudio.com). He also has several stand alone stories, mostly in the hardboiled and noir genres. He is an award winning screenplay writer with an option on a horror film. In 2009, he was a contributing writer for one new play festival and a featured writer in another.

On *Emerald City Confidential*, Jack writes:

I've always had a penchant for crime stories. With everything that is known about Oz and all the stories that exist in the series, it seemed only natural that there would be a dark underbelly in the wonderful land of L. Frank Baum's creation. I always felt there were struggles amongst the classes of the characters, a caste system built on differences amongst the inhabitants, and only those who lived within the shimmering green walls were safe. This story is about what happens when those walls are threatened and to the cowards who hid behind them.
(hardnosedsleuth.blogspot.com)

David F. Mason is the winner of the RCCC Creative Writing Award, and a student at UNCC. He has no dogs, cats, or pet raccoons, but is married to a wonderful woman named Chloe. The better part of his youth was spent hiding inside books like a convict inside the hollow of a tree; and in all his various escapes he discovered the power of authors to capture life, and lead the willing across vast, impossible landscapes in pursuit of it. Thus, with knowledge armed, he has commenced to build worlds of his own- ink blacks skies that glisten dark over white paper horizons- to surround himself with Words, breathed to life in the hope that one day he might aid the Lost in finding the same refuge he needed: shelter from Them That Would Devour.

On *The Last Battle of Trewis*, David writes:

Like any story, mine went where it wanted and did as it pleased. And like any author, I hurried behind, picking up the pieces of the brokenness it left. (davidfmason.webs.com)

David Steffen When David isn't writing code or spending time with his wife and two dogs, he's usually staring out the window, imagining what the future holds: like phones that are living symbiotes, or gods made of satellites. He's a writer, a media enthusiast, and a lover of all things Oz. His fiction is scheduled to be published in *Pseudopod* and his non-fiction has appeared in *Fantasy Magazine*.

On *The Utility of Love*, David writes:

I've never been completely satisfied with incarnations of the Tin Man. The whole basis of his character is heartlessness, but not a single version of him is heartless. The original Tin Woodsman is downright kind! So I set out to create a heartless Tin Man. He's not cruel—he doesn't hurt others for pleasure—he is just purely pragmatic, doing things for his own gain and not caring what happens to anyone else.
Dorothy's quest wouldn't have been so easy with such a companion...
(www.diabolicalplots.com)

T. L. Barrett is a writer of speculative fiction. He lives with his wife, Sandra, and their five children in Vermont's Northeast Kingdom. *The China People of Oz* is his first published story.

On *The China People of Oz*, T.L. writes:

Intrigued by the submissions call for the anthology, I thumbed through our well-read copy of Baums's book. When I came to chapter twenty, "The Dainty China Country", an idea started to form. Having a chronically sick child at home, I decided to confront the most terrible fear of any parent. Writing the story put me in a dark frame of mind for some days. There's something about watching your child waste away that it feels like they are being pulled from you into unknown territory. The story still haunts me. Maybe, it will do the same for you.
(tlbarrett.blogspot.com)

JW Schnarr is the Evil Mastermind behind Northern Frights Publishing. He lives with his daughter Aurora and a grumpy turtle in Calgary, Alberta Canada...a corporate city full of lions and tin men. While putting this anthology together he had originally opted out of putting his own story in; friends and family persuaded, cajoled, and finally threatened him with bodily harm if he didn't do otherwise.

On *Dorothy of Kansas*, JW writes:

In Dorothy of Kansas I wanted to create kind of a reverse story to the original Oz journey. I had just spent a few days in a camper reading Cormac Mcarthy's The Road *by candlelight (occasionally using it to kill spiders) so I was thinking dark things about the end of the world. As Baum always intended Oz to be a real place somewhere, it occured to me that with Nuclear Armageddon prevailing fallout would sooner or later end up in Oz. Now...what would they find in Kansas...*
(jwschnarr.blogspot.com)

Frank Dutkiewicz is a middle-aged Michigander with a lovely wife and two equal lovely teenage daughters. He took up writing as a hobby two years ago. He has eight publishing credits to his name (most recent for the 2009 August issue of *Space Squid*). *One Wicked Day* is my first non-flash fiction sale.

On *One Wicked Day*, Frank writes:

An online friend made me aware of the anthology when he asked if I could look at his submission. I thought about the squished witch under Dorothy's house and knew there had to be story there. While researching Baum's late 19th century novel, I read of the implied political meaning behind the tale. One Wicked Day is a satirical marriage of both ideas.

Jason Rubis lives in the Washington, DC area with his wife and a Shih Tzu named Dupree who could give Toto a run for his money. His fiction has appeared in a number of venues, most recently the anthologies *Like Clockwork* from Circlet Press and *Needles and Bones* from Drollerie Press. He is a self-confessed and unrepentant humbug.

On *Chopper's Tale*, Jason writes:

The tale the Tin Woodman told of his origins had always intrigued me; I wasn't particularly disturbed by it as a child because violent as it was, it had a fairy tale's simplicity and logic. Yet upon re-reading Baum as an adult—an adult who had watched a great many zombie movies, need I add—I experienced the inevitable shock. It seemed perfect for a horror story, but I wasn't sure how to make it work. Then I remembered the Powder of Life *from* The Land of Oz *and it all came together.* (jason-rubis.livejournal.com)

E.M. MacCallum Raised in Del Bonita, Alberta Canada E.M. MacCallum spent most of her days entertaining herself with her imagination on the farm and in school. At the age of seven she developed a passion for reading and writing. She wrote her first story in grade two and has been creating new worlds and stories ever since.

On *The Perfect Fit*, Erin writes:

After reading 'The Wonderful Wizard of Oz' *something struck me as curious. No one seemed to know where the slippers came from or what they did exactly. So, I took it upon myself to find out precisely what they could do and found a dark little beginning to Oz in the back of my mind.*

Mari Ness lives in central Florida, quite near the land of Mickey Mouse. This isn't as scary as you might think. Her work has previously appeared in numerous print and online venues, including *Fantasy Magazine*, *Hub Fiction*, and *Farrago's Wainscot*.

On *The Fuddles of Oz*, Mari writes:

Reading The Emerald City of Oz *gave me absolute nightmares as a child. The thought of scattering myself into thousands and thousands of pieces for the entertainment of others was bad enough; the realization that I might never be put back together again was particularly horrifying. This story has been softly bubbling in the shadows of my mind ever since.*

(mariness.livejournal.com)

H.F. Gibbard is a lawyer by day and a writer of speculative fiction by night. Several dozen of his short stories, poems, and essays have appeared or are forthcoming in various print and electronic venues. He is a member of the Horror Writer's Association.

On *Four AM at the Emerald City Windsor*, H.F. writes:

"Four AM" was originally written as a generic hotel room horror story. When I read the submission guidelines for the Oz anthology I realized it fit really well as an Oz story. In fact, details I had originally included without thinking of Oz specifically, such as the green colour of the hotel room lights, translated easily to the Oz setting. I have always found the Tin Man intimidating at a subconscious level, so he fit in nicely as well.

Gef Fox grew up in the southern hillocks of Nova Scotia's Annapolis Valley. Raised in a rural setting, his imagination became his main source of entertainment. Now, knee-deep in this information age—still calling the valley home after all these years—he's putting that imagination to work through writing. The first steps began one weekend when he sat down to write a ghost story. It grew byond its original boundaries to become the rough draft of a horror novel. Since then, he's been hooked on the craft of writing. *Scarecrow's Sunrise* is his first published story.

On *Scarecrow's Sunrise*, Gef writes:

Origin tales have always been an interest of mine, particularly when it comes to long-established characters with a clouded history. In thinking of a story to contribute to this Anthology, I imagined how the scarecrow came to be. Only two days old when Dorothy met him on the Yellow Brick Road, little is told of the Scarecrow's brief history before their meeting, especially his creation. I imagine a living strawman was a rarity even in the land of Oz. And a great shock to the farmer who made him.
(waggingthefox.blogspot.com)

Lori T. Strongin learned to hold a pencil long before she understood the magic that tool held. There has never been a time in her life when she didn't want to be a writer—armed with the power to take words and ideas and mold them into something that can create, end, or change lives. Lori has been published in several literary journals, trade magazines, and anthologies, including *Tip o' the Tongue*, *Reflections of the Flatirons*, *Beneath the Harvest Moon*, *The Florida Palm*, *The Florida Writer*, *Literary Liftoffs*, *Tales of the Talisman*, and most recently in *Renard's Menagerie*.

On *Not in Kansas Anymore*, Lori writes:

After a school production where the high points were the Yorkie playing Toto got flattened by the cardboard Oz's jaw falling off, a promiscuous Dorothy not being able to sing, the Tin Man not being able to act, and Oz himself delivering his lines in Spanish, in his underwear, to the low point of my hair catching on fire when my crystal ball-slash-garden lantern blew up, I've always had a bit of a sore spot where The Wizard of Oz *was concerned. I consider* Not in Kansas Anymore *my revenge.* (www.loristrongin.com)

Martin Rose began life dyslexic, until he picked up a pen at the age of 12 and hasn't put it down since. A steady diet of Alexandre Dumas, Anne Rice and Stephen King, marinated in a Donna Tartt sauce, kept him nourished during his grammar school years; he holds a degree in the visual arts and works as a graphic designer/copy editor for local publications where he currently resides, in coastal New Jersey. Look for his work in forthcoming publications such as the anthology *Hideous Evermore*.

On *King of Oz*, Martin writes:

I kicked around this story for several years when I heard about the Shadows of the Emerald City, and thought it would provide the setting I needed to get it off the ground. I pulled on my real life experiences with my father, who set a cornfield on fire with a gas can and a match, and the story came out of a need to convey my terror of becoming my father. Words like "straw" and "scarecrow" became synonyms for "crazy" and "schizophrenic" as the character of David Gale explores my own private terrors. (www.martinrosehorror.com)

Northern Frights Publishing

In the Great White North, Blood Runs Colder...

www.northernfrightspublishing.webs.com